Aniruddha Bahal is the found[er of]
Cobrapost.com, an Indian news w[ebsite. He was a]
founder and former CEO of Tehelk[a.com, the website]
famous for Operation Westend, which [exposed] widespread
corruption in defence procurement in [Ind]ia. Bahal was one of
the reporters who broke that story and is equally famous for
his exposure of match-fixing in international cricket. He has
worked for *India Today* and *Outlook*, among other publications,
and lives in Noida, near New Dehli. He can be contacted at
Bunker13@cobrapost.com

Further praise for *Bunker 13*:

'Bahal deploys some wonderfully idiosyncratic writing . . .
All of this combined with a bravura twist makes *Bunker 13*
one of the most enjoyably demented books I have read in a
long time. In fact, it is so demented that it is probably as near
as damn it to truth.' *The Times*

'Simply hums with authenticity . . . Written with commend-
able pace and a neat line in black humour, Bahal's novel
provides a fascinating account of just how crooked the subcontinent's two governments might be.' Geoffrey Wansall,
Daily Mail

'A gripping drugs 'n' espionage nail-biter, which introduces
one of the most memorable anti-heroes to come our way in a
long time: investigative journalist and all-out adrenaline
junkie Minty Mehta.' *Glasgow Herald*

'*Bunker 13* is gripping, stylish and so mystifying you don't see the twists coming. Do believe the hype.' *The List*

'An intense, action-packed espionage thriller, it's a satirical time bomb full of high-tech weaponry, military corruption and hedonistic debauchery that brings the Indian novel kicking, screaming, drug running and arms-dealing into the twenty-first century.' *Metro*

'Drug-rattled reporters and soldiers in embattled Kashmir double- and triple-cross each other and their subcontinental governments – in a . . . frightening thriller from an Indian journalist who knows far too much.' *Kirkus Reviews*

ANIRUDDHA BAHAL

Bunker 13

faber and faber

First published in 2003
by Faber and Faber Limited
3 Queen Square London WC1N 3AU
This paperback edition first published in 2004

Typeset by Faber and Faber
Printed in England by Bookmarque Ltd, Croydon

A CIP record for this book
is available from the British Library

ISBN 0–571–21742–7

2 4 6 8 10 9 7 5 3 1

For His Holiness Jagadguru Shankaracharya Bharati Teertha Mahaswamiji of Sharada Peetham, Sringeri

Acknowledgements

Satya Pramod Shastriji for his prayers. Monu and Dwark-anathji for their well wishes and suffering my numerous phone calls; Dada and Lakshmi for some big favours; the fish I have enjoyed feeding at the river that runs through the Sharada Peetham at Sringeri, Babaji, Dada in Allahabad, Livleen, and Dr Kashyap.

My daughters, Rhea and Esha, for sitting on my lap on occasion as I worked at my computer – Rhea being mes-merised by the screen and Esha by the keyboard; Reema, for her good-natured tolerance of the many hours I have been immersed in word machines over the years; Tarun and Vinod Mehta for sanctioning me two months' unpaid leave way back in 1996 when this novel started; Gillon Aitken and Antony Harwood, for seeing some promise – they have to now suffer this; Jonathan and Jon for some splendid editing; Anne Korin and Stephen Farrel for making some sugges-tions; the many dozens of books that I used for research and whose names I was too sloppy to take down for a proper mention; and Mita for egging me to complete it.

Also, to all the lawyers and others who have supported us at Tehelka over the last two years and more. I would have had no time, inclination or peace of mind for any creative pursuit had it not been for their pro bono work and extraordinary support. In order of appearance (based on my chaotic memory) I profusely thank Viraj Dattar; Pravin Anand; Kavin Gulati, my schoolfriend whose general equanimity and common-sense have seen us through many months of legal turmoil; Siddharth Dave; Nishith Desai; Ashni; John Holton; Medhanshu Tripathi – if law failed us he could double as our chief muscleman; Kapil

Sibal, the nuke in our arsenal; Prashant Bhushan, who has a conscience few lawyers equal; Vishal; Sidharth Luthra, who put in many dozens of hours of frenzied work and held the fort on days when the vandals were screeching at the gates; Pramod Dubey, for showering us with his precious Bihari insights; Dushyant Dave, who can dictate a twenty-page application in about fifteen minutes while listening to Mozart; Shanti Bhushan, whose mere presence gave us minions at Tehelka many million volts of confidence; Rani Jethmalani, who gave us much required moral support along with delicious sandwiches; Baldev Malik, Gitanjali; Ram Jethmalani – when you have him on your side it doesn't matter how many thugs the Union of India has arrayed against you, his voice is enough; Meet Malhotra – you can give him any task and forget about it; Satyanarain Vashisth, Amit Prasad; Madhukar Pandey; Kapoorji; Smriti; Vaibhav, Uttara; C.V. Nagesh, the genius from Bangalore; R.K. Anand, who could give Sherlock Holmes a run for his money; Rajiv Dhawan, who can untie a legal knot in real time but who isn't quite enamoured of our tendency to disappear for weeks without notice; Gopal Chaturvedi, who can regale you with anecdotes all day; Anil Diwan, for moral support and agreeing to be our General in reserve and; Rakesh Dwivedi.

Of course, this list wouldn't be complete without mentioning some Tehelka staffers, former and current, who put in many hours of toil: Anu Nair, for her industry; Arun Bhanot – without him we would have been at sea; Sanjeev Kapur, for his meticulousness and reliability; Kumar Badal, a very special colleague and one who, realistically speaking, has shouldered the bulk of the government's vendetta against Tehelka – maybe someday there shall be an inquiry against the CBI for his malicious prosecution; Arnab Pratim Datta, a tireless and most loyal colleague; Shamya Dasgupta, for being on call; the late and dear Arun Nair, for staying on and helping us in the most crucial of phases; Brij, our one-man army; Neena, for her energy when she's around; Parsa

Venkateshwar Rao Jr and Venkat Parsa for believing in Tehelka; Hemendra Singh; Ajay; Minty, Prawal; Matthew Samuel, without whose heroic deeds many of the above wouldn't have been employed; Shoma Chaudhary, for being one of the few pleasant sights as I laboured for a month on the witness stand; and Rakesh, for managing the cumbersome logistics of lunch.

Which brings me straight to put on record my special thanks to Sir V.S. Naipaul, Lady Nadira Naipaul, Pradeep Kishan, Uma Shankar, Upendra Baxi, Anand Patwardhan, Madhu Kishwar, Mark Tully, Admiral Purohit and Prem Shankar Jha, for speaking their minds without fear or favour.

It would also have been difficult for us at Tehelka to survive so far without friends like Madanjit Singh of the Rainbow Foundation, Carl Pope of the Sierra Foundation, Shenaz, H.S. Vedi, Satya Sheel, Arundhati Roy, Nilanjan Tolia, Manoj Prabhakar, Biswadeep Moitra, Manish Tiwari, Carin Fischer, Deven Verma, Mahim Mehra, Mahesh Jethmalani, Madhavan Kutty, Devanshu, Vijay Raman, Shekhar Bhatia, Billy Singh, Arun Lamba, the late Priya Tendulkar, Sudhir Varma, our number cruncher, and Pavan Sethi (may everybody have a landlord like him).

Last, but not the least, Shankar and Devina, for they have taught me the meaning of courage in the face of evil, and all my friends in the media.

BUNKER 13

You have soldiering boots stuck between your teeth so you don't maul your tongue. Major (Dr) Sandy is lancing a blister on your toe at the turning point of your twenty-kilogram tab. The others have overtaken you. After fixing you up, even Sandy goes on ahead. You are left alone to pull on your boots, and you tense with pain as you dig your toes in and put some weight on them. You are increasingly feeling that you needn't have got into the shit you find yourself in right now, tabbing twenty kilometres with a twenty-kilogram rucksack burning your back.

But out of the many ways that a *homo sapiens* with an IQ of 130 can fuck himself in the flagging end of the twentieth century is by writing the following to his country's army chief:

Dear sir

With reference to our telephone conversation of a few days back, I am hereby forwarding a written proposal for your perusal. We at *The Post* would like to do a photo feature on the making of an Indian paratrooper: to put one of our writers through the course and see whether he can make it. In the competitive news environment we face, the treatment that we give to our feature stories is important, hence the rather off-beat request. But it's our sincere belief that the piece would be a great image-building exercise for the army and do much to bolster its own efforts to draw top-notch talent through its gates.

Yours sincerely
MM

The request was granted in February 1999, after you pushed hard and greased the army's public relations officer, who – an ex-9 Para himself but now an army headquarter memorandum expert – kept looking at you weirdly on each of the three times you met him and asked, 'Are you sure of this?' Of course you were, then. If he had spelled out in vivid terms what you were getting into, you might have been a little less sure.

But now that your sorry ass is in, you plan to stick it out to the end, make your jumps, even if you have a kilo of blisters on each foot. You have your reasons.

Sergeant Major Islamuddin is really enjoying putting you through your paces. He thinks of guys like you as soft ass to regulate, to show what a tough guy he is. Do some show-off. He is now coming back through the runners to see what's with you. He thinks you are regular army grade four.

'What's up?' he asks. 'Running out of gas? You want to go back a week, repeat the whole fucking thing with the next batch coming in?'

It's in Sergeant Major Islamuddin's interest to kick your ass through the fitness course before the army lets you even touch a parachute. Maybe that gives him some career motion. But the talk is he likes only new faces in his basic fitness programme. He doesn't like leftovers to fill in the new guys in advance about what a bastard he is. He likes them to discover it for themselves.

You are not part of the regular 9 Para course, but the one they run for officers from other regiments, a kind of contingency reserve they have a policy of building up. That saves you all the 9 Para advanced hocus-pocus, which you are convinced would send you all straight to sick bay in two days flat. But even though they have condensed their drills and tabs into a diluted version of the big-fuck routine they run on their own lads, it's still enough to screw your biocycle, give you a high-fatigue RPM.

What no one wants to do is have a second crack at

Sergeant Major Islamuddin's fitness regimen, give him the opportunity to tinker with your biorhythm, reprogramme it permanently with his 5 a.m. PT.

You get up and wobble along on the one and a half legs at your disposal, but then you say, 'What the hell, fuck the toe,' and pick up speed, and you find you can move into higher gear because the pain isn't as bad as before. Major (Dr) Sandy has worked some magic.

It's a different point altogether that none of this blister shit would have happened if Sergeant Major Islamuddin hadn't told you to stuff your Nike power joggers in your locker the first day of your hitting base. The army likes its boys in leather boots. Likes to give them a shot at stress fracture in their first fortnight of marching and tabs. The guys in your batch have been wearing them for years. You haven't.

'Watch out for tendinitis,' one of your batch mates from 9 Jat Regiment warns you. 'That's even worse than stress fracture.'

'What's that?' you ask him. 'It sounds like a cow disease.'

He looks at you with pity. 'The muscles at the back of your ankles flame up from stretching too much. You be careful. I got it at Academy. Got it in both legs. Couldn't walk for a week.'

You don't know how to be careful to avoid tendinitis, but it's at the back of your head and you try some fancy running steps that you think will keep you free from it. So you get blisters instead. That's not as bad as all four of you, who are packed into this L-shaped army hostel accommodation, taking off your boots at one go after a tab. Dogs, you read somewhere, pack a sense of smell that's a thousand times more sensitive than us humans have. You are sure if a dog came sniffing in at that time it would die.

For the last week you have had to attend theory plus practical. A two-day dose of airborne history precedes the technical stuff. You learn about the Airborne Brotherhood, the International Standard Organisation 1000 mark that is the Red Beret.

5

The instructor reads out from his notes:

The Italians raised the first para force in 1928. In 1930 the Soviet Union formed its first battalion. In April 1940, however, it was the Germans who first opened the eyes of the world to the successful use of paratroops. Germany used her paratroop force, the Fallschirmjaeger, on Norway and then a month later in the Netherlands, with spectacular success.

The Allied forces, particularly Britain, were quick to realise the potential of the paratrooper. The British set up their parachute training school at Manchester in 1940, after Winston Churchill called for the immediate creation of a five-thousand-strong para force. Within a year an Indian parachute battalion was approved and soon other Commonwealth countries followed suit. The Canadians followed in 1942. Although many of these para forces were started and trained independently, the common unifying trait of the forces in Commonwealth countries was the Red Beret emblem. But this was just the outward sign of the bond that formed between paratroops of different countries as a result of combined operations during World War Two. The two most famous are the June 6 landings in 1944, part of the Allied invasion force, and Operation Market Garden later that year.

Here Instructor Bhaumik hangs his reading spectacles around his neck and throttles his memory. He narrates for us the street battle of Arnhem, where the British 1st Airborne Division was ordered to capture and hold the road bridge over the lower Rhine for forty-eight hours. First the British fuck up by air-dropping just half the task force on the first day while chuting the rest too late in the battle. But they land and find that intelligence fucked up even worse and that the forces whose defences they had to smash through included an elite SS panzer corps. But in spite of having the SS nuts right up their ass, about seven-hundred-odd men

6

make it to the bridge and take on German tank and infantry attacks for three days and nights. Until finally the SS decides that enough is enough and that you can't let so few men keep bothering you for so long. So they chase the 1st Airborne from the burning houses they were holed up in. Instead of surrendering, the paras disperse. After nine days of fighting the 1st Airborne finally pulls back across the Rhine: 2,163 survivors out of 10,095 troops.

However, the British parachute regiment, you hear, established its Red Devil lore in north Africa as part of the 1942 Allied offensive in Morocco and Algeria, where battalions were air-dropped to capture runways and road networks ahead of the ground forces, which were later supposed to come and relieve them. This, you learn, is vintage Airborne initiative.

But on one occasion at least the ground forces forgot to link up with 2 Para and the poor guys found themselves eighty kilometres inside Rommel territory and had to make a two-day march to join their own forces. Only a quarter made it.

The regiment also established an early reputation for botching up its drops. For instance, in an operation in Sicily in 1943, just three-hundred-odd men out of 1,800 plus that jumped off planes landed in the Drop Zone. This allowed the three-hundred-odd guys an opportunity to become heroes by defending the Primosole bridge for one whole day. Instructor Bhaumik's historical erudition regarding the paras doesn't include telling you why the bridge was important for the Allies to hold for a day. Maybe they couldn't find enough whores around the bridge for their officers to bounce before retreating.

While the British have just an airborne brigade, the US airborne freaks have an order of battle that contains the 82nd Airborne Division, a mechanised infantry division, an armoured brigade, an anti-tank air cavalry brigade and the 101st Air Assault Division.

The 82nd Airborne Division, of course, are the designated out-of-area motherfuckers who first took on this role in Normandy on D-Day. With about seventeen thousand nuts on its rolls, the 82nd also packs enough wing power in C-130s, C-5 Galaxies and C-141 Star Lifters to lift and deliver their load of nuts to any point on an atlas. They train at Fort Benning, Georgia, and take up their dates on AH-1S Huey Cobras, which you can mount TOWs on.

But if the US parachute forces dwarf those of the British, the Russians are in a league of their own. They are quantum motherfuckers. The Vozdushno-Desantnyye Voyska is over a hundred thousand strong. In case NATO does something really pissy, the guys are going to chute down in western Europe behind enemy lines and riddle French and German ass with 73 mm hardware, the AT-4 Spigot anti-tank missiles, the 120 mm self-propelled 2S9 guns and whatever handy thing they can mount on some turretless shit called the BMD M1979.

The reason they will be running into the French early on is because part of the brief of the French paras is to go save German ass if the Russians come paying a visit. The French airborne strength in the 11th Parachute Division is about fourteen thousand men and is based at Tarbes. That includes the 2 REP from the French Foreign Legion, which carried out the assault on Kolwezi in 1978. These élite motherfuckers have about four companies of assault paratroopers. They are so élite they don't talk to civilians.

The unique aspect of the French paras is that they have undertaken more operational jumps than any other para force in the world. They have seen action in Indo-China, Suez and Africa, particularly Algeria. The French campaign in Indo-China saw them make 156 operational drops, culminating in the historic jump in the valley near Dien Bien Phu where General Giap's Viet Minh took the French out of the battle and eventually out of the region in 1955.

In 1957 the French paras returned to combat. This time the

10th Parachute Division took over the city of Algiers and restored order within a month. But the force received a setback by involving itself in the attempted overthrow of General Charles de Gaulle in 1960 and has been looked upon with suspicion ever since. Yet it produced two very striking generals in Jacques Massu and Marcel Bigeard. The latter's appearance at Dien Bien Phu did much to raise morale in the beleaguered garrison. The trademark that distinguished him from other generals was his habit of arriving to inspect units by parachute, his hands at the salute as he landed in front of the honour guard.

The Indian para strength is modest by comparison: a token force of nine battalions with a total of 5,500 men. Of the nine para battalions, 1, 9 and 10 are para commandos and have most recently seen action in Sri Lanka and the Maldives, but the 50th Indian Parachute Brigade was formed way back in 1941 and saw action mostly in Burma and the North East. The Gurkhas were the first Indian troops to wear the para wings. When para forces were still in development, the British found it easiest to sucker the Gurkhas into jumping.

The 152nd and 153rd Gurkha Parachute Battalions saw magnificent action against the Japanese at Sangshak when they were on their way to Imphal. Bearing the brunt of the flanking attacks by the Japanese on the retreating 14th Army, the battalions gained time for the garrison at Imphal to reorganise its defences.

Later, the brigade distinguished itself in the British efforts to recapture Rangoon from the Japanese. The paras jumped over Tawhai, south of Rangoon, to clear Japanese coastal defences on the Rangoon River to make way for the 26th Indian Division that headed upriver in the amphibious operation code-named Dracula.

After you are through with theory (an area in which you intend taking an unassailable lead over Major Rodriguez, with whom you have a bet to top the course), they herd you into landing practice. You learn to touch ground in a dozen different ways. The standard – elbows tucked in, feet and knees together and legs loose like box springs – has the potential to save you from all but the heaviest of landings. But since army-issue chutes are non-steerable, giving you scant control over the direction of your approach, you have to learn how to land forwards, sideways and backwards, buck with the way the wind brings you down. You are told never to break your S position. The army has even developed laid-down procedures for fuck-ups you can see coming, like hitting a church wall. It wants you injury free for the screwball mission it sends you on. It teaches you how to reduce impact. It teaches you to avoid frontal collisions with stationary objects. It's better, they tell you, to bust your ribs than smack your face on concrete.

For two hours the Parachute Jumping Instructor (PJI) makes you do about forty parachute rolls from any angle he hollers out. Next to you Major Rodriguez whispers, 'Hey, MM, what about a dick landing? Do they teach that too? What could happen to a guy like Islamuddin on an emergency dick landing?'

That, you agree, is a tremendous theoretical point of concern. Islamuddin has an organ the size of a forty-pound dumb-bell. Your stick of ten men saw it once when Islamuddin put you through compulsory showers to build comradeship.

But you forbear from responding to Major Rodriguez for fear of attracting the PJI's attention. You are familiar with the major's unscrupulous tactics. For Major Rodriguez there are just two categories of the living: players and fucked-up eggheads. Major Rodriguez fancies himself as a player. While you don't grudge him that status or doubt the merits of his claim, what you have strong reservations about is the fucked-up classification that the major's social theory will shove you into should you lose the bet with him. You have observed the major at close quarters when you were together at Siachen in December 1998. He'll do anything to come out on top. So you want to make him sweat till the last moment. Your only chance lies in squeezing an error out of the major by cramping his style, throwing him off his game.

What immediately follows your landing period is an introduction to canopy: the special nylon that stops you falling like a stone from up above. The main chute of the Indian paras, you learn, is the Paratrooper Main (PTRM), a non-steerable parachute with a destiny you cannot control except by lifting the webbing on one side to allow air to hiss through so you don't crash into other jumpers on the way down. The PTRM is modelled on the American T-5, but the cords play out before the canopy locks so you don't get that body jerk that the American T-10 gives you. On the other hand, the American T-10 is fully steerable, with the canopy opening out even before your cords tauten up.

'But,' throws Major Rodriguez into one of your stick's drinking sessions, 'the T-10 is actually a military disadvantage in certain situations.' None in your stick can figure out any obvious disadvantage in the T-10. Better to steer to a DZ of your choice than land on electric wires and have yourself barbecued. The major, however, has been putting in some extra time in the library, getting some solid purchase over you in theory.

He explains: 'It could create problems when you have sim sticks on both port and starboard sides of the aircraft. Every steerable chute has a bias. It doesn't drop you straight down the way a PTRM or a PX4 does.'

The rest of you nod intelligently.

Right now, your batch is simulating aircraft door sim launches. You drop through a door slowed by a giant fan. You have to indulge in skilful manipulation to avoid having the major right after you in your stick of six, or you might find yourself catapulted out with more force than necessary – an unnerving contingency, even if the drop is only thirty feet.

But you flow through the fan trainer with ease, and the next step in your training takes you to the tower, where you hurl yourself down forty yards on a harness that connects you to two wires, a kind of aerial runway. A bit like a slide, only the ride's a lot more bumpy. You slide a cool hundred yards. It's the nearest you can get to knowing what it's like to jump into an AN-32 slipstream. For three days you have also been practising harness release and drag. You are given tips on how to avoid being dragged on the ground by the canopy after landing.

The next day you are supposed to go up for your first jump. Everybody in your stick is at Major Rodriguez's quarters taking turns sipping rum from paper cups. Through cigarette smoke and rum fumes Major Rodriguez is giving us a blow-by-blow account of an accident that took place yesterday in a simulated runway raid.

'Jumping on an airfield you have to be quick. But if you are too quick you could end up like those two guys yesterday. The second guy out got right above the first guy out. He went into an air lock. His chute candled. That's what happened.'

'You mean they went into an entanglement?' Major Sandy tries to clear the technical fog in his brain.

'Yeah. Two guys right on top of each other, rigging lines kissing each other,' says Major Rodriguez. 'The guy on top had an air steal all the way down till two hundred feet and then the guy below tried to get his lines straight but then his chute went limp and both of them came down from two hundred feet. They tried pulling their reserves but all the chute did was blow up in their faces and get entangled in their rigging.'

'Are they dead?' you ask, before you can help it.

'No,' says Major Rodriguez, 'they're having tea with the base commander. Broken legs, broken pelvises, fractured backs, heads, hands, every fucking bone. DOI case.'

'DOI?' asks Sandy.

'Dead On Impact,' Major Rodriguez says. And the way he rolls the 'impact' over his tongue has everybody silent for a while. 'One of the worst incidents these guys have had in a while. The other day they had this group up on first jump and the last guy on the stick wouldn't jump. He just caught hold of the door frame and wouldn't budge. The PJI whacks him on his wrists and kicks him way the hell out to make him go. The guy got a fractured right wrist and he doesn't remember how he got it. He's in a blank. You go into shock out there sometimes when you see the ground and you can't remember shit from then.'

'The PJIs are not supposed to force someone out on the first jump, I guess,' you say.

'Who the fuck knows what the PJIs are supposed to do or not do?' asks Major Rodriguez. 'We got this rookie asshole anyways. We are his first stick. Maybe the guy kicks us all out. Maybe we all go into shock up there. Bring the fucking plane down.'

It's para practice to have a full-blown morale-building battalion drop within twenty-four hours of some freak para accident. It's also general para practice not to club first jumpers with veterans. But one of the IL-76s gets a bird hit, a hawk through the jet turbines, and three greenhorn sticks have to crowd in with 5 Para doing a sixty-kilogram kit jump. The big boys keep lugging these containers all over the aircraft, falling over everybody else. And the joker sitting next to you goes to sleep before the bird starts taxiing. Then you have this dispatcher nearly walking over everybody's head to check things out.

But all you are thinking of is to stay ahead of Major Rodriguez after the light turns green. Your bet with the major stipulates a significant points bonus for whoever hits the ground first. A little game within a bet. The major's own game, of course, has been to up on benzedrine. That's his thing. A speed booster to up his confidence level, tone his central nervous system for the high-stress manoeuvres ahead.

The way he's done it is to roll the sulphate in a Wills cigarette paper and swallow it. He chases it down his gullet with chilled beer in the mess before arriving at the rendezvous point.

The bomber takes hold of him in half an hour and you can see his eyes light up. You don't like to swallow the stuff. That, you feel, dilutes the hit. You want your rush faster, so you do a few lines on your shaving-kit mirror, chopped fine to reduce the burn and sniffed through a rolled tenner. Of course, you got the stuff from Major Rodriguez. Where he got it from is his business.

All the chatter stops when the green comes on. Your three sticks are right at the back, sweating it out, waiting for the big guys to jump in the wind. The thing about jumping, you remember, is to go out with a thrust. That stops the slipstream from getting a hold over you and banging you against the AN-32 body, loading your face full of aluminium rivets.

Major Rodriguez is the last on your stick. You are two guys ahead of him. The major's giving the works to Sandy, who's behind you.

'Hey, Sandy, you checked your chute? Looks very bad to me. Looks like your cord's stuck in your harness,' says Major Rodriguez.

Major Sandy starts sweating like a pig.

'Fuck you, Rodriguez,' he says. 'You got stones in your nylon.'

'Man, this is serious, you ought to have a look. There's this gooey stuff sticking all over your pack,' Major Rodriguez says.

He's got Sandy fidgeting like mad. Then there's this other guy on your stick, Captain Prem Prakash, who's behind Sandy but in front of Rodriguez, and Sandy looks up at him for psychological support but the young captain is having none of that. He's clearly having some kind of quiet freakout of his own, and is fully preoccupied with keeping himself sane.

Rodriguez keeps on at Sandy. He yells at the PJI to have a look at Sandy's pack. And when your stick gets the Go, Major Sandy's so tripped he starts yelling and unhooks himself from the line.

You, of course, are only too aware of what Rodriguez is up to. Narrowing the numbers between you and him. Reducing the three-second advantage you have over him. But still you figure victory is yours. You are still going to have a lead of fifty feet by the time Rodriguez jumps.

But you haven't counted on Sandy blowing all the fuses in his head. He's howling a demented howl, making all sorts of gestures at Rodriguez. It's then you realise fleetingly that maybe Sandy's on a bomber too. Only he doesn't know it. You see your PJI leave the door and come to Sandy. Keep him in grip. It's then that your turn comes and you exit the AN-32, pushed out by one of the three PJIs standing at the door with monkey harnesses.

'Go, go, go, go!' they all shout.

And as you go past the slipstream and feel the reassuring jerk of the canopy, amidst all the new sensations that rush in and stall your thinking for a while, you still feel the need to glance up and flash the V sign at Major Rodriguez.

You hear the crack of canopies opening. Rodriguez is forty feet above you. You can see the concentration on his face. You also see him go for his parachute release mechanism, the two levers on his shoulders. Rodriguez is free falling now. He goes below you. You can't believe what you are seeing. You see him pull the ripcord on his chest where the reserve lies and you wait what seems an interminable moment before the lines deploy and the nylon balloons. His body jerks up 150 feet from impact. The lines pull him taut at his chest. Rodriguez goes horizontal. You see him pull the lines down, stall his chute, go vertical at the moment of impact.

You chew the cud on what you just saw. In the catalogue of crazies it has been your fate to meet, you decide Major

Rodriguez is in a class of his own. And then the ground comes at you much faster than expected and you are concerned about your own fate. You tense your limbs. You go into the S formation. What you have to avoid doing is falling like a bag of shit. That's what they have taught you. They have also taught you about harness release and drag. What they haven't taught you is what to do if there's no wind and the sonofabitch of a canopy falls right over you. It takes you about a million minutes to come out of that.

Kudos comes Rodriguez's way after the news of his presence of mind during his first descent filters through. Surviving a reserve chute landing on first jump is unprecedented in Indian para history and ensures Rodriguez's name in the battalion hall of fame. The major, of course, is smart enough to locate his released main chute immediately after landing and knife through five compartments. The blowing of panels on the main canopy is a well-documented hazard. The 5 Para hard-boiled nuts came and shook his hand and congratulated him on his narrow escape. Major Rodriguez took these things in stride.

He couldn't duck an inquiry because of the thing with Sandy. But nobody – except Rodriguez himself, Sandy and you – quite knows what took place and so the major's version goes uncontested. You have your reasons for sealing up on Rodriguez and they aren't the ones that Rodriguez thinks they are.

Importantly, nobody got hurt. If anyone came close to squeezing the ghost out of his frame it was Major Rodriguez himself. There is no reason not to believe what he says, especially since Sandy didn't crack, though he knew what it was all about. He just packed his stuff and went back to 9 Rajput Rifles like nothing had happened.

The good thing about army training, you discover, is that it's geared for eventualities like Sandy's. There was nothing fishy in chickening out at first jump. Para drops are scary and there is nothing wrong in getting scared. Fear management is essential para drill. The only surprise is that Sandy had made it so far. The army is good at filtering the scum at first stage. They pick guys who can piss high. Where it's weak in tackle is when it has to deal with fringe bastards of the Rodriguez variety.

The major's testimony was a lot of horse-shit but it sank well. He claimed he thought Sandy's pack looked kind of funny from behind and all he did was warn him about it. Since Sandy flung his pack aside and diddled with it while in flight, the pin cracked and burst his chute in the fuselage. He was lucky he wasn't anywhere near the door. He got his chute so messed up nobody really doubted Major Rodriguez's version of events. That just left the question of Major Rodriguez's shoving of the PJI at the door to leap into the slipstream. Not an ordinary shove but one that cracked his ribs against the fuselage and snapped his collarbone. This Rodriguez did to gain some vital fractions of a second in his pursuit of you.

Major Rodriguez's deposition was electric: 'From the moment the green light went I wanted to Go. I sat crouched during jump run, my eyes locked on to the light, and nobody could stop me from jumping. I was in an aggressive, relaxed, concentrated state of mind. That really helps me on with things. I don't remember the incident with the PJI. After all that waiting, the fear and the apprehension, I just needed to Go. I went into a kind of blackout after the jump. I didn't know what was happening. Then I felt the jerks on my two shoulders and when I looked up I saw the panels begin to rip. That's when my training took over. I am thankful to all my PJIs for the innumerable drill sessions. I am alive because of them.'

That is what he said, or thereabouts. You got it from the garrison commandant, whom you met just before you left and who was so impressed by the wordage he jotted it down in his diary. He planned to recommend Rodriguez for a Republic Day medal. He was the one who got the base psychiatrist off Rodriguez's back. He was poking at Rodriguez for a while, getting his fun. But Rodriguez came out flying from all the psychological traps he sprang on him.

If you don't know what you are looking for, chances are you won't find anything interesting. He ranked him top beef. What the medics didn't do was check his blood after the jump. Or yours or Sandy's for that matter. That might have shaken the set up a bit.

Of course, you lost your bet with Major Rodriguez. He did top your batch. He took a hundred bucks off you. But you know it wasn't the money Rodriguez was after.

Four jumps later Rodriguez volunteers for Pathfinder Company, the military free fallers. A club so élite it's an active force of just a hundred people. While your basic para course took you twenty-one gruelling days, military free falling, you learn, is a place for the truly mad. A full-length course strings you up for three months. But the para forces are raising a show jump team on the line of Britain's Red Devils and are prospecting for talent a little farther afield than the regular para battalions.

You aren't keen on continuing at the Agra para base, four hours from New Delhi, but your business is to bait Major Rodriguez and you are left with no choice but to tap your own sources and let the army trim you a vacancy in the free fallers. You sell the army chief the idea of a glossy book this time. To sound convincing, you make your editor and publishers fax him a bogus contract letter including a clause for all royalties to go to the Army Women's Welfare Association. You know people who can push the army chief's hand but you prefer to play it this way. You want to pull zero fucking confrontation. A war on two fronts is not your way to conduct business.

As a professional you have already broken rules. You are neck-deep with Rodriguez into pumping your veins with all kinds of mind-blowing pharmaceuticals. Bumping into each other again ten years after Academy you recognised this common weakness. It let you strike up an instantaneous rapport. Just because one day in the near future you may feel the need to shut him up permanently, speed-post him to Goa to lie in his family burial yard, it doesn't take the pleasure out of your dealings with him. Instead, it introduces a sense of contrast. It's a tussle that you enjoy.

You are back to the drawing board again. Free falling, the PJI explains, is all about oxygen, thermal wear, air pressure and flying. If you don't get your basics right you might end up in a bullet drop, a 200 kilometres per hour base hit, but at 200 kph the air rush is full of convertible energy. And if you learn to direct this air-flow you do not fall. You fly.

'You have to have a feel for the air,' PJI Malhotra tells you as he puts you through the wires to post you on the basic positions.

Your bread-and-butter position on the way down is the spread eagle, legs and arms in V, face down, back arched in a hollow to maintain equilibrium. Lose this position and you might drop through space in involuntary loops, somersaults, barrel rolls or the vicious flat spin which would centrifuge the blood out of your brain and whip you unconscious.

This is where you are taught the principle of controlled bypass from your symmetrical poise, which is possible through a rearrangement of air-flow against your body surface.

'You can initiate movement by bending one or both legs, your hands, arching your body, even angling your palms,' says Malhotra. For four days Malhotra hangs each one of you on suspension wires and you learn various body geometries. A head-down or a no-lift dive, for instance, increases vertical speed by reducing the area of body surface presented to air-flow. In skydiver jargon it's called a delta, track or max-track approach. Or you can fly horizontally by sloping your body at an angle to the air. Or if you are one for show jumping positions you could take the Canarrozzo Position, a head-down dive with legs apart and hands folded across the chest.

To come out of delta dives you practise the reverse arch: body balanced on fingertips and toes, cupping your body to catch the air full on.

'This is a dangerous position, though,' warns Malhotra. 'If you don't have enough feel for the air you could end up on your back all the way down.' To flip out of your back-down position you have to arch your back upwards and let the air do the rest. If you fail, and pull the ripcord in panic, you are likely to wrap the main chute around your body, with little chance of firing your reserve.

The way the army starts you off on free-fall jumps is by dropping you on static lines from 12,000 feet for the first five jumps. Canopy control is what you have to master before getting high on ground rush. The Pathfinders' rectangular, steerable canopy is a revelation, a flying machine with a forward speed of twenty-nine nautical miles per hour in zero wind conditions and a ratio of three to one. It imparts a forward thrust of three feet for every foot it takes you down. What is impressive is the degree of manoeuvrability you can exercise at this speed. The toggles serve as your brakes and accelerators as well as your steering wheel. Because of them, Pathfinder platoons can be dropped kilometres away from the DZ and from big heights.

Malhotra builds up your mentality. 'You don't have to know everything about physics, Newton's law of action and reaction or your dive angles. The important thing is to think flying rather than falling. That goes for landing too. You have to drive towards touchdown on a downwind approach, your toggles at shoulder levels. If you are over-shooting you press the levers further. If you are falling short you let them loose. Piece of cake.'

But stalling, you are told, is the main killing statistic for free fallers. Braking the toggles beyond a certain point takes the air out of your chute and you go down like a stone from that point.

The history of parachuting is, however, more colourful than that of the paratroopers alone. The para school occasionally invites veteran sports enthusiasts to fill you in on the trial and error methods of early pioneers, some even going back all the way to the eighteenth century. The whole of the nineteenth century and the early part of the twentieth were crammed with great aeronautical expectation. People launched themselves from balloons, off bridges and spires, anything that let them fly. The current safety levels in the descents, lecturers tell you, owe much to trendsetters who risked cracking their skulls and backs and lives in experimental jumps.

You are particularly enthralled by the era of show jumpers and the trail-blazing free fallers who got the hang of controlled free fall by simply climbing out of cockpits and letting go. These are people after your own heart.

Two mammoth jumps stand out for you. First, Joe Kittinger's in Operation Excelsior, which was launched to inspect endurance at the frontiers of the atmosphere. In 1960, on his second jump, strapping his Beaupre multi-stage stabilisation parachute, Kittinger stepped from an open gondola 103,000 feet above New Mexico, thirty kilometres above earth. He reached a speed of 1,000 kph at 90,000 feet, slowing down as the air became thicker, and opened his chute after four and a half minutes of free fall. He landed safely in the desert thirteen and a half minutes after stepping down from the gondola. No man has jumped from those heights since.

But there have been attempts. A crazy bloke by the name of Nick Piantanida tried in 1966. The New Jersey truck driver had big ambitions. He wanted to be the first skydiver in history to crack through the sound barrier. For this he had to attempt his jump from 120,000 feet above sea level, which would take him to Mach 1 before he hit thick air. The attempt ended in tragedy at 57,000 feet when the face shield blew out of his pressure suit. Piantanida died four months later, without ever coming out of coma.

Rodriguez has been a quiet participant in the training and lecture sessions. It's like the calm before a storm. He hasn't picked your bait yet and it's making you nervous. People like Rodriguez are fast movers. His patience gives you cause for alarm, although you are careful not to bring up matters yourself. From what you know of Rodriguez, he can sniff a trap in his sleep and you don't want the scent to lead to you.

Instead you have left letters and invitations on your bed that should indicate to him your presence at international seminars involving issues like defence and environment: the fixer-journalist with heavy connections. Even clinchers like inducements from the US Institute of Peace and the Carnegie Foundation to accept year-long fellowships. You have been heedful not to flaunt these personally. And Rodriguez has been careful not to let on if he has snooped on your documents, and he's far too cautious to let you catch him in the act.

Your strategy has been three-pronged. Besides your document display you have shown significant willingness to dilute your moral standards. In fact, you have been at pains to indicate none at all. You know he has appreciated your silence in the matter with Major (Dr) Sandy. Complicity in minor intrigues is a great bond with sizeable rogues like Rodriguez. So too are drugs. There you are as degenerate as Rodriguez. You need no special preparation for shooting and snorting yourself to high altitudes. You feel a solidarity there that levers you free from your long-term plans.

Third, you have given him evidence of your criminal genes. The bogus NGO that you floated to siphon off a Swedish grant committed enough foreign exchange violations to put you behind bars for five years, not even counting forging cheques. You left the fake clearance certificates lying unattended in the hostel you shared with him. Rodriguez quizzed you on the procedure but he stopped at that. It was enough; you've given him his edge. You want Rodriguez to get heady on that. Let him get an uppity feeling.

You also let it be known you're looking for a big score. A tally large enough to set up in a mansion in the English countryside. You drew the line at this. Any more perfume in the air and warning bells might ring in Rodriguez's ears.

But the closest connection between you comes from the game of danger you are involved in and the new dimensions that Rodriguez brings to it. You discover that the airborne brotherhood is a place for togetherness of a high order. It brings you specially close to play this new game, waiting to see who will drop lowest before pulling the cord. This came a little later, after you first started snorting on lady H at 10,000 feet. (Actually, even this was a little ahead in the sequence of things.)

First came the death of Captain Prakash. You have numerous hypotheses concerning Prakash's death. But first the facts. The timer on Prakash's chute activated at 8,000 feet in a Cessna when he was standing near the door. The pilot chute dragged Prakash out of the exit and his head banged on the side before he was plucked into thin air. At that height Prakash had forty-five seconds before impact. Captain Prakash's main chute wrapped itself around his spinning body and since reserves have no timers and he was unconscious, he hit earth at terminal velocity, a small matter of 190 kph.

To Rodriguez's credit, he displayed great presence of mind, fast reactions and supreme courage. He deltaed after Prakash in the vain hope of catching up with him at a sufficient height to pull his reserve cord. Rodriguez was nearest to the door, in jumping gear and one whose responsive hands Prakash desperately lunged for but failed to meet when he saw that his life's plug had just been pulled. Rodriguez came within twenty yards of Prakash, but the creep of the altimeter reminded him at 800 feet that he had better leave Prakash to his own fate. There was nothing anybody could do to save his skin.

Your first hypothesis regarding Prakash's death is that he forgot to switch off the timer on his chute after the pilot was forced to turn around from launching point by a murderous-looking cumulonimbus with enough water to outweigh a couple of aircraft carriers. A single wind from the cloud-swept mass could have cracked the Cessna like a tin box. In a hurry to get away, the pilot forgot to issue the compulsory warning when the plane descended. Timers operate on the barometric principle and activate at the air pressure you have set. It is part of procedure to deactivate your timer in the case of an aborted run and it seemed to have slipped Prakash's mind.

Or the timer malfunctioned. But they are reliable gadgets.

Your third hypothesis, and the most troubling one, is that somebody else activated Prakash's timer after he had switched it off. Somebody who stayed focused while the rest of you gazed through the Cessna's portholes at the ready distraction provided by the swirling black mass.

In spite of Rodriguez's gallant act, something which even PJIs with over a thousand jumps to their name are scared to attempt, the needle of your suspicion swings to him. Prakash's rag doll death doesn't have the look of a technology fuck-up or human error. Somebody wanted him out of action. And you figure Captain Prakash had something on him which made Rodriguez desperate enough to go after it. Also, all you have is Rodriguez's version of Captain Prakash's fall. By the time the Cessna turned around and swung below the cloud cover everything was over. Maybe Prakash's reserve did open and Rodriguez jumped to ensure that he stayed dead even if he survived the drop.

You don't discount such ominous possibilities. Especially when you take into account Captain Prakash's background. Captain Prakash was an officer from the 7 Sikh, which right now is based in Kashmir's Kupwara sector, the same area as Major Rodriguez's 5 Kumaon.

A week before, you heard a heated argument of some sort between the two as you entered Captain Prakash's room, which terminated abruptly as soon as you made your appearance. You never bought Rodriguez's explanation that Prakash was upset because he (that is, Rodriguez) was mainlining in his room. He had all the toking paraphernalia spread in front of him. Whatever else Captain Prakash might have been he was pretty cool about high octane levels in somebody else's bloodstream. He wasn't a snitch either.

He knew what you and Rodriguez were up to when you chose to be the last to jump into the slipstream of the AN-32. Snorting H at terminal velocity is hardly an efficient way to get your rush. Since there is no way you can nose in an appreciable quantity the regular way, you have to smear your thumb and forefinger with powder before you jump and stick them up your nostrils after you have cleared the air cushion from the plane.

There are a few drawbacks inherent in the method. You have never taken to the taste of heroin. It's bitter and you have to drag it one nostril at a time. Besides, though the powder hits in a minute, you get none of the blinding buzz that comes when you mainline. You also have to take into account the wastage of material that occurs with lots of it remaining in your nostrils, plus the amount that you lose in the wind. And H is gold dust as far as you are concerned.

The injecting rush is intrinsic to your pharma-diving plans. Though the rush is something that veteran users are immune to, you have not let the drug run away with you and you don't fall under the addict classification. You want to let the whooz hit you even as the air is blowing past. You want to run with life and death forces before you pull your cord. Of course, mainlining at ground level itself is a sufficiently complex procedure. It depends upon the purity of the heroin you can corner from retail. If it's prime grade you spread it on a spoon with a small amount of water. Your next step is to flame the solution so that the particles dissolve easily. Then you suck it up through a syringe and hit a vein in your forearm. Of course, if all you can get hold of on street corners is brown, your kit will have to include citric acid or ascorbic acid to ensure powder assimilation. To sift the impurities further you have to syringe the solution through a cigarette filter.

An attempt to go through these steps during sixty seconds of free fall is fraught with various unknowns. But that is hardly a deterrent for you and Rodriguez. You test a few breeze-proof lighters in flight but they aren't designed with free fall in mind. You go for a battery-operated wire lighter souped up by Rodriguez to include an additional pair of pencil batteries.

'It's cold as a morgue up there. We need some supplementary power heating to get us by,' says Major Rodriguez.

You have to dig your glucose disposable into a forearm vein before taking flight and keep it in place with a smartly wound Velcro. You have the syringe taped right next to the tube opening, which is capped. You take the precaution of corking the needle tip. You carry your premixed ammunition in a small bottle and attach a paper clip to use as a handle. Theoretically, all you have to do is get on your back, heat the bottle, detach the syringe from its holster, suck the solution through, unhinge the syringe and depress the plunger in your tube.

Because of the precarious nature of your circumstances, you have to keep glancing at the altimeter strapped to your midriff. Altitude has a way of creeping up on you unawares. It also teaches you in unambiguous terms the direct relation between cause and effect. Your head elevates more than is necessary and the spin works on you, you go into uninvited somersaults, losing the tenuous hold over your kit.

You try streamlining your procedure at ground level. Rehearse after dinner on the suspension wires. Pick up Formula 1 pit stop speeds in your routine. For all of Rodriguez's automated bluster, he's at heart a risk management expert. He accepts the hazards involved but he works at blunting the luck factor. That's the way you operate, too. You believe in giving yourself sufficient chances to pull things off.

You come up with the idea of falling together, just having one man go for the needle. This way you have a watchdog to pull your cord should the hit take you too deep into the game to bother. Heroin puts the troubles of the world at a great distance – you fall in a beautiful bubble of stupefaction. And one of the uncorrectable things it can do to you at 2,000 feet, the recommended safe height for pulling your cord, is sink in you the belief that life is too complicated to manage and the best way out is the free ticket to oblivion.

You spin a coin to decide who's going to take first shot. You call right. The first time you do it, Providence smiles your way. You are not on a regular training run, but are doing an unofficial exit from an IL-76 on a pilot training sortie. It's just the two of you in the whole wide bay of the 160-seater. You bend your routine a bit. You take your shot at the door itself before yahooing into space. The major goes non-nuclear. You lacked the foresight to keep some spare ammunition.

At moderate doses of H, your brain retains its distinctness and dynamism. You go into sharp focus and the warm feeling that emanates from your belly steers you clear without any effort from the everyday clutter that ping-pongs in your head. You gravitate to a spiritual exactness. You are like a seer soaring and swooping in heaven. You are into NOW. You are into nothing. You see the ground rush into you and when you pull the cord it's an afterthought, with none of the urgency and fear that categorised this action for you in the past. When the nylon jerks you violently into deceleration you hardly feel the cords bite into the bruises at your shoulders.

The only luck that comes Rodriguez's way is that you manage another training sortie ride but this time the seats are full with veteran Pathfinders from 10 Para commando battalion who are sneaking a joy jump free of military encumbrances. For 12,000-feet plus jumps you need thermal suits, oxygen masks and cylinders and acclimatisation routines. You talk in hand signals at these heights, and although you have jumped with all that gear it makes your dives too technical for you to think of introducing the Afghan soldiers into your bloodstream. Even though you get more time with a mask on your face you can't see for shit.

The advantage that informal leaps give you is there's no PJI breathing over your neck when you fall a couple of kilometres away from drop zone. You can never make it to the designated drop zone and punch your way to God at the same time – your chute opens too low for you to get much glide momentum.

But this time you're going to drop close to a highway and hitch a ride back to base.

Rodriguez slips in the mid-air engagements with robotic accuracy and speed. 'Nobody goes face up,' he keeps mumbling to himself, his mantra. The two of you jump together.

After mainlining with swift efficiency, he gives you the thumbs up sign, chucks the syringe into the air, and you can see it sharing the ride with you twenty feet away. Before you split, you check the major one last time and you see symptoms that you recognise as signs of an overdose. Rodriguez is slipping into a daze, his eyes falling shut and his chin slipping to his chest.

You realise that the H Rodriguez has mixed today is purer than both of you thought. You have been so used to the inferior dimorphine base stepped with glucose, lactose, chalk and talcum powder that the real thing has put you in a spot. Brown has purity levels ranging from 20 to 40 per cent. The same quantum with weapons-grade heroin can steer you into some serious side effects, all perfectly visible in Rodriguez's case. His head begins to roll uncontrollably.

You realise that if you don't do something for Rodriguez, and quickly, he'll go the way of Captain Prakash. A part of you sees justice in such a scheme of things, but you also understand that Rodriguez is your only overpass to more sinister happenings in Kashmir, and he is worth more to you alive than dead. Still, there's only so much you can do, since even after you pulled his cord and split, his chute would launch from a face-up position and tangle him hopelessly in its lines.

But people like Rodriguez aren't what they are without residual survival syndromes. Even as you pull the cord and before the pilot chute comes flapping out, some aboriginal instinct tunes Rodriguez to the danger he is in and you see him bend in a reverse arch and flip over as his main chute shoots up. You take a look at your altimeter as you open up. You have dipped 500 feet below expedient altitude.

Rodriguez survives the landing with his bones intact, though he is in and out when you reach him in a tomato field. The experience of the fall makes the two of you abort future heroin skydiving. Instead you go on speed, which you snort in the loo next to the briefing hall and it fortifies you in your resolve to pull your lifeline at heights below 1,000 feet or whoever cracks up first. It is here in the loo that the two of you first shoot methedrine and you discover that the hit is much more powerful than H, doesn't last long and won't put you to sleep in mid-air.

But you don't want to push your luck with methedrine. One of its effects is that it makes you feel omnipotent. It doesn't, like H, give you an insight into things – it becomes the insight. You become God. And flying with that fiery brand of philosophy in your head is, you decide, a prelude to dangerous consequences.

But you command an emotion from Rodriguez after bailing him out which you thought lay outside his repertoire. He occasionally flashes you a look of something like gratitude, even respect.

And one day he feels the need to confide, his way of handing you his balls. A motherfucker's reciprocatory gesture.

'Hey, MM,' he says. 'You know why Prakash died?'

'Because the timer fucked on him,' you offer, with a poker face.

He looks straight into your eyes. A bastard's piercing gaze. 'Because if you play out of your depth, and you don't pack what it takes to get you out of a hole, you just sign up for what's headed your way.'

This is as far as he goes in his confession. But it is easy to take things from there. For you, the shark had sunk its teeth into the bait. Now it is a question of giving a lot of slack and reeling in at a propitious moment. Rodriguez taps you on your intents, tempts you with the big score, and you, in turn, nibble on the enticement offered your way.

The two of you don't stick around at para school after this. There's no need to. For one, you aren't part of the para crowd and are pissing off the regular bunch with your fucked-up attitude to free falling. Also, sticking around meant falling eventually to another bout of pharma-diving, which might well lead you in the footsteps of Captain Prakash.

You give them reason to tick you out of base. You botch three consecutive DZs, and PJI Malhotra decides that he isn't in the mood for another casualty so soon after the Prakash incident. Even if the Army Women's Welfare Association could use the royalties.

When you next meet him, two months down the line, it's in a very changed locale. You are in Kashmir, partly to shoot a documentary on the Line of Control at Kupwara, where 5 Kumaon and Major Rodriguez are posted, but you haven't sought him out just yet. Although there is a lot of pressure on you to whip up the pace in your dealings with him, you want things to develop naturally.

It's late April 1999 and you have come a few days ahead with half your crew, a sound engineer called Siddy. You have to push paper with the 15th Corps at Srinagar, part of the Northern Command at Udhampur, get them to sort out the logistics.

Siddy is the son of a veteran with a distinguished record of service in the 1971 East Pakistan war. Right now he has with him a manual which he has pinched from Major General Mahalingam's office at 15th Corps, *Standard Operation Procedure in Low Intensity Conflict Areas, Volume 1*.

'We have fucked it up from the start,' he says.

'Fucked what up?' you ask, alarmed. In your life you have fucked up many things, often with painful results, and you like to stitch up the loose ends in your control.

You realise after Siddy hands you over the *SOPLICA* manual that your beginning in Kashmir has been both illiterate and dangerous.

Rule 1 of *SOPLICA* warns you not to arrive in Low Intensity Conflict areas in military aircraft. That might single you out as part of a Special Forces Group. You and Siddy had hopped a ride in an army Avro. Siddy's red London Fog jacket must have been visible for kilometres around. You learn that airports in LIC areas are usually where the

Mossies sponge for tips on arrivals. Rule 2 of *SOPLICA* warns you not to stay in street-level hotel rooms, as they are easier to get into and easier to throw something through your windows. Right now you are freezing your ass in room 101, ground level, soft target for loony Mossies.

You have assiduously refused army guest house accommodation. You are in the mood for some luxury, and even though the hotel you have pitched camp in, bordering the Dal Lake, isn't luxurious, it is better than the squatter mess settlements that the Western Command is most likely to put at your disposal. You also learn in detail about soft and hard targets. Soft targets don't stay alert, aren't aware of what is happening around them, are predictable, don't blend with the environment, are high-key jerks and don't stay informed. Conversely, hard targets are inaccessible, unpredictable, aware, low key and own a dog.

This was knowledge. All you had to do to become a hard target was start acting like a low-key jerk, buy a dachshund and adhere to individual protective measures. Two of these being not opening doors to strangers and wedging a one-inch screw between the door jamb and the door. So you tell Siddy to go hunt for a screw and jam the door up. You tell him to find a screw and what he does is use the tin top of your black Cherry Blossom boot polish. That's Siddy for you. You can't get him to do a thing straight.

If you delay entry of the terrorist, *SOPLICA* explains, you get time to rush to alternative exits or lock yourself in the bathroom, where you can get into the bathtub and start raising hell. That's if the tub's not made of porcelain or something, in which case it wouldn't be enough protection against gunfire. The bathroom in 101 doesn't have a tub.

You are also supposed to learn sentences like 'Help', 'I need a doctor' and 'Where is the police station?' in the local language. The best way, however, to keep from being selected as a target is – and here you quote – 'not to say, do, wear, display, or drive anything that will help the terrorists identify you as non-Kashmiri. Wearing military uniform, for example, will identify you as an Indian. When a uniform is required at work, wear civilian clothes while travelling to and from work.'

Even if you do merge in with the locals this way, not observing local customs and habits will give you away.

You have started reading the manual aloud and Siddy, who's dusting the lenses of his Panavision video camera, is getting more and more agitated. Part of the reason for his perturbation is, of course, your own put-on about the whole thing. The main reason, however, is that after a binge last night on Tibetan Temple Balls, nuggets of hash he periodically gets from Dharmshala, he is a little edgy. He has run out of the stuff.

If you are locked in a hotel room a thousand kilometres from home with a guy like Siddy, one of the ways of entertaining yourself would be to read documents like the SOPLICA.

You may also, just for the hell of it, try following some of the less bizarre recommendations. For instance, when room service knocks on your door to clear your American breakfast, you tell the guy (through the door) to come back later. Meanwhile, you have Siddy wrench the Cherry Blossom tin top out from under the door, which takes him ten times longer than to insert the stupid thing and renders it useless as a tin top in the process.

Out in the lobby, where you hang around for a while with Siddy, you bump into Sally Jennings of *The Times*, London. Sally seems hugely interested in what Siddy and you are up to in Kashmir. She's chasing the story of the four foreign hostages taken by militants. Nobody is quite sure whether they are alive or dead. You, of course, know the fate that befell them and when and at whose behest, but this is not the time to spread any free enlightenment. When you tell her you are here on a film project, she gets even nosier. At first it strikes you as suspicious when Sally says she's heard of you, but you have learnt that the big reason journalists talk to other journalists is to get story ideas, and Kashmir in April is a bit silent, and Sally from London seems more than a little desperate.

So you spread some bait. You mention a survey you would like to show her later, after she has spent her seventh day chasing army and police bureaucracy. There's this unpublished sex survey that *The Post* commissioned. You have been carrying it around in your leather satchel for well over a month. A sneak preview in a London paper would give the magazine some welcome publicity, besides forcing Digs, your editor, to slot the survey and your lead essay on priority form. It's one of your weaknesses to want to see yourself in print every now and then.

Besides, there is always sex. Your strike rate in alien territory is something you are proud of. It beats reading *SOPLICA* manuals in the hotel room with Siddy jamming doors with Cherry Blossom tin tops. So you exchange some more pleasantries with Sally before heading out with Siddy to pick up tomorrow's itinerary at Northern Command's local HQ and lobby for a chopper ride to the Kupwara sector. Going by road would be time consuming and uncomfortable. More important, you want to sound out military top brass on your editor's questionnaire.

Srinagar, when you are high on acid and *SOPLICA*, isn't much fun. Especially when you remember that one of the *SOPLICA* clauses relates to inspecting your car, even if it's a taxi, for tell-tale signs of a bomb. You have to look underneath as you approach, walk around the outside and examine for smudges, marks and fingerprints at the doors, the bonnet and the boot. A careless Mossie might have dropped something on the ground – electrical tape, a broken circuit board or a detonator. There may even be wires hanging out that weren't there earlier.

Hard targets are also supposed to look around the interior of the car and not dump their personal stuff around on the back seat. That makes it easier for some Mossie to conceal his explosive mechanism. Try explaining that to Siddy. You are even supposed to look under the front seat and the dashboard before you sit in the car.

It's a tedious routine, and since you went through all the initial manoeuvres without noticing that your driver was watching you all the while from inside the taxi, you feel like a fool once you and Siddy get in. It's only the 250 micrograms that's holding your shit together.

But *SOPLICA* is on you like a demon. There are these bold clauses about keeping your windows rolled up when coming to checkpoints and just rolling down the one at the driver's side about four inches to show the pass. But the van you are riding in has no air conditioning and this is Srinagar in April. Siddy has half his face hanging out his side of the Ambassador like a dog.

But your paranoia levels are revving up. Acid sometimes does funny things to you. You try checking on other *SOPLICA* transit desirables. You are supposed to have a first-aid kit and a fire extinguisher stashed within the vehicle. Zero. The gas tank has to be topped off to minimise explosive effects. Condition unknown. Have two good side-view mirrors outside and one long rear-view mirror inside. The van, you observe in a psychedelic haze, has no side-view mirrors and the one inside is cracked.

On roads, drive in the centre to avoid being boxed in. The checkpoints wouldn't let anyone do that. You count ten that you have to cross before you reach HQ, a grim reminder of the war zone you are in.

You leave Siddy in the little magazine-filled cubicle that Major General Suresh Mahalingam's personal staff passes off as the waiting room. Siddy, at best, is unpresentable in delicate situations like the one you are about to negotiate.

When you last met Major General Mahalingam he was running the National Security Guard in Delhi. Your persistent image of him is when he tried opening a 747 wing emergency door from the outside in front of the minister of state for defence, who had, at Mahalingam's insistence, made a courtesy appearance to watch a Quick Reaction Team make a dummy run on the plane. Mahalingam yanked the handle so hard his hand slipped, and the momentum took his heels from under him, sprawling him on the wing, from where he had to take a ride on a stretcher.

Clearly, it had been decided that his inherent potential for fuck-ups would have less impact on national security in a FUBAR area like Kashmir than in the nation's premier special force. You interviewed him once, for a documentary on the NSG. To get clearance you showed him rushes that included a long uninterrupted sequence of his talking mug, which pleased him no end. But since you snipped all of that in the version that finally aired, the brigadier has nursed a silent grouse against you for not raising his career curve.

And right now, as you discuss your editor Digs's wheel questionnaire with him, the only ammunition you have at your disposal is a letter from the Defence Research and Development Organisation certifying the psychological methodology you have adapted to snapshot the souls of the people running the army's LoC patrols. Yes, and a letter from the vice-chief of the army requesting co-operation with personnel from *The Post*.

It was part of Digs's editorial brainwave, based on your subtle input, to peg a defence cover for the magazine on a morale poll of the army, with special focus in LIC areas like Kashmir. Give the readers souped-up psychological statistics that would tell them something. Needless to say, in a scheme as grandiose as this, a lot depended upon army co-operation. Or your ingenuity in slipping it in through their bureaucratic set-up, an act equivalent to passing RDX through airport security.

But you have plans. You have a two-part questionnaire. The first, which is Digs's creation, is essentially your smokescreen.

You explain the intricacies of this open-ended question-naire to Major General Mahalingam.

'Sir,' you begin, 'the good part about this questionnaire is that it can be administered individually or in groups. It's the first time that military psychologists have devised such an analytical and psychological tool.'

'I didn't know we had military psychologists,' comments Major General Mahalingam.

'They just started the wing at the DRDO. It's a small one. In fact, our editor, Ashok Mehra, helped them manufacture this open-ended structure appraisal and coping assessment technique. He's got a degree in psychology from Cornell University,' you say.

'What's open-ended?' asks Mahalingam suspiciously.

'It's a questionnaire which opens and ends,' you say rather lamely.

'Doesn't every questionnaire do that?'

'I guess not, sir. Or they wouldn't have called it that. Most of the assessing techniques developed so far start midway. Not this one. Also, you can't go on listing thousands of factors or there would be no end. The subjects are asked to write down just twelve factors that are most characteristic of the war situation. There is also a time limit. Most psychological tools don't have that. This is a new generation PsyOps. Please have a look at it, sir,' you say and push Digs's wheel questionnaire right up the major general's nose.

Mahalingam looks at the three sheets of paper the way a cobra stares at a snake charmer's stationary gourd stem.

'What are these segments?' he asks at last.

'Those, sir, are for the twelve factors that the subject will write in the wheel that he thinks are typical war characteristics. There are twelve of them,' you say.

'But there's no war?'

'The psychologists maintain that an LIC situation is sometimes even more stressful than a regular field war, sir,' you say.

But Mahalingam is not listening to you right now. He's intrigued by certain signs. 'What are these plus and minus signs here?'

'Those are the rankings, sir. The soldiers are supposed to rank the factors in order of importance. Two or more factors can have the same rankings. For instance, a soldier might say that fear of death has the same order of importance for him as the fear of maiming himself.'

'What are these plus and minus signs here? What do they mean?' The major general was getting inquisitive.

'They, sir, are the negative or positive evaluation of the factor itself by the subject. For instance, if he listed not letting his comrades down as a factor in a war situation, he might cite that as a positive factor and fear of death as a negative factor. So he might rank the positive factor as a + + + + on a five-point scale and the negative as – – – –,' you say.

'What good is it going to do?' asks Major General Mahalingam. His eyes don't blink as he peers at you.

'Sir, the test is designed to index the motivational, coping, emotional balance and ambiguity levels in the subject,' you say.

'Ambiguity levels. What does that mean?'

'That's the effectiveness of differentiation, sir. The degree to which perceived elements are distinct and unique,' you say. You have learnt in your experience with army brass that one sure-shot method to freeze hostility levels is to become unintelligible.

'What's this?' asks Major General Mahalingam, looking at the second part of the questionnaire, the toxic one.

'That's the backgrounder, sir,' you explain. 'Its purpose is to glean over the fault levels of the wheel questionnaire. See whether the subject is answering questions truthfully or not. It's for the psychologist's own use.'

But amongst the questions that you have listed there are many that could embarrass the military. One that you have hidden somewhere in the middle goes: Have you ever indulged in self-mutilation to duck the border patrol? Your sources report high levels of self-mutilation as yet undeclared and not accepted by army authorities as fact.

Another is a set of three variously dispersed questions about drugs. Have you ever taken drugs on the border or seen other military personnel take them? If so, how frequently do you take them or see other personnel take them? How do you finance your drug habit? Do you sell captured arms or loot in cordon and search operations?

But before this set of questions come the more generic ones. What for you is the most frightening aspect of battle – letting dependants down, death, injury, letting the unit down, being a coward? Are you happy with your officer, or do you think he should be replaced?

Midway Major General Mahalingam's brows net a little and you think you have fucked up – but you needn't have worried.

'MM, do you think we could add an extra question?' asks Mahalingam.

'Certainly, sir, anything you suggest.'

'Something about whether the soldiers would feel better if they had on 9 mm body armour when they were doing cordon and search operations,' says he. 'We have had ten deaths in the past month. All close-range shots.'

One of the most satisfying moments in Major General Mahalingam's career has been when he designed shock pads and shrapnel glue for the 'Tiger Steel' 9 mm bullet-proof vests developed by the DRDO. He gave you a demonstration of the vest for the documentary, then he took the shock pads and shrapnel glue out of the vest and had a dummy shot. The dummy went back five yards and had a head full of shrapnel.

You remember him saying, 'Vests are no fun if they stop slugs but still can't keep metal out of your face. You also have to keep your balance, for a bullet hitting you is like five mule kicks. The shock pads spread the force of the slug over your whole torso and the glue on the steel grabs the lead.' It's been Mahalingam's constant lament that the value of his inventions has been given short shrift by the DRDO. It's also been his relentless endeavour to publicise himself as the chief designer of the vest.

'I guess that's an excellent idea, sir. It would establish the degree of fear psychosis present in cordon and search operations,' you say. 'If you are in agreement, sir, we could also toss in a question about whether the soldiers would like to wear the Tiger Steel 9 mm vest during border patrols, too. It would make the job tough for snipers on the other side.'

'Yes. It would reduce casualties, too. Besides, if they had to make so many vests they might put some money into research and come up with a lighter variety of steel,' says Major General Mahalingam. His eyes sparkle.

'Yes, sir. Nine kilograms is a little heavy right now. They might come up with something as light as a Goretex jacket,' you say.

'What's a Goretex jacket?' asks Mahalingam.

'It's a brand name, sir. They specialise in mountain gear.'

'Oh.'

'Another thing, sir,' you begin. You like to strike when the iron's hot. 'One of the statistical components of the test is to administer a few of them in battlefield-like conditions. Like a little before, after or during a cordon and search operation, or even after a Special Forces operation. I was wondering if you could have something organised in the Kupwara sector in the next two days, sir.'

'Why do you want to do that?' asks a perplexed Mahalingam. His idea of a psychology test slickly administered would be to herd his unit into battalion HQ and hand out test sheets to the men to fill in, squatting in the open field. Military style.

'Well, you see, sir, soldiers are in different mood frames in battlefield conditions. They answer questions in a different manner when the action's all under their nose rather than far

41

away. We want to map the fluctuation levels, sir,' you say.

'Well, MM,' says Major General Mahalingam. 'I wouldn't mind letting you do that, but frankly, as you will understand, it's all a little out of my hands. I mean, you don't know what's going to happen.' Then, a little wickedly, 'But maybe I will go through last evening's SITREPs and see what can be done. If anything's possible I will have my aide contact you.'

'Yes, sir,' you say. 'That would be just perfect. By the way, sir, we are also planning a documentary on the twenty best inventions in India in the last five years. Even the BBC is interested. We were thinking of putting the Tiger Steel vest in the top ten. I hope you don't have any objection to that, sir?'

'BBC? When is this?' asks Mahalingam. You can actually see his nostrils quiver.

'As soon as we get back from Kashmir, sir,' you say. 'We would like to send a crew up to shoot you with the vest and all, sir. It would be very impactful.'

'Certainly,' says Major General Mahalingam. His chest swells and he twirls his moustache.

Then you decide to fuck the major general a bit for a little parting entertainment.

'Actually, sir, what the producer of our documentary wants is for each inventor to use his invention in front of the camera,' you say. 'I hope you are OK with that, sir.'

'With *what*?' asks Major General Mahalingam nervously. You notice about half the blood disappear from his face.

'Like we would want you to wear the vest and have a soldier shoot at you with an AK-47 or something. Makes the whole thing dramatic. Like, in your case, the inventor, putting his life on the line behind his invention,' you say.

'I am too old for that kind of thing, MM,' says Major General Mahalingam and he laughs a sickly kind of laugh.

Your face falls. You behave as if this attitude of the major brigadier might cause you some major problems with BBC.

'It's part of the film format, sir. And it's kind of approved by the BBC, which has bought first airing rights for the documentary. You can't change the grid of the thing. BBC would throw a fit. Like we have this guy in Bangalore who's featuring in the show, who's developed this special putty for making bricks that are stronger and cheaper than the regular ones. We have him making the bricks himself. And he has to step up to his neck in mud mixing the bloody thing,' you say.

You wait a bit for the thing to sink in. Watch the clash between opportunity and fear in Major General Mahalingam before you decide to bail him out.

'But I will see what I can do, sir,' you say. 'I might get them to agree to a wooden dummy or even a volunteer from one of your battalions.'

Siddy is rather upset with you. If your limited range of emotions included empathy, you might be tempted to feel more charitable.

Siddy has spent the day in Major General Mahalingam's outer office working the Tiger Steel vest question into the wheel questionnaire. After he's typed the whole goddamn thing in (and Siddy types with about half a finger and takes two minutes to search for a letter), there was still the logistics of rolling a thousand-odd printouts. Mahalingam's laser jet had just enough toner to reel out a hundred copies. The rest Siddy had to photostat and it took him all evening to get to four figures because the power kept tripping on him, and the machine kept heating up, spitting out copies that looked as if they'd been distorted by magic mirrors. All this you got to know via Siddy's periodic, abusive telephone updates.

Then Siddy's return to civilisation wasn't much better. You poked your head out of 101 just long enough to tell him to buzz off. One thing you dislike with intensity is someone watching you turn the smile for half a chick. Sally Jennings just about makes it to the half-way mark: her thin upper lip gives her a flat, stupid grin, as if she smiled by stretching and clenching her upper lip in her mouth.

That is the reason you aren't giving her a reason to smile. You couldn't take that smile even on LSD. Instead you are discussing the sex survey, the first and only one of its kind to be conducted in India, you tell her.

The survey itself you have discussed threadbare in its many intriguing details. Starting with the multiplicity of sex partners, you have reeled off the figures on pre-marital sex.

Of course, you never let her read the survey herself. That would be giving away the mystery. But you let her absorb the occasional pie chart, throw enough numbers at her to keep her scribbling madly.

'Don't you think it's amazing that Calcutta's India's sex capital? I mean, all the numbers are so high out there,' says Sally.

'Yes,' you say. 'You never would have thought the Bengalis had it in them. Actually, I think it's just the women who are more into it.' Yours is a subjective opinion.

'But women are only into it with men,' clarifies Sally rather wickedly.

You begin to notice her break into the preparations for a grin. You forestall that with a grim outbreak of statistics.

'Our respondent base in the survey has been close to three thousand. We spread them over twenty cities. Even in cities we had a minimum of twenty clusters from which we selected them,' you inform her. You begin to feel rather unequal to the task. You have never done it before, play a seduction game with this taxing parameter of not having the woman smile.

But her lithe form is rather setting you off and what you do is get your sunglasses out from your suitcase and put them on, so if she did grin it wouldn't grab you that bad. 'I have this problem with my eyes,' you tell her. 'It's a kind of allergy. They start to water without notice. Would you like some Kashmiri tea?'

'No, thanks,' says Sally.

You get up to go to the loo for a chemical infusion. The acid in your bloodstream is weakening. Acid lowers your threshold, lets you distract yourself with almost any woman. You have been in love just once, but that was way back during your Academy days. Afterwards there were some in college.

Then you got into drugs. Grass first, acid later. Mercifully, you could muster enough control not to reach escape velocity,

45

and you didn't quite graduate into heroin. Instead you took up interests like mountaineering and soon realised that you had to cut down on the chemicals to keep your muscles trim and nourished. But you never lost the taste for the rush. For you it isn't just a chemical wonder. It's what happens to you when you are in the game with an adversary like Major Rodriguez. When you are free falling from 10,000 feet or holding on to life from a slender crevice at 18,000 feet on the Nuptse face.

Your quality of life is defined by the rushes you can generate without short-circuiting your system. You have yet to reach optimum levels of efficiency. This is one of the reasons you live the way you do. A hole, a vacuum, that sucks your life in between two rushes. This is where you sense the danger lies.

Right now, for instance, it lies in your search for sex without intimacy. Though it's nothing new for you, the various permutations and combinations of danger this lifestyle can generate aren't beyond your capacity to grasp. For one, you could get AIDS, for you are out of raincoats for your apparatus. Two – and here lay the real danger – you are prone to indiscretions when you lie in bed with a warm body wrapped around you. It does things to your head. It makes you talk about Shomali, your sweetheart many years before. Perhaps one of the reasons you go to bed with women you don't love is to talk about what happened. It only happens after the temporary cleansing that sex brings about, after you ride a woman.

Sally is jotting masturbation statistics from your survey when you come back from the loo, chemically invigorated.

'It's funny,' she says, 'how 40 per cent of the women left this query unanswered. Why is it that much of a taboo?'

This is the kind of opening you look forward to to give a crank to the proceedings.

'I thought even the Kinsey Report had a low response to this question,' you say. 'Would you answer this question?'

'Yes, of course,' says Sally. 'There's nothing wrong in answering the question.'

'Do you masturbate, Sally Jennings? If so, what's your frequency? At what age did you first start masturbating? Do you indulge in clitoral stimulation only or do you use insertion devices? If insertion devices are unavailable, would you be content with using just your fingers to achieve penetration? Have you ever masturbated in a group? Do you think it's more satisfying than the act of sex? Have you told your boyfriend or husband about this habit of yours? If so, what has his reaction been?' you ask.

'You mean it went like *that*, the questionnaire?' Sally asks. You can feel her self-composure thin a bit.

'I am asking you,' you say impishly.

For a while you feel that she isn't up to it. But she rallies, though you never would have thought that she would fall to the obvious bait of answering your series of questions. She takes a deep breath and reels out some very private statistics.

'Yes, I masturbate. My average should work out to something quite above your Indian women mean average of five times a month. I first started masturbating at the age of thirteen. I indulge in both clitoral as well as penetrative stimulation but my favourite remains clitoral. I am content to use my fingers for stimulation. I haven't masturbated in a group, though I have had frequent fantasies of doing so with males. There's nothing that can beat the act of sex. I have never talked about this habit of mine with any of my boyfriends,' says Sally.

That's how you start up on her. But it takes a while to soften her enough to get her to ride the night in your company. For that you have to lace the late-night coffee you order with an ampoule, after which you have things running easy and in control.

The key to control, you have worked out, is being in lesser need than the person you seek to control. The way to work on it is not to decrease your own need, for that may or may not be possible, but to increase the need of the other. What, however, you have learnt from experience is that while it is possible to induce a physical need, that's not what you are looking for in someone you happen to fall in love with. For instance, the need that makes someone take you for what you are is something you can always be sure to fail to induce.

The way you like to take your girls is to begin on them slow. If you are in a freaky mood you work on giving them the shave. You specially like to lather girls with compressed foam from Gillette canisters. You are armed with a Bentex double-edged razor blade that you keep enclosed in your shaving kit for encounters like these.

Shaving pubic hair is an art in itself. The skill lies in making it an enjoyable experience for the woman. You ease Sally's stiffness and apprehension by spraying on her a liberal dose of foam. Then you start rubbing the foam on her mound till she stops giggling. That's when you know that she has entered the pleasure zone. You have to allow ten minutes for the foam to soften the hair roots. Most shavers don't have the patience to work this time into their schedule and that makes the razor work tough.

But once you weave this bit of technicality into the proceedings your razor movements become silky and slice through the hairs as though they were cobwebs. The other trick is to keep on stimulating the girl even as you shave, to swamp any prickly and unsavoury sensations your shaving might be giving her.

While generally your shaving posture is ankles under the girl's thigh and knees bent as you crouch over her mound, you try an innovation with Sally. You face the other way with your knees digging beside her waist and your head bent over the mound the wrong way up. This gives you the de luxe facility of having Sally stroke the base of your dick with her fingers, rub it against her breasts or take you in her mouth.

Although it upsets your concentration on a couple of occasions, especially when she suckles you in one deep and lasting lip squeeze, it is not enough to shake your shaving hand.

After you are through with shaving you wipe Sally clean with a towel and uncap the bottle of olive oil you use for post-shaving interludes. You drop a few drops on her clitoris and spread the puddle over in smooth strokes. The secret of your olive oil is that it has half a dozen poppers dissolved in it, making it a lethal arousal fluid – the nitroglycerine of pussy.

You stop during your rhythmic stroking to make her cry for you to continue. The begging acts like an aphrodisiac on you. The more you leave off the more she begs and the more you feel strong enough to move into your entering routine without bursting a popper under your nose.

But you haven't taken into account the ghost that roams your mind. The hurt that's there and won't let go for those few brief moments that bring with them the joy of oblivion. But first you feel a compulsion to make Sally come harder than she ever has before, and as you rub the oil on her smooth mound you start finger fucking her. One, two and then three fingers and when she is nearly shouting for you to mount and perform the final rites you burst a popper under her nose with your left hand even as you increase the speed of your lubrication and you glimpse first-hand the frightening sexuality of a woman fully aroused and in the act.

What you regret is that the sight hasn't the impetus to move your own drive into top gear. You lie shrunken and handicapped beside Sally as she comes back from her shudders and you ask her when she lets go the tight hug she has you in, 'Have you ever been in love?'

'What?' she asks. The timing of the question produces a little incomprehension. But she rallies. 'Yes,' she says.

'What was it like?'

'It was like being in perpetual pain,' she says.

You think you might have to rethink her philosophical potential. You become curious. 'And why was that?'

'I wanted to possess him and when I couldn't it turned into pain,' says Sally.

'Why did you want to possess him?'

'My love is like that. It doesn't seek a moment or a fuck. It wants all of something. And very few people can give all of theirs to somebody. They want to keep a lot of it for themselves,' she says. 'What about you? Why didn't you come? Should I work on you?'

Sally tries to blow some air into your limp shooter but it's got a puncture she doesn't know about.

'Are you still in love with him?' you ask.

'Yes, but I don't think about it. It's over,' she says.

'How can you still be in love and say that it's over?' you ask. Such things are always great puzzles for you.

'What I mean is I still have a soft corner for him but there hasn't been any motion on the thing for a couple of years now,' says Sally.

'So how can you say it's over if you still have a soft corner for him?' you persist.

'Because there's no pain any more. I don't have to start hating him to get him out of my system.' That's what all emotional recuperation is, you figure, getting the pain out of the nerve cells.

'But what if you can't get somebody out of your system and you continue loving that person even though it gives you pain?'

'Then I would say you have a problem,' says Sally and rubs her tits on your side.

'Who's talking about me?'

'So what if it's you? People have to have problems. What would they be without them?' she says and goes off to sleep snuggling against your chest.

But in the middle of the night, when you think about Shomali even as you lie with your hand sandwiched between Sally's freshly shaved crotch, there's a problem you would rather do without. It's Sally. She wakes up and asks you, 'Will you stuff ice in my cunt?'

The woman starts howling. Captain Satish Warrier, aide de camp to Major General Mahalingam, who's been eyeing you cagily, finds it difficult to carry on with his insulated composure.

Mahalingam had gone through the various situation reports on his desk and singled out three districts you could take a chopper to: Kupwara, Baramulla and Poonch. You are interested only in Kupwara, where both the 5 Kumaon and 7 Sikh are based, one hour's drive apart on the LoC. As it happened, Major Rodriguez himself was in Srinagar, on his way back from home leave in Goa. Division HQ at Kupwara immediately assigned him the task of interrogating certain Mossies caught by the 7 Sikh. Though 5 Kumaon and 7 Sikh report to different brigade headquarters at Kupwara, they are both part of the 27th Division, which in turn is part of the 15th Corps. You travel with Rodriguez in the chopper with Siddy and Captain Warrier for company.

You try including Warrier in the conversation you are having with the others, but Warrier is still smarting from the *SOPLICA* doctrine you had sprung on him when he knocked at your door with two packets under his arms.

'Thanks a lot, Captain Warrier,' you said. 'But don't you think you put yourself in danger bringing these?'

Captain Warrier was perplexed. His scope blinked off. Civilian asshole with some Major General Mahalingam connection was telling him he was in danger bringing in the packets. He found it difficult to shuffle the information in place, get his scope back on alternate power supply.

'It's there in *SOPLICA*,' you said, hoping to bail him out. Captain Warrier looked at you from a very military posture.

His gaze said a lot of things. His scope hummed back with light and he identified his quarry as a jerk from Mars whom unfortunately he had to humour because he was under orders from his CO to escort him to Kupwara.

'I don't think I understand, Mr Mehta,' he said.

'Oh, it's your own guys who made up the stuff,' you said, going to the table and picking up the manual. 'Section B. "Do not load yourself with packages in civilian areas so you can react with speed in case you are attacked."'

Here you chucked the *SOPLICA* manual right at Warrier's chest. He dropped your two packets, containing photostat copies of your questionnaire, in panic. He couldn't latch on to the manual either.

'There, Captain,' you said. 'The manual's right. It could have been a knife coming your way. You shouldn't burden yourself with such things when there's a war going on. Do you know that human beings can't react faster than a thirtieth of a second. A second. I mean, that's the fucking fastest they can react to anything happening around them. And even guys like Billy the Kid didn't have those reflexes. Not carrying that packet might have meant the difference between life and death to you. You roger?'

Captain Warrier was pretty shaken.

The arrival of Major Rodriguez spares him further embarrassment. He begins to think you are from Military Intelligence. He asks Major Rodriguez that over the rotors when he thinks you can't hear, and the major has such a laugh that he nearly rips off his seat harness. The major doesn't tell him anything and Warrier's dilemma continues.

Of course, right now he is standing right beside you and you are watching soldiers from the 7 Sikh search a household in the village of Nunkar. The Mossies Major Rodriguez has interrogated have squealed on the village. The Rodriguez preliminary interrogation chemotherapy involves the use of pliers and bandages, hot and cold stuff to get the assholes on the information highway. Prior to this is the emphasis on psychological stress to break down a prisoner's resistance. If the major has time on his side, conditioning of the prisoner starts under solitary confinement, where the prisoner's conception of place and time slowly begins to dissipate. According to the Rodriguez doctrine, removal from reality can be further advanced by the application of the technique of total immersion of the prisoner in warm, black and neutral water. The tank is designed for total sensory deprivation. It's easily portable in a truck as well. You can also increase the level of noise followed by periods of silence to heighten a prisoner's sense of danger.

Of course, the advanced Rodriguez pyrotechnics involve Soviet techniques. This hyper-accelerates the whole process and is right up the major's sleeve. It means using drugs. Hallucinogens and tranquillisers deepen a prisoner's disorientation and begin the onset of phobias that break a prisoner's mental resistance. Rodriguez's speciality is the use of tubocurarine, a muscle relaxant that in increased doses results in a paralysis of the diaphragm. Hooked to artificial ventilation, the prisoner becomes beholden to his interrogator for every life-giving breath.

You haven't yet seen the major's skills with tubocurarine first-hand. But you don't doubt them. He acquired his expertise at a training programme in Moscow. That's the reason HQ called him in to help the 7 Sikh. HQ doesn't care about turf.

There is a significant cache of arms somewhere in the village and the 7 Sikh has gone through every single one of the fifty houses like a comb and come up with nothing more than a used truck battery which, try as they may, they cannot link to the cache.

And now there is this motherly woman howling the village down and soldiers from the 7 Sikh coming out of her house with their faces sheepish and the search half done. This is when Captain Warrier is provoked enough to come up to you and gesticulate.

'Jesus, she's like my mother. These guys can't behave like that with her,' he says.

Warrier is as green as they come. Even you, from the looks of it, are inclined to give the woman the benefit of the doubt. But it's here that Major Raunaq Singh makes an entry. Counterpart of Major Rodriguez in 7 Sikh, he has been watching his troops work the ropes.

'Get the woman out, search the fucking place down, break anything you want,' barks Major Raunaq Singh.

Even Rodriguez, who himself has been straggling, a mercenary working in a hostile command, perks up. The two majors are reading something in the situation that is escaping the others. Rodriguez, too, goes into command mode.

He takes the safety off his Glock. 'Be careful. We might have company,' he barks.

Captain Warrier's a little taken aback. The woman's silent now but you recognise a new fear in her eyes. You can almost hear her heartbeat. Then there comes the moment that shapes Captain Warrier's destiny. He goes up to Major Rodriguez and enquires in a soft tone, 'Don't you think you might be making a mistake here? Overreacting a bit?'

Rodriguez blushes a little. You don't know whether it is because Warrier omits the 'sir' or a few 7 Sikh soldiers are glancing his way. Then Major Raunaq Singh smirks at Rodriguez. He has no option after that. Rodriguez hands over his Glock to Warrier, who was unarmed, and orders him to lead the way. Major Raunaq relinquishes territory, a little puzzled.

'It's for you to find out,' says Major Rodriguez, and Warrier, who wasn't expecting this flow of events, leads four soldiers of the 7 Sikh into the house. He does it with attitude too. And you see that smirk on his face through one of the windows right till a dumdum knocks his head off.

It happens like this. First, one of the soldiers inside drags a chest of drawers some way and Warrier notices something and bends down. Right then you notice the woman turn deathly pale, and Major Rodriguez, who's been watching her all the while, is about to bark something, but it's too late. The first bullet of the Mossie, who's hiding beneath the trap door under the chest of drawers, takes Warrier smack on his face.

You see him spin and hit the floor with a thud. The rest turn around and start emptying their AK-47 magazines into the trap door till Major Rodriguez goes inside in a gallop and pulls them out. He doesn't want them blowing up the dump. They drag the Mossie out from the trap door and though he might have taken about thirty slugs he's still got a pulse.

'*Afghan gandu hai*,' says one of the soldiers.

They search in the little alcove behind the trap door and they come up with radio control sets – the kind that are used to explode mines – detonators, fuses, grenades, five AK-47 rifles, four boxes of ammunition and two RPG-7V rocket launchers with ten projectiles. Enough stuff to take out an entire convoy.

Major Rodriguez is hunched over Warrier's body. One of the men has to tie his bandanna around Warrier's head to keep his brains from dropping out. They take the woman into custody. Nobody talks to her. As a parting gift they shoot the place up. Furniture, walls, beds, cupboards, even the cutlery.

'How did *you* know, Major?' you ask. You are stuck with the 7 Sikh for the night. Some time early morning you will be moving with Rodriguez to the 5 Kumaon camp. Rodriguez himself is a little tense at having to give up a five-minute chopper ride to his base but it can't be helped. The chopper is flying in the bodies to Srinagar. His place has been taken up by Siddy, who wants some aerial shots of the village. On the army field telephone Major General Mahalingam is livid that Rodriguez hadn't taken better care of his aide. But Rodriguez's tension has more to do with having to be in 7 Sikh environs, even though on division work.

'Seen it a couple of times. A woman crying loudly means there's a dump near by,' says Major Rodriguez.

'You should have gone yourself,' you say.

'I was going. But you can't stop someone who wants to get his head blown off,' says Major Rodriguez. You can't really pick holes in Rodriguez's reasoning. 'First fucking commandment of life. Live and observe. Don't make a play if you don't know the moves.'

But in the night you break Major Rodriguez's first commandment. You go out on a patrol with him. Even this has come about because of the departure of 7 Sikh from the area. The two of you will be spending the night at a nearby Border Security Force camp. You realise that, for the major, going on patrol is a fundamental necessity as vital as the morning shit. But you are greener than grass. It's a new rush for you and what you sense is that Rodriguez's rush in the thing lay in going out with someone green. Or, to put it more accurately, someone he thought was green.

Major Rodriguez has hold of some intelligence that some Mossies might come for the cache the 7 Sikh just cracked and he's plotted an intercept course. 7 Sikh had the same intelligence but disregarded it. Why put yourself in danger when the booty is already yours? This, you surmise, could have been their line of thinking. A philosophy at distinct variance with that of the major from 5 Kumaon.

Rodriguez is packing an AK-47 and two knives. The major is a very basic hardware man. No fancy technology for him when he moves in the night. What you have is the Glock Rodriguez loaned Warrier. You try not to look superstitious as the major watches you wipe the muck off the grey handle. You are familiar with the weapon. You have checked the magazine. Its big grip fits your palm size. The major makes you change your shoes too.

'We don't want your Woodland sole patterns in the woods,' he says.

You remind him that it's night, but the major's firm. He wants to be sound on patrol basics. So you have to do with Siddy's plimsoll trainers. They have flat soles and nearly no patterns. Because of the irregular nature of what you are doing you have to slip out unobserved from the BSF camp.

In the woods, Major Rodriguez tries to get you up to date on patrol psychology.

'It's not enough to just gawk around. You have to train yourself to look right through the static,' says Major Rodriguez. Static for him is trees, the shrubbery, the grass, the noise. There's not much of a jungle in Kashmir. 'Once you get the hang of looking through it all, your eyes will go down that extra dozen yards. Mossie camps here are not in the open. So you don't have to sniff the air for their socks. What you have to do is listen for static that doesn't fit in. That's the odd guy out for you.'

Major Rodriguez picks a place by a stream where he thinks the Mossies might cross. He knows the topography well. 5 Kumaon has been here before. Grass, thick shrubs and trees conceal you from the stream and even though it's a moonlit night, the place scores nine out of ten for an ambush site.

Just to be with the major is an education. It's business, too. You are also of a kind for whom the nearness of death doesn't matter. Warrier's death hadn't put a damper on your plans for the evening. It isn't that you don't know fear. But the way it hits you is like a popper in your veins. Amyl fucking nitrate. Arousal and fear, you think, go together.

In the night Major Rodriguez talks about insurgency in Kashmir. You have never before heard him exercise his tongue so much. He starts in a whisper.

'When it all started in 1989, it would take, on an average, five hundred hours of patrolling for a soldier to have his first encounter with the assholes. For the normal regimental unit the figure's come down to three hundred hours. With 5 Kumaon it's seventy-five hours. If you haven't had your first taste of live fire by then, you start getting an inferiority complex.'

'And your first kill?' you ask.

'Usually about the same time. But we were the first guys that started going after the Mossies instead of waiting for them to bump into us. That was new to them. We first brought down our firing initiation average to a hundred and fifty hours by organising our patrols better. The more erratic and disorganised our second- and third-tier patrols were, the more chances we had of running into the Mossies, getting to fry the bastards. Then HQ sent us these five ground-surveillance radars for trial evaluation. The LMT RB12A solid-state radio transmitter you can fit in your rucksack and move on. It can be operated by remote and it picks moving targets two kilometres away. It gives you bearing and range and, if you want, it even plots an intercept graph for you. Five are too few for the border but we started having excellent results. They even cut down on our casualties. Understandably, we posted a negative on the equipment to HQ. We said we needed more time to assess them. We didn't want other units getting the same edge. It would mess with the flow of inventory we were piling up. Later, we reported them as damaged beyond repair in a bomb blast.'

'What about the stress, the people around here? The minimum-force army doctrine?' you ask.

'That's something for assholes at the LIC school at Udhampur to work out in their textbooks. For us . . . we try to find the bullets before they find us. The problem starts after the first few weeks that you come in fresh. You are all psyched up to fight terrorists and all you get to do is knock civilians on the head. The locals look on you like an occupation force . . .

'So you don't know who's the enemy. First thing one learns is each civilian is a potential asshole. Some try to worm their way into our hearts. But they could be friends today and throw a bomb at you tomorrow. A twelve-year-old could be playing cricket with you in the morning, in the night he could be burying you with cutter slugs. Sometimes they use special ammunition, which at exit makes holes the size of fists. But even with all this there comes a time when you're not sure of the rightness of your actions.'

'What happens then?' you ask. 'When you're not sure of the rightness of your actions.'

'You heard about the Bell-rat experiment?' asks Major Rodriguez. He takes out one of his knives and starts working his nails.

'No.'

'They keep rats on one of these plates they run a voltage on. The rats run on to the next plate but that too gives them a shock. They keep going to the next plate but can't find one that's normal. Once they come to understand that moving to another plate isn't going to help they accept the situation. They learn to live with the shock. So once your morality gets the right hook, your values become more fluid and malleable. Even at command level. Your reaction towards unacceptable behaviour becomes softer and more understanding,' explains Major Rodriguez.

'You turn beast.'

'That's too harsh, MM. What you start doing is latching on to anything that dehumanises the enemy and dilutes your sense of responsibility,' says Major Rodriguez. 'You also become cruel. That comes with the feeling of power. You feel mighty with respect to the civilian. You realise how easy it would be to misuse that power. You start destroying property at the first excuse. Since there's not one particular direction the Mossies are supposed to come from, you are forced to have a light trigger finger. You need to have lightning responses, which of course increase your chances of hitting innocents. And once you hit them you go into that trap. You dehumanise them.'

'And that makes your job easier?' you ask.

'If you get a justification for anything, your job turns easier,' explains Major Rodriguez. He raises a finger to his lips.

This is when you first hear the swish-swash sound coming from the opposite end of the stream. A big bulk emerges from the trees on the other side. He comes cautiously to the edge of the water and swings his Kalashnikov over his shoulders so the barrel doesn't come in the way of his drinking from the stream.

Four dark forms follow him. They are too far for you to catch the white in their eyes, but you file the fact that they all pack Kalashnikovs. You remember with alarm that you haven't cocked your Glock. Silence, as you well know, is the essence of a successful ambush, and though mathematics has never been one of your strong points, it doesn't take you long to calculate that the two seconds you'd need to cock your personal weapon would give enough time to a single AK-47 packing Mossie to push twelve rounds into your rib cage at 2,330 feet per second. You figure that would be mortal even if the Mossie pressed the trigger at three hundred yards. One of the AK-47's highlights is its low recoil, which allows for the weapon to be controllable at auto.

Your memory also retrieves for you the fact that Mossies have sometimes been known to fire at every bit of shrubbery that looks like a potential ambush site and falls on their trail. This you had picked up in an apparently erudite article on Kashmiri militant training camps across the border.

The only thing you are reasonably content about is that you aren't on acid. That would have amplified the series of horrors unfolding before you. You may have given the game away by hollering at them. Also, that you have a proven Mossie decimator in Major Rodriguez.

You hope that the Mossie squad doesn't cross where you are. When two of them proceed a little downstream to check the water flow you start easing up. But it's a short-lived relief, for you observe the group make preparations to cross right under your nose. Three of the five hang back at the edge of the trees on the other side, prepared to give covering fire for the advance party of two. This creates battlefield complications. Do you take out the two up front, which would be the easiest thing to do, or do you wait for the entire party to come across? If you plug the two advance Mossies there is every chance the rest will escape. You realise you would, too.

But Major Rodriguez, you know by now, isn't a bits and pieces man. He's a wholesale connoisseur, the all or nothing man. You look at him for strategy confirmation and it's a shock to discover that the major is no longer where you thought he was. While you have been busy watching the progress of the Mossie squad you haven't noticed the major disappear, leaving you to your own resources.

This unexpected twist in proceedings puts a crimp in your mental equilibrium. You go through your list of options. Your escape route at the rear is clean as a whistle and you still have time to crawl away to safety. If you don't, you may slowly get sucked into a situation known as 'isolated individual fighting with his back to the wall' or 'hero fights to the last bullet' syndrome. Only you have serious doubts whether you will get to fire anywhere near your last bullet.

Naturally, you hold no animosity towards the Mossie squad. Your work was with the major and those he represents. And even though you think you have cracked the major at Agra in your sky-diving sessions it is proving a little harder than expected. You want to win Rodriguez over by deeds he appreciates, even though it makes you commit acts that don't, in the longer run, help your cause.

You strain against the darkness to get a bearing on Rodriguez's position, but all you can see is a lot of bark. You look back at the squad just in time to see one of the front men chuck something right where you are. Even as you try to figure what it could be, you fail to pick the downward curve of the object and it lands right on your face. Grenade, you think. What saves you from pressing the panic button is the smell of the thing. It is the Mossie's pair of sneakers tied together, with his socks right in them. He wants to keep them from getting wet. 'Sonofabitch,' you mutter. He could have hung them around his neck.

Your last and most dangerous alternative, of course, is to hope they won't see you. That would be risking your neck for nothing at all, and unless you plan to take out the guys, the better option is to slime out of the whole thing, retreat while you still have time. Besides, there is the business of the sneakers. Lying low doesn't sound like too healthy a possibility with one of the Mossies flashing his hooded pencil light in your direction to hunt for his footwear.

But what, you wonder, is the major's game? Your guess is that Major Rodriguez is throwing you into the deep end to see the balls you pack. Trust is an important factor in the kind of business you and he are involved in. Maybe he's testing you. Or so you think.

It could also be that the major is indulging his perverse sense of humour. Watching you sweat till the last possible moment.

Either way, you don't want to give the major the mental edge, confirm his role as chief chemist in a laboratory situation he's cooked up. Even though you are outgunned and outnumbered you plan to stick it out. Observe the way the Zen flows out of the next few moments. You are beginning to get the rush.

And you are banking on an instinct that the major hasn't deserted you but is around somewhere waiting for his moment. According to Major Rodriguez, things turn out for the best only when you recognise which moment to seize on and turn to your advantage. For the major, the play doesn't work unless it's at the ripe instant. If there is to be a skirmish it will begin at the moment of the major's choosing. It will also begin depending on what Rodriguez wants. Right now, you don't know what he wants. But when the forward party of two cross the stream with their AK-47s held over their heads and the major doesn't make his play you know that he's going to stretch the game right till the end. All you can do is tense yourself for the moment or let it come and grab you.

The Mossie who chucked his shoes is in no hurry to come and get them. He's covering up for his buddies at the other end whose turn it is to cross. The other goes behind a tree and takes a pee.

While you have manoeuvred away from the shoes you are still only three yards from the Mossie taking his leak. He has the barrel of his rifle pointed right where he is aiming his pee and as the vapours hit you in the night you think how easily you could take him and the other guy but you wait patiently for the major's move.

What you don't want to do at any cost is start your play before the major starts his, let the Mossies see you and blow whatever the major was planning. You don't have any affinity with moments. The ripe one could pass and you wouldn't know it.

Soon the two become five and while four have crossed with their shoes hung around their necks, the single Mossie comes looking for his sneakers. He spits once, about four yards, before he comes by his sneakers and the spray from it hits your forehead. It creates prickly sensations on your face. Ambushing, you figure, is full of the unexpected. It rains things from above that you could do nothing about.

You also, as the spray starts making your nose itch, see for the first time the major's knife still on the stone where he was trimming his nails. The discovery is something that is shared by the Mossie as he drags on his socks. He lets out a whisper of surprise. As he does that and the other Mossies perk up, you feel the moment coming, even though it's your first patrol and you have the antennae of an amateur.

You don't hear the roar of the AK-47 in auto. The major's rifle is on single fire. You hug the ground. You see four Mossies folding up and falling on the grass. You cock your Glock for the Mossie who was dragging his socks and lift yourself from the ditch you were in. His eyes turn wide with terror, his mouth yawns open. Gritting your teeth you fire a round from your hip. You don't intend to hit him but you suddenly realise that firing has a calming effect on you after the sustained rush you have had. You empty your magazine at his feet, around his face, at the Mossie's sneaker. What you don't do is fire to kill. You fire to overcome and control your fear. Or, perhaps, you fire to give the major the impression that you do so to administer your fear.

You also see, as you fire like a maniac, Major Rodriguez eyeing you from your right. He has a look of unconcern on his face. All he says once you have run out of rounds is, 'What a waste, what a fucking waste.' Then he straightens his arm and before you can gear up to what he is about to do he fires his fifth into the Mossie's head and fluid comes spraying on to your face once again.

You are somewhere in Kupwara, Kashmir, guests of the 5 Kumaon. You are progressing towards your target in steady bounds. Quarry like Major Rodriguez and his confederates is to be stalked over months. The snow has started melting and the reason you are here with two of your colleagues is ostensibly to finish your border patrol documentary on the LoC. That and the thing with the questionnaire, which has yielded rich dividends. A camerawoman has flown in for the mission, a troop increase, a girl called Teresa. Siddy, your main cameraman, who also doubles as sound recordist, is still with you.

Right now you are working yourself up to be pissed with him. You can't do anything except glare, because if you so much as took a deep breath you might get your head blown all the way to Rangoon. There are four of you in the bushes, and ringed around you and converging at top speed in a semicircular arc are about a dozen, or maybe a few less, Mossies from the Islamic side of things.

It's night and that's what saves you, for your two armed escorts pack Panavision night viewers, gizmos that give them all-weather data in magnified green blurs. You and Siddy were doing a cursory terrain scout to pick an advantageous position for your twenty-kilogram remote-operated video camera. What, in fact, saves you from running smack into the Mossies is your having borrowed the night viewer from one of your escorts, who has it slung on his left shoulder, to indulge in a little private peek, and when you see an assortment of green blurs that could be carbon-based life forms similar to your own, you raise a quiet alarm.

Advantageously, all of you are in army greens and have

complexions that can do without black camouflage paint. And you have enough time to huddle into a four-by-six-foot ditch that no Kashmiri, Mossie or otherwise, should have reason to cut across. It's out of the way and surrounded by pines.

They go past you and beyond in a silent but fast flurry of feet. You lay low for a further three minutes to keep out of the way of any slow tail, then you hear one of the escorts use his walkie-talkie to warn the inner perimeter patrol about the baggage coming their way. You tell Siddy what a jerk you think he is for not loading the battery in the control handset.

'We could have had all the shots we wanted the first day if you had just done what you have been brought here to do,' you tell him. 'And now we don't know whether we will bump into another bunch.'

'We can stay here for a few more days,' says Siddy.

'That says nothing. You could be here the whole year and never be closer than this,' you say.

'Jesus, we weren't expecting anything like this, MM. It wasn't even a dry run.'

'That's the point,' you say, backing him into a tree. 'Each time you hold a camera, remember you are on. If you spot the heat around the corner there's nothing that should take you more than fifteen seconds to get fixed.'

'Be glad you are alive,' says Siddy.

He's still shaking and sweating. He's never been in anything this tight. He's so traumatised he can't carry the camera straight from where he left it on the trail back to our bunker. You carry it for him. Digs wouldn't like to hear that a probationer jerk went and screwed a rented, uninsured $150,000 camera. For your part you are smug in the knowledge that you had voiced your objection in distinct, unambiguous terms to being saddled with two greenhorns on a run like this.

But Digs had pulled rank on this one. 'There's always the first one. You had yours. It's time for the others now,' he had said. And you didn't really push all that hard, since you didn't want to provoke him into knocking you off the list. Your plans are too important to let Digs foul them up. You meet Major Rodriguez and seven men from 5 Kumaon halfway to Bunker 13, the name 5 Kumaon has given to the underground shelter they have built for officers to duck in if shelling becomes incessant. They are going to be sealing off the retreat of the Mossies you just watched go past. They are the men you are here to watch.

'I hear you had flying guests,' says Major Rodriguez. 'Got any on film?'

'Junior here fucked it up, Major. Forgot some batteries back at the bunker,' you say.

Then the major turns around to one of your escorts and slings on his AK-47. The major now packs two. 'Hey, MM,' he says as he pokes the butt of the spare AK-47 in your abdomen, 'you got the stomach for this?'

It's easy once you get the direction the game is taking. 'You bet,' you say, smiling, as you hand over the camera to one of your escorts with explicit instructions to drop it by Teresa in the bunker. You ignore Siddy.

The run is nothing like you have ever done before. It's part of the major's ploy, you guess, to soften you up to gain the upper deck in the negotiations that would follow. A little dose to bean you, numb your intelligence.

But you can feel he hadn't expected this calf and thigh response. This fast 20 kilometres per hour through Kupwara geology, matching pace for pace and stealth for stealth. You have the capacity to outgun them, steal a march on pure gas. But you are unfamiliar with the play. The desperation of cornered Kashmiri Mossies might not be to your liking. Nobody's briefed you on the cute little tactics they might employ. The little tricks that might trip you up on your life expectancy. So you run with your pack but bring up the rear. You don't want the first burst of lead to kiss your anatomy. Your bones and flesh are something you like to strut, and they work out for you even when your mind is in low gear, doing its best to screw things up yet again.

Amongst the things that come high on the list is misplaced initiative. You know from experience what high energy levels, erroneously directed, can do. You found that out one fine summer in 1985, during your first semester in the National Defence Academy at Khadakvasla, when you decided to form a cadets' union after the excesses of a drill sergeant led to the death of a roommate. Nothing more avant-garde had ever happened at the Academy. You lasted four long weeks because the commander of the Academy, in the note he had forwarded to the general in command, had added a few lines in the margins: 'Though recommend dismissal would like your permission to let things be for a while because the subject in question offers immense research richness that could come in handy keeping in mind long-term army training procedures. We would also get to know the names of some of the other ringleaders, if any do exist.'

So, in fact, the fogies were on to you long before you ever imagined. You suspect the only reason they gave you a long rope was to determine the toxicity coefficient of a single cadet preaching mutiny.

Of course, when two whole semesters did not turn up for drill one fine Monday morning, the general thought enough was enough and handed you your letter of discharge. At that point, you remember talking of the orders as 'such a sham', because even though you, in your teenage perspicacity, had set the ball rolling, new faces had taken over – cadets who were your batchmates or a little senior. Some of them in Kashmir and now in positions to strike some lucrative alignments with you.

You have been running for a full forty-five minutes. For the past fifteen minutes you can hear sporadic automatic fire. Major Rodriguez calls for a halt.

'MM,' he asks, 'what's your fear gradient? Does it hang low?'

You get your breath back first, balance your ass at a stub of pine root. 'As low as it can get, Major. I got a high chassis. You make me turn tight and you got a peacetime statistic to deal with.'

'Peacetime! It's so hot in here you get blisters while dreaming,' hisses Major Rodriguez.

'So, tell your lads not to dream, Major. Dreaming's bad for soul mechanics. REM upsets your biorhythm,' you say.

'What also upsets it is trying to dodge AK-47 lead that's bent on drilling you a back-up asshole each time you take your compulsory shit,' says Major Rodriguez.

'Bunker politics. Part of the game,' you say.

'Maybe,' says Major Rodriguez. 'But try shitting in polythene for a week and you are going to evolve a new world view. You will forge new insights into geopolitics and your own survival schemes in the sea of shit around you.'

'The shit could be your own making,' you say, checking your magazine. These are things you learnt to do a long time ago.

'We didn't go load these Kashmiris with independence doctrine. Some people have some half-assed abstract notions they deserve the half-assed state knee-jerkers coming their way. It's physics. Seventh grade. First law of Newton and our first rule of survival.'

'What's the second?'

There's a crackle on the radio being carried on his back by one of the lads. A squeaky voice comes on air: 'Delta calling Dhatak Company, we are under attack. Need reinforcements quickly. Over and out.'

A kilometre up ahead you can hear the fireworks shift to a higher gear. You and your pals need to speed up your act or the plan to trap the Mossies in a pincer might fall through. The major, though, maintains radio silence. He takes a packet of Wills Classic out of his dungarees and one of the men lights his stick for him. You didn't know smoking had the green at night. Give some trigger-happy, two-legged

69

mammal the chance to know where you are at. But the major covers the lighted portion with his palm.

You fidget. You want to rush in, help the crowd in trouble. More important, to appear to want to do so. You wait with interest to see the course of action that Rodriguez will embark on. Whether he will indulge in some mutual regimental-level back-scratch. You are trying to figure out the major's game plan when the message is repeated. This time the voice is desperate. There are gunshots close to the radio and then high, continuous static.

'Funeral time,' says one of Major Rodriguez's sidekicks. He has a four-inch scar on his forehead. A scowl that shows some satisfaction at what is going on.

'Shouldn't you be helping, Major?' you ask. 'Use some of the skills you draw your pay for? The 7 Sikh is calling for help.'

Major Rodriguez takes a drag on his cancer stick. 'This is our second rule of survival, MM. Newton's first law in reverse. For every action there's an equal and opposite inaction. You don't shoot, you don't get shot at, because the Mossies wouldn't know where you are.'

Your adrenaline level is undergoing a metamorphosis. 'Are you a genetic asshole, Major, or do you feel the need to be one on specific occasions?' The firing comes closer to you. 'It's your side out there, Major. They need help.'

'My side's here, MM. That's a Sikh outfit,' the major says quietly.

'What's the difference? What is this, regiment politics? Today it's their ass. Tomorrow it could be yours and they could be in smoking stand-by.'

'Our ass has been taken and gone, MM. This is judgement time. The equalising hand of fate,' says Major Rodriguez.

'I am going in, Major, with or without you. You want to send any of your sidekicks with me?' Of course, your wanting to join the action has much deeper implications than anybody out there with you, including Rodriguez, can fathom. It's not the rush or patriotic affinity with the 7 Sikh that's moulding your actions the way you make out. In time, if the major is astute enough, he might know. But in the job you are in, it will be your business to ensure that it's too late for him to do anything about it, if and when he does manage to put two and two together.

The major hadn't seen this coming. A journalist with mad responses is not what he has been trained to handle in pressure situations. Specially when there's more to the journalist than profession dictates.

'Trying to be a hero, MM?' he says, smiling. He doesn't look all that confident. 'You know what, sometimes it's better to be an asshole than try to be a hero. You stay alive. But be my guest.'

You have no option after that. You don't particularly relish what you are about to do – on the face of it, a solo run to save a Sikh patrol platoon – but one talent that you pride yourself on is concentrating on the job at hand. And when you are doing that there's no time for rumination.

'Fuck you, Rodriguez,' you say and head for the danger zone. You hear some rustling behind you, but the major could be collecting leaves for all you care, toilet paper substitutes to smooth the rough ends of bunker politics.

You hit the turf running full tilt. You hear cries, shouts of pain. Sensory information from which you can deduce the mortality of human affairs, the agenda of death that's the permanent milestone beyond all other individual manifestos.

Suddenly you're in the shooting, you are shooting and you trip over a body (dead or wounded you don't know, except it's the still remains of one of the cross-border Mossies) to go head first into a tank-size ditch that, even as you crash, you see is manned by a turbaned life form of the 7 Sikh, bleeding but still there. At least you have the consolation of knowing, as you phase out, the side you have managed to sling your hero's ass into.

* * *

When you regain consciousness you feel the poke of metal in your ribs. Unfriendly jabs that swell the panic in your arteries, bringing you alive to the fate that is likely to be yours.

'Indian army dog,' says a Mossie and thumps his rifle butt on your ribs. You find that such minor pain-relieving options as squirming and twisting are denied you because of two Mossies holding you down by your arms. 'Seven of my friends you dogs killed. The time is not far off when you dogs will have to give up Kashmir.'

Kashmir. You are too fused out to counter a Mossie's political-science predictions. All you can lock on to is visual, ground realities. A rifle butt going up comes down. Law of gravity. You tense your abdomen, beef your ribs for the blow. But the butt is moving in semantics you can't hang a pulse to. What is up, for instance, you learn quite late in life, can cruise down in unpredictable trajectories. Your left temple in this case. And then a little combination therapy of ISI-issue boots, a blur of fists and the butts of rifles.

Finally, time for the climax. A barrel is slanted and you can run your tongue over hot iron as you tense for the high-velocity lead that's going to tear you a ticket for heaven or hell or your next life as the Panchen Lama. You close your eyes and prepare for what is coming. Only you feel a body slump on your chest and gunfire that keeps reverberating in your tympanums. You know some miracle has happened. You open your eyes. You see Major Rodriguez glaring at you with strong disapproval.

Kashmir in May has a strong smell of something you can't put a name to. Teresa is tending to your bruises in Bunker 13, aghast that you could possibly cross the line from recorder of events to participant, even if the breach was on the patriotic side of things.

'Some things you just don't do as a journalist,' she says. 'You don't take sides. You don't erode your status as an independent player.'

You keep quiet. You don't have the time for crunching ethics with amateurs in the game who have little clue to the many factors cooking the broth.

Right now you are soaking in the few luxuries that Bunker 13 afforded you. A rickety water cooler whirred eight feet away, powered by a clump of batteries. Lit by weak bulbs, the rooms in the bunker also have a permanent odour of sweat and curry. The organisational acumen of 5 Kumaon hasn't extended yet to converting their officers' bunker into an underground resort. The enormous kitchen tent overground has an unstoppable ability to waft down the smells of spices, charcoal, condiments and other cooking paraphernalia.

A flight of forty steps leads into the bunker. The first time you entered the concrete fixture it took you many minutes to adjust to the dim light. The bunker is like a military barracks underground. Four rooms lead into one another. Two are bedrooms, the two others have feeble pretensions to being an officers' mess. A makeshift bar, a *carrom* board and a reading table, adorned with two-month-old magazines, are the sum total of recreational embellishments.

The USP of Bunker 13 is that somebody has to point out its existence for you. Or nobody would notice. A column of

men could march past it and not know of the facility underground. At ground level it's covered with thick vegetation.
From the air you would just see the trees. Of course, to the
trained eye there would be tell-tale signs of shelling. Trees
split in half, enormous holes in the ground, shattered wood
and, further afield, local village houses smashed by shelling
and lying abandoned.

After a while you walk up the steps and proceed to Major
Rodriguez's tent, one of the five below and behind the concrete bulwark that faces down on the stream separating you
from the neighbouring nation of the Mossies.

You raise the flap and go in. The major has company.

'Ah, who do we have here? Our hero from the forest. So
eager to have his head blown off in the pursuit of some
higher calling, a one-man rescue army trying to save the
hide of three left-over Sikhs,' says Major Rodriguez.

You give him a thumbs-up sign, gratuity for pulling the
cord on someone about to hole you.

On the way back the major had taken the lead with a
vengeance, and though you were giddy from the beating
you had survived, you could still muster the reserve not to
ask for limb support. That was one of the ways to salvage
your respect. The 5 Kumaon squad, you learnt fast, didn't
give a hoot for misplaced initiative, particularly if they had
to come and bail you out of the hole which, according to
them, you had no business digging in the first place. You
also think maybe if you had come out with your gun blazing, piling the Mossies in a bloody, tattered heap at your
feet, what then? Deny the major the chance to tool his I-told-
you-so sneer? But maybe it's better this way, better to have a
crazy reputation than one that makes the other fear you as
an independent player.

'They were on your side, Major,' you say, observing the uniformed colonel in the shadows. You have counted the stripes.

'Are you accusing me of anything, MM?' asks Major
Rodriguez. He's spinning this stirrer he has in a martini he

has just fixed himself. The colonel's loaded with a glass of Scotch. The 5 Kumaon seems well stocked in the spirits department.

'Not offering an injured guest a drink?'

'My apologies,' says Major Rodriguez. 'Shall it be Scotch or a dash of vodka?'

'If you could spare some Old Monk, it would be just perfect,' you say. Nobody's offered you a chair yet, so you lift the only one remaining away from the gas lantern in the tent. You don't particularly relish these pump lights. They have a built-in destruction mechanism and you don't want your face to be the only casualty in the vicinity. And you want your features to be in the shadows, away from the sharp eyes of the major and his accomplice, whoever he may be.

'Ah, Old Monk. The favourite brand of the soldiers. Your taste is a trifle too close to earth, MM. But it goes with your labour leader image. But you shall have what you want,' says Major Rodriguez, pouring the liquid into a steel cup. 'I hope you don't mind the steel. We can't keep you in city comfort.'

You ignore this dig. 'You haven't introduced me to the colonel yet.'

'Ah, what's happening to my sense of propriety?' queries Major Rodriguez as he turns around with your drink. 'Colonel Sangma, light of 5 Kumaon, and Minty Mehta, journalist at *The Post*.'

You shake hands with a reluctant Colonel Sangma. You understand why. He has two fingers missing in his right hand. You know this man. The powder pusher in Assam and Mizoram. The colonel had been transferred from a Madras regiment posted in the north-east to the 5 Kumaon six years back after developing a spoken reputation for being involved in the drug trade. The colonel, then a rank below, had carved a retail market for heroin in Mizoram with the help of thugs from his unit. So you have been told.

Of course, Sangma soon infected Rodriguez and other officers from his new unit with his brand of criminality.

But Colonel Sangma is a minor-league player. His ambitions don't extend beyond retail. Rodriguez, on the other hand, doesn't look to you the type to even consider running a loose-change dealership. He's a major-league bastard.

'A toast,' Major Rodriguez proposes and as he lets the words hang in there a few seconds too long, you fill in the blanks.

'To mutual gain and long-term association,' you say.

'Cheers,' says Major Rodriguez.

'Cheers,' says Colonel Sangma.

'Cheers,' you say but you don't like the taste of rum coursing through your gullet. You pour in some more water. What you observe is that, even though the 5 Kumaon is tanked on liquor, they have no supply of ice.

The major switches moods. He drops his patronising air, shifts smoothly into speech mode, 5 Kumaon philosophy and peacetime economics, a development of decade-long, low-intensity conflict. You at last are about to get your reward for many months on Rodriguez's trail.

'MM,' says Major Rodriguez, 'let's get one thing straight. The war's not of our making. 5 Kumaon is but one of many de luxe strike arms of the northern command keeping its claws sharp by engaging Mossies with numerous agendas. Our one and only mandate is to keep the Mossies plugged on their side of the fence and to issue shoot and search warrants for those who manage to spill over, trying to upset the delicate power equilibrium in the valley. Of course, as you have discovered, we are just not any other army unit on the border. We have been here eighteen months and along the way we have hooked ourselves to gun economics, white dust mobility and other such unlawful distractions that, apart from keeping us sane, exhilarate us with the profit motive. And as our returns are linked to the number of Mossies we bust, our energy isn't an evil force to the nation to which we belong. 5 Kumaon has the distinction of hauling in 2,500 armed mercenaries so far, twenty times more than any other unit in this part of the world. Officially, that is. We have busted about two thousand more that nobody knows about save our parallel economy bookkeeper. Our contribution to the Indian nation's long-term stability is perhaps right there at the top and . . .'

'What we want is just a slice of the GNP commensurate with the toil we put in,' you finish for him.

'Well said,' says Colonel Sangma. You were starting to think the colonel couldn't talk, but the major's speech is like a syringe of steroids straight in his larynx. 'What we have faced here we alone know. All of us have lost buddies. The army, MM, fights at the company level on personal bonds. Flimsy constructs like nationalism mean nothing to us. You hit at that bond and you have a bunch of angry men to deal with who suddenly go about asking themselves what this rigmarole is all about. Why do they have to risk their lives for a nation that's insulated to their hardships? Who's skimming the milk and where's their share of the cream? It's certainly more than the basic 2,000 rupees (Rs) take-home plus C-grade rations that include eight eggs a week. Would you risk even a single finger for that, MM?'

'No, Colonel,' you say. You don't want to embark on any impertinent digressions or disagreements, especially when what is on tap is a prime-grade peep into the motives of the 5 Kumaon brains trust.

'Well, this is just the premium I paid a little more than a year back,' continues Colonel Sangma, waving his three-digit hand. 'For a policy that's going to retire me four years from now and dispatch me, at age fifty-four, to quiet civilian repose, when I shall no longer have the shelter of a uniform to hide my low social mobility from the Nokia asshole next door. It's not a fact of life we are content to live with. Major here lost his wife and kid recently. Casualty of 5 Kumaon over-confidence, but a casualty nevertheless. Family is never permitted to travel in convoy. But ours was the first to be taken on by the Mossies. They took out the jeep with a rocket. We didn't find enough flesh to fill an envelope. We have lost a hundred men so far, figures that don't make their way into newspaper ink, and no reporter has ever had the initiative to lever out any such statistics from the Central Defence pension office at Allahabad. We don't matter is the message we get. 5 Kumaon could lose a trained patriot once every two days and the nation wouldn't pause in its stride. We are sick of being just expendables, peacetime attrition arithmetic. The scars of hate run deep and long in us too, and we don't know the fate that may be ours when all this will be over, when we no longer will have the licence to hate. We don't want the millennium to glide by us and our children. What we want is minimum grease to stay afloat with some dignity and you know where you plug in so we can all make the leap.'

'Colonel, with due apologies,' you begin, 'could we just bypass the motives? We might just lose focus. Could we have some idea of the quantum we are talking? The booty we seek to peddle so we can all upholster our lifestyle? You don't need to sell me your ideology. I am a convert. What's the game?'

You know of Rodriguez's personal loss. You have sometimes broached the topic but the major hasn't encouraged you. The recent spurt in the major's drug habits you put down to that. Also his buccaneering spirit almost bordering on suicide.

'We will come to that when the time's ripe,' intervenes Major Rodriguez. 'First, we would like to know the kind of collateral you can toss our way to make us breathe easy a thousand kilometres away.'

'How about a few snaps you can circulate within the police forces to help track me better if I fly off with your retirement cache?' you say.

'Come on, MM, you can offer better than that. We would rest easy if we had a fix on you. It's safety dynamics. Circus net routine. You wouldn't like to do a two and a half without the netting, would you?' asks Major Rodriguez.

'Major, I do things for the ride. The bigger the spin the better.'

'Is that why you slipped in your solo today? A fix to keep your chemicals in shape?' asks Major Rodriguez. You notice he isn't smiling. The motives of your solo run have eluded him.

'I don't like people on our side dying without my extending a helping hand. Especially if I can influence the pattern of things,' you say with a straight eye.

'Not even if the guys asking for help did in one of your officers and a *jawan* in a joint patrol? Slimed out of a mission and the guys didn't know till very late. So late that they had their epidermis taken off as trophy, little Mossie knick-knack for drawing-room exhibition,' says Major Rodriguez.

'You have a brother, MM?' asks Colonel Sangma.

'No.'

'Would you go to help some people if you knew for a fact that they had delivered your brother to guys who skinned him alive? Would you?' asks Colonel Sangma.

'No,' you say.

'You remember the guy with the scar today in our chase? On his forehead?' asks Major Rodriguez. 'His name's Indramani. The *jawan* was his brother.'

'Why did you venture out at all, Major?' you ask.

'You have to play by the rules, MM. But if you're late on the draw it's not bayonet time,' says Major Rodriguez.

'And there's the booty, of course,' you say.

'That wasn't the case here. But that too,' says Major Rodriguez with a smile.

'And all yours. You wouldn't have to share it with some parallel Sikh operation,' you say. Sometimes you have to hit blind to get the ball where you want.

'Competition we can handle, MM. Not that there is any. All you need bother yourself about is whether you can handle bulk. Or do your skills and ambitions lie in retail? We don't want to piecemeal our inventory, increase our overheads,' says Major Rodriguez.

'Which again brings us to the load factor, Major. Even genius has to know what's coming. You have to give advance warning or the system overloads,' you say.

'All we can tell you right now is we are talking big. Very big. So sleep well tonight. At dawn we are raiding the village of Ur. We like to provide some entertainment for guests. Memories they can chew on back home,' says Major Rodriguez.

And as the major's dismissal chimes with the end of your drink, you nod and step out into the chill of a starry night.

Major Kohli of 5 Kumaon comes to deliver your next day's itinerary before the three of you turn in for the day. Little dos and don'ts to brighten your perspective, enlighten your ignorance.

'You all know where the shit pits are. There, behind the mound. It's beyond sniper range. We don't usually mortar each other's pits. It's a mutual agreement. Earlier it wasn't so and all of us used to have a tough time. It used to get so hot sometimes you had to stay holed in for days. Same on the other side. But then we thrashed out a pact with the guys at a border meeting. We call it our shit truce. We have a meeting every month. Of course, if we have something pressing to discuss we use mirrors. We can have no radio contacts with the enemy,' says Major Kohli.

'Something pressing?' interrupts Teresa.

'Yes. You see, if the major's birthday comes up or something, we organise a little celebration. Or somebody becomes a father,' says Major Kohli. 'We wouldn't like to be chasing Mossies on a night like that. So the pact is that they don't push anything on mutually agreed dates.'

'And they don't?' asks Siddy. He has a four-cylinder incredulity quotient.

'Well, except for once. But we taught them a lesson for that on Id, the Mossie festival. You see, they had their goats stashed in this tent for the big day. But we put four snipers on twenty-four-hour alert on the tent and they couldn't get to their fucking goats. Then we knocked the tent off and picked out the goats. That taught them an important lesson. Violence is a game two can play at,' says Major Kohli.

'A very basic lesson,' says Siddy.

'Yes. But you see, units keep in rotation. The guy you are dealing with might not be there tomorrow. And it takes the new guys some time to learn the law of the region,' says Major Kohli.

'And what's the law?' you ask.

'The law is what you agree upon. The rest is a game of chess,' says Major Kohli.

'How do you win?' Siddy asks.

'By being ahead. Using deception to kill deception,' says Major Kohli.

'How do you do that?' Kupwara has been the biggest fucking thing that's happened to Siddy's career. The bold lettering on his CV.

'You see, for a long time the jerks would shell point X and then slip the Mossies in at point Y. It took us some time to figure out that the shelling was a red herring, a whore dance to make you look in the wrong place. They used to wait for us to go on our wild goose chase before moving in, so that even if we wised up we would be too scattered to crack some muscle. Of course, once we understood the game we started moving small decoy parties towards the shelling while the bulk of us lay in wait at the right place. For a long time they didn't know what was going wrong. Now, of course, they just try to figure out where the 5 Kumaon patrols are and avoid them at all costs, even if it means taking other units head on. We have really botched up the Mossie slippage schedule. Sometimes they have to cool it their side for two to three weeks, trying to work out what patrol timings we are keeping. But Rodriguez thought up these random patrol runs. We would pick little chits out from a helmet with some time written on them. That keeps them on a real hop. Confuses their reconnaissance. That's what increased our take,' says Major Kohli.

'*Take*?' asks Teresa. You have to be sharp around that girl. Siddy, he's got stone-age IQ. Just knows what hole's for what.

'Yes,' says Major Kohli, eyeballing me steadily, 'the Mossie capture tally.'

'Oh,' says Teresa. 'What do you do with the captured men?'

'Some we post in big black plastic sheets to mother earth. No one wants to buy stiffs around this place. The hospitals are too far off. The hardcore parcels we kick ass all the way to Srinagar. The dopeys we chase back where they came from after relieving them of their hardware. You see, there's no place we have to pen them down and it would weigh too heavy on our souls if we put a hole apiece in their heads all the time. Besides, we would have to dig graves and we like to avoid unnecessary labour to keep our fatigue levels low.'

'So you let them go?' asks Siddy.

'Why, you want us to mail them to you? Bunny boys for the night. Handsome, hairy cuties to keep your mean temperature going,' asks Major Kohli. He smiles to keep us guessing.

'No, I mean they might come back,' argues Siddy.

'We want them to. They are the soft ones. You can nail them with your eyes closed,' explains Major Kohli.

'But what moves these guys? Why do they keep coming? What's their problem in life?' asks Teresa.

'You mean the Mossies?' clarifies Major Kohli.

'Yes,' says Teresa. You can see she was getting a little sheepish with the word Mossie.

'Rationality is not one of their strong points. Certain races are born without logic. Or maybe the DNA has got a kink that boots their logic into deep freeze. Like that gay gene they are talking about these days. But in the long run, I think, some people just like getting fucked. They don't know it, but they do.'

'That's absurd,' decides Teresa.

'That's a fact of life,' defends Major Kohli.

'Nobody likes being tortured,' says Teresa.

'Who's torturing anybody?' asks Major Kohli, looking at you for moral support. 'We kill some dumbasses who are shooting at us, because if we don't get them first, they are going to get us. We pack some off to Srinagar, the state capital, where the government can do anything they want with them, make them Members of Parliament or anything. And we chase some back. That's what we are doing to keep you guys down south in good health. So you can sleep easy in the night.'

'What about the interrogations and torture?' persists Teresa with embarrassing obstinacy. But Major Kohli's had his training.

'Who's got time for interrogation? You interrogate only when you know the answers are going to help you,' says he.

'But how do you know what answers you are going to get if you don't interrogate?' asks Siddy. He's a little confused.

'Because we are psychic. We know all we want to know to run the border. The locals coming back after three months of Mossie mumbo-jumbo and basic arms training know no secrets that we can squeeze out of them. We just ask them their name. They don't want to tell us, we don't waste our calories kicking their balls. We cook some name up. Exercise our imagination. Shift our workload to Srinagar, where the guys are trained for sorting out confusion. They have procedures. They open a file in the name we have given the Mossie. Maybe it happens to be his real name, or he likes it so much he takes it on. Then they interrogate the fucker twice a day for three months, sponge him of all he knows and transcribe what he says on to white sheets of paper and run it through their encryption machines or whatever the fuck they have there. But the basic problem remains – the guy knows nothing. So he has to keep inventing stuff to keep the guys off his back. And when you are tossing data out of the blue you don't often remember it the same way the second time around and you end up contradicting yourself. That's the opening the interrogator is looking for to prove to himself that you are hiding something and so he extends your interrogation schedule by another month. At the end of it your average Mossie just goes dumb, he has a problem getting even the alphabets right. When you reach that stage, the interrogators at Papa 2 jump you to the list of hardcore nuts. Once you get that status you have fat fucks coming from the Ministry of Home Affairs in Delhi to talk elections and strategies with you. Some would like to delete their hardcore status but their new-found privileges are too tempting to give up. Your new status fetches you extra dietary supplements, pieces of animal protein to boost your immune system, give you enough calories to thumb through a week-old *Times of India*, your factual update on national-level horse shit,' says Major Kohli. At some level even he's riled.

'You are nuts,' says Teresa. Such candid spelling out of policy is more than she is equipped to handle.

'That's why I am still alive and a hundred of my unit are dead. They weren't nuts. They took life seriously. It isn't worth it. Your line of duty is what keeps you breathing,' says Kohli.

'So chasing Mossies through Kupwara is your key to being alive?' you ask.

'My way. I chase them my fucking way,' emphasises Major Kohli.

'What's the difference?' you ask.

'Difference is I know where they hide and seek,' says Major Kohli.

Intelligence is that forty-odd Mossies are playing hide and seek in the three-hundred-house village that is Ur, eight kilometres from Bunker 13. Chased a long way by the 7 Sikh, the Mossies had splintered and recollected at Ur.

A cordon and search operation involving the dimensions of Ur calls for major logistical planning. You have to congregate the different 5 Kumaon companies, some in dispersed locations. You have to post sentries round the clock to keep an eye on the village so that you know if the Mossies try to make a break for it before dawn. They all want to reach a big town where they can merge and start payback time. But the army's job is to prevent them from doing that. Plus, 5 Kumaon likes an even flow of inventory increase. No highs and slumps for them. They want to reel in the hardware at a steady trot.

Speed is essential. You want to swoop before the Mossies get any advance warning of what's coming and zip their flies and run for the woods. Things even out in the woods. It's difficult to chase splintered groups. And there's always the fear you could catch some stray bullet, have your photograph printed in the biannual regimental signpost column that housewives use to wrap their kids' lunch in.

An operation starts at 4 a.m. in the summer. A little later in the winter, but there's not much loot in that season and things are lax. Summers are make-up time and business booms.

The danger, of course, in these Gestapo-style manoeuvres is that if a trigger-happy Mossie decides to open up in front of civilians, the casualties are the innocents, the crossfire victims. But since the Mossies never stay bunched together

86

in one house but scattered in twos and threes in houses all over the village, the trick is to not give them time to regroup. Achieving isolation, the army has learnt through experience, fucks the morale of the Mossies. Springs a leak in their adrenaline reservoir. Makes them amenable to surrender and putting their faith in army amnesty.

So speed is the key. For if you are slow, things start happening in reverse. The Mossies bunch up. Try punching a hole through the net the army has woven around them. While some escape, the rest come back to the village and take civvies hostage. They are scared of army retaliation because the group that got through has inflicted some terminal statistics on the predator. It's even worse if one in the unit is just wounded, because helicopter evacuations take time and the soldier's out there howling away for his buddies to hear. And then hell breaks on the village. Hostage or no hostage, an SLR slug can take three guys out standing head to head.

Amongst the memories you carry is 5 Kumaon fucking up on Operation Ur. If your success rate touches the sky a fuckup's round the corner. That's established morphology. But nobody really anticipated the direction from which the heavy shit came.

First, Bravo Company, whose job it is to cordon the village, is late in coming. They had to take a detour because of unforeseen landslides. So instead of hitting at four in the morning, Colonel Sangma, who was commanding the operation, found himself digging the village ninety minutes too late. Shit-taking time for Kashmiri shepherds. Who raise such a racket before the troops get into position that the Mossies have time for a five-minute assembly bang in the middle of the village. And this time the Mossies the major's men are trying to outsmart aren't all local Baramulla – misguided Mossies – but have a dozen-odd share of Afghan mercenaries, Islamic muscle export to aid *jihad* at trouble spots around the globe where Mossie fortunes have taken a nosedive.

The first move to break through the cordon comes right where you are. Next to the command centre, five yards from Major Rodriguez on the walkie-talkie getting his troops to move door to door. Tighten the lid. You have positioned Siddy and Teresa two hundred yards away from the village to get shots of peaceful surrender, images to make Indians sleep easy at night. The major has detailed four soldiers to look after the security concerns of your two colleagues.

But the first salvo here is a rocket that takes out Major Rodriguez's jeep with his driver still in it. Casualty number 101 for 5 Kumaon. Then the automatics start sending buzzers around your head and you and the major have to hug the grass. The major drags his driver's body around the bend to feel his pulse without having a Harkat ul Ansar asshole line him in his sights. You help the major as your support group gives you covering fire.

At the other end of the village, where the 5 Kumaon presence is in diffused numbers, the Harkat ul Ansar strives to gain its freedom. A small but potent rearguard keeps the troops engaged towards the south. You watch the mayhem with the awe of a kid in a museum.

A rocket misfires, blowing the roof off a house fifty yards from you. People come scurrying out. Scared women, children and men howling and running for cover.

A Mossie emerges from a burning house. His skin's hanging from his face but with his right hand he's emptying his AK-47 magazine into the troops taking him on. You watch, the major watches. He keeps taking bullets, but the mule kicks don't slow the momentum he has developed in his running. His left hand rips off his body. Just like that, a piece of wool in the wind. Blood rushes out like a spring but his leg muscles keep pounding. The whoof of battle and the hate give him unknown sources of energy. Then his head, suddenly, is no longer there. It's rolling backwards, two pieces of it. But the legs still have it for two more paces as the automatic goes silent and clatters to the ground.

'Holy shit,' you say. This is beyond anything you have ever seen. You feel like puking.

The major looks transfixed. It's clear he hasn't seen anything like this either. You wonder whether Teresa got the action on betacam.

For a moment things stand still. Clearly, a surreal episode makes for a pause on both sides. But the fire is spreading and the roofs are catching it all at once, throwing people out of their wooden doors with two minds, to run for water or save their bodies from lead. The women have no choice. They run with little girls and boys into fields. The men take stock, crowd around a well, watch the conflagration. This is war.

Colonel Sangma is a little fazed, out of his depth with the ferocity of the events. Major Rodriguez has more or less taken over. He is barking orders into his wireless.

'Stop firing,' he's shouting.

Civilian casualties are something he would like to avoid. It's a black mark in your confidential report. It might also signal the end of the road for 5 Kumaon's stay in the neighbourhood. Get army brass to move them to the north-east or something, where they might learn that messing with the Naga rebels was a different piece of cake. Also the terrain – a pound of leeches sticking in your boots if you took ten paces.

The Harkat ul Ansar seize on this window of opportunity. This lull in the proceedings. They ram a corridor north-west in the welter of confusion of women, children, shrieks and cries and sprint for the woods before the major can lower the gates on the leak.

More bad news. While the troops are busy plugging the gap a splinter group of radical Mossies sneaks up south-east, undetected, a kilometre down to the metalled road where 5 Kumaon have a few of their trucks parked. They make off with one after suitably incapacitating four others by tossing grenades into their gas tanks, standard guerrilla policy practised to good effect on retreating Russians. Hit-and-run, using the enemy's own wheels, ancient Shaktiman six-tonners that bounce you like ping-pong balls in the back. But better to toss around like a white ball than have the troops break your bones for pleasure, or worse, have five dozen 5 Kumaon veteran motherfuckers, led by Major Kohli, chase you through the woods determined to plug lead two times your body weight into your frame, give you a heavy send-off.

Meanwhile, things get sad and ugly at Ur. The troops have knocked two houses out with mortars to stop the whole village torching up. Knots of brave civilians try salvaging stuff from ashes, inferno and smoke.

In the midst of the confusion Major Rodriguez remains resolute. He starts rounding up villagers, trying to grind out information about the arms and ammunition store dump of the Mossies the 5 Kumaon just flushed from Ur. Apart from wanting to increase the 5 Kumaon inventory, the major doesn't want it blown up in the fire. A profit smashed to bits under his nose. A percentage decrease in the cut for all the dealers.

But the people feign ignorance. The major follows unwritten army procedure for civil disobedience in disturbed territories adjacent to the national border. Step 1: separate the population by sex. It's easier for rape.

You see troops put a ring around the women, who cling to each other in fear of the wave of lust around them, cutting out their escape route. Your superior vantage point allows you to monitor facial signals, little subtleties that you have to be alert to tune in to. What you see is the major jog his jaw about two inches in the direction of the non-commissioned officer in charge of hustling the women, and two burly 5 Kumaon veterans tear two teenage girls from the swirling mass and push them into the nearest unburnt interiors of a single-storey construction.

The movement is fast, too fast to register on the retina unless you were looking for it and it's escaped most of the frightened villagers. But it's locked on the mother – you assume the relationship because she's the solitary one pushing and screeching at the cordon even as the troops switch modes to automatic and let loose bursts in the air to add to the confusion.

You look inwards to see how you feel but, of all the images in your head, there's just one turbocharged visual, the memory of the one-handed and headless assault of a nameless Mossie. As a general rule, when you are numbed by blood and mayhem, rape shifts to low gear, a sour taste in the mouth you can brush away with Colgate.

Major Rodriguez now switches to Step 2, in normal circumstances the first step but now, in action mode, in tandem behind Step 1. Get the civvies in formation and run them single file in front of an army Jonga jeep with black-tinted windows, inside which sits an informant, a village dickhead in army pay, to spot your leftover Mossies for you. The smartest don't go for the break but stick on, try to pass as harmless locals.

Step 2 pays off handsomely. A catch of three prize Mossies pointed out with little hesitation by the informant. Of course, the danger here is that the informant could be settling personal scores. But the test here is to see whether some howling mothers come to snatch their wards away from custody. Then you might be on the wrong track and would have to further exercise your judgement. Basically, it's no skin off the 5 Kumaon. Sometimes a Mossie or a local is all the same. You just need a butt for your toe to sink into.

The village of Ur is relieved when the cache is found. It's stacked in the attic of one of the houses. Enough hardware to take on Mauritius – two hundred AK-47 rifles, twenty thousand rounds of ammunition, four hundred grenades, a hundred anti-personnel mines, walkie-talkie sets, detonators, IEDs, RDX and, for the first time, an item long suspected: five Stinger missiles, shoulder-fired surface-to-air motherfuckers with an operational range of ten kilometres.

The major is a happy man. As happy as a man can be whose driver has taken a rocket hit. The day's not a complete snafu, though three in the major's unit have been killed. The Mossies have taken a heavy knock. Eight in the village and the rest being chased through the woods.

The blips on the radar, though, are the civilian casualties. Fourteen villagers have died in the crossfire and twenty are wounded. The army doctors are stuffing plasma and glucose into the injured, trying to keep the Ur casualties from spilling over into a human rights fiasco. This besides the rape victims. You count six but there could have been more.

By eight in the morning Operation Ur is history. You return to Bunker 13, hitching a ride on one of the returning trucks, where two sulking colleagues confront you.

'They didn't let us shoot after the jeep got knocked off. Did you see that?' asks Siddy.

'They just herded us off, didn't even let us stay. Watch the fun,' says Teresa.

'It wasn't any fun. It was dangerous,' you say.

'What happened?' asks Teresa.

'Usual stuff,' you say. 'Some died, some lived.'

Your socialising instincts are below ignition level. There's something new biting you. The eyes of the mother who saw her daughter dragged in. What you are wondering is which one of the two the daughter was. Or were they both?

You are with Major Kohli. You have volunteered to be part of a special mission, saying you want to experience the thrill of the chase. Although Major Rodriguez was initially disinclined to accede to your request – for the very convincing reason that to lose you would be to lose the sole conduit he trusts to peddle his inventory – he shows the green after assigning a section with the specific duty of getting you back alive.

Major Kohli knows where his quarry's headed and he plans to outsmart them by being the first one there. You yourself are there as a field academic. To observe, at close quarters, the Indian army's Mossie-capturing techniques. You plan to write a book some day.

'MM, what do you think is the main ingredient in the LIC situation we have right now?' asks Major Kohli. The major, you feel, is trying to assess your jargon compatibility.

'To prepare a Threat Situation Template of the LIC situation,' you say.

'Wrong. That's for the armchair guys at Academy. You have to get your terrain analysis right. What do you think the Mossies need most right now?'

'Shelter,' you say.

'Shelter, yes. But for what?'

You duck the question. Major Kohli enlightens you.

'For food and medicine supplies,' he says. 'Sometimes terrain that has no tactical importance becomes important for a Mossie force's key logistical needs.'

'OK,' you say. 'So what are we going to do about it?'

'We are going to get a little ahead in the game. Integrate our terrain analysis with our anticipation template.'

'What does that mean?'

'It means you might be the first civilian in history to be part of an army ambush force,' says Major Kohli as he twists his Disruptive Combat Material combat cap from front to back. 'That's my personal code, you see. My men now know what's up.'

You hope so. For your furious clip through Kupwara to reach Rajor, the town that Major Kohli insists the Mossies are heading for, is like nothing you have ever done before. First, you go on a slight detour – confusion tactics for any Mossie rear recce teams – and then cut north-west again, a diagonal that should get you there ninety minutes ahead of the Mossies to prepare for their reception.

You arrive at seven in the evening and it's time again for you to receive an enlightening discourse from Major Kohli, beef up your theory first-hand.

'Where do you think you are standing, MM?' asks Major Kohli.

'On a stream bed,' you say.

'No. You are standing in the central ambush zone. Our principal "hello" area for the Mossies, where our ambush shall be initiated with a maximum personnel casualty-producing device. In short, Claymore mines,' says Major Kohli.

'What's this, an area ambush or a point ambush?' you ask, a lame effort on your part to beef up your end of the exchange.

'Ah, I am impressed. This is going to be an area ambush but with a high technical rating. In keeping with the superior nature of our Mossie threat, this time we are planning very fluid assault formations, a 5 Kumaon speciality,' says Major Kohli.

'What, a line formation?' you ask.

'No, MM. We will begin with a line formation and then switch to an L assault on the west side and then L and Y again at the bend in the stream bed and then the Y and Z formation, nail the Mossies on the river bed,' says Major Kohli.

'Why the Z?' you ask.

'No point taking chances. The Mossies might have high-frequency radios and could have called for reinforcements or help. We need the additional side of the Z to keep off a reinforcement force and seal the end of the kill zone,' explains Major Kohli.

'What about a chopper? Why don't you just pick them up from the air?' you ask.

'Too risky. You never know when they might be packing a Stinger. Also, the air force is always on a frequency that doesn't match the army's. You have to knife through a lot of red tape to requisition one,' says Major Kohli.

You nod your head. Then you watch the *jawans* lay the stream bed with waterproof mines. Swiftly, two pits are dug for placing machine guns, one on each side of the stream but with a limited arc of functioning so that the *jawans* coming in through the three access lanes are not caught in the crossfire.

'Every properly prepared ambush should have three elements, MM. The assault force, the back-up group and the perimeter party. The back-up group functions as the secondary assault force and the perimeter party secure outlying ambush zones, where leftover Mossies dispersing from the central ambush zone are mopped up,' says Major Kohli.

'What if outlying ambushes are discovered by the Mossies before they walk into the main killing area?'

'Good question, MM. The *jawans* are under orders to open fire if discovered but not to yell or shout,' says Major Kohli. 'But, of course, the whole purpose is to lure the Mossies into the main killing area and draw any relieving forces into our multiple ambush points. Get the fuckers from all sides. Zap them with our hardware.'

'We aren't supposed to capture them alive? Make them surrender or something?'

'Frankly, MM, that's not an option. It only increases your casualties. Also, I am not in the mood. They got three of our men. We are out to get their ass,' says Major Kohli. Then he does a bit of landscape survey. 'Besides, for that we would have to have a harassing kind of ambush, but the terrain here is not suited for a T-formation assault where the attack element is deployed at right angles to the movement of the Mossies so that the attack element and the Mossies form the letter L. With this formation a small platoon can skew and harass a much larger force without at any moment becoming decisively engaged and thus suffering losses.'

'There might be more casualties on your side.'

'No. Even though it's night, we know the direction they are going to come from. If we hadn't known that, we would have deployed the triangle formation, small-unit strong point to counter night movement of Mossies when Mossie approach route is unknown. A General Purpose Machine Gun placed at each point of the triangle with a 30-degree arc-of-fire so that it can be shifted quickly to form criss-crossing fields of fire with the two other GPMGs. And then alternate flank firing, just before you break into the T, sub-ject them to interlocking fire. Fry their flesh for them,' says Major Kohli.

Well, the Mossies come, but from the wrong direction. And though Major Kohli's command to his men to take their safeties off is given at eight, it isn't till nine that the moon-light shines off the first of them. Major Kohli has you placed in sniper position. Away from the approach or assault zones but on the left bank of the stream, on the top of an embank-ment twenty yards high. There, with the knowledge that mines guarded the escape route up the embankment, besides the presence of a multi-directional machine gun, a certified widow-maker, you eye the Mossies through your AK-47 sights, flanked by your bodyguards, waiting for the major to signal the shit to start.

But what happens is that one of the Mossies trips on the green nylon cord that connects lead members of assault teams on the right bank of the stream to co-ordinate timing for the blowing up of the mines. This much Major Kohli has pieced together for you in the aftermath.

So, the soldier in charge of blowing up the mines blows the whistle prematurely, thinking the tug on the cord came from Major Kohli. What this does is start the game before hardly 20 per cent of the Mossies are in the central ambush zone.

It's for the first time that you see what a personnel mine bursting under the groins of a group of three Mossies can do. It blows them about fifteen feet in the air. Each comes down with either just one leg on or no face at all, depending upon his body angle at the time he was negotiating the stream – that is, whether he was looking downward or at the moon or somewhere else.

In case he was looking anywhere else but down and his face is still intact, once he's come down he has it in him to start screaming a very special kind of scream that makes even his Mossie buddies stick him one in the head to take him out of his pain. If no one's around, he keeps screaming till he goes unconscious and then bleeds to death. Yes, he also gets splattered remnants of his balls popped up in a shower which could land anywhere within a radius of a hundred yards. You say that with confidence because you are somewhere at the sixty-yard mark and your cheek gets some of it from the sky.

Now, with the mines going up, the GPMGs start their slaughter and, because the Mossies came the opposite way from the one expected, they could, if they had the presence of mind, run to the end of the stream, for this isn't as efficiently bottled up as the one they just passed on their way coming in, when nobody was firing.

But with guys screaming that special scream, something happens to your head and the Mossies who are at the perimeter, still with remote chances of giving the whole thing the slip, keep getting drawn in, an example of suicidal comradeship.

You let loose a couple of shots in the air, your contribution not to Mossie mortality but to the confusion. You get more from the scene by just lying low and watching, a benefit of your location.

But this soon alters.

The Mossies organise amidst the slaughter and go for a counter assault through the right bank. They try to beat lead with lead, following the access lanes the assault teams were using. They chant their battle hymns. You can hear them over the din of the automatics, though they keep getting feebler and feebler. You have been too busy following the massacre below to notice two Mossies climbing the bank on your side. Your bodyguards are busy giving covering fire to the line formation on your side of the bank and are too far to your left to have intercepted them even if they had noticed.

The first time you notice their presence is when soldiers on the right bank start picking the dust on the embankment below you.

You see a turban and then a face red with blood. Then you see the brown eyes and they belong to someone very young, maybe eighteen, perhaps younger.

You feel like helping him up, a solitary jab of sanity in the murder around you, but then you see the terror in his eyes. You realise what you look like. The threat you represent. And even as the Mossie is trying to raise the barrel of his automatic from down below and level it at your chest you see what you have to do, for there is no time to explain to him the ridiculousness of your position. You have no option but to pull the trigger and you see a big empty hole where you once saw a pair of brown eyes.

Your bodyguards pick off the Mossie below him.

The next day, in the evening, Major Rodriguez summons you to his tent. Business time. He is alone and his feet are stuck up on his desk.

'Ah, MM,' he says, 'things are grim.'

You have got a bit of your starch back.

'War is grim,' you say.

'This is not war. This is Battalion Headquarters. They don't like what happened at Ur,' says Major Rodriguez, clicking his heels.

'Neither do the people of Ur,' you point out.

'We didn't ask them to give bed and board to forty Mossies,' defends Major Rodriguez.

'You don't say no to men with guns,' you enlighten the major.

'You have to make your choice. Us or them,' explains the major.

'That's not much to go by, Major,' you say.

'It's enough. You have to understand who can fuck you more. Play your game in that light.'

'You don't need to burn half a village down to show who's boss. The army's got some cannons, somebody breathing down their neck in Battalion HQ.'

'We didn't burn the village down, MM. Asshole equipment error. Maybe the rocket was aimed at your ribs. You should go bury the Mossie personally, thank him for letting you be.'

'Maybe somebody let things get out of hand on the women's side,' you say. That catches the major a bit off guard. The rhythms of lust are not something he thought you picked up in the din.

'Maybe they ought to let you run a unit in this area on St Paul precepts. Get you started with ideas to baptise the Mossies, convert them if you cannot catch them. MM, tit for tat is the only Tao principle that plugs with the blood groups down here. What you say you saw is an old weapon of war. They have done us worse. It's good to have them fear us. Make them reorganise their priorities for next time,' says Major Rodriguez.

'Hate you is more likely,' you say.

'That's good enough for me. When you hate you slip up. Keeps my men out of the barracks to straighten you up,' says Major Rodriguez.

'And levitate the inventory,' you add.

'That's one of the perks,' admits a smiling Major Rodriguez.

'So what's grim?' you ask.

'Battalion HQ doesn't like burnt-up places. They set up inquiry committees who go around asking embarrassing questions. It's bad PR for them. Loses them brownie points with the state government. And these human rights assholes,' says Major Rodriguez.

'I thought the state government was on your side,' you say.

'The government is on nobody's side but their own. Besides, they have a little balancing act to do. Give no reason for Amnesty International to make some noise. Or worse, invite the New Delhi diplomats down their throat. Make them shift their offices from Chanakyapuri to Kashmir.'

'Nobody should know anything, Major. Ur's nowhere from anywhere.'

'News travels, MM. You can't brush the fire and the civilian casualties under the carpet. I would love to, but it's not going to happen. This is our first fuck-up and it looks like it's going to be our last in this region.'

'You shouldn't have forced your way in. Just laid a long-term siege.'

'What? And get the media at my door. Lose control of my operation. Have everybody know we got Stingers? No way.'

'You are going to swallow them up, too?' you ask, a little taken aback at this daring.

'What do you think? Give it up to the warehouse guys?'

'Sometimes there might be more gain in giving something up. Deflect attention from what happened. Create a scare that makes you a hero and has the Ministry of Home Affairs shitting in their pants. Stingers can take out planes flying the hotshots into Srinagar. It will make them stay put in Delhi, keep their ideas to themselves.'

The major muses on this a while.

'Won't do,' he concludes. 'It's tempting, but it won't help the unit stay on beyond normal schedule, get us some more time.'

'There's no harm trying,' you say.

'And lose the cash due from the Stingers in the bargain. No way. A bird in hand is worth two in the bush. But we will play the Pathans up. The Taliban from Kabul looking for a kick in this part of the world. That may suit our purpose. We wouldn't mind losing them,' says Major Rodriguez.

'But you have only stiffs. You have none alive. Major Kohli saw to that,' you say.

'Yes. Twenty stiffs. But the problem is they don't speak. If only you guys had flushed a few alive, we might have had a good TV talk show,' says Major Rodriguez. 'I hear you knocked one out yourself, MM?'

'You heard right,' you say. You have locked that scene right out of your mind. You may get back to it one day when the world isn't looking but you aren't doing it now.

'You OK?' asks Major Rodriguez. You sense that what you may say now is crucial for whatever the major has called you for.

'Mossie's about to poke his AK-47 in your face. You blow his face off. Nothing in it that should make you feel the need to ask whether things were OK or not,' you say. 'Cause and effect. Cause: Mossie lines his gun. Effect: you blow his brains into the stream. As long as you got the effect all sewn up your side of the game, everything's OK.'

The major sizes you up for a good thirty seconds, as if he's making his mind up one last time.

'Now to the point, MM. Ur was sad and unforeseen. It's expedited certain decisions that we had hoped wouldn't have to be taken so soon.'

'Who's we?' You don't like the knowledge of faceless players.

'That's something you needn't concern yourself with. You were concerned about bulk yesterday. You can chew on some of the numbers before you leave. We are talking big. We are talking thirty thousand AK-47s, one million rounds of ammunition, a hundred kilos of RDX, detonators, five thousand grenades, a hundred Uzis, twenty automatic grenade launchers, fifty state-of-the-art mortars, five Stingers and the big cake, four hundred kilos of heroin that we captured from the Mossies over a period of two years. You ready for this?' asks Major Rodriguez.

'Major,' you say as you whistle, 'you are talking big league. You are talking my language. We could take over Africa with that kind of stuff.'

Your job brief as Executive Producer of Putman Offshore involves working for Digs's television company, called Media Vision. Here you are directly in charge of the documentary division. For complex tax reasons, which you could never quite figure out, Digs never uses his TV company to hire staff, preferring instead to wire your salary through Putman, an arrangement that quite often leads people to think you are working for a finance company.

As part of the special deal you have cut with Digs you also hold the post of Features Editor in his weekly news magazine *The Post*, which Digs started a year ago. You are primarily a print man, but you started flirting with television a few years back because of the profile it brought you. You needed that profile to stay ahead in the information game.

You met Major Rodriguez again after many years in December 1998 at Siachen glacier in Jammu and Kashmir, where you were crafting the first-ever documentary on the region. That is, after the National Defence Academy in Khadakvasla in 1985. You knew him there, but you weren't friends.

Siachen was one of the ideas you had sold Digs, before you got in, to get him interested in you. Your expertise in defence and environment reporting made you ideal for the job. High-altitude mountain warfare has lately become an Indian speciality. The Yanks have been wanting joint exercises in the region to cut in on what's happening, but the chiefs have been reluctant, so you figured it was a bright commercial idea to feed Yank curiosity, have them know what it takes to hold on to a barren piece of land twenty-one thousand feet above sea level, stop the Mossies from building the highest piece of mosque in human history.

You got to sit next to the major on the chopper from Leh to base camp, the training area for the troops moving up, the place where the first thing they teach you is how to walk on ice and how not to fall into a crevasse. You, of course, are familiar with this rigmarole: you have been as high as Camp 1 with a US team on Mount Everest.

The major was on the advisory committee to the glacier think tank that meets annually to reassess the long-term glacier situation. He was too junior to be on it but he was a special case. He had honed some warfare techniques that busted five Islamic choppers, one with a brigadier on it. 5 Kumaon had seen action at Siachen. It was the major's first posting as a raw second lieutenant straight out of Academy.

You haven't any pleasant memories of Rodriguez from your revolutionary days at Academy, but at Siachen you vibe well. Those were the days, just six months back, when the major's family was still intact. He showed you a snap of his wife, a honeymoon shot at Lakshwadeep. The major comes in handy. Your stay permit for your crew at the glacier is just five days, this after all the strings you pulled at the Ministry. But you were thankful you got in at all. The major sees your point of view. He sympathises with your concerns for quality. He has the chopper pilot pull out a flight due to technical reasons the day you were booked for return. And that extends your stay for five days, by which time the weather screws up and you get another five days. You end up owing Rodriguez ten days.

Of course, the major had his reasons for slowing you down. You were bunkered with him and he did his sonar booms on your personality, listening for shallow reefs and sand heads he should steer clear of. The general message he got, you guess, was that you were open to new ideas, exciting rides to punctuate the monotony of life.

That's when he baited you on pushing certain hardware, a sample run to test the market and see the depth you packed. In that deal you netted Kumaon $500,000. Your share was a cool 10 per cent.

You used to be a guy with scruples, but in your early thirties you have started hitching on to things for the ride. Illicit gun-running simply came your way.

What made you up to this enterprise was your international mobility, the contacts you had nurtured overseas in seminars by spreading half-truths about the nuclear position in south Asia, the subject of your dissertation and later of your articles when you were Defence Correspondent at *News Today*. You were the first to break news about your country's ambitions in the nuclear submarine field. A news report that had put you under the surveillance of the Research and Analysis Wing for a month, until one day you just walked into the RAW chief's office and cleared things up, gave him reason to believe in your innocence. So much for India's premier foreign intelligence agency.

Along the way, when you ran out of stories on defence, you widened your scope of operations to include the environment, specifically toxic waste, climate conventions and ozone. Toxic waste you developed as your forte, your tag to establish journalistic currency. India is huge, and who knows who is dumping what? You made it your business to find out. Not everybody wanted to depend upon Greenpeace alone to give them estimates of Indian scrap metal imports, the trading lacunae companies abroad were using to dump a lot of stuff they couldn't cram into their neighbourhood landfills.

You also expanded your brief a bit by including your concerns about indigenous poison generated in places like Gujarat and Maharashtra. You realised that foreign expertise was needed to teach Indians what not to do with their industrial excreta. So you submitted a proposal to the Swiss Development Authority to help you understand the holistic approach to inorganic and organic waste disposal in developed countries, specifically Switzerland. The Swiss were only too happy – for months they had been agonising over how to spend their aid grant and here was this guy walking in with a concrete proposal, even if it was not a part of their charter. You got a grant of $20,000, a four-month stay in Europe.

It was then that you developed your acquaintance with Dinesh Patel, at the time just a diamond merchant. You interviewed him for a story about Indian diamond dealers in Antwerp, written for *News Today* just to let everyone back home know you were still alive. Patel, his money-making schemes in diamonds exhausted, soon rose to become the second largest arms dealer in Bosnia and, later, Kosovo. Nobody knew about this development then, nobody knows about it now, the Indian connection in the Serbian wars. For your own reasons you never got around to doing a profile on Patel. Perhaps you intended to store the intelligence for future encashment. Stories didn't give you a fix any more unless they served your larger agenda.

It was Patel who took your first consignment of five hundred AK-47s and other little knick-knacks. The advantage of dealing with Patel was that he picked up your merchandise in Delhi. You didn't have to work out the sea route or bother your head about the end user. Your stuff went 30 per cent cheaper but you liked it this low-risk way. It didn't push you into unfamiliar territory.

But now you were getting into high-risk manoeuvres. Major Rodriguez has the first heroin shipment delivered to your apartment by 5 Kumaon personnel on leave. Wooden crates with red outer markings saying they are Government of India disaster relief, medical consignments, glucose powder for the dehydrated.

Your immediate problem is to hunt for a safe hibernation zone for your white packets. They have given you two sleepless nights and you can't take two more.

You sort your shit at work, rack your brains and decide to stash the packets in the air-conditioning vents of Digs's News Vision office, neutral, unexploited space where the H can't be traced back to you. You can crawl into them from the mezzanine floor. The aluminium is thick and strong enough to bear the weight of a man on hands and knees. You know this because you have seen the electrician do it. Yes, as part of your preparation you plan to take him out. Indispose him for a couple of months and in his place recruit one of the two muscle men Major Rodriguez has provided you as backup – Indramani, with the scar, and Gulab Chand. Both from 5 Kumaon's Alpha Company, are eating their annual two-month army leave to earn their part of the cut.

It's Chand you have in mind as designated temporary electrician. He knows his circuits and when you have Brandish, the electrician, knocked off his Suzuki Samurai at night by a speeding army Jonga jeep with Indramani on the steering, you create the opening for Chand to come the next day and flash his fake CV, work experience in your friend Jumbo's fictional air-conditioner dealership. The guy knows everything about air conditioning, he can keep your ass cool through an Indian summer provided the power's coming. He's hired on the spot.

Once you have your man on the mezzanine, guarding the ducts, it's easy work getting the packets in piecemeal, an inch-thick white carpet over twenty yards of aluminium. You hope media premises would be the last place the Narcotics Control Bureau would poke their nose into. At night the doors are double locked and nobody has the keys except Chand. You have a copy made, in case of emergencies.

A few days after you return from Bunker 13, Digs takes a walk upstairs to your cabin. As a rule he stays clear of the TV floor, the logistics confound him. He feels out of synch. But today he has things on his mind.

'MM,' says Digs, 'I want you to hire some new staff. Features has the highest turnover. This time, no experienced staff. Just trainees you can run around and get some honest work done. And what's happening to the border thing? I hear you got some good rushes for the LoC documentary.'

'Plenty,' you say, but before you can elaborate Digs nods his head and walks off. Digs's attention span is shorter than a pigeon's. He can't switch it on for longer than fifteen seconds. If you have to pitch a story to him you have to run the whole knickerless can-can routine in ten seconds flat. Grab his attention and get him to sign whatever you want in that period. Or he is going to shelve your proposal. Sit on it for two months till you forget what it was.

He drives the regular *Post* guys nuts. He fancies himself as an editor. He is, because he owns the damn thing, but he has ambitions to leave his mark on Indian journalism. The kind of editing he does is to snoop around the place with his neck lowered. If you didn't know him you would think he was the floor inspector or something. It always takes the news guys a while to get used to him. He gives them the creeps. He stares over their shoulders at their computer screens and half the time when they look up he is there grinning at them. It cracks them up so fast they keep looking over their shoulders. In the end they kind of get addicted to his presence.

He doesn't do this much with the senior guys. Instead he keeps them off balance when he brushes shoulders with them in the loo. He asks what they are doing. Most of the guys are doing nothing, naturally, and start to hem and haw, waving their big whales over their trousers, making interesting patterns. Then he pushes them into his office and assigns them some update on the whore district or crime nonsense, and there goes their week. Even the reporters who are doing something forget what it is until Digs has just slapped them with some shitty assignment. They end up having to do both Digs's stuff and theirs as well.

The trick is to burst into an answer. Say you're doing a story on floriculture exports. That kind of thing cuts him dead in mid-sentence. He loses his vowels. 'Yeah, OK,' he says and walks off. His memory's shorter than his attention span. He's never going to come up to you and ask how the floriculture thing is going. In case he does, you tell him your section editor put you on this or that. The thing is, once you start talking he isn't interested in listening.

But you like Digs. He got his nickname because he digs his nose in public. That's only second to his burping in your face when you are talking. But Burps didn't sound as good.

While you are contemplating your hiring methodology, Digs comes by once again for a twenty-second verbal burst.

'Oh, I forgot to tell you. My daughter Karnam's back from the US. She wants to see how this place works. See if you can take her in features. Show her around,' he says.

'OK,' you say. She won't be picking a hole in your salary is how you console yourself. But you find it odd that Digs can't do his own hiring. He does all the sacking. Recruitment doesn't contribute to his blood pressure. It wouldn't fray his hypertension.

You place calls to journos on the circuit, leave word around that you need a couple of trainees to beef up your features division. (You don't want to run an advertisement and get a million CVs to read.)

You tip your chair back, gazing up at your safe, invisible stash. Kashmir feels a million kilometres away. And that's when the call comes from RAW, the call you always knew would come.

'Hello,' says Colonel Ray Chowdhary, your RAW godfather, who thinks he runs you. You have run for him and RAW on occasion. These days your loyalty could only be called sporadic.

'Yes,' you say.

'What's the news, pal? You remember your friends?'

'Always.'

'What's the score? You have anything to help us nab the bastards?'

'Not yet.'

'What the fuck have you been doing up there? We have been hearing things.'

'Ears are for hearing. That's what God made them for.'

'I am in no mood for your cockiness. You get to go where you want, we dropped you a line to Bunker 13. We want to know what the weather is up there.'

'I told you. Nothing. The place is clean as a whistle. Just the usual army bullshit. They went and razed that village, Ur. But you don't need that from me. That's everywhere. Even the media's got it.'

'You sure?'

'About what?'

'About the weather up there?'

'You couldn't fry an omelette.'

'We have been hearing talk about some Stingers they found on the raid.'

'Not that I know of. They shooed us off when it started getting shirty.'

'It's not your business to shoo off.'

'It's also not in my interest to have a Mossie tear holes in my chest.'

'Is that why they bounced off all the Afghans? Stop them singing about the Stingers under interrogation?'

'Doesn't make sense. They took a few local Mossies in,

110

alive and kicking. They too must have seen what was going on.'

'Those are the guys that told us,' he says.

'You guys pump Mossies so bad they start inventing stuff. You see, if, as you say, they had found Stingers, they wouldn't have left any Mossies alive to tell the tale.'

'Maybe. Maybe they slipped. You got anything at all?'

'They haven't taken my bait yet. Give me some more time.'

'Time is running out, my friend. It's time for you to press their hand. You stay wired.' Colonel Chowdhary hangs up.

For all your bluster you take a long breath and mop your face.

Later in the day, Digs's daughter comes by. She isn't what you have been expecting. You have been imagining someone with Digs's porky looks, a pest you would have to put up with. But it looks as if Digs had someone else turn in the rod, squirt some prime-time genetic fluid.

'My dad said to come and see you,' Karnam says.

'Yes, I was planning to call you. He says you want to have a look around, see the levers.'

'Actually, I was planning a bit more than that. I was hoping I could pitch in somewhere, get some work experience.'

'What have you been up to? I hear you have been chasing some piece of paper back in Texas.'

'Yes, I just finished my MBA.'

You feel the first shiver of need seep into your veins.

'M fucking BA. You could be barking up the wrong tree, you know. You should be sharing the latest you have in circulation technique with our marketing guys. They can't seem to be able to push it beyond the five-digit barrier. Make them go sonic.'

'No. Actually, I hate marketing. I don't want to whip up soap or something like that. I want to be a journalist. I want to make a difference.'

'You too? Another member of the caring brigade. Maybe somebody ought to tell you there's not enough foam you can hose in out there.'

'You are so cynical. Are all of you like this? Journalists, I mean,' she asks.

'No. I haven't progressed to the point where it's just another job for me. If you are only cut out for doing some particular chore in life, it makes the choice easy.'

'They should put you in career counselling,' comments Karnam.

'That's my in-house speciality. The crowd comes to me for straightening out their change-the-world kinks. Change yourself, I say, save the world from your brand of revolution.'

'Would features be a good place to start off?' asks Karnam.

'Well, actually, no. The desk would be ideal, but that would be grade four, third-world pay. We'll start you off in features and then maybe you can move to business once you get the hang of things,' you say.

'Marketing sounds so boring,' she comments.

'Boring is as boring does. You could pack some action there if you got the right ideas,' you say.

'What's the basic tip? I mean the Zen of journalism. No ten-minute speech,' she asks.

'Well, it's like any other job. Just don't fuck up. Get your Ws right – the why, what, where and who – and you should chip along fine,' you say.

'That's it?'

'What did you expect, a warden's monologue? It's more than I got.'

'What did you get?'

'A test trial, the first day I walk in for this interview at *The Statesman*. The editor asks, "So you want to write?" "Yes, sir," I say. "What's the time right now?" he asks me. "Nineten, sir," I say. "Well, writer boy," he says, "get me three exclusives by five in the evening and you have your job." "Yes, sir," I say and walk out of his office. I didn't even know what he meant by exclusives. I checked it out with some blokes who seemed to know. This was in Calcutta. I hang around Esplanade for a while figuring what to do. I can't figure out shit. I walk in the sun hoping to bump into something. And bump I did. I find myself kicking a packet of something by Ho Chi Minh, this little side street they have by Tata Centre. It's a packet of letters some postman chucked into the drain that had four-month-old postmarks. That's my first story.

'I hang around a bit hoping to latch on to something else, but it's all fucking dead around there and so I call this friend of mine for some help. He gives me a lead on this guy that can light electric bulbs anywhere on his body. Nobody's ever done him in press, he tells me. So I go all the way to Jadavpur to meet this man and plead with him to get into the mood to show some of his stuff. And right there he takes a bulb out of a socket and presses the slim end on his nipples. Then he sits like that for five minutes with his eyes closed and the filament glows up. I mean, it isn't bright or anything but it's heated up. He shifts it to his tummy and bingo. He does it about five different places. I ask him whether he can do it on his dick, he chases me out. I try to get an explanation of the phenomenon from a physics professor and he thinks I am wasting his time. But I have two stories and when I am coming down in the lift from meeting the professor this guy next to me gets his hand jammed into the gate grille. It rips his wrists off before I can push the stop button on the lift. I and some others take him to hospital and when I am free from all that, it's late afternoon and I don't even have time to change my shirt before returning to the office. "So what do you have for me, trainee boy?" the editor asks me. I give him my two stories. "Where's the third?" he asks. I tell him I don't have a third. "I didn't get the time after taking this guy to hospital," I tell him. "That's your bloody third," he tells me. The best human interest shit you have. Then he packs me off to get a quote from the guy's wife. How she felt seeing her husband's wrist knocked off? That's how my interview went. You want something like that?' you finish.

'Jesus!' she says. 'Who was the editor?'

'His name was Suman Sinha. One of the maddest I ever worked with. He was fifty-seven then. He drank himself to death,' you say.

You're cooking the stuff as you go along. Sinha was indeed your first boss, but the way you got your first footing was through a sedate copy test that the old man gave you. A thing to gauge your precise writing skills and whether you could locate the state of Mizoram in the atlas.

'How old were you?'

'Eighteen,' you say to sustain the myth, though you were hitting twenty. 'That's how we started off in those days.'

'When can I start?' asks Karnam.

'Any time. Now,' you say. You shrug your shoulders. 'It's up to you.'

'OK, now,' she says, smiling.

'Fine, I want you to give me four story ideas first thing tomorrow morning. Let's see what's in you,' you say.

'Could you show me around a bit?' she asks. 'Like what happens where. A conducted tour. I am kind of nervous.'

So you take her for a three-floor spin. You start with the Desk.

'This is the Desk. The last net. You don't have it and you end up looking stupid after print. Basic job function: cleaning copy, giving headlines, intros, captions, and cutting copy to length. If you've copy needs fixing they may or may not end up running the story. They may reassign it to one of the staff writers.'

'Sounds like a lot of dull work,' says Karnam.

'It is. But if you go through the grind for a year it will fill the holes in your system, make you a better journalist,' you say.

With such penetrative insights you begin the tour.

You are out drinking with the lads at Moets, in Defence Colony: Karim, Matthew, Dravid and Jolly. You aren't so pally with your crowd up at documentary, Siddy, Teresa and the others, as you are with features. Dilip from systems hops on your gang. He has some news for you. But first Karim has to do some takedown.

'Hey, MM boss, hear you're hiring a million-volt broad for features. You have to develop a two-guy recruitment panel for these tasks, boss. Get yourself a second opinion,' advises Karim.

Karim's a cunt you have to tolerate. He hails from Bihar. But the thing is, he's a workhorse. He's also plugged into the corporate world. And on occasions, it's in your scheme of things to organise sponsorship for events. That's where Karim fits in.

'She is Digs's daughter,' you inform your crowd. Your thousand-dollar chip for the evening.

'You kidding!' says Karim.

'Serious?' asks Jolly, her turf as sole belle of the department threatened.

'No jokes. Ask Dilip,' you say.

'Yeah, I had to give her a password for the system,' says Dilip. 'She couldn't make up her mind for ten minutes.'

'What did she choose?' asks Dravid.

'What did she choose?' mimics Dilip. 'What are you going to do? Look up her files for sexual preferences? She hasn't any yet.'

'What, files or preferences?' you ask. The others laugh.

'Give me a break, MM,' says Dilip.

'OK, tell me how many letters,' persists Dravid.

'Fuck off,' says Dilip.

'Letters, for Chrissake. It would still take me a million years,' says Dravid.

'Four,' says Dilip.

'What's her ID?' asks Matthew.

'Karnam,' says Dilip. 'The same as her name.'

Soon they forget her and Dravid starts complaining about the Desk.

'Hey, MM, you got to prune their hormones a bit. Give them some reality programming. There's this new bitch they have who called me at *two* in the night asking whether this quote I have of Perreira on this Zakir guy was *on the record* or not. It went, "Zakir scalps his clients out for the ten minutes he spends thinking about them on his shit pot. It's shit thought, something the companies can well do without." She asks me first whether I was sure he said it. I mean, *I* am the reporter. I filed the stuff five days ago.'

'I had this other guy – what's his name, the guy with hair down to his balls?' begins Karim.

'Aiyar,' helps out Matthew.

'Yes, this Tamil Nadu fuck. The hard metal asshole plays the drums on this Chakra band. He calls me up on this real estate story I filed. He says editorial policy is to have all measurements in square metres, not yards. I tell him the whole north Indian market ticks on yards. You say metres and everybody's going to have calculators out to understand the story. He says no, he has got to have his metres. He showers me stuff about *The Economist* and their metric style sheet. Then he branches off into pounds and kilograms and prepositions and God knows what else till I tell him to do what he wanted, double-decker the fucking masthead, bring in a design revolution. But he says no, he doesn't have to do the conversion, *I* have to do it. I said, Sorry, I thought that was the Desk's load of shit. He says even if it was, though it wasn't, he couldn't find any conversion table and he was most likely to botch it all up. I said the software was all there on the system. All he had to do was enter "Calculate" on Advance but he said if he could do that he would be working with Bill Gates not *The Post*,' complains Karim.

'Guy's got a point,' you say.

'He didn't, boss,' says Karim. 'He was just playing hockey, trimming his workload.'

'How's Nonita doing these days?' you ask. You have been out of office gossip for a while on the copy editor. 'Is she still humping Digs?'

'As far as I can see. One of the drivers dropped them at the Imperial at ten in the night after the political snapshot pages went to bed,' says Karim.

'God, he's so hooked on her, you should have seen him last Monday when the Atex started playing funny,' says Dilip. 'She was fixing this Momin special report on the fodder scam in Bihar and swoosh the system goes down and she can't recall her file. She does a search on it and system says there's no such file. I mean, you guys know how the Atex behaves sometimes. You need some time to coax things out of it after it trips. In the first place they have thirty terminals going when the mainframe's just built for twenty-two. Then they have this news co-ordinator asshole doing H&Js on files as big as *Middlemarch*. The system can only take that much load at one go. Anyways, the Atex tripped about thrice in the evening and twice Digs was affected because he's writing his comment piece. But he doesn't flap. He sits in his own office, corrupting his lungs with his Marlboros. But Nonita gets running to him the third time, saying the system administrator should be sacked, she's lost her file and all that crap. And Digs comes running out of his office like somebody keyed his buttocks up. He just lights into me, gives me hell. The bitch. Somebody lend her a spare tit, loan her some silicon, she might give Digs something to hold on to.'

'She lost the little she had, rubbed this pimple cleanser on them,' bitches Matthew.

'Yeah, Reinhold Messner would find it tough to climb on those nipple holds,' says Karim.

'No, now these silicon babes have this new scare. They can't go Concorde,' you say.

'How's that?' asks Matthew.

'The silicon explodes the moment you break the sound barrier,' you say.

'Serious?' asks Jolly.

'As hell. Straight out of *New Scientist*. You get a silicon job on your boobs and you get a job as an air hostess in the Concorde, you could end up serving nipple pie,' you say. Everybody laughs. Your contribution to the evening's humour.

'Now you look at Minnie, that's where all the action in the office is now. A woman has to have tits like her to shoot her stock up, get her beyond competition,' says Dravid. Minnie's this designer beauty at *The Post* whom Karim has been zoning in on for about two months, but without much apparent success.

'I think this is getting sick,' says Jolly.

'How are things with you, Karim, you make any progress?' you ask.

'No progress, boss. Biggest luck I have had so far is taking her out for a pizza. I had to eat half of hers as well. She wouldn't leave unless I had the whole thing mopped up,' says Karim.

'You should have ordered the dump down. Monopolised the call numbers, hogged all the trays. Made Slice of Italy work overtime. Taken yourself a year to finish the stuff,' advises Matthew.

'And pay off washing their dishes,' Karim finishes with sarcasm. 'What I get out of that luck is this business fuck we have, this Jain asshole, come needling me all afternoon because he has seen us coming back together. He goes into this ankle-biting routine and Minnie happens to pass by and hears some of the stuff and the next thing she says to me when

I call her is, "So you have been bragging that you took me out." It takes me a week to explain Jain psychology to her.'

'The problem with you, Karim, is that your strategy is out-dated. Fucking *pizzas*. You got your brain scrambled. Take her out for some of this band stuff. Like the Ricky Martin show that happened some time back. Take her to see Ricky fucking Martin,' you say.

'That Jain asshole's been giving me a headache, too. He gets me to input on this story, how the white skins are squeezing out Indian managers, and I slog my ass for two days, get the dope on the thing, file him a thousand words, no fluff, and he doesn't even give me a joint by-line. He stuffs my name at the bottom, takes his own above in Helvetica bold. He uses all my stuff, it's better than he could fish out himself in one week. I do it to him as a favour because he comes whining to me. He says his own crowd's on leave. Slime,' says Matthew.

'You should have told me,' you say.

'Well, I didn't want to blow things out of proportion,' says Matthew.

'Hey, MM, you got any load on this new design thing? The guys are going nuts. Leaving about an inch for copy. Some gag these marketing guys are playing on Digs about the reading habits of Indians. They have had some survey done which shows the letters are too much for the readers to absorb. The picture's all they can take, colour their time in the loo. I mean, if somebody doesn't play the right song Digs's going to buy it all, make us take our golden hand-shake,' complains Jolly.

'Digs's too cautious to innovate in a hurry, whatever that dope Leslie might sell him,' you explain.

Leslie's *The Post*'s art director and chief in-house, bull-goose loony. You had got him in in the first place, but the career motion he engineered once he got in had taken him way beyond all reasonable expectation. You remember how you had taken Digs out to lunch to check on Leslie, somebody you got pally with in the Press Club. You remember, with admiration, the kind of wholesale shit Leslie had sprayed all over Digs, stuff about design, type size, typeface, grids and other incomprehensible designer lingo that you'd think was some pig disease. But seeing Digs in solid listener mode, the kind of attention that he gave to people about twice a year, you had to alter your thinking. Leslie got hired on the spot. You got a lesson in bullshitting.

'He can't make a decision, either,' comments Karim. 'I tossed up this idea at the meeting about *breaking* into a prison illegally, taking photographs and coming out, just to prove the kind of shit that goes around in jails here. How prisoners are committing crimes and using jail as an alibi. He's put that on hold.'

It isn't till the second round of beer is gone and the crowd splits up, leaving you alone with Dilip and Jolly, that you get to know what's on their mind.

'MM boss,' says Jolly. 'We have this scoop.'

'What?' you ask. You have known many hot stories start this way. But this, you get the feel, is different. Dilip's your resident Kevin Mitnick. Mitnick, of course, was for years the world's most notorious cybercriminal. Dilip, though not in that league, started off as a ham enthusiast but had eventually fleshed his skills in cellular phone eavesdropping. The gizmos had just come home and Dilip had already busted Airtel phone software, giving him unlimited free-time access to the airwaves. Right now, however, he was giving an unofficial helping hand to Jolly, trying to bust her man for her and get some pussy into the bargain.

You have put Jolly on to doing this investigative piece on the 120 MiG-21 Bis avionics and armament upgrade deal which has gone to Russia. This after three other countries, Israel included, slogged their ass off trying to swing it. But the Russians get the nod because, as Jolly's sources have tipped her, the Price Negotiation Committee got an all-expenses-paid tour of Russia, with their fair quota of ballerinas and St

Petersburg whores. Which happens all the time, but this time with a difference: the Russian mafia tailed the contingent across the whole place taking photographs of air marshals and additional defence secretaries from the Ministry of Defence snorting powder and feeling ass. All of which were given to them as souvenirs to admire in the choked Aeroflot loo on the flight back home, colour prints to remind them of their promises.

What Jolly had got hold of were a few of the prints from one of the air marshals who came clean. Howling the story out, risking his pension. The only catch was that the Russians were the lowest bidders – so why, Jolly wanted to learn, had they thrown in all the perks, not to mention blackmail?

But here the story really hotted up. What Jolly had come to know was that the Ministry of External Affairs had taken the matter up with the Russian ambassador and the latter was due for dinner at Defence Minister Suresh Yadav's house, to clear the static in the air and reaffirm commitment to the Indo-Russian friendship treaty, notwithstanding the damage done by some hired Chechens.

So what Jolly does is park her car fifty yards from the minister's house, hoping to sandbag the Russian ambassador for a comment right on Yadav's doorstep. Dilip's with her, just tagging along for fun with all his eavesdropping truffle cart in place from yesterday because he was doing some test runs in Vasant Vihar, fine-tuning his technique. But just for the heck of it he switches on his stuff and starts playing with his antenna outside the window and bang they are on to this power conversation between Suresh Yadav, who also holds the power portfolio, and some Korean fuck, deal co-ordinator of a Seoul power conglomerate, whose voice Jolly recognises. The company just struck a power deal with Uttar Pradesh to throw a plant in the Terai region, bordering Nepal.

Jolly plays portions of the tape for you, they get it somewhere in the middle.

'We regret the mistake,' the Korean is saying. You can feel him bowing in the phone, lifting his ass. 'We confuse between bank. I get information you call, I call you immediately. We rectify mistake tomorrow. We will pay you the whole amount. OK, sir. *Gam sa nida.*'

You can feel the minister edgy on the phone, he hadn't expected it on this number.

'Yes, yes,' he says, but forgets caution for a brief while. 'Could you repeat the number, please?'

'78910123,' says the Korean.

'That's right. Please do the needful. I need two million dollars immediately,' says Yadav.

'OK, sir. *Gam sa nida,*' says the Korean and the line goes dead.

'Well,' says Jolly. 'What do you say to that? You recognise Suresh Yadav's voice or not? I think it's him.'

'I don't know. It's too brief a conversation to go by,' you say. In fact you recognise the minister's audio from the moment he says, 'Yes, yes', you just don't commit yourself to anything.

'I will talk with Digs,' you say. 'Let me keep the tape. You got copies?' You look at Dilip.

'No,' says Dilip.

'OK, I will get one made,' you say.

'The thing is, can I go ahead with my MiG story or should I wait a bit, coat-tail an angle on this tape, rake mud at two places and reel the minister in?' asks Jolly.

'No, you go ahead with the MiG thing. The tape, let's think about it. I will get the legal angle. Besides, we can't just honk the tape. We would have to show how it dropped in our lap and that would lynch us, get both your asses too,' you say. 'Just be careful where you wave your antenna next time around. You could come on the radar of the Special Protection Group the next time you use your equipment. They could antenna your shit hole, get the friction in your mucus, if you aren't careful.'

'They wouldn't know a computer from a TV,' says Dilip.

'You think too much of that and you'll be the first Indian arrested on cellular eavesdropping charges.'

'You too,' you say to Jolly, getting up. 'Don't lead him on. This is no back-seat Ambassador power fuck.'

'You are gross, MM,' says Jolly. Dilip grins.

'Tell me something I don't know,' you say.

Outside, you get in your Defender, a power chip in your pocket. A fucking bonanza. A tool to soften the minister should the game hot up. You feel the tape with pleasure.

A van tails you all the way home. You don't floor your pedal. This wasn't the time for lane dog-fights. You don't spill your cards so early in the game.

Saturdays you usually spend with Jumbo, go swimming at the Sheraton or dig Djinn's if you feel like it. Or the Dragonball, where you can do any of Jumbo's girls that takes your fancy.

You don't like taking your prey home. It clouds your neighbourhood image, messes up the sheets as well, and you do your own laundry. Your help is limited to a Nepali cook-cum-house cleaner, who comes in the morning, does his stuff while you are around and packs up for the day after he polishes your Defender. You love vehicles from the Land-Rover family. You bought it second-hand from a British diplomat.

Today you find yourself making small talk with Jaspreet, in the back seat of Jumbo's Mercedes. She is in a sleeveless something that could be doing wonders to her figure. Only you are too fucked up to give her points for that. You have done today what you never did before. You snorted some of the stuff that Jumbo does about four times a day. He said there had to be a phase in everybody's life which they could turn around to and say, 'That's when we popped the Burmese talc.' Especially you, he said, when you are holding some of the stuff. You hadn't told him how much yet. Jumbo's generally into the Orient except for things like transportation and the Russian mafia, whom he has to keep in good humour because he's also the boss of the company that handles the Russian plane charters into Delhi, carting in the hordes for shopping and holidays.

You feel things happening to you. You watch your hair standing on end. You want to rip the leather off the front seat but Jaspreet's reading your palms, mumbling prophecies about your sexual affairs, playing seduction games that have the firepower of BB guns.

You want the wind to hit your frame, loosen you up. You can't push the right button for the glass, so you say what the hell and open the door and stand on the rim where the door fits the way you have seen the American secret service do, in which movie you can't remember. Your brain doesn't want to tell you that right now. But the Mercedes is doing 120. You don't remember the presidential limousine going that fast. You think maybe they were, but the producers had to slow it down using digital cinematic make-believe. This new stuff that can have Tom Cruise shake his digits with Hitler or anybody.

Jaspreet is tugging at your trousers trying to pull you in. Jumbo hits on the road to the airport where Dragonball is but he doesn't slow down. You yell at a 747 lining up for final approach. 'Hey, Jumbo,' you shout, 'your twin brother's up in the air.'

You feel you have been funny. You retreat next to Jaspreet to laugh. She's looking at you in a very startled way, as if you are wriggling your ears. The ushers at the invitational discotheque check you in. Jumbo's partner so far on this Saturday expedition is a striking Russian girl, angular features, all legs, no English. You get her to repeat her name about three times. It's Catherina or Rina or Tsarina or something. You are too fucked up to listen properly. Jaspreet is tugging at your sleeves, urging you to take on a *bhangra* sizzler but your movements on the floor are painfully arthritic unless rum's raiding your circulatory network. And now there's this something new that you have tried and your footsteps on the stairs to the bar echo like gongs in your head.

The trapezium shape of the bar appeals to your sense of post-heroin aesthetics, but you distinctly remember running it down about a month back in a learned geometric exposition in front of female models who didn't understand what a protractor was. You remember telling them something, but you can't remember what. Heroin, you get the feeling, is all about not being able to remember things. Though now the word 'protractor' sticks in your head you can't figure out what to connect it with. It sounds to you like a dinosaur species.

You try to bounce it off on Jaspreet, but you have oddly lost her in the maze. You are sitting in the bar next to a miniskirted mammal on the lap of a sonofabitch in a silk shirt. A sweaty silk shirt. He's massaging her thighs with one hand and the other holds something red, maybe a Bloody Mary, which he gazes at when he's finished ogling the multitudinous shapes and forms down on the dance floor while the DJ launches into *Cotton-Eye Joe* by Rednex.

To your right, gazing philosophically at something very whiskyish in a glass, sits what you could get away with calling a *homo sapiens* of indistinct sex contemplating some big fuck-up that happened or was about to happen and could be countered by an urgency in gaze.

You wonder how you got here and how others are gauging you when Jaspreet rejoins you from wherever she was roving. You ask her if she knows what a tractor is. She looks puzzled. You know you have got the word wrong but you don't know how or where. She nods her head. Maybe she thinks it's some new game you are playing. Something she's been too dumb to pick up. But you take comfort in the knowledge that at least she knows whatever it is you have asked her.

You start looking around for Jumbo. You suddenly need insulation, for a while, from this girl.

But her non-heroin status is making her restless in a different way. She's tapping her feet to the music and soon she pulls you, even as you try to hold your rum aloft, to the floor, where you spot Jumbo in full swing with the Russian, whose height, you just notice, clears Jumbo by six inches.

The Russian's throwing some fancy footwork that you infer could be a major new dance step that still hadn't diffused in your part of the world. You try to match her for a while, which amuses her, but you can't copy the rhythm and you step on about four toes.

You grin at the aggrieved faces you see, soothing their fears by renouncing your flamboyance. You jerk about in your own space, now energised by the bra-less tits of your partner in motion.

But denied an uninterrupted supply of photo images because of her habit of spinning around and disappearing for vital seconds into the adjacent medley, you gravitate consciously towards the perimeters of the dance floor where, on a waist-level ledge, you have deposited your half-full glass of rum. Expectedly, some asshole's discovered it and the glass is now empty. But there's a full one next to it of something that you take a big gulp of anyway, hoping to boost your morale for the evening, which you feel could have reached its apogee.

The DJ, in his own way, is trying his best to get you into the spirit of it all. Jumbo beckons you. He is doing a three-some with the Russian and Jaspreet. Dick to ass and cunt to ass and when you join, another dick to ass. A foursome now, swaying like an independent entity to some guitar pyrotech-nic that has scores of eyes glancing enviously at the massing of flesh and bone that isn't their own.

Then some dickhead takes it into his head to join the movement by pressing his dick in your ass and there's a scramble and soon there's a chug-chug train around the perimeter that you do once and then disengage because that's the rule you have learnt of any temporary innovation.

When the train loses momentum and the people merge and you can't locate your partners any more, you split for a while to get some fresh air outside and you spot someone who you think resembles in left-side profile the brief image you had of the guy trailing you in a van a few days back. But it bothers you just enough to get you to go back to the action you just jettisoned. And the music suddenly is such that you don't want to waste time looking for Jaspreet. You cut a direct route to the centre of the floor and start an exhibition of a solo something, muscle power responding in tandem to something that cuts to 2 Unlimited and then opens in samba country. Others, by now recognising the wild spirit in you, provide you space for your antics.

The Russian girl emerges at your side. From which direction, you don't know, because you have your eyes closed. But she gets you into a pelvic grinding number, front to front in circular vectors, and from the way her flesh rubs you in the chest, you, for the first time in the evening, feel the emergence of an erection.

And then by some strange, unargued, silent, hedonistic compliance Jumbo and you switch your evening partners. You suddenly discover increased compatibility even though you can't figure out what Tsarina or Catherina is saying. But it's the language of the heart and body, which doesn't need linguistic embellishments.

Soon you have had your fill of Dragonball. You ache to see action elsewhere. Jumbo suggests a jump in ethos and character and, five minutes later, this time with you driving and Catherina or Tsarina in front with her arms around your shoulders, you accelerate to make up about thirty-odd kilometres before the action dissipates at the Kamal cabaret joint in west Delhi.

At a traffic light at Naraina a cop waves you to the kerb. It's past midnight and you surmise that he has taken offence at the blaring stereos. But whatever his agenda before he stops your Mercedes, he now switches it to an inspection of your front passenger's passport, whose sensual deportment isn't chiming with his sense of road discipline or personal unfulfilment.

You wave your press card, which dilutes his sense of investigation. You point your finger to the MP sticker on the windscreen. He hesitates. You take that as a green, release your clutch slowly and then, as a passing gift, watch Catherina or Tsarina flash her left breast at the night sentry. He doesn't like it, or thinks he can eye more of it by delaying us some more, but you floor the gas and leave him behind.

At Kamal you watch as the doorman winks at Jumbo, calls him sir, salutes you and opens a brass door to admit your group to a 50-by-100-foot joint that's in full swing, your timing perfect. An unslim Eve, clad skimpily, is in the throes of some daring callisthenics in the middle of the cabaret floor. She walks up to some individual tables and performs some powerful brand of breast tectonics, which the live band finds hard to keep up with. She gets currency notes stuffed into her mirrory bra.

'Now this is what I call real action,' says Jumbo. 'You take too much of that Dragonball stuff and it will fuck up your taste.'

'It's pathetic,' says Jaspreet.

'It's different. It's not sanitised the way you want it,' says Jumbo.

You are here for the first time. The two girls too. You arrange your chair in the dark and at the back so you can do things to Tsarina or Catherina that people would have to turn their necks to see. She has a mass of zip slits on her dress that allow you easy access. What you are interested in knowing, the way your dirty mind works, is whether Tsarina or Catherina has panties or not. You suspect not. You are just confirming a hypothesis, ironing out a doubt tinkering with your mind. It's as you have guessed. Lingerie either comes too expensive back in the place Tsarina or Catherina comes from or she leaves them in her suitcase at her hotel so that guys like you can have a little quiz.

On the floor the girl transfers her currency collection to her underwear and then jerks off her bra in one fluid motion. The band marks the event by letting its drums go berserk for a while, reaching a crescendo in disorganised sound. Jumbo has Jaspreet's tits cupped and he asks her, 'Like that?'

You don't know whether he means the action on the floor or what he is doing to Jaspreet. Jaspreet says, 'Yes.' You don't know which question she's answering. Such evening ambiguity keeps you from descending to low spirits.

'Do they go any further?' you ask Jumbo about the floor-girl.

'Some days they do if they don't spot any plainclothes cop,' says Jumbo.

All of you sit and wait in dim hope as you taste some snacks that Jumbo orders. You wonder how much anticipation you would have if you were waiting out a gigolo to kick his pants and whether it was the same for the two girls with you. How much were they putting up with? You realise the complexity of explaining your query to Tsarina or Catherina. And Jaspreet is busy with Jumbo.

You try concentrating on the floor but the sight doesn't excite you. The woman's only interested in going to tables and stuffing currency notes in her undies. The guys who wave five-hundred-buck greens she allows to do the stuffing themselves. They keep their fingers in there till the girl has to pick them out delicately. Tsarina or Catherina is trying to feel your armament but today you have on buttoned Levi's and that's posing insurmountable problems for her back-hand grope. You don't feel like helping out Tsarina or Catherina. Instead you start nibbling at her ears. She starts giggling. She says something to you. For once you understand. Tsarina or Catherina wants to dance on the floor. Maybe, you think, she has an act in Moscow.

'Hey, Jumbo, she wants to dance,' you inform Jumbo. You don't want to have a hand in such advance decisions, help her with something whose chemistry you can't control. For all you know, the in-house girls shot foreigners who cut in on their take. But you suspect that Tsarina or Catherina wouldn't be interested in the green wads. She might be a show-off instead. Inform us Indians about what we're missing.

131

'Why not?' Jumbo asks and beckons to someone who looks to you like the guy who was responsible for the shit on the floor. He's never had so outrageous a request. He doesn't know whether to say yes or no. He's in a bind. Jumbo says something to Jaspreet and she gives a feel to the guy's trumpet. He jumps about two feet, looks at our crowd like we were the best weirdos he's had in the months or years he's been working in the joint.

Meanwhile, Tsarina or Catherina is under the table snorting something that Jumbo has passed to her. She snorts it off a mirror in her handbag. She comes up and tells Jumbo to call off the whole thing. She wants to sit on your lap instead and you worry about what this means in her current state and after you worry some more you signal to Jumbo that it is time to abort the setting, leave the place intact even if it means not getting to see the kind of dynamite the floor-girl packed below her waist. Some things you could leave to the future.

Outside, it's a question of where now? Jumbo's suggesting his place, but you want something very neutral. You don't want to use his neighbourhood. You suggest this Golf Links guest house you know that has big rooms and is ideal for the kind of thing that is now left to do in the night. Once again, peculiarly, your group compatibility undergoes a metamorphosis. You think it has to do with the something the traces of which you can still see on Tsarina or Catherina's nose. You sit in the rear with Jaspreet and this time you have your arms interlinked with hers. You feel the heat of her breasts on your elbow. For the second time in the evening you feel your blood surge below your waist. You are not sure whether or not you have condoms in your wallet. You don't remember a recent refill.

You keep a lookout for some open chemist's shop as Jumbo knifes through the streets. But it's too late for commerce to cater to your software needs. You hope Jaspreet or your other two companions have some to spare. In this day and age it's the women who go loaded.

You are still in the hit zone. It's over three hours since you made your heroin hit and the impact on your system is still considerable. There's a strange taste in your mouth, you don't feel like lifting your arms sometimes.

You guide Jumbo through Golf Links to the place you have in mind. There's just one free room, which means that you have just one room vacant to try out any stuff that you might have planned. It means that for the first time in your life you find yourself one of the participating cogs in a foursome.

Clothes, you feel, once you have your room secured, are something irritating your state of mind. You feel more relaxed in your BVDs. You look at yourself in the mirror. You want to see whether heroin has done any visible damage to your frame. You feel your eyes are a little puffy, the kind that you are accustomed to see after a night that lasts till six in the morning. But otherwise your systems seem to be pulling on.

In the mirror you can see Jumbo start on his programme. Have Tsarina or Catherina peel the layers off him. Jaspreet, you sense, is a little unsure of what is about to happen. She, it registers on you, is the only one not on Burmese talc. Which perhaps aggravates her nose for suspense.

And Jumbo is in the mood for something really kinky. He's egging Tsarina or Catherina on to something and she's begun to giggle like mad as she unstraps what's hers to discard even as she gives Jaspreet some lascivious glances. You can guess what's coming, but Jaspreet is still clueless. But when Tsarina or Catherina starts helping her loosen her stuff her instinct rings the right bell and, though she is not taking a puritan stand, she does feel a mild panic which induces her to say, 'I haven't done this kind of thing before.'

'There's always the first time,' Jumbo tells her, and you view the sight which develops within the next few minutes with not a small degree of interest, even though, as things stand, you aren't the one finger-fucking Jaspreet on the king-sized double bed, but Tsarina or Catherina, and it is not your hardware that Jaspreet is swallowing and sliding on with immaculate timing and sense of purpose, but Jumbo's.

For two minutes you stand and watch the scene the way any triple-X director would have done, trying to spot the weaknesses in the frame, any loose ends to tie up, and you conclude that, even though cinematically you might just be missing the camera's acute angle, the daisy chain won't be complete until you accept Tsarina or Catherina's desperate pleadings to bury your stick in any of the orifices she offered.

Her body language makes it clear it doesn't matter to her which hole you choose. Still, you take the one you know best.

You do it slowly and rhythmically at first, trying to work out a thrust that squeezes the maximum out of your exertions, then you work up a pace the likes of which has your end of the chain arching up spasmodically, forgetting all about Jaspreet. Who soon complains, until you work out a count that doesn't disrupt the harmony of your group.

But soon you feel the urge to innovate and you break up the formation to realign in a different combination.

A triple sandwich with you at the bottom, Jaspreet digging you and Jumbo working on Jaspreet, while Tsarina or Catherina has you lick her. Then she turns around and fixes her butt between your face and Jaspreet's, offering you the same place but requiring Jaspreet to pay some attention to her other hole.

All of which continues for some bewildering length of minutes. Jaspreet is the first to come and Jumbo soon follows, which leaves Tsarina or Catherina and you to take your time and prolong your increments of pleasure. For her, a shudder and then release, but for you a wave of nausea and a convulsion that sends you straight to the pot. Tsarina or Catherina follows you inside to see you don't choke to death and from the room Jumbo shouts, 'How's he, Nina?'

This time the heroin doesn't fuzzy your hearing. At least you vomit in the comfort of the intelligence that you have cracked Tsarina or Catherina's real goddamn name.

You are in Moscow. Jumbo's with you but you're worried. Yesterday, you had an evening rendezvous with a Chechen mafia head, Rustam Akramov, but his henchmen never showed up. You were supposed to be at Dolls, a strip joint on the Krasnya Presnyaul, between seven and eight in the evening. You took a corner table and it took you and Jumbo till half past ten to finish your beef stroganoff and have a dozen lap dances but nobody turned up.

Though Jumbo has a liaison office in Moscow to run his air charter deals, you haven't used his contacts to tune on Akramov. You touched Dinesh Patel. The way you communicate with Patel is through encrypted software on the internet. You have a decoder your end. It's costly software but you cannot do without it.

Akramov is one of Patel's point men in Russia. Nobody's seen him for the past ten years, since he was stabbed by a Byelorussian. Even Patel. So Patel has told you. But when you are in a foreign land trying to work out a channel for four hundred kilos of heroin worth two hundred million dollars retail you don't easily believe what anybody tells you. Though Major Rodriguez has delivered just half of that quantity so far, there's no reason for the future not to be promising. 5 Kumaon is going to be judging you by the price you nail for them. And you don't want to disappoint. They have held half the heroin load back as an insurance policy.

Patel's sent you a file on Akramov. You have done your own research, too. Talked to a Tambov gang chief from St Petersburg under whose protection Jumbo runs his office on the Polyarnya UL.

What you know about Akramov is interesting. He made his reputation and first few millions staging traffic accidents against middle-class Muscovites owning cars and homes. The modus operandi was simple. It was so simple he duplicated the operation in Brighton Beach for three years before insurance companies got wise, but not before they had forked out nearly eight million dollars.

But while sponging big insurance companies in the US has nobody complaining except the companies themselves, in Moscow the unfortunate victim is made to settle the accident claim with Akramov's muscle men. The price set is high enough for the victim to have to sign over his house for sale on Moscow's tight real estate market. Nobody goes to the police. They are in league with guys like Akramov.

But Akramov's real killing came after *perestroika* struck roots and Russia boomed with entrepreneurs having their first shot at business. The starchy communist bureaucrats looked with disdain at these new upstarts, but it soon turned to unease when they discovered that the change to a market economy was not only viable but lucrative. Then began the huge tussle for control of the successful enterprises. The old bureaucrats tried to muscle in on entrepreneurs, and goons like Akramov stepped in to stave them off.

Of course, Akramov didn't step in for charity. He got a cut from each entrepreneur for his services and in 1988 something wonderful happened which sent Akramov Inc through the roof. The government, for the first time, allowed the export of metals that home industries couldn't process. Akramov was the first to seize on the economic opportunity this new export law presented. He became the copper king of Russia. In two years he, almost single-handedly, was responsible for making Estonia, the Baltic nation where he originated his complex shipping patterns, the sixth largest copper exporter in the world.

The Russians woke up when their ordnance factories had

to halt production because there was no raw material for bullets, but Akra-mov had shifted to arms and armament by then, which is where, you presume, he first established links with Patel.

It was here that he got into RM 20/20 or 'red mercury', the trading metal of the 1980s and early 1990s, and established his reputation for ruthlessness. Middle Eastern Mossies were willing to pay $400,000 for a single kilogram. RM 20/20, with the chemical formula $Hg_2SB_2O_7$ and a flare temperature of 180.5 degrees centigrade, has special properties as a neutron reflector. It increases the efficiency of the nuclear fission process. It allows you to make nuclear grenades the size of apples that can knock aircraft carriers right out of the sea. Some versions also leave no residual radioactivity. You can move in right after a land blast and find skyscrapers still in place and the lifts working.

But the ex-KGB officers who shipped Akramov his red mercury, who in turn had sourced it from production bases in Ekaterinburg, stepped on one of his consignments: a hundred-kilogram batch headed, by way of an unknown UK firm, for South Africa, the biggest end user of the product in the world. The $40 million deal fell through when part of the consignment turned out to be red nail polish.

With a forfeit clause in the contract, Akramov was forced to dish out $10 million for his inability to supply the original amount.

Akramov traced the four former KGB officers to Germany, where they met such violent ends that he acquired the title of The Ruthless. Red mercury dried up after the Gulf War, with governments launching secret clamp-downs on traders, and the product disappeared from the world market.

It was then that Akramov switched to drugs. He became the biggest Russian conduit for South American drugs passing through the former Soviet Union on their way to Europe and the US. What you were about to offer him was another supply source, a pipeline so fresh that the international narcotics trade would take some time to analyse the new push in the market.

Today you are not at Sputnik. You are at a smoky joint called Mothball, which is on the outskirts of Moscow. You are hoping to be picked out by Akramov's crowd, for the whole day you have been spamming on the net, posting coded adverts with the names of the four ex-KGB officers that Akramov liquidated in Berlin on 13 June 1991. The file Patel sent you had their names.

You are not really happy bringing Jumbo in on this. Especially as it could get dangerous and you might end up needing some outside help. But you have taken care of that. What you are a little nervous about right now is carrying two hundred grams of your white powder in the inner pockets of your blue Savile Row suit. In a Russian neighbourhood it's like carrying $100,000 in cash. Very fearful things can happen if a person continues to be so foolish for the second consecutive evening.

You were given an introduction to the fear psychosis the mafia had built up in the city when you negotiated for a cab to one of the city's Western-style hotels from Moscow's Domod-edego Airport. The going mafia take for one such ride was $200 but you paid $70 to a gypsy cab driver. He was too scared to take the money in the open. He took you to the kerbside and made you part with your cash away from all prying eyes. He showed you the penalty inflicted on him for disobeying an airport shark once. He had just half a little finger on his left hand. Not too horrific by Moscow standards, but the only warning he would get before the Azerbaijani mafia, whose turf included the international airport, where they did their money-changing, decided to pass the death sentence.

All around you in Mothball are members of mafia families dining on bortsch. On the fringes of the room scar-faced bodyguards keep a close watch and gab on their cell phones.

What you are thinking is that Akramov may not be in town, and that you have to cast a wider net in your search for a pipeline, when the room visibly tenses. A thug straight out of a Martin Scorsese film pulls up the third chair at your table and sits down without an invitation.

'I hope I am not disturbing you, gentlemen,' he says.

'Depends on who's saying it,' you say.

'Let's say netiquette demands people don't spam or post in the wrong newsgroup,' he says. 'We like people to check on their FAQs before shouting on the net,' he says.

You had posted your advert in all caps.

'People have their ways. I have mine,' you say.

'Sometimes the ways of people take them very close to being flamed,' he says. You take notice of the double play in the last word.

'Some people have exaggerated notions of what others could be capable of,' you say. 'It shows a lack of confidence. It hurts, too, especially if people have contacted through mutual friends.'

'It's a crazy world,' he says.

'So am I,' you say.

'The corner of Robosky and Vosidonya, beside the fire station, in fifteen minutes. Ask the time from the person in a red coat,' he says. Then he looks at Jumbo. 'Who's he?'

'A friend,' you say.

'We like our friends to come alone,' he says and goes.

'That's cool,' you tell him. 'How far's the place?' you ask Jumbo.

'How the fuck should I know?' says Jumbo.

But your Hertz chauffeur is a local and understands the need for punctuality. You make your corner with a minute to spare, feeling surprisingly calm. Seeing a gangster movie, you feel, was different from acting in one.

You spot your red coat honcho as you light one of your Marlboros. You go up to him and ask the time. Somewhere a car screeches, wheels leaving their rubber on the road. A black-glass Mercedes lines up alongside you and the red coat extends the courtesy of opening the back door. You grind your just-lighted cigarette with your leather boot. The red coat sits next to you. The bearded flunky beside the driver turns and tosses you a balaclava.

'That wasn't mentioned as part of the plan,' you protest.

'It's the price for meeting Arkamov,' he says.

'I would prefer to keep my eyes closed,' you say.

'Have it your way,' concedes your escort but he barks something in Russian to the red coat. 'I have given him instructions to blow your brains if you open your eyes without permission,' he explains for your benefit. You hear the cocking of an Uzi, the preferred weapon of the *shabaskniki*.

All that stuff you read in books about heroes keeping track of where they were headed when they have a cloth over their head is all for nutcases who haven't tried it themselves. The real pro drivers take you once round the block and then take a couple of 180-degree spins on the wheel before they shoot the hood the right way. By the time you hit the second block you aren't even trying. Working out Akramov's HQ isn't on your immediate agenda. You're busy concentrating on keeping your eyes closed. You don't want to call any bluff with your head at stake. The Mercedes slows. You hear some gravel bounce off the chassis. Then the light dims and you figure you could be in some kind of garage or tunnel. The car weaves its way down an incline. A basement, you think. Your front seat guy has to gabber at some guy. You hear a gate clicking open. The Merc comes to a halt. A twenty-minute ride, give or take a few minutes.

'Hey, Mr Red Coat, you still got your Uzi at my head?' you ask as the door on your side opens. He stays silent. Maybe he doesn't know English, you think. But what he does is sneak the balaclava over your head this time and prod you out.

'Hey, that was sneaky,' you say.

'I am sorry, Mr Mehta,' says the voice you recognise as the bearded guy up front, 'but we can't take chances now. Nobody sees Mr Akramov. You only hear him.'

'I could have kept my eyes closed,' you say.

'But you might open them. And if you did and Mr Akramov didn't like what you had to say, you would take permanent residence in the Volga,' he says.

'I am prepared to take the chance,' you say. You have now walked into a room with a carpet that nearly sinks you to your ankles.

'You are a courageous man, Mr Mehta,' says a voice. 'And have a strange way of contacting us.'

'You didn't keep to the meeting yesterday. I had little choice, Mr Akramov.'

'You must be desperate. What other things did you find out in that little research of yours about the KGB officers?' asks Akramov.

'Nothing you don't already know.'

'Do you know, for instance, how they died?'

'No,' you say. You hear him draw up a chair. You are hustled into one.

'Do you want to know?' asks Akramov. 'How they died.'

'I am listening.'

'Ninov Arkady, Dimitri Shubasenko, Rudolf Karenin and Boris Yegeney. Do you know who was the leader, Mr Mehta?'

'No.'

'Can you tell, from the way the names sound, the name of the leader? I am told some Hindus are good at this sort of thing.'

'I am not one of them,' you say.

'That's a pity. Well, the leader was Rudolf Karenin. He was built like an ox. He was a Graeco-Roman wrestler. He used to practise in the Nuyayev stadium. How well built do you think I am, Mr Mehta?'

'I can't see through the hood,' you say.

'That's just as well or you won't live to tell the tale. Now my deal was with ARMSCOR. Armaments Corporation of South Africa Ltd. They were to pay for part of the consignment in Swiftarrow missiles. You know what those missiles can do?'

141

'No.'

'They can burn their way through one metre of steel armour. They use red mercury in the nose of the missile. Once it is ignited it creates a super-high-temperature blow-torch. The Iraqis were willing to pay me three times the market price for them. But the problem was, Rudolf was running this other deal with the Saudi Arabians around the same time that I didn't know about. You know how red mercury is packed, Mr Mehta? I hope you haven't come here to sell me red mercury.'

'No, Mr Akramov.'

'Just as well. Red mercury is packed in containers weighing two, seven, ten and forty kilograms. It's highly radioactive and carcinogenic. It's got various names depending on the type of mercury. Burning Rogue comes with a stick of uranium down the middle. Red Glitter is the 45/50 variety that's much in demand. So Rudolf gets these fucking Arabs to Berlin. You know how these guys travel?'

'On camels,' you say.

Akramov ignores you. He is too engrossed in his tale. The chair they have you on is more like a stool, about four inches from the ground. Motherfucker strategy to keep you in a low launch position, a gravitational disadvantage. Akramov's voice hits you from the top of an inclined plane. More of mafia PsyOps to disorientate you.

'These days they come on Falcons The guys in Riyadh are the biggest buyers of red mercury. Nobody knows what they do with all the stuff they buy, but they buy like hell. They have this lead-lined laboratory at the back of the Falcon jet which has fancy metal analysis equipment and even robots for handling radioactive material. They have the jet sitting at Riyadh ready to fly within two hours anywhere in the world. Rudolf is selling them fifty kilos of Moulin Rouge, a 100/100 type that goes into the making of a clean atomic bomb. A bomb that leaves no residual radioactivity. His initial plan was to con the Arabs. Land them with two ten-kilo containers of mercury nail polish. But he didn't know anything about this flying lab that the Arabs had and they were testing every sample before payment. So he tells Arkady to fly two genuine containers, the ones meant for us, into Berlin. You know how they went in?'

'No.'

'Lufthansa. Diplomatic baggage,' he says. 'A little of this stuff leaks and your Boeing electronics couldn't run a pocket calculator. Boris flies back this nail polish in lead containers to Moscow and the German immigration creates a big racket. They hold the thing up for two days. Now you know why Hitler lost the war. Anyway, Boris and Dimitri play a con on Rudolf. They tell him they have contacted some scientists at Nalchik-44 who can refresh some of the out-of-date mercury we had. You know what Nalchik-44 is?'

'No.'

'It's a closed military city. It doesn't even exist on the map. That's the place they make their red mercury in,' says Akramov. 'Do you have any such cities in India, Mr Mehta?'

'No.'

'Then it would be no fun for a guy like me to do business there, would it?'

Patience is in order.

'You need a nuclear reactor to restore red mercury properties. But what Boris and Dimitri do is pass on the old stock to me. Even the old stock has some value these days, but you can sell it only to governments. For, unlike us in Russia, only governments have access to nuclear reactors in other countries. Maybe if they had done that, passed me the old stock, they might still be alive. But I doubt it. In our business some rules are not made to be broken. It's the only way we can survive. But they don't even do that. Rudolf now plays a con on Boris and Dimitri. He switches the containers that he thinks contain the recharged stock with the nail polish and makes his team deliver the consignment to me. Now Arkady comes and tells me the whole story. He thinks there will be some reward for him. But he too dies. I don't like squealers. Do you?'

'Not particularly,' you say.

'What does that mean? That in some situations you like them and in some you don't?'

'How did they die?'

'Have you heard of the Rooivalk attack helicopter? This super chopper that the South Africans have developed? They were giving us a demo at the Angolan border. Do you know that the South Africans have developed a variant of red mercury that's more powerful than the Russian one?'

'No.'

'You don't know many things, Mr Mehta. It would be fun doing business with you. I could teach you a lot. Well, they showed me some of the stuff. They have a membrane separating two chemicals and that increases the shelf life of their product. They gave me a hundred-gram sample after the demo. You know what they did in the demo? They took about ten grams of the stuff and mixed it with ten grams of the other stuff and blew a bulldozer tank away. You understand? Blew it away. It just disappeared. Of course, I brought this sample home to Moscow. And one day my four friends are playing basketball at Rudolf's house. He had a little court in his house next to the subway at Krasnopresnenskaya. You see, I put about four grams of my sample inside the ball they are playing with. It came to the size of half a ball bearing, the kind they use in cycle axles. The rest you can guess . . . So what brings you to Moscow, my friend?'

'Business,' you say.

'Buying or selling?'

'Selling.'

'What does India have to offer us that we don't already have, Mr Mehta?'

'Hospitality for one, Mr Akramov. When we talk to guests we look them in the eye,' you say.

144

'In my business it's better that few people know what you look like,' says Akramov.

'Are you that ugly, Mr Akramov?' you ask. 'Did the Byelorussian leave a big souvenir on your face?'

'If you don't watch your tongue it's going to get you into big trouble.'

'Story of my life.'

'What do you have on offer? My time is valuable. Yours could be running out.' You don't miss the sinister tone.

'I have a gift for you,' you say.

'Aha,' says Akramov. A friendly blip on the radar. All stations hold firing.

'It's in my breast pocket,' you say.

'Ninov,' barks Akramov and you smell the special cologne of the red coat as he reaches inside for the packet.

'Heroin,' you say. 'Ninety-seven per cent pure. A special token of affection.'

You feel the room going silent. Russian motherfuckers getting a toke on the situation. A Hindu asshole doing the overtake, leading the pack. 'The people I work for want to know whether you can play big numbers.'

'What numbers could you be talking about, Mr Mehta?' asks Akramov. 'Ninov, please take the balaclava off our guest.'

'Two hundred kilos to begin with,' you say. 'And much more to come.' You notice the two stitched-up sutures on Akramov's cheeks. You take note of his eyes. Glassy and small, but with a gaze like a pair of pistols.

'Welcome to Moscow, Mr Mehta,' says Akramov. 'Tell me, do Bengal tigers shit in the same place twice?'

You make it back from Moscow in time for Digs's weekly edit meeting on Monday. The 10 a.m. assembly that Digs orchestrates in the conference room. On other weekdays Digs goes by quorum, a battle of turf limited to section heads. But on Monday he has an open house, gives all kinds of scumbags an opportunity to punch holes in editorial policy.

Your standard operating procedure at all edit meetings is to perform a holding operation, ricochet arrowheads winging your way. What you really specialise in is neutering your threat template before the meeting. That way you have an easy glide on your Marlboros. View all the butchering through the haze of smoke you exhale. You have seen careers go up in smoke in these meetings. What helps you is your reputation for neutrality when the point at issue is not your own turf. You are happy to see the minnows slug it out without taking sides yourself that could nip at their rudders.

The others realise that your Vatican stance is dependent on them playing by the book, bypassing your territory as they launch their assaults. On occasions when you have your own programme, a battle of space with the political badasses, you maintain your observer status by letting your henchmen argue the case.

But today you walk right into an unexpected combination. A Leslie, Jain motherfucker and Digs triumvirate, a fucking rear para assault. While Digs's accepted role at these meetings is to stick to his thermostat function, not letting temperatures blow the machinery in place, when he does join battle it's usually a swift annihilation of the opposition. A mosquito kill.

But your battlefield acumen makes you a worthy opponent. Right now it's not the magazine's interests you are worried about. You are concerned that your ace in the hole, the tape that you hold on the defence minister, is common editorial knowledge. Jolly has fucked up. She has gone and talked to Digs about the tape. Digs gets overexcited when he smells a scoop. It does wonders to his biomechanism. His attention span profligates and you suspect the switch on his sex drive flicks to turbo.

You can smell the urgency in his system to get on with it, get the scoop in print. He can't sustain excitement levels. Take a course on long-term orgasms, prolong his journalistic stimulation. He likes the sharp thrust, the flood that over-comes the system. Right now he is arguing that *The Post* should get on with the raw tape, and nail Defence Minister Suresh Yadav. There's also economics at work. The timing of the next issue, where Digs wants his scoop in banner head-lines. It's the anniversary issue and with all the hoopla planned for it, plus the ABC media audit coming up, Digs wants a steroid boost in the works, to take the circulation soaring above the five-digit mark.

What's heating you up on the inside is Leslie throwing his hat in the ring, aligning himself with the trouble-shooters. A stab in the back from someone you were responsible for bringing in. Jain is new to the game. He's swinging along for the fun of it. He's too blind to see the fist you were preparing to shove up his ass, to split him in two.

The highest form of generalship, you have read in Sun Tzu's *The Art of War*, is to prevent the junction of the enemy's forces. Along with that, you plan to generate a few allies of your own, try to increase your numbers.

'A problem we will have if we want to run the tape the next issue is what to drop,' you say. You consult the printing form in your hand. 'We will have to drop four pages of crime. Can you do that, Mukherjee? Condense your story to three pages?'

Mukherjee is a political badass with whom you vibe at a very street level. Nothing hurts anybody more at meetings than a tangle with him. The tape issue was, strictly speaking, a turf squabble that should concern no one except Mukherjee and you. Till the time you drag him in, Mukherjee was watching the proceedings from the fence but now, with your special gambit, you hope to convert him to your side in the skirmish.

You know that Mukherjee's crime story is very dear to him. He has been nurturing it for two months, building his file on politicians with mafia connections. He has had to contend with the frustration of seeing Digs put the story on hold on two occasions and just when he thought he was past any last-minute hurdles, some tape looms large to screw his seven-page investigative report to three piddly pages.

You, of course, have a few other Machiavellian considerations in drawing Mukherjee into the field of mayhem. You have given allowance for the ethnic ramifications it will allow you to create. Having Mukherjee on your side allows you to pick up the Bengali votes in the conference hall, and there were two in crucial positions to blow some wind into your sail. Saurabh Sen, the news co-ordinator, and Mahesh Deb, who as production manager was vital to your immediate strategy, where you were attacking the triumvirate not on editorial grounds but on the sheer impracticality of their logistics.

The other consideration was simple. On the two occasions when Mukherjee's story was held back, it was because Jain had argued and won his case for some telecom crap. On one of those story holds you had given the signal to Karim to argue in favour of Mukherjee but with no success. Now you were simply providing Mukherjee with a target and reminding him of past favours.

'Absolutely not,' says Mukherjee. '*News Today* is working on a similar story. I don't want us to come out after them, specially when we have cracked it earlier.'

You look at the form with new concentration. 'Then I don't see how we can squeeze in the tape unless we drop four advertisements in first form,' you say. Any mention of dropping advertisements hits Digs in the lower guts. The wind gasps out of his frame. You feel you have your flanks covered adroitly. But Jain, the motherfucker, is on a suicide mission.

'I won't mind if you held back four of my pages. You can junk the Bangalore crash,' says Jain. He's willing for his pages to be taken out. You figure either the guy wants your ass bad or he's plain dumb.

'What's it about?' asks Digs. That's Digs's editorial hold. A story's on form and he doesn't know what it's about.

'It's about software companies going bust,' explains Jain.

'Oh yeah,' says Digs.

'It would save time, too. The Bangalore courier is running late. We haven't got the slides yet. The tape thing we can do with stock photos,' says Leslie.

You feel the swing in momentum. But Mukherjee provides you some temporary covering fire.

'But I think we should run the software story. The Singapore delegation is coming to town next week. They have invested over a billion dollars in Bangalore's software set-up. Besides, did you read Bill Gates's interview, Jain?'

Jain feels the need to take off his glasses. As Business Editor he is supposed to know these things. Not have a political badass like Mukherjee take him blind.

'Ahem,' he goes. 'What interview?' He wipes his glasses on his tie. You figure he wouldn't be so prized an asshole if he didn't come wearing a tie. It sets the tone against him.

Mukherjee likes to rub these things in. Get the salt in while he can.

'Don't tell me you haven't seen it,' he says with shock. 'It was all over the net. It was this live internet session he had with some college guys. He mentioned Bangalore as the next destination for the software industry.'

Jain wipes his glasses. This was not perhaps as big a goof-up as it could have been had it come in one of the

149

Indian papers. The net was something very fringy in the Digs mental framework.

'Oh, that,' he rallies. But Mukherjee presses his advantage.

'If the facts are right in your story and you can really show that the software industry might go bust, you have a story, pal. The right time to do it would be when these Chinese are here from Singapore. Make a lot of noise. But I don't know how strong you are on the facts,' comments Mukherjee and lets the thing hang. On your part you aren't so sure whether there is really a delegation coming and even if the interview wasn't a rapid creation of Mukherjee's imagination. But right now the triumvirate was ducking under his armour-piercing slugs.

Jain looks like he is about to cry. He goes on the back foot.

'No,' he begins, 'we are pretty solid on the facts. Real solid.' He clenches his fists. He feels like he can hide behind the word 'solid'. He wants to regain lost ground. He opens his fists and grabs his chair arms tightly. He modifies his position. 'Well, I hadn't thought of it this way. Maybe we could drop the letter pages this time and the diary as well. That should give us four.'

Digs snorts from his chair. Jain realises too late how dear the diary pages are to Digs. Next only to the advertisements. He lifts himself one side. You suspect he's so nervous he's breaking wind.

'No, not the diary,' barks Digs.

'I still think we can hold Bangalore. How long is the delegation going to stay, Mukherjee?' asks Leslie.

'A week or so, I guess,' says Mukherjee.

'Then there's no problem holding the thing up till the issue after next. It will still be current,' says Leslie.

'I think let's not be guided by which delegation is in town or isn't,' decides Digs. 'If the story holds it holds even after they have left.' Jain gets some starch back into his shoulders. 'I don't particularly relish timing the two things.' Jain nods in agreement. A trifle early. 'But I think the story might act as a demoraliser on India's liberalisation efforts. We should avoid doing these negative stories if we can.'

Digs's commercial antenna opens up to anything which could cut into his advertisement intake.

'Let's run the tape stuff. We will club it with the air force story. What do you think, MM?' asks Digs.

Mukherjee throws a glance at you. You sense the ball is in your court.

'It's OK by me, except I was thinking on a slightly different line, Mr Mehra,' you say. Mukherjee's covering fire has given you some time to reorganise your editorial geopolitik. 'I was thinking, instead of running the tape cover we could go instead with the sex survey in our anniversary issue. It's bound to be a hit, Mr Mehra, specially with the kind of statistics we have. Also, if we don't run it this issue, *News Today* would be stumping us to it. They have got wind of our survey and are getting MARG to do one for them. Let's drop the Bangalore story and the letters and run a seven-page sex survey as cover.'

You can see Leslie panicking. You place the missing piece in the jigsaw puzzle. Leslie's coming out into the open to root for the tape becomes clearer every second. He has seen you come into the meeting with the sex survey and he doesn't have his layouts ready. The illustrations that you had given him to do a month back. Digs likes to see all cover layouts the hour after the meeting. You press home your advantage.

'Leslie has some deadly illustrations ready for the thing. I told him to merge the Kama Sutra elements into a modern kind of collage with sepia borderlines. We can be out with the form by noon tomorrow,' you say.

Digs chews on this awhile. Leslie sweats.

'I think it's a great anniversary idea,' says Mukherjee.

'Yeah, it's going to be a sell-out,' says Deb.

'When did you get this done, MM?' asks Karim.

'I didn't. It was Mr Mehra's idea. We had it done three months back,' you say. Digs colours. God, you think, he didn't want to be recognised as the originator of the idea. You know, for instance, that Digs took a whole week over framing questions for the survey. He spit on and polished them and ran them on you to show off his meticulousness in the matter.

'It would be great timing, MM, but my only concern is that we might not be able to do justice to it in just seven pages. We need at least five more to make an impact. Let's not piss off a great spread in a hurry,' says Leslie. He still has fight left in him.

'I would love to, Leslie, but we don't want to be "us too" journos, do we? What's the point if you let *News Today* steal all the thunder? We have spent five lakh* on the poll,' you say.

'We can't be "us too" journalists,' says Mukherjee. 'I think we have to keep the importance of the anniversary issue in mind. What do you say, Mr Mehra?'

You have set Digs's mind in motion. You can see it whirring, deliberating, little weights falling on and off the scale.

'I think let's go for both,' says Digs. Nobody in your knowledge can set different people on the route to a coronary faster than Digs.

'Both?' asks Leslie. There is still fog around.

You feel the need to tap your third Marlboro out. Get a puff of nicotine to boost your brainpower.

'Yes, let's run the sex survey as well as the tape,' says Digs.

Deb pales. 'We don't have the space for both, sir,' he says. 'We would have to drop a lot of advertisements.'

'Who's talking about dropping advertisements? Let's add more editorial pages,' says Digs. In living history Digs hasn't taken such a decision – whack more newsprint into the issue than he needed to maintain the edit–ad ratio at 60:40. 'That takes care of all the problems. After all, it's the anniversary issue. We have to come out with a bang.'

---

*A lakh is a Hindi denomination for Rs 100,000.

You take a long drag on your stick. It's not that you haven't prepared for contingencies like this. But the nuke you have in reserve is the last shot you have to halt Digs in his tracks. You punch in the code, clear your throat. Deb, however, is beefing Digs on the economics. You want him to soften Digs up for the kill.

'That would be a cost overrun of Rs 11 lakh, sir. We could also end up a little late on the stands,' says Deb. 'I will have to check whether they have the extra newsprint. We are really going issue-to-issue on the imported glaze we are using.'

The blood withdraws from Digs's face. Cost overruns in percentages are things he is used to handling, but a recognisable two-digit hole in his pocket is screwing up his body language. He wipes his palms on his trousers, looks at his belly, sends his forefinger up his nasal cavity and gets his spine straight. 'If it's to be done it's to be done,' he says. He makes a brave face. You figure it's time to bail him out.

'But there's a problem, Mr Mehra. I hadn't wanted to bring this out in the open but I think you will need to change your decision,' you say.

'What's it?' asks Digs. A lifeboat to the rescue.

'You see, Mr Mehra, I have dispatched the tape for a VMA. They don't do that kind of stuff here in India. There's a laboratory in Phoenix, Arizona, that does it on a commercial basis. The earliest we can have a positive confirmation is within a fortnight. I thought in such a sensitive issue as this it's better to have a lab back what we say, give us a certificate we can flash in court in case we get sued for libel. After all, we don't want to demolish somebody's reputation without a scientific backup,' you say.

'VMA? What's that?' asks Digs.

'Oh, sorry. That's a Voice Match Analysis. The intelligence agencies do it all the time,' you explain.

Nothing this fancy has ever happened in Digs's journalistic career. He is intimidated. The others too take time digesting the information.

'How much does it cost?' asks Digs. You, of course, don't want to take any chances with Digs's stinginess. You have it all worked out.

'It's not costing us anything. I have a friend from school-days working as a technician there. He's doing it free for us. Otherwise, I think they have a flat fee of $1,500,' you say. Digs beams at you.

'What are they matching it with?' asks Digs.

'I got a recording of one of the minister's All India Radio speeches,' you say.

'I guess we will have to hold the tape then,' says Digs.

'Yes, Mr Mehra. I think there's no point in increasing the size of the issue,' you say.

Your coup is, however, incomplete right now. Leslie's just returned from a month-long stint at *Time*, New York, where Digs sponsored his stay to see how the design department worked. Digs was planning on a design overhaul a year into the stands.

'When do we get to see the dummy design?' you ask Leslie. The dummy design has become a sore issue with Digs. Leslie's overshot on his deadline by a month. He tightens up, gears for the assault.

'Just got a few more pages to crack. We are developing a gutter design for the news pages. It's taking time,' says Leslie.

'I was wondering, Mr Mehra, if Leslie could circulate a paper on the design concept he is working on so that all of us could contribute. I know these few designers at the National Institute of Design who would be eager to pitch in. Even come and give Leslie a helping hand as part of their semester work experience,' you say. The two ways to fuck up Leslie badly were to make him write something beyond a margin note and get a couple of eager-to-contribute designers on a summer job loitering in his set-up. That drove his blood pressure through the roof.

'That's a good idea,' says Digs. 'It would speed up things.'

Digs puts great store by institutions like the NID.

Leslie's aghast and before he can voice his dissent Digs breaks up the meeting and says to Leslie, 'Could I have a look at the sex survey layouts? I will be out of the office for a couple of days.'

Nothing like coming out of an editorial meeting with all the blood sticking elsewhere.

A week after you have first met Karnam, you feel a tremendous urge to know the key to her. Actually, come to think of it, you can also say that it was she really who set the ball rolling, fencing you with this schoolgirl drill on the office stairs. You saw her coming up the steps and she wouldn't let you pass, blocking the way, daring you to detour her. And you played the game her way. You have taken her out to lunch four times in the week, a record of sorts in your romantic history.

And today she's your date at Jumbo's birthday bash. You are waiting in Digs's sitting room for Karnam to get ready. You have invited the rest of Features as well for Jumbo's party.

You look at the miniature paintings hanging on the walls, the brass fixtures getting at you from all angles. The banisters, doors, planters, candle-stands and even a brass sofa set. Digs is a brass maniac. In his next reincarnation he might settle for an evolutionary downgrade, come merged in brass, become an electrical frame in a high-class strip joint.

You have a look at Digs's music system. Bose speakers, a silver frame tape deck, a collection of CDs ranging from American country music to Nusrat Fateh Ali Khan. A liveried asshole breaks up your inspection. He comes pushing a cart arrayed with tea paraphernalia. 'Lemon, Darjeeling, iced or herbal tea, sir?' he asks. You go for a Darjeeling brew. You have never had tea that sells at $300 a kilo. You want to test it for psychotropic properties. Check out the motives of the gentry buying the stuff.

Something catches your eye. An album counter, photographic archives of the Digs family tree. You flip open a few albums. Digs puts great store by pumping the hands of sports celebrities. You see him in a two-paw grab with a reluctant Sunil Gavaskar, a ribbon opportunity with Greg Norman. Digs is divorced. He split eight years back, but the divorce hasn't made him junk history. His ex looks pretty, but she has no contours that match Karnam's.

You look for early snaps of Karnam, see what she was like as a kid, but you draw a blank. The only photo you see is recent. Digs giving her a hug at the airport. Strange, you think. A significant flaw in memorabilia.

You have finished your tea. It was faintly bitter. Someone walks down the curved banisters. You see Digs coming towards you.

'Hello, MM,' he says. His eyes are cold, as if he's taking the intrusion as a breach of protocol. 'There's something I want to talk to you about.'

'Yeah,' you say. You still have the empty cup in your hand. You place it delicately on one of Digs's brass side tables.

'The army's been up my ears all day. They are getting pretty worked up about the wheel questionnaire. They are saying it was unauthorised. That if we go ahead and publish it they will bust us with both the Official Secrets Act and the National Security Act,' he says.

'The more the merrier,' you offer.

At Srinagar and Kupwara, Siddy's career graphics had performed hot-air manoeuvres. He had managed to set up sessions with eight hundred soldiers from seven different regiments. *The Post* had eight hundred pieces of paper telling whoever wanted to know the FUBAR status of the personnel in charge of protecting the nation's borders. Amongst the things that you tabulated, had keyed in and analysed: 90 per cent of the enlisted men outside 5 Kumaon considered their officers to be a bunch of fuck-ups. Morale was at an all-time low. Seventy per cent honestly thought they couldn't win a war against a crowd of worked-up

Mossies. Ninety-five per cent hated what they were doing. A significant 7 per cent were punching holes in their veins. The army was so heavily right wing they hated the guts of all civilian Mossies in Kashmir.

'But they wouldn't dare,' you add.

'Yes, they will,' says Digs. He's in a confrontation mode. He presses charges. 'You told me it was authorised.'

Digs, you feel, needed a crash course in army psychology.

'Mr Mehra, no army in the world will ever authorise any civilian to sink shrink probes into the minds of their soldiers. If somebody gets to do it, he slips in unobserved by the top brass,' you say. 'It has to be civilian sleuthing at its best.'

'That's the point. They are calling our tests highly illegal,' says Digs.

'We have a piece of paper from the army PRO requesting assistance to *The Post* personnel for the poll. It would help in court,' you say.

'That's not the point. What we don't need is a toe-on-toe situation. If they think it's sensitive we should respect their view,' says Digs.

A prima facie case by the government would, of course, see Digs as the first one chargesheeted. Lawsuits upset Digs's constitution. And this promised to be much more, a collection of army crooks cracking the NSA in his shithole. A job many sizes too big for his in-house legal cell to handle.

'You know the way armies think. They call all kinds of junk sensitive. What we aren't doing is going to tell the world the force break-up in Kashmir or the kind of hardware they pack behind their backs. The Pakistanis know it anyway. Our job is to give our readers an honest Situation Report. We owe it to them. We didn't tool what we found. And right now they don't know it anyway,' you say.

'They want all the test papers back and a written statement saying we haven't made any copies,' informs Digs.

'Tell them to stuff it,' you say.

Digs reddens. 'There's something else, too,' he says.

'What?'

'They have complained against you. Military Intelligence wants to have a chat with you about certain killings on the border,' says Digs.

'The army ambushes?' you ask.

'From the looks of it, you were where you weren't supposed to be. There's an official complaint from the 7 Sikh,' says Digs.

'I was where the army took me. What are they complaining about?' you ask.

'The army vice-chief wants you to come by for a chat, sort out things. They are saying we are all for an independent media but some co-operation is in order,' says Digs.

'Why don't you go pay him a visit?' you suggest.

'It's you they want,' says Digs. You don't like the tone, the smell of putting distance. 'It would be a good idea to junk the wheel Q. The long shot of it all is we are all Indians.'

Karnam walks downstairs. 'Let's go,' she says. She kisses Digs.

'Take care, sweetheart,' says Digs. 'You, MM, I hope you are taking my daughter to a decent place.'

'Don't worry, Mr Mehra. The army won't be around,' you say. Digs looks at you suspiciously.

'What was all that about?' asks Karnam as you turn your Defender around the first bend after Dig's house.

'The army's getting your pop on the hop.'

'You too,' says Karnam.

'Me? I am an innocent little motherfucker.'

'My father says to watch out. He doesn't trust you.'

'Fathers never trust guys that take their daughters out for the evening.'

'It's not that.'

'Then?'

'He says you might be involved in something big. I mean bad.'

Your hand tightens on the wheel. You turn and smile at her.

'And how is that?' you ask.

'You should know,' she says. 'He said you did some shit while you were at the border.'

'What shit?'

'How should I know? You were moving around carrying guns with patrol units.'

'That was my job.'

'Your job was to make a documentary.'

'The only way you can make your subjects easy in front of the camera is to start behaving like them. Become one with the lads. Merge with them. They don't teach you that at business school.'

'They don't teach you to shoot people either.'

So, you think, that was what it was all about. You relax a bit. It was better than her knowing how deep you were in the works.

'Mossies,' you say.

'What?'

'Mossies. Not people. Terrorists if you like to go by official nomenclature.'

'You shot some terrorists?'

'One.'

'You killed a man?'

'It was me or him.'

She stays silent for a while.

'What was it like?' she asks.

'There are some things you just lock in your brains and throw the key away.'

'You know, when I was in high school in Texas I used to go around with a Syrian. Second generation. We were friendly and one day he took me to a roller-coaster ride and proposed right when we were going through a dinosaur's belly. I was seventeen. I said yes. I told my mother. She moved me to California the same week. She said she had had enough trouble with my father to have her daughter start the same way,' she says. 'I didn't have the guts to stand up to her.'

160

'What happened?'

'He tracked me down three months later. My mother called the cops and had him thrown out. He came back a month later. My mother wasn't in. He said, "It's me or you. Choose." I said, "I choose me. I am sorry but I don't think it can work. Our religions don't match." "What has religion to do with it?" he asks. "It matters to my parents," I say. "If I don't care what my parents have to say on this, why do you?" he asks. "Well, I am Indian," I say. "Well then, choose Indian," he says. "Choose me or you." "What's all this rubbish about choosing?" I ask him. "Indian," he says, "if you choose me, both of us live. If you choose you, one of us has to die." "I choose me," I say. You know what he did?'

'You are alive is what I can go by,' you say.

'He shot himself with a pistol right there on our balcony. You could have swum in the blood,' she says. There's a mist in her eyes but no tears trickle down. She hasn't finished.

'Yes?' you say.

'You know, you looked the same way when you said, "It was me or him," like when Yakub said, "It's me or you. Choose." Only you chose you.'

'We are sailing in the same boat,' you say.

'Difference is you pulled the trigger,' she says.

'You pulled it with what you said,' you say.

What you know is that every person has a thing. Major Rodriguez's thing was on the patrols, in the woods that he said you could never trace echoes in, and the rush of execution. Your own thing was that you lived for rushes and didn't care where they came from. The similarity between your thing and the major's was that both of you were addicted to risk. You got high on adrenaline amongst other things. The bigger the risk the bigger your addiction. Life for you and the major was just the rushes. The thing you did in between was a lot of waiting. Akramov's thing was that he provided a code for business in a country where government was still without regulation. Jain the motherfucker's thing was that he was an asshole and didn't know any better. Karnam's thing right now was to bush you with her past.

What's also true is that sometimes the thing that people strut doesn't give you a hold on the surface underneath, the hand they might be holding that never comes out in their temporary thing. For your things are like little acts in movies. Most of the time you know where the script's headed but there's always the deal that surprises you in the end. What you are trying to say is that when you poked to find Karnam's deeper thing all you got was an engaged tone.

At Gurgaon, in the farmhouse where Jumbo's throwing his party, the cars are already in rows of twenty and five layers thick. This is Jumbo's fifth experiment in raves. He's teamed up with Cedric, a veteran in setting up raves at Goa's Bagga beach. Cedric supplies Jumbo with all the E, the speed and other chemical knick-knacks while Jumbo looks after the logistics of the operation.

He's had the place wired with Bose speakers. His favourite. You can't tell the difference. The music itself is DJ-orchestrated. It patches synthesised percussion tracks with the latest in disco hits, volatile Eurobeat sounds, bleep-teep jungle and trance-producing Om renditions that mix with Osho chants. An Acid House clone.

The music isn't the only draw. There are laser beams, eleven video monitors, smoke machines and private rooms on the third floor where you can do your own stuff, buff a girl or mainline into your system. There's even karaoke. And Jumbo plans some video conferencing in some of the rooms, to spin his rave global. As a precaution there's also a medic in case some shooters mess it up. When it's a mixed bunch of pros and amateurs you have to look out for the initiates.

You have split with Jumbo on the expenses, taken a silent partnership. Though the main hall's big enough to squeeze in a thousand the maximum you have taken so far is about half. You don't get the London warehouse kind of numbers here. Not even the attitude. Here guys dress to pull in birds. No headbands, slogan T-shirts or Day-Glo outfits. You, however, flash an I LOVE GRAVITY T-shirt.

Though Jumbo and you have immediate commercial motives for the place, the setting gives you an ideal location to surreptitiously film important people in compromising situations. Tapes you could then archive for future use.

Your promotion right now is limited to word of mouth. It's Jumbo's invitations on the phone that bring in most of the crowd. Though gatecrashers are not unknown. But the chemicals are available just to the cool heads, the professionals that Cedric and his gang think can handle the mood elevation.

For an initiation the customer has to be known to the main handlers.

Till now, however, seeing the nascent nature of the operation, you aren't charging for the hits. You are farming out friendlies to establish a clientele, build a base. The way you have financed your side of the operation is by selling Cedric five hundred grams of heroin from the load you hold. With him you are exploring the possibilities of a distributorship in Goa. The Germans and Scandinavians, you are told, can sustain the bottom line in retail, move a dealer's stock at sonic speed.

You have always dreamed of a home in Goa. A place where you can recuperate from sustained chemical abuse, get your bloodstream on keel. In your fantasies you aren't alone. You have a woman. Sometimes it's Shomali, sometimes someone whose face is a blur. But she always wears white, your favourite colour. You also have a couple of kids playing around. Yours or somebody else's, it doesn't matter to you. What matters right then in the fantasy is that for a while you are happy with the little concerns of life. A baby on the lap and early morning swims in the Arabian Sea. A lunch of rice and prawn curry. A night with your woman. Just lying, no sex.

But even there, as the fantasy arcs towards exit point, you feel inundated by restlessness. You feel you don't belong there in that cosiness. The hooks in your back reeling you out of that scene are big and deep. For you it's just a place to sit and get your breath back.

As you enter the hall you spot the E guys and the blokes on speed on the dance floor. It's a hidden talent you have. Ecstasy does something to the face. It eats into your sex appeal. It does that because when you are on E you get so freakish that sex somehow recedes into the background. It is to do with the precise pharmacological thrust that E delivers, excessive dance energy and an absurdist view of the world that makes you empathise and dance the night through.

Speed, on the other hand, is like an additional supply of voltage to your central nervous system. A six-hour high that starts with a tickle in your guts and floods you with the confidence of God. You flow with witticisms and your libido increases in horsepower. You feel you can fuck a horse and get away with it.

You have to work your way through the floor to get upstairs. But Karnam pulls you into the crowd. The thing with raves is you have to get your air conditioning working overtime or the heat starts flooding the floor. It's more of a problem than in your normal kick and shake discos. Here, once you are on a trip, you stay in. You don't even feel the need to empty your bladder.

And Karnam soon discovers basic rave tectonics. You pull her to the side of the hall into a low-density area cordoned off with a wooden screen. She clings to you and that triggers in you a question.

'What's your thing, Karnam? I can't get a reading on your pulse,' you say. Karnam smiles.

'I heard you went parachuting with the army,' she says.

It's difficult to talk above the music. You have to shout.

'I think you are a mystery woman,' you say.

'What was it like?' she asks.

'Fun.'

'I don't think it was just that.'

'It was lots of other things but fun's the best word.'

'What was the first jump like?'

'You don't know what's going to happen, so it's the easiest. You just put a lot of faith in your equipment and tell yourself what you need to hear to get yourself out of the AN-32,' you say.

'That doesn't sound like fun.'

'Fun, my dear, is a lot of things. One of them is fear when you don't know the invariables in a given situation. There are basically two kinds of people. People who can do fun and people who can't,' you say.

'Where do I fit in?'

'That's what I would like to know,' you say.

'I love fun,' says Karnam.

'Prove it,' you say.

'How?'

'Kiss me now,' you say. That's when you spin her right into the middle of the hall where the lights hit the strongest and you can have your crowd watch the fun. And she does it all right. She doesn't go for your cheeks or anything. She sinks it right on your lips and what you feel is like what you felt when you took your first jump without the static. When you forced the hand of destiny and came back in one piece.

Karnam doesn't let go till the end of the song and when you do break up you carry over the sweetness of her mouth upstairs where the rave is picking gas.

Your Features crowd and some others you find in the room next to the snooker table. Journalists, you think, need to be told where the action is. Jolly, Dilip, Matthew, Dravid and Karim sit on chairs watching video. Karim's managed to swing his desk girl Minnie over to the place and she's smoking a menthol. At least she's smoking, you think.

Siddy's there too and already screwed up on acid. He looks at you dispiritedly.

'What's the action, guys?' you ask. You push Karnam ahead of you and put an arm around her hips.

'Siddy here knows some guys who are throwing Ecstasy tabs for free,' informs Jolly. She is in diaphanous black. Her tits, you observe, are more out than in.

'Any of you guys want a trip? Something to smooth your Saturday,' you ask. Your crowd, you figure, hasn't gone beyond prep school where mind benders are concerned.

'Jesus, MM, it's scary down there. I mean, some of the blokes are dancing like they have four legs or something,' says Dravid.

'One dose of MDMA gives you insights into the world that you won't get in twenty years of journalism,' you say. 'It makes you believe in the oneness of body and spirit.'

'I would rather go for old-fashioned sex,' says Matthew. 'It's proven technology and it gets you right up there believing in the oneness of body and soul and all that crap.'

'Yeah. When was the last time you cracked the whip?' asks Karim.

Matthew blushes. Karim, you deduce, is still a virgin. His question has the agony of expectation.

'Less time than you can even think of or would like to know,' says Matthew. You are the only one that sees Minnie blush. Oh me, you think, what's going on here?

'Ha, ha,' goes Siddy. It's an acid laugh, manic and loud. No amount of booze drinking can make a person throw the acid kind of laugh. Or even, for that matter, the peculiar shine that it brings to the eyes.

'Well, let me see,' says Karim. You know what's coming next and before you can glide the moment into neutral by continuing with your discourse on expanding the mind's horizons, Karim gets his foot in. 'When was it that you went to Japan?'

You were responsible for sending Matthew on a Suzuki

junket to Japan, a year back, where he struck gold as far as pussy went in some very peculiar circumstances which rather blows your head even now. Matthew patted the cheeks of a two-year-old girl on a Tokyo subway and the mother threw kidnapping charges on him.

It was the best thing that ever happened to him, in hindsight. The Japanese had to keep him in detention for a week till the charges came up for hearing and Suzuki and the Indian embassy got their act organised. In confinement he struck up a friendship with a Jap policewoman who expressed commiseration with his plight. To make amends for his introduction to Japanese culture she invited him to stay at her flat for the remainder of his stay. Matthew got to do things that blew his mind. His conquest wasn't limited to the Japanese police force. It spread to Suzuki, where he got friendly with the PR assistant assigned to him, and he claims to have given her an introductory course in ancient Indian gymnastics with reference to the Kama Sutra. The reason everybody knows the details is he went around with snaps in his wallet for a while. The strange thing was his golden run had continued after he returned.

'I think you are full of shit, Karim,' says Matthew.

'I think it's time to give you guys a course in the recreational use of drugs,' you say. You see Cedric passing by. You yell for him. 'Hey, Cedric, how about an alphabet course for my friends here? A group lecture in divinity.'

Cedric's down to his sleeveless vest. Rivers of sweat are flowing down his steroid-pumped muscles. But from the way his jaws are locked and he's jerking his arms around you figure he's in the first phase of a 1,500 mg dose of acid and still half an hour away from going on autopilot. The thing about acid is the first rush takes some time evening out, getting the fin stabilisers in place. And Cedric looks like he is on a real twister.

'Who's this?' says Cedric and peers at you closely. 'Is it MM?' He's having trouble focusing.

'Relax, Cedric,' you say. 'Do you have our lecture visuals on you?'

A gleam of intelligence raids Cedric's eyes.

'It's here in this fucking locker,' he says.

Strangely, it isn't locked. You locate your drug folio beneath the warranty papers for the video system. You withdraw it.

'Now this, guys, is what I call the different aspects of God,' you say as you unveil your folio. Your crowd creeps up. You kick the door to the room shut. 'The first eight letters of the alphabet. What's missing is F but you leave that blank. Because F's for fuck only and the whole world knows it.'

Siddy claps. 'F's for fog too,' he says and laughs.

'That's when you are funked on acid,' you say. 'Then it's float too.'

'Fly agaric,' says Karnam.

'My, what do we have here? The Narcotics Control Board,' you say. Karnam smiles.

'What's fly agaric?' asks Minnie. She's smoked her Moore. Karim's carrying around the ashtray for her.

'Mushroom. *Amanita muscaria*. Grows mostly at the bottom of trees. Identifiable by its bright red cap. Eaten for its psychotropic properties but passes through the body mostly unmetabolised. Makes a good case for siphoning off your urine, which is what Siberian tribesmen do,' you say.

'Ugh,' says Jolly.

'But let's start with A. Amphetamine sulphate. Commonly known as speed. It's the favourite of all punks and Nazi shitheads. It gives your whole CNS a buzz,' you say.

'What's CNS?' asks Dravid.

'Jesus, what are you guys? Nursery school? Central nervous system. B here's for barbiturates. They're downers. They depress the CNS. One barb that's guaranteed to fuck you up is Seconal. It's a Lilly product. If you resist the inclination to sleep you become a mean bastard, specially if you chase it down with a dose of Benzedrine,' you say.

'C's for crack, I presume,' says Dilip.

'I don't need to tell you about that, do I? D's for Diconal. It's a synthetic opioid. Dangerous too. It's rich in silicon. You try injecting it and your veins fill up. They get as hard as steel. But if you tab it down it gives you a rush as good as H. Now E here's for Ecstasy. It's a rave special. You can dance the night through on this but you have to see that you don't heat up. You lose fluid fast and you could end up with blood clotting your lungs. All you have to do is keep standing under the vents every now and then to chill out.'

'You also blank out on E. I read in the papers. You go blind or something,' says Karnam.

'Now, please don't scare my flock like that, Karnam. It's called a "head rush". You just go blank for a couple of minutes. But you take Jolly here. She would love the E. It would make her lose all that lard on her hips because this thing puts you on a diet like nothing else.'

'Shut up, MM. I have no lard on my hips,' says Jolly.

'Hey, look who's here,' says Karim. You turn to the video monitor. You see Leslie and Jain dancing in the hall with two British embassy staffers.

'Who the hell got these guys here?' you ask.

'None of us did,' says Matthew.

'Hey, Cedric, you know those two guys? The white-shirt assholes,' you ask.

But Cedric is busy calling Siddy the mother of twenty bastards and Siddy's pushing him off his chest.

'Get away, you bat,' Siddy's shouting. Two chemical casualties. You don't like to see your main chemical man grounded so early in the gig.

'Are those two married?' asks Karnam.

'Leslie is,' says Minnie. 'Don't know about Jain.'

'He's married, all right. He has two kids, the asshole,' says Karim.

'Now with G you can either go for ganja or GBH. Ganja you all know about. GBH is a powerful anaesthetic. Not as dopey as Ketamine, which takes you right up after you start sliding on E, but nearly there,' you say.

'I have smoked ganja a few times,' says Dravid.

'Attaboy, Dravid. That's the spirit,' you say.

'It just cooled me up for a couple of hours. The thing it does is it shrivels your pecker up,' says Dravid.

'Shut up,' says Jolly.

'You can't get a guy to shut up if he's got his facts right,' you say.

'You are a corrupting influence, MM,' says Karnam. But she slips her hand in your palms.

'Hey, MM, I want five days off starting this Monday,' says Dravid.

'Crazy fucking Jesus. Here we are just about to get to the H word and you come up with this leave business.'

'My mom will be in town,' says Dravid.

'What's up?' asks Jolly. 'She's trying to fix you up again?'

'Sort of,' says Dravid.

Dravid's mother lands up in Delhi from Bangalore every six months trying to find him a girl to settle down with. She inserts a matrimonial advertisement in the *Hindustan Times* and checks the responses out.

'Hey, Dravid, you done it yet or are you waiting for your mom to fix you up?' you ask. You really are curious. How can a person remain sane if he's a virgin till the age of twenty-five? What substitute does he have in place?

'Shut up,' says Karnam. 'It's personal.'

'The fuck it's personal,' you say. 'The guy's either done it or he hasn't. All Features present raise hands if they have done it.'

Everybody raises hands. Dravid half lifts his.

'What's this half-mast thing?' you ask. Everybody laughs. Dravid goes sheepish. But he has the glow that comes from a child suddenly under extra attention. He plays to the gallery.

'I did half of it,' says Dravid.

'Now this sounds too interesting to miss. Can anybody do half of it?' you ask generally. Then you look specifically at Matthew. 'Can you, Matthew, seeing your experience on the international scene? Can you do it half?'

'Not me,' says Matthew.

'It's some new thing,' says Karim. 'Dravid's invented some new manoeuvres.'

'Do you want the girls in on this?' you ask.

Dravid takes a new red. It's getting out of hand for him. 'I mean, I just didn't go all the way, guys. I mean, I could but I didn't. I wasn't in the mood,' says Dravid. Minnie giggles. Karnam looks like she wants to empathise with Dravid.

'He could but he didn't,' echoes Jolly.

'The guy needs some counselling,' says Dilip.

'Fuck off,' says Dravid. He's getting some colour back. Confidence on a rearguard action.

'What you need is some chemical support. A dose of speed that will make you rip it up. Keep your serotonin levels at the red mark, check your mood fluctuations,' you say.

'What I need is my own concern,' says Dravid. 'I am going to get me some dancing.'

'You're too hard on him,' says Karnam.

'Hard! We were soft as butter.'

'Look at Jain and Leslie,' says Karim. And all of you look at the closed-circuit monitor. Jain's got his shirt unbuttoned and Leslie is smooching his partner.

'Let's go down and give our friends a welcome,' you say.

'Can't we like lace their drinks with something?' suggests Karim. 'Give them the trip of their lives.'

'Good idea,' you say. You take out two blotters with 30 mcg of LSD. 'Acid with alcohol is, you know, a dangerous combination, especially on a first trip. You guys want to try something. Let's work out a lottery with speed, E and acid. OK?'

'OK by me,' says Karim. 'You have to try it some time. See what it's about.'

'Just put it under your tongue,' you say as you hand out a blotter to Karim. This was your amateur dose. A two-hour binge. A bit of a laugh rather than a six-hour escape-velocity thrust. A 100 mcg-plus dose at first shot, you know, is a recipe for sensory battering that not all people can contain. After four years of tutelage, acid has taught you that its best effects depend upon proper mood and setting. A sober and attractive room. No wild bats around. An introspection into the nature of self before you pop the dose, which acts like a throttling of the system or you will be in flight without preparation.

Since what the drug is going to shout loud and clear in your mind is that your self is an invention and that you are just part of a whole. Acid's taught you that you have to absorb this constructive lesson graciously, for if you don't, and attempt to go fist on fist with a few grains of rye fungus, you get a big puncture in your confidence for your efforts which it could take a few weeks to recover from.

There's also this little secret that veteran acid trippers are familiar with. The anticipation you carry for the experience controls its effects as much as acid itself. And that if you go into it with a sense of fear and hundreds of people around shouting like maniacs and have a run of *The Silence of the Lambs* on the television in front of you, the experience could be traumatic.

'What's happening?' asks Jolly. The rest look at Karim expectantly. But take-off thrust is till fifteen minutes away for Karim.

'Nothing's happening right now, guys. Cool it, will you? Tap in one yourself,' says Karim. The initiative swings. Jolly's the next to fall in with the mood and soon you reach critical mass. Your whole herd is into acid but you abstain. You take the responsibility to shepherd your lot, steer them away from precipices, check their paranoia levels.

'Should I?' Karnam asks you.

'Of course,' you say. 'I am here. There's nothing to worry about. No one ever got hooked on a single dose of acid.'

You go downstairs for a while, greet Jain and Leslie.

'Hi there,' you say.

Leslie's jaw drops. You know his wife well. Jain's a little too stoned on Johnnie Walker to look at you straight. Life for him was getting too complicated without getting stoned. A dot of acid in his whisky, you figure, would take him to a new planet. For Leslie, a source of new visions that would energise his design concepts. For acid makes you evolve visions from almost any background and object and even some that aren't there.

By the time you usher Leslie and Jain into the snooker room, where you have them run *Aliens*, the two are waving their arms like propeller blades, trying to ward off the crazy beasts. There's just one thing good about LSD when you are on a bad trip. It's not an immobilising drug. You can make use of your legs if you think there are a couple of dozen monsters giving you the chase. You can run out of the room like a bat out of hell.

Choosing ammunition when you have to hop police HQ near the Income Tax Office, where Major Kohli finds himself temporarily locked up for careless driving, can be a tedious process. Kohli has the keys to the warehouse where 5 Kumaon's delivery of inventory has begun. The advance party of the regiment has already come in with half the hardware. Crates full of AK-47s, machine guns, assorted ammo, wireless sets, rocket launchers, grenades, explosives, detonators. Though you have solved the problem of the small entrance door at the warehouse by blowing its hinges with Hatton rounds and having the door fixed back with new locks, Kohli is in a rather delicate position. If wind of his location gets around to Military Intelligence it could blow the whistle on your operation. With Kohli you are doubly worried because, through your sources, you know that he is on deputation with an élite agency nobody knows anything about. And even in your last meeting with him at Kupwara he was basically on leave from the agency and not supposed to be with his parent unit, 5 Kumaon. Though you don't tell him you know, you are worried about the position he is in.

Breach of discipline by army personnel invites a new kind of wrath from divisional HQ. Specially if you have been yahoo enough to ram into a police wireless van broadside at 60 kilometres an hour, breaking about thirty bones in three night-beat constables, a 1,000 kilometres from where you are supposed to be. It raises all manner of questions.

All of which qualified personnel will try to answer through Kohli's interrogation. The scrutiny will be relentless and revealing. Right now Kohli is in police custody. Within twenty-four hours he will have to be produced before a judicial magistrate, who could send him to further police custody for a maximum of two weeks. He could also be given bail. But even though Major Kohli was travelling under the alias of Major Joseph, exposing him to a police interrogation at this delicate stage of your operations is fraught with risk. Different intelligence agencies might start getting wind of things. Especially if they began examining the crates at the back of Major Kohli's truck.

Even though Kohli might be your man to organise ambushes, his skills won't extend to staving off mind probes by the likes of Colonel Chowdhary.

And the colonel, you fear, might be closer to the gig than you gave him credit for. In which case Kohli will be like a bone to a pack of dingoes.

But time is on your side. It is three hours since Kohli went in and it's still just five in the morning. If only he hadn't hit the police van right in front of police HQ. On any of the other local beats things could have been quietly settled with a bit of monetary incentive. You can hit and run a lot of the locals in this part of the world if you have a little cash to spare. Besides, it was a wireless van, the thing with an antenna on the top. You can't hush one of those. The sound bytes were in the air and HQ preserves a recording for three straight days running of talk on the air. This you know from having been on the crime beat as a cub reporter for the *Indian Express*.

But these sorts of unforeseen eventualities you have to deal with if you want to keep up your part of the game.

You view the spread before you. Your personal weapon these days is the Glock that Major Rodriguez gave you when you left Kupwara. It's the same weapon he had handed over to Captain Satish Warrier with rather tragic consequences. You were able to fly it out from Srinagar because you didn't use civilian transport. The army doesn't bother frisking you on its runs to Delhi.

You are taking in your hardware purely as a last option, the nuke on your shoulders if the situation gets unpleasant. The last thing you want is a shoot-out at police HQ. Although you aren't too nervous of the outcome. You have confidence in your superior firepower and the intrinsic motherfucking capabilities of Gulab Chand, Indramani and yourself. What you would like to be spared are the negative fallouts that would accrue from the shooting. Unnecessary media attention plus the fact of the casualties themselves.

Still, the motherfucked nature of the police calls for specialist treatment. This you have to weigh against the fact that you would be leaving tell-tale evidence behind in the shape of lead in victims. Not very many people have access to the kind of ammunition you plan to go in with.

You look at the options at your disposal. The hollow-point projectile designed to expand on impact, ensuring high-energy transfer in human tissue. But the jackets on these are too weak. They could rupture even if they hit the chain around your neck or a brass button. There's also the semi-wad cutter bullet, which cuts a core out of your flesh rather than letting the wound channel close after it. In short, you bleed to death. But that's not your choice. What you are looking for is a slug that combines maximum speed of incapacitation with zero sneak-out capability. Of course, that assumes maximum body penetration, which gets a black mark in your standard police manual.

You have the luxury to go for fourth-generation special forces ammo. The high-energy dump, reliable, no ricochet, no shoot-through projectile. You could choose the Glaser safety slug. Fired at 1,900 feet per second, its cap ruptures, releasing spheres in your body causing systematic shock and immediate liquidation. The thing with this bullet is that you get no chance to walk up to the guy and say, 'Sorry, buddy. I was actually aiming at the guy next to you.' It's also costly at $8 a round but that's the least of your worries.

Another option for you is to use an Accelerated Energy Transfer slug. The German Gecko action or the British Equally. Gecko's a hollow bullet with a plastic core. The core's displaced as you fire the bullet and once it hits the target its construction causes it to tumble through. But it cannot penetrate angled cover. Equally, on the other hand, has a specialist anti-hijack role but it can only be fired from a revolver. The advantage of this slug is that you can stop it in four inches of Lux soap.

But what you load are French THV rounds. Its reverse ogive ballistics make it the closest to the perfect CQC round ever made. With a forward protrusion and a velocity of 2,700 feet per second it has an AET profile in a ninety-degree arc throughout the bullet's path. It causes hydrostatic damage of grave dimensions.

You also pack a Remington 870 shotgun. The advantage of twelve-gauge is that you can shoot a variety of cartridges from grenades to the Hatton to the CS gas Ferret. Gas, you think, could be your ace in the hole. Keeping that in mind you have also packed a MARK-12C tear gas-cum-fog generator that can pulse-jet fifty thousand cubic feet of gas in about ten seconds. An anti-riot weapon, which you presume Major Rodriguez used to flush out Mossies from attics and under floor planks. If you take gas you cannot but throw in three rubberised respirators for your rescue team.

Your main weapon in case Operation Flush Out went sour was the Heckler & Koch MP5SD submachine-gun. The silent version of the MP5, it has a laser lock device and its primary feature is that it lets off its slugs below the speed of sound, which prevents your bullet boom. You also throw in a dozen E182 multi-burst disorientation grenades with high decibel levels and half a dozen rapid-opening Dart cord frame charges to blow precision holes through steel frameworks and concrete.

All these you pack in two Nike tennis bags. Though your hardware back-up is of GSG9 quality you are a little low on planning. You have had one of the 5 Kumaon lads nick a staff Gypsy from the motor pool at 16 Brigade headquarters, which is twenty minutes' driving time from the warehouse. The ones that have red flashers on the top and a siren. You plan to ride into police HQ with siren blazing and numb the DSP on duty with your audio-visual entrance. You wear a colonel's army uniform and Gulab Chand and Indramani dress in NSG regalia. An army officer flanked with two black cats, siren on and light flashing with some kind of funky music emanating from the Gypsy, which you discover has a stereo system, was your plan to disable police brainpower and introduce a high compliance factor.

You have typed an impressive release order on regular army stationery with a bogus name, stamping it with a very authoritative-looking seal. You could also have forged a bail release order from the court of a night magistrate at New Delhi but that would have looked even more dubious. You have a back-up team of two following you in a stolen Maruti assigned with just one primary function: to speed off with the impounded truck, which was still parked outside on the main street instead of in the police garage.

Yes, you have dark glasses on and a fake moustache.

You couldn't pull off anything with a cuckoo plan like this at, say, Scotland Yard but Delhi police HQ was a softer proposition, a mazeland of Jats who might take your MARK-12C gas generator as some kind of fancy television apparatus. Besides, you also have a basic reason why you want to push with the plan fast, instead of waiting for the imminent arrival of Major Rodriguez, who would be more adept at thinking these things out. So far he has come out superior on every gig the two of you have slung. Operation Flush Out you plan as your own spunk, a leadership gambit to draw level.

And as Gulab Chand hits the porch of police HQ running with his motherfucker gear on and you get off the Gypsy with the air of one who was used to such things, the sleepy police personnel in the complaints area look at it as a moment of beauty the like of which they haven't seen in their lifetimes. Indramani covers you from the rear and you walk with crisp steps to the desk of the inspector on duty, who gets up and salutes you. You hand over the impressive-looking envelope. Half a dozen civilian stragglers hang about the reception area absorbing the scene. You ignore them.

'Yes, sir,' he says. He handles the envelope like a piece of porcelain, afraid it might fall down.

'Release orders for Major Joseph,' you say. 'From the Prime Minister's Office.'

'Yes, sir,' he says again. You notice his pants are falling down from having his belt unbuckled. His feet were way up on the counter when you came bursting upon him, displacing the cool of the place. But his eyes are riveted by the MP5SD that is hanging loosely from Gulab Chand's shoulder. From his right suspends the Nike bag.

'Where is he?' you ask. You nod at Gulab Chand and he zips open the Nike, moving out the barrel of the MARK-12C. Next, he and Indramani slip on their rubberised gas respirators. 'There's very little time.'

You plan at getting the inspector from every direction. Give him no time to get his faculties in place. Already his eyes have switched to the MARK-12C barrel. He looks at it with awe. Gulab Chand lets off a little squirt of gas, a quarter of a second squeeze. About three feet of gas whooshes into the media briefing room. The civilians squatting on the bench at the reception get up in panic.

'What's that?' asks the inspector. He hauls his pants up, tightens his belt. The letter's tucked under his chin. Sleepy police constables gather in a knot.

'DDT,' says a civilian trying to be helpful.

You glare at him. 'Who's the seniormost officer here right now?' you ask. Your voice is tinged with impatience.

'The Deputy Commissioner of Police has left for home. You can talk to me,' he says.

You move behind the counter, put your arm around his shoulder, take the letter from his fingers and tear open the envelope.

'This is the release order of Major Joseph whose truck hit a police wireless van early morning,' you say in a whisper. 'The truck was carrying radioactive material. You understand we have to decontaminate the place.'

The inspector looks at you blankly. Evidently, the search engine in his brain was drawing a big neurotransmitter failure with words like radioactive and decontaminate.

'Nuclear material,' you say, nodding your head.

His eyes widen. He's heard of nuclear. 'The army man is downstairs in the basement lock-up,' he says.

'Good,' you say. 'Let him out.'

He understands the order. The thing with all forces is to keep telling personnel what to do, for things crack up if they have time to think. He pulls a drawer to get a bunch of keys out and walks downstairs rapidly. You follow him. So does your two-man crew.

'How many people got hurt?' you ask. You attempt to show the considerate face of the army. And yourself. The tough officer with a heart warm enough to care for the health of minor minions.

'Three,' he says.

'How did it happen?' you ask.

'Nobody saw it,' he says. 'There was a big bang. The van got smashed,' says the inspector.

'How are the men?'

'Leg and chest injuries,' he says.

'Nobody in coma, I hope,' you say.

'No,' he says.

'That's good,' you say. 'Where's the truck?' you ask, though you have seen it outside.

'It's parked on the road,' he says.

'*On the road*. Shit,' you say, 'Indramani, go secure the truck.'

The inspector watches Indramani go.

'Not to worry. We have guards there,' he says. 'I saw the crates inside the truck after the accident and put a guard.'

'I hope you didn't touch the truck?' you ask.

The inspector falters. He exhibits traits of neurotransmitter failure once again.

'I don't remember,' he says.

'Just stand here,' you say. You take your rubberised respirator from your pocket and pull it over his head. You push him face first into the walls of the stairs, knock his legs apart and spread his hands. 'We are going to decontaminate you. Just stand still.'

The inspector's shivering. 'What are you doing, sir?' he asks.

Gulab Chand's also slow to pick up. But you grab the barrel yourself and press the pulse trigger from ten feet away. The inspector disappears in a cloud of smoke.

'You can walk down now,' you tell him. 'This smoke is special. It kills all the radioactivity. You don't want to get cancer, do you?'

You see Major Kohli pacing in the lock-up. He looks at you with considerable surprise. The inspector hands the keys over to the constable on duty. He unlocks the steel cage. It takes three keys. You slip the mask off the inspector and hand it to Kohli. The inspector sneezes.

'Captain Joseph, stand by for decontamination,' you say. Kohli, who's watched the whole game from his cell, looks distinctly uncomfortable, but you repeat your orders.

'Captain Joseph, stand by for immediate decontamination,' you say.

Kohli pulls on the respirator reluctantly and then you whoosh him with a dose, too. You're beginning to enjoy this.

You walk up. Everything under control. But then a bit of leftover smoke drifts into you and you borrow Gulab Chand's respirator. It is when you are taking the mask off, about to impress on the inspector the necessity of keeping all this under wrap for the next hour at least, that your moustache comes off with the rubber. What you have also failed to do for about three minutes since the release of Kohli is put the inspector under constant sensory confusion. You have given him time to get his breathing rhythm back. You smile at the inspector. For the first time you glance at the name plate on his uniform. Ruknam Singh.

Ruknam's face hardens. His instinct tells him there's something funny going on here. You can almost feel the whirring and clicking going on his head, the jingling of alarm bells. You stick the moustache back even as he is looking, giving him time to make his play.

'I will have to consult with my superiors first,' says Ruknam. You notice that the air of obeisance has disappeared. Logic is making a comeback. He reads the letter for the first time. It has got an army HQ logo. 'We are not supposed to take orders from the army. You said PMO. We will be producing him at the court of the Metropolitan Magistrate in the morning.'

At the porch Indramani has already backed the Gypsy. You look at Gulab Chand. Kohli relieves him of the Nike bag. Indramani switches on the light and the siren. Ruknam stiffens. The cops start smelling the tension in the air.

'I think it's time we decontaminated the place,' says Major Kohli.

But you want a very quiet exit. You move behind the counter once again. You put an arm behind Inspector Ruknam Singh. Ruknam shrugs it off. But he's listening.

'We are Officers on Special Duty,' you say. 'OSD. Heard of that?' Ruknam nods his head. 'We have to use disguises so that people don't recognise us.'

'But I just want to check with my superiors first,' he says. 'It will take two minutes.' He picks up the receiver of his push-button BelTel.

'We can't stay,' you tell him. You walk to the door. Gulab Chand and Kohli follow you.

'*Hello*,' says the inspector. 'Ay, hello.' He's not talking into the phone. He's shouting after you. You try not to hear.

'Hello, hands up,' he shouts when you are two feet away from the main entrance. Three constables come hustling by. They block your exit. Ruknam is levelling his revolver straight at Major Kohli's chest.

'Cool it, will you?' says Kohli. But Ruknam is in his Jat element. The scene, you figure, is getting fucked by the minute. Gulab Chand's levelling his SMG at Ruknam. He still can't see it because Major Kohli's in the way, but then he moves, gives Gulab Chand a clear shot at Ruknam. You are thinking, Hell, this wasn't part of the plan, maybe he won't go for the heart. He doesn't. There's a small pop, a cork falling limply off a champagne bottle, and the inspector's right wrist blows away. The revolver clatters on the floor. A triple-hammer precision maiming blow with THV rounds. Ruknam's stump starts bubbling blood. He is staring in shock at his wrist. He clutches the tip with his spare hand. He starts howling. A few sleeping cops in magenta drawers come rushing out from an adjacent room. They walk right into a river of smoke.

Kohli's taken out the three constables blocking your way, who are still unsure about what happened, by putting the MARK-12C on full release. He turns the barrel on the new arrivals. Even a little savoury dose for the civvies on the bench, who scramble downstairs. You rush to the Gypsy. In ten seconds police HQ looks like the place is on fire. Only there are no flames. Gulab Chand discourages any chasers by dropping a few stun grenades. Boom, boom, boom they go. Lightning flashes, one-million-candela levels. Gas billows out of the building.

You provide your own touch to the party. With your Remington 870 you knock out a tyre each from the four police jeeps standing by the porch. Then all of you get into the Gypsy and get the hell out of there.

'Fuck,' you say to no one in particular. 'Why did my moustache have to come off?' You rip it off and chuck it out of the window. 'Where's the truck?' you ask Indramani.

'They should be halfway to the warehouse by now,' he says.

'Thanks, MM,' says Major Kohli. He grins at you then slaps Gulab Chand's back. You are happy to have done a good turn for Major Kohli. In the days ahead, you know, the time will come to reel in your favours.

At home you find Karnam sleeping on your settee. You are surprised. One arm rests on her forehead, the other hangs down. In sleep many things swim to the face that lie moored deep down during moments of consciousness. In the contours of her face you see an innocence that reminds you of another face, another time. Or maybe you put the innocence there. Sometimes you see what you want to see.

Lately, the woman in the one dream that you have has metamorphosed into Karnam. For the first time since Shomali went her way, you have begun to see some hope for yourself.

The highway you are on leads to doom sooner or later. What brought you on was your own sense of melodrama and the defeat and rejection you felt when Shomali went her way leaving you with a void, a waiting, that you filled with the chemical demands your body made, natural or artificial. You began to see life as a little movie in which your thing was to get a bang out of the play. Squeeze the juice out of the moves.

But always, even in that, there was also a sense of waiting for something that would put an end to it all, a tether line stretching taut, putting brakes on your soaring. You think Karnam could be that tether. You haven't known her long but in such things it's the lava flow that matters.

You let her sleep. You slip out of uniform. You go to the kitchen and make some coffee. You are pouring the brew in a cup when you feel her hands encircle your waist, a body press against your own. A voice ask, 'Nothing for me?'

'Honey, all of mine is yours,' you say. You kiss her. Your lips brush her forehead. 'How did you get in?'

'I came here late at night. Your door was open. I waited for you. I fell asleep,' says Karnam.

'Lucky me,' you say. You begin fixing another cup.

'Where were you?' she asks.

'Me? I am a night bird. I hunt for fun,' you say.

'So, where's your prey? Should I be jealous?'

But you are moved from kissing her and aren't really listening. Incredibly, your eyes get wet and you catch a burst of sunshine through the sink window.

'Is something bothering you?' A hand rests on your shoulder.

'Lots of things,' you say. But your weakness is just a passing spasm, a little dust in the eyes. You regain control. 'Sugar?' you ask.

'Let me finish it,' she says. You let her take over. A woman in your kitchen. You go over to the hammock that stretches on your balcony. You swing in soft rhythms of memory. Karnam comes and sits at your feet. With one hand she sips her coffee, with the other she halts your swinging.

'You remind me of someone I once knew,' you say.

'Someone close?'

'Very.'

'What happened?'

'Who can tell? It's over.'

'Then why does it keep coming back?' she asks.

'Memory is something you cannot kill,' you say. 'What brought you here?'

'I thought maybe we could go somewhere.'

'Your father must be worried to see you mixed up with someone like me.'

'I doubt whether he's even noticed my absence,' says Karnam.

'What happened between him and your mother?' Karnam's eyes falter for an instant and she ducks your gaze. There is something in this movement that warns you, but you

186

can't get it right, and when you do, many days later, it's too late. 'It's OK if you don't want to answer.'

'No, it's not that. It's just that nobody ever asked before. They just assumed I wouldn't want to talk,' says Karnam. 'He developed this drinking problem and with that came a lot of other things. You know what I mean. When we were here together and I was in school I didn't understand but I think my mother did the right thing by leaving. My grandfather was in the US. My mother went to him.'

'How did they meet at all?' you ask.

'Oh, it was an arranged marriage. Lots of dowry and stuff. That's the money that started off Father's printing press and his publishing business,' says Karnam.

'Your mother married again?' you ask.

'No. But she had her flings after grandfather passed away,' says Karnam.

'Around the same time that you met the Syrian?' you ask.

'Yes. Why did you ask about Yakub?'

'Strange fucking guy. You didn't make that one up, did you?' Karnam looks hurt. 'I'm just asking.'

'Why would I make it up?' asks Karnam.

'Women have their reasons,' you say.

'Not death.'

'You got a photograph of the guy?' you ask.

'Not here. I mean, not in India. It was a painful episode,' says Karnam. 'But what's that snap of yours there in uniform?'

'National Defence Academy, 1985,' you say.

'You were in the army?'

'Training to be there,' you say.

'Tell me about yourself. Why did you leave?'

'Nobody leaves the army. I got sacked.'

'What for?'

'It's part of a long story. It begins way back. I don't think you would have the patience,' you say.

'Try me,' pleads Karnam.

So you tell her the crazy fucking story of your life. Not the *whole* story but very close to it. In your life rebellious patterns emerged at the age of thirteen. One fine day you boated all the way from Allahabad to Benares on the Ganges with four other buddies, a physical jamboree that took you all of five days. While your friends were part of the National Cadets Corp rowing team and earned valuable credits for their actions, your presence had more to do with the spirit of expedition. In the holy city, you split and embarked upon a project of self-discovery.

One of the good things about life is that you never can tell what is going to come next, and when one day you sat next to a Dutch plumber on a six-month trip to India things suddenly changed. You sat watching the boats slip by on the river and the wrestlers doing their evening routine, when he suddenly turned to you and revealed why he liked the Ghats so much. 'This is the only place in the world,' he said, 'where you can have a conversation and a goat can come and sit next to you. No problem.' His name was Juster. You couldn't get the pronunciation right but he liked you well enough to invite you to the seedy hotel he was staying in to meet his wife Patricia. Your own staying arrangements were a matter of chance and convenience. Strangely, the couple didn't mind you shifting in with them for the remaining five days that you planned to stay in town. It was Patricia who gave your impulsiveness a new direction altogether.

And it all began in a quirky sort of way. She sat sketching the fishermen on the river and when she finished she showed you the sketches she had done in the past four months. Of the rains in Gauhati, the tea gardens at Darjeeling, tigers at Corbett, gypsies on the trail in Rajasthan. In the desert two camels mating under the sun.

'They couldn't do it by themselves,' said Patricia, mischievously. 'They had to be helped by the people. They were too clumsy.' You looked at her with all the seductive hope of a thirteen-year-old and asked, 'Are you?' The first time you did it was the same afternoon when Juster went to Bodh Gaya alone because you and Patricia, with tacit connivance, dropped out of the cultural trip. You were about the same height as her, and her breasts made a perfect fit in your palms. You couldn't come this first time but she did and you remember this with pride even today. You also remember her scent that first time – it was somehow different from the other times that you went with her over the next two months. It was a mix of jasmine and lavender, that's the closest you can come to describe it.

Over the next four days in Benares, Patricia, besides keeping you tubed, was the first person to introduce you to the thrill of risks. You discovered that sex in itself was great but that it somehow became greater if you did it while Juster was having his bath or had gone to the local shop to get some mosquito repellent. The risk of discovery and all that followed with it spurred the pleasure factor to unimaginable heights. And soon, when the time came to say goodbye, Patricia invited you to come with her to Cochin. She was splitting with Juster for the remaining part of the trip, he going to Sikkim and Patricia longing for the greens of Kerala.

Of course, you had school. You argued that sex and tourism for two months was a better choice than sharpening your trigonometry. The kind of school you were in didn't bust you on attendance. They just asked you to pay a fine of fifty bucks for every day your rolls drew a blank. Also, your old man gave you a reason when you landed up home with Patricia in tow and made your intentions open. He got depressed and sulky and then threatened to chuck you out of the house. Your mother wasn't in that evening and even though she wouldn't have been able to stop your father, he might have been more considerate with her around. Your father seemed to have given up on you. Of course, you didn't know then how troubling your juvenile escapades were to your father.

So you split south. Though Patricia was exactly double your age it didn't put any noticeable crimp in your relationship. Sex, you discovered, was a universal language. It didn't need a cultural unipolarity to get itself going, nor did the Dutch do it places where any enterprising couple anywhere wouldn't, given opportunity and a feeling of privacy. Sometimes, when need was great, you felt that privacy itself was a discountable commodity. For instance, on the train trip to Kerala the loo wasn't often the best place to satisfy your urges. Balance was difficult and the smell and sights were mood suppressers. So one night the two of you said, Fuck it, and huddled together on a second-class air-conditioned upper berth. You drew the blanket around you and innovated an angle that could do without the luxury of space. There was a thrill here, too. In the berth facing you an old man in his sixties snored. His closed eyes faced you and your moments of decadence were punctuated by anxious looks in his direction.

The next morning there was the strong smell of spunk in your cubicle and the young mother on the lower berth looked at the two of you with great disgust and refused to be drawn into your unfinished conversation from the day before. But then as now, social casualties didn't ruffle your feathers.

Patricia checked into a backwater hotel in Cochin and the first thing the two of you did was go on a backwater cruise to Allepey and then all the way down to Trivandrum. The tourists hadn't discovered the ride till then. The two of you rode alone in a thatched grain boat with a crew of two who cooked you rice and curry and kept Patricia high on local toddy.

At Cochin you became friendly with Nicky, who ran an antique furniture shop in the Jewish area of Matanacheri. Nicky soon warmed to your bantering skills and asked you to help out in his shop for a few weeks since his deputy had gone on leave. You sold beds, desks, chairs, drawers with fancy mirrors, pillars, tables – anything. Two-hundred-year-old Malabar teak was a great selling point with foreigners, who had the stuff shipped out to Europe and the Americas. Nicky bought the stuff from ancestral houses in villages at dirt-cheap prices, had his carpenters spruce up the piece, then arranged for the shipping.

Your part in the scam was to provide a historical perspective to the wooden pieces, sell them as an exalted heritage. It was at Nicky's that you first learnt the art of bullshitting. You took a 5 per cent cut on each piece you sold. Your style of operation was simple.

This is how you would spin your yarn: 'The term antique is very loosely focused these days, sir. What most dealers might pass off as an antique will not be more than forty years old. But if you look in the dictionary, sir, it is described as a work of art or handicraft that is more than a hundred years old. It's not that they want to cheat you, but history, except in a very superficial sense, is not one of their strong points. There's a new trend these days, sir, to buy furniture not because of its good quality or for the love of it but as an investment or as a show-off. But you don't look that type, sir. We don't encourage this kind of buyer.

'Now, I don't know the reason you are looking for a heavily carved piece. Restorers like us don't like those kinds of pieces. It's the dealers who love them. They make easy money on them. But we call them "dust gatherers". We like the pieces we sell to be well cared for, and bulky and impractical constructions, our research shows, are the most neglected in the homes of people. Besides, with space becoming a constraint these days, simple designs that take very little space and are easy to maintain are what most people look for. But I guess, sir, if you are insisting on a heavily carved writing bureau it must be because you want to make it the central controlling aspect of your living room or study. That is usually recommended, for then the furniture complements the living space and because of having a function it doesn't look stressful to the eyes. Now this piece here, sir, is what I would suggest you take a good look at. It's a rose-wood construction with, as you can see, ten side drawers. The legs are carved in floral motif and on the sides you can notice delicate brass inlay. It's a very heavy piece. We like to show all our buyers the raw pieces before we restore them so that you can judge for yourself whether it is genuine. Now you can estimate the age of this piece by a look at the joinery, sir, and the age of the bolts and the hinges. This is from the Wadiyar period, sir. My great-grandfather was a minor functionary in their state. You can see, sir, this is seasoned wood and at least 150 years old. The wood isn't bent or cracked. While restoring it we take care of the fact that we don't alter the original proportions, for that violates the basic design principle of the antique. We also don't believe in painting or varnishing furniture. That's not part of our philosophy. We like to highlight the natural grain in the wood and that comes out best if we give a sandpaper finish and wax polish the wood. But the piece is expensive, sir. It will cost you Rs 100,000 plus cartage.

'If you want a reproduction we have another branch that deals exclusively in that, sir. We are fortunate enough to have an excellent team of duplicators who make some of the most elegant reproductions of all periods, even Western. But even that would be about half the price. You see, sir, we don't compromise on the quality of wood we use. There are some dealers around here who would try to pass you off red paduk wood as teak and you wouldn't know the difference. But you will in five years when your piece cracks right down the middle. What we use here is white cedar, not even rosewood. And white cedar has so many knots on the surface that you have to go right down to get a smooth surface. It takes a lot of work. Also, we don't ever reproduce furniture on the basis of photographs. South Indian furniture is so structurally correct that unless you have an authentic life-size piece it's a fallacy to think that you could reproduce the design.

'Of course, you can do it with the French, Portuguese and Dutch colonial furniture because that's well documented. What I would like to tip you off with, sir, is that the real antiques are selling off in the market like hot cakes. There are so few of them around these days. If you came again next year there might not be any left. You see, most of the stuff you are seeing here is sold. That hat stand, for instance, is going to a London connoisseur. He's crazy about hats and where you put them. And camphor chests with the strong fragrance are so rare you have buyers killing each other to get hold of one of them. Then you have these interior decorators from Bombay coming here with their aesthetic ideas. They could sell their mother for these Vasco da Gama teak barrels that we have. They are willing to pay any price to us to convert about five of them into a bar counter. My brother Nicky told them to get lost. He considers them family heirlooms. You see, sir, Vasco da Gama was this Portuguese guy whose grave you will see right down the road in a church. It's a tourist spot. He came here in the sixteenth century. The barrels are from that period. My family has this special secret of keeping wood intact. It's like an invisible paint. It's a combination of formaldehyde and secret herbs that only we know about. My brother Nicky goes and collects them once a year from the Nilgiri Mountains. He is supposed to pass on the secret to his son but he isn't married yet. He has got a girlfriend, though. We are hoping something will happen soon. You see, sir, ours is a very traditional family. For us furniture is a passion, sir. We make a living out of it and when you make a living out of something in India it becomes a religious kind of thing. You wouldn't believe it, sir, but we have things laid down by our ancestors. Like, for example, the kind of bed my brother Nicky has to sleep in on the first night of his wedding. It's a Chettinad-style bed. It has got inserts for old ceramic tiles. An Austrian was here a couple of months back and my brother invited him over for lunch. We took him around the house and he came upon the bed. He offered us $50,000 for the bed straight away, Visa card. We told him no. Dealers around here, they consider us crazy for holding on to principles like that. But my brother Nicky says if a guy doesn't respect what his family told him he is like a straw in the wind. He is going to be tossed all over the place. He's going to have no peace.'

You could hardly believe it when people fell for this kind of spiel. Nicky himself couldn't. He made me write down my speeches once so he could have a go. To his bad luck he ran into Major Ed Friske of Edwards Air Force Base. Friske was a test pilot and he flew jets at twice the speed of sound over the Mojave Desert to see if all the nuts and bolts in the aircraft were still tight if he pointed the nose of his flying bird down at the ground and pressed the throttle. These test pilots, you learnt at the age of fourteen, were a special breed of men. What brought him to Cochin was his girlfriend, who was Jewish and who was doing her doctorate on the Jews of Cochin. There were about three hundred of them around and they came to India at the time of the Crusades. All Friske was interested in was shipping a *chaise longue* back home to Edwards Air Force Base, when Nicky opened up on him with your speech, which he had got by rote. This one was about adapting antiques into pieces of furniture for everyday use. 'You could, for instance,' Nicky was tearing into Friske, 'turn this wooden nineteenth-century bucket into an umbrella stand.' Friske stared at him the way you guess he might stare at a Lockheed aerodynamics engineer who had just sent him up on a plane with a faulty left wing.

But Nicky went on. 'We could turn these carved legs from the Queen Anne-style four-poster bed into table lamps.'

Friske shivered. 'Will you shut the fuck up?' he said. 'All I want is a *chaise longue*. I want to use it like a love seat. What the fuck will I do with lamps?'

But Nicky couldn't take hints even of this magnitude. He pressed on. 'We could take the headboards of this Victorian-style bed and craft a crockery case for you. No problem. Or see this low Burma teak trunk. We could turn it into a drum seat for your bar.'

By now you could see that Friske had had about enough of it all. 'You see this palm of mine,' he said, 'I can turn it into a stone-age nutcracker.' Then he grabbed Nicky by the balls and set him up on a wooden elephant with ivory work from the Warrangal period. That was the end of Nicky polishing up on your speeches. But you got pally with Major Friske and travelled with him around Cochin in your spare time. He instilled in you the desire to fly supersonic jets.

And now three months of selling antiques had netted you enough dough to put you through university in style. You didn't stretch it long with Nicky, though, after Patricia split home. She discovered that she was pregnant. That was the end of your relationship. She freaked out. Even you got scared. She didn't want to abort in India. She didn't trust Indian medical facilities. She flew home. That was the last time you saw her and now when you try to remember her face it doesn't come to you in one piece but like a fragmented negative that you have to piece together, a visual jigsaw puzzle. That was like the end of a period in your life.

You went back home and things had changed between you and your parents. You swam in a deluge of space. You caught your father on a couple of occasions brushing up on a child-rearing book. One day he even called you over in a gruff voice and told you about the facts of life, while you listened with proper decorum. Life, he told you, was about rules and following them. He wanted you to focus on the days and years ahead. For some strange reason he wanted you to join the armed forces. Like father, like son. Over the last many months you had given him cause for too much hypertension. You loved your old man. Even more so your mother.

And in 1985, at the behest of both, you took the Academy papers and cleared them. Only the air force guys busted you in the medicals for the lack of stress-bearing capabilities in your spinal column. They said your vertebrae were stuck so close together, ejection would be a problem. You tried some humour. You said you had been ejecting since thirteen with hardly any mechanical problems at all but they cold shouldered you and shunted you to the army, which you had given as second preference. You weren't really keen on joining the army, but your father prevailed. This was the second stage of your learning process.

It was at NDA that you first fell in love. You met Shomali. She was Instructor Lieutenant Colonel Ravi Kumar's thirty-year-old wife. You were eighteen. The way you first met was when Colonel Kumar requested you to chauffeur Shomali to Bombay and back one weekend. Shomali's mother was in bad shape. Severe asthma. She was stuck up in an oxygen tent at Jaslok Hospital. Your deportment was the very best. You drove considerately, offered the right kind of commiseration, brought medicines and spent time with her mother. That made her start off with a special feeling towards you, the kind that comes your way when you help people in need.

But gratitude is not what you look for when you fall for a woman. Though it helps in sneaking an entry through the perimeter fences. You soon discovered that Shomali was a very lonely woman. Colonel Kumar was a fitness freak. One of the things that he introduced at Academy was archery. But for all his flowing deltoids he couldn't swing it in bed. This is where you came in. Shomali was the best thing that happened to you after Patricia. Even better. You felt a torrent of passion sweeping over you and she developed in you her need for a confidant.

One of the things she showed you after the first few weeks was the handkerchief she had embroidered with the names of men she had been with. Your name was eighth and last. She got you by your initials, MM. There was no name that you recognised except Colonel Kumar's and that made it a little less painful for you. But she volunteered the information that Sammy was the best she ever had. He was sixth on the list. She never told you who he was and you never asked.

The way you would work out your timings is she would call you at the phone by mess hall and pretend to be your mother long distance. But she couldn't always do that with the colonel around, specially after he took to setting up a twenty-yard archery range in the backyard of his house. He would insist she help him out and try the sport herself. Then when he got out of the way you wouldn't always be around the mess hall. You worked around this in a highly ingenious way. You got Cadet Milind, a fresh batcher, to swing a flare packet out of the rafting and hiking club. The flares went up three thousand feet and fell under a parachute half the size of a lady's umbrella. They took about one minute to come down and were visible five kilometres away. Academy was half that distance.

On weekends when the colonel tried his hand on the golf course things were a little smoother. You had time and because the colonel went in the evening and stuck around there close to three hours polishing his drive under the lights, you often took Shomali out for a little drive to a hill point near Lonovala, one hour away. For you, Shomali was everything you had ever wanted in life. Your dreams fired on all cylinders. You probed the possibility of a serious alliance but she would laugh it off.

'This is it,' she would say after a toss on the bed. 'MM, learn to live NOW. I am here and so are you and that's what there is to it.' That was how she lived and that's what is left in you of her after these many years. But even she crossed into the future and that one transgression gave destiny the opening it was looking for.

'MM, I want your child,' she said one fine day. You were combing your hair. The colonel was sterile. He fired blanks, and not even that lately.

'Why me?' you asked.

'Because I want my child to grow up like you,' she said. That's how her moods were.

'Me. I am a born scumbag. What about Sammy?' you asked.

'No, not Sammy. You are wild but it's a wildness I like. Sammy, he's *too* wild. And dangerous,' she said. Then she laughed. 'Sammy as a father. Ravi will kill me even if it's you but maybe not as fast as with Sammy. You see, they are close. Sammy is Ravi's nephew from his sister's side.'

'You serious?' you asked. You finished combing your hair and looked in her eyes.

'Very,' she said.

'Better sort out the colonel first,' you said.

'We will see when the time comes,' she said.

That's how she planned things. But then you didn't see things that way. You saw in this an opportunity to make her your own. That's when you reassessed your priorities in life. You were getting sick of Academy and now Shomali was giving you a reason to move on. The thing about getting out of Academy is to make them chuck you out, for though you can leave of your own free will they make you fork out a pile of money to be able to do that. And right now you were having cosy little dreams of setting up an antique store in Bombay with Nicky's help. Cash in on the leftover liquidity from three years back. That's when you recognised the opportunity that the shit-kicking of Cadet Milind presented to your plans. Cadet Milind was the favourite kick-bag of cadets in the senior dorm. Was Cadet Milind really as dumb as he looked, or could you provoke from him some deed that would outshine his previous misdemeanours, like asking a senior cadet to pass the salt on the mess table?

That was early on and the first time that Cadet Milind got an introduction to the Academy's predator–prey balance. Cadet Milind was designated salt in charge and for a fortnight his energies were channelled into fetching salt for any senior that felt the need to sprinkle some sodium chloride in his soup or lentils.

'Hey, you motherfucker, the salt's all stuck up in here.'

'You asshole, can't you see whether the cap's screwed on tight before you tap the dumb thing over my soup? Now drink this fucking soup yourself.'

'You got a problem with my face, asshole? You take two fucking minutes to come to my table with salt.'

'You, Milind. Sister fucker. Stand up when you pass me the salt.'

Cadet Milind never got to eat that fortnight. The mileage he logged in fifteen days at mess hall could have taken him all the way to Madras. You interceded on his behalf and got him off the hook, and since then Cadet Milind's gaze had alighted upon you with great gratitude. But there was nothing you could do about the genetic dumbness in Cadet Milind. His legend grew by leaps and bounds. He could dismantle and reassemble the Indian SLR in flat time but he couldn't hit a TV at forty yards. In drill he passed out three times in a week. He got caught out by the warden about half a dozen times for keeping smokes and rubbers in his room. Cadet Milind didn't smoke but he took no security measures to disallow his room being used as a contraband storage dump. Cadet Milind didn't fuck either and from the way he looked at girls you knew that he was as fresh as they went.

You were around when the warden busted him for the rubbers. 'What do you do with so many of them, three fucking dozen?' asked the warden.

Cadet Milind squeezed the packing. Maybe he thought it was chewing gum inside the squeezy plastic with the slinky woman-on-the-beach photo. He gave the warden a dumb look. But the warden marked him out as a slimy deal, an operator he had to keep under constant surveillance. On top of that, Cadet Milind came and confided to you one day that he had a heart condition. Angina strikes the young too sometimes and he just about managed to give the doctors the slip at selection.

You tried to smooth things out for Cadet Milind by taking him on your amateur movie assignment as assistant camera-man. That way he could duck evening games for a month, a compulsory for all cadets, and give his heart a break. One of the philosophies at Academy was to really splatter money at the cadets to sharpen their minds and bring out leadership qualities. One of the ways and means of doing that, the Academy thought, was handing over a video camera to a cadet and asking him to have a crack at celluloid. You had duly submitted your documentary proposal and Colonel Kumar had approved it. You wanted to replace the existing sixty-minute video on life at Academy, which was all a bore, with an updated version, one that would film faculty too, specially something as interesting as the colonel's archery range in the backyard of his house. That's what got the colonel hooked to your proposal amongst a dozen others.

You made Cadet Milind do all the shit work. You taught him the camera basics and discovered that his special powers lay in things mechanical, gadgets that whirred and purred and which you could set up on tripods. Within a week you even felt confident enough to send Cadet Milind to Shomali's place to shoot the colonel twanging his bowstring.

That's when things first started to go out of keel. You, however, only came to know a couple of days later when you sneaked out Shomali's embroidered handkerchief from the handbag she kept it in to have one of your periodic checks. You read a ninth initial. It's the same as yours and it takes you a little time to place things in perspective. You realise that Cadet Milind Mohan had notched his first score in life.

'The guy just kept looking at my bra strap,' said Shomali. 'I felt sorry for him.' That's how she was. She felt sorry for Cadet Milind because he hadn't got to use his dick for any-thing other than pissing. She even got Cadet Milind to get the whole thing on tape and she played it for you on the colonel's Sony VCR. Cadet Milind's ineptitude in the whole matter made you feel embarrassed for Academy. Amongst the many blunders that you got to see on tape the first one stood out. Cadet Milind got so jerky in his movements as his excitement levels compounded that he went on cruise without taking off his trousers and, in the process, because of the series of complicated manoeuvres that he involved himself in, he bruised his dick on the zipper of his pants.

'How could you do it with a guy like him?' you asked, hurt.

'It didn't mean anything, sweetie,' said Shomali.

'It does to me,' you said.

Of late, you had been harbouring a delusion that there wouldn't ever be any ninth name and that you could put a lid on her promiscuity with the evident zealousness of your love. The insight you drew was that maybe promiscuity was as genetic a factor as complexion. Also, for you to be happy with her all you needed to have was enough moments to tip the scale on your side. For Shomali, you realised, life consisted of a series of moments and she had to drain each one dry. To think you could be there in all of them was an idea you had to get rid of.

'I want your child, remember,' said Shomali.

And you went to work on that. You had been working on that the past three weeks. For you it was the building of a complex emotional web that would help you entrap her. For her, it was one of the things she felt her womanhood was incomplete without. And one day the paper turned pink. Life had struck root. You were happy. She was delirious for the first week but then her fear index started rising to the red mark.

In the meantime you put your Academy-leaving plans in active mode. You keyed up Cadet Milind to a confrontational stance with the seniors. Cadet Milind was swimming in new confidence after his path-breaking tryst and you found it easy to harden his resolve. Cadet Milind simply waited for an opportunity to defy a senior. He chose a particularly nasty specimen.

'Hey you, asshole, bring down the cricket kit from gym,' ordered Cadet Gaurav Bhanot.

Cadet Milind swung around, gave his chin a military bearing and said, 'Asshole yourself, asshole. And get your own fucking kit.' Then he walked out of the net area where Cadet Gaurav was nailing down the spikes to anchor the matting.

Cadet Milind showed considerable initiative to get out of spike-throwing range. After this suicidal show of aggression Cadet Milind's life at Academy became living hell. He was shunned by all and sundry and one night they boxed him in a wooden crate and nailed it shut. You were the one who crowbarred him loose the next morning. At this point in the game you decided to play your hand. You crafted a letter of complaint addressed to the general in command and took up cudgels on behalf of Cadet Milind. This is how it went.

Sir, this is with special reference to the treatment of Cadet Milind at the hands of senior cadets in the Academy, which happens to fall directly under your command. Cadet Milind is an exceptionally sincere cadet and joined the Academy with every intention to subsequently be commissioned in the army to be posted wherever he might be taken in the line of duty. As you might be aware of the rough initiation process that every new cadet has to endure at Academy I need not take it upon myself to brief you on that subject. But what has happened, sir, with respect to Cadet Milind is that his initiation period seems to have been unnecessarily extended by certain misguided elements at Academy. While I wouldn't have bothered to apprise you of the case if the ragging had been within bounds, in Cadet Milind's case it has exceeded all traditionally accepted parameters. Cadet Milind is in grave physical danger. The other day he was locked up in a wooden crate and if I hadn't come upon the scene he might have suffocated to death leading to an inquiry that would have brought great ignominy upon our great Academy. I beseech that you seize upon the matter immediately and send a fact-finding mission of your own that will help you identify the mischievous cadets and issue necessary warnings. You might also, sir, once and for all issue Academy warnings on this pernicious practice of ragging which is the only blemish in this world-standard Academy we Indians are proud to have.

You posted copies of the letter up at mess hall and left one at Colonel Kumar's office. You became a new point of hostility at Academy. But fresh cadets with little brainpower came up to you from the shadows and shook your hand to compliment your brave stand. Your batch-mates looked at you like the rivets in your head were coming loose at one shot. Stage two in your plan was to increase hostility levels to a boiling pitch and divide the Academy into two clear factions.

But events moved beyond your control at this stage.

Shomali started harbouring these big doubts that the baby might be Cadet Milind's after all. Which eventuality was not something that even a broad-minded soul like yourself was willing to swallow. Fighting wars for Cadet Milind on two fronts was not something you were keen to do. And even though there were dim statistical probabilities in Cadet Milind's favour the two of you decided it was better to nip such a possibility in the bud and start afresh. With this in mind you arranged for an abortion at an upmarket clinic in Pune near Hotel Blue Diamond. The clinic catered to the demands and needs of Bhagwan Rajneesh's many thousands of disciples, who congregated in the city from all over the world. The doc you chose confided in you that nearly fifteen international couples came to him in a knocked-up condition every fortnight.

Perhaps the series of coincidences that eventually took place started from your choice of clinic, because Bhagwan Rajneesh's ashram was a stone's throw away and three months back you had introduced Colonel Kumar to the Korean Zen archer Myung Mong who taught his craft at the ashram. You had read about the archer in a local paper and it became your strategy to have the colonel interested in him too. Not only was it a power-packed career move on your part, but it performed the excellent function of hauling the colonel away from home and providing you with many adulterous moments.

Events, however, became a matter of conjecture for you after the point you dropped Shomali off at the clinic over a weekend when the colonel was supposed to take off to Bombay with Mong, who had invited him to attend a series of his lectures on Zen and the Art of Archery.

That was the last time you saw Shomali but you never knew that it would be so. She asked you whether there was a phone she could use in case she felt like calling you. You told her there was one down the hall. You left a couple of coins with her. The last image you carry of her is one where she is flipping through the latest issue of *India Today*. You kissed her on the forehead and you promised to return by evening when the doctor had scheduled her in the operating theatre. And then as you were leaving she called you and gave you the best moment of your life. She took a case out from under her pillow. Her fingers eased a gold ring out of the case. 'I was planning to give it to you later today in the evening. But wear it now,' she said. That was the first time you saw tears roll down her eyes. 'I am scared.'

Those were her last words to you: I am scared. You slipped the ring on to your finger. You still have it. But strangely, the way you remember her in the last few scenes is how she flipped through the magazine rather than when she gave you the ring.

You doubt she ever made it to OT. This is what you think happened from the bits and pieces that you heard and what came out in the papers. Nobody bothered to ask you the important questions and you didn't volunteer to give leading answers. The colonel, you know for a fact, in his new-found enthusiasm looked to tape archer Mong's lectures at the YMCA in Bombay. He had come and collected the video camera from you for that very purpose. Though relations between you and the colonel had become a little frosty after your letter to the general, it didn't stop him commissioning the services of Cadet Milind for handling the camera in Bombay.

Some time during the day – after the colonel had collected the camera and before Cadet Milind was supposed to join him at his place, from where they were to proceed to the hotel Mong put up in and leave in the bus he had hired – you suspect that the colonel checked Shomali's drawers for an empty video cassette. And that led him unsuspectingly to the tape which recorded in explicit detail the sexual bungling of Cadet Milind. You figure it was foolish of Shomali not to have erased it or kept it in a discreet place, but her whole personality was one big self-destruct button. That was the way she was wired. The colonel lost it after that. But he maintained his outward composure.

You don't think the colonel really planned out the violent things that happened at this stage. That is, before Cadet Milind dropped in on him. But Cadet Milind's immediate presence might have been too much pressure for the colonel's disturbed sensibilities. It pressed some trigger in him somewhere, a secret spring that set a vendetta in motion. Then again it might have been limited just to Cadet Milind if not for another evil coincidence. As the colonel dropped by Mong's hotel, which was right across from the clinic you had brought Shomali to, you suspect he spotted her across the road in the hallway where the coin phone was. You also infer that Cadet Milind must have seen her too and since he was too dumb to put two and two together to take precautionary skin-saving measures, he might have been the first person to go across and say hello right under the colonel's nose and in this act sealed his own fate.

The next you know from Mong's statement to the police. He said, 'The colonel told me to proceed without him. He said he would catch up with me in Bombay the next day. He said he wanted to film something very interesting, which I could show in one of my archery lectures.'

So maybe the colonel swung some filming number and took Shomali and Cadet Milind back home. You don't know what story Shomali sprang of her being there. She was ingenious in these matters. She couldn't have known that the colonel's gunpowder was dry and the cannonballs were on their way.

At this point you have the colonel's statement to aid you. He said, 'I wanted to pick an apple off Cadet Milind's head. I wanted to surprise Myung Mong with the proficiency I had reached under his guidance. Only, as luck would have it, the arrow slipped from my hands and it went through Cadet Milind's chest.'

The tip came through the other side. It split the ventricles in Cadet Milind's heart from ten yards. You don't know how long death took in coming for Cadet Milind but he got no medical attention.

Of course, Cadet Milind's death was no mournful matter for anybody but his parents, and you used it to arm-twist Academy to gain you a swift release. You hinted that maybe there was a link between Cadet Milind's death and what you had warned the authorities about. You didn't do it to fuck Colonel Ravi Kumar. You had no need to. He blew his own head off two days later with a Browning. And you figured, with him gone, you could use even his death to help your case.

You claimed you feared for your life. The army bigwigs, already swimming in a lot of mud from the episode involving the colonel, thought it prudent to cut your lines for fear you might talk to the press, give them some gibberish that would skewer them some more over the coals. It had become a national media event. The colonel's archery range became a coveted visual on the Doordarshan TV network.

You aren't quite sure why the colonel whacked his brains out. He couldn't have got sorrowful over the killing of Cadet Milind. That must have been the one big pleasant memory he carried to his cremation pyre. Maybe it was Shomali's lack of fidelity. You don't know what transpired between the colonel and Shomali after Cadet Milind's departure from earthly life. Maybe she told him about her impregnation. Maybe he guessed it already. Maybe she told him about her plans with you. Or maybe just the shock of seeing somebody as fucked-up as Cadet Milind doing his wife was the last straw.

Shomali learnt about her husband's death while the MPs were questioning her about Cadet Milind. They were considerate enough to understand the fucked-up dimensions in the case and let her go home to attend to Colonel Kumar's limp anatomy before they took it away for an autopsy. Cadet Rodriguez and Cadet Kohli escorted her home in the company of MPs. Some time in the night Shomali overdosed on 4,000 mg of Amytal. They had to break open the doors to the house in the morning.

Why, you might ask, didn't you make an effort to meet Shomali in those crucial two days? The answer is simple. You didn't want to give the army or police a reason to step on you, fuck your chances of walking through the exit door at Academy. You decided to wait out the storm. Besides, Colonel Kumar's death was a bonus to your future plans and you didn't for a moment think that it would rattle Shomali in the way that it apparently did.

* * *

You break your narration for Karnam here. There were many other things that happened in the episode with Shomali and also later with RAW. But those are your own memories. You don't tell Karnam about the posted note that you received from Shomali the day of her funeral:

> Hi sweetheart, what a mess. But I guess we could go ahead with the baby now. Let's take a leap of faith. Rest later. Love, S.

That threw you out of the daze of incomprehension you were dwelling in after you got news of her overdose. Things fell into place for you when the priest performed her last rites and you heard Cadet Kohli consoling Cadet Rodriguez. 'Come on, Sammy,' he said in a whisper, 'you did what you had to do.' That was the first time you got wind of Cadet Rodriguez's first name. It explained a lot of things to you, and life after this piece of intelligence was never the same for you. You never knew Cadet Rodriguez or Cadet Kohli personally. But a week later, a few days before you left Academy for good, you walk into the room that Cadet Kohli shares with Cadet Rodriguez with your video camera. Cadet Kohli is sitting alone in the room. He is polishing his marching boots.

'I hear you have some interest in amateur filming. I was wondering if you could finish this documentary that I was working on. You know I am leaving Academy,' you say.

'Me, filming? You must be crazy.'

'It's easy. All I want is someone who knows the difference between a video camera and a MILAN anti-tank system,' you say. 'Point and fire is not the only thing that there's to go by.'

'My Minolta fits in my palms. All I have to do is press the shutter. It's auto everything. Does all your focusing for you. This thing looks like a rhino's ass to me,' says Cadet Kohli.

'It's the same principle. All you have to use is common sense. If Cadet Milind could figure it out, so can you,' you say.

But before Cadet Kohli can answer, Rodriguez coughs from the door. He's been hearing for some time.

'How much have you shot already?' asks Cadet Rodriguez.

'Almost all of it. Just needed a few more shots of the colonel ripping his arrows to cap it all, but now, I guess, someone will have to think of something else,' you say. 'Funny why the colonel's hand slipped. I have seen him do better than knock apples off people's heads. He could nail a lizard at forty yards, upwind.'

'You have shots of his archery range?' asks Cadet Rodriguez.

'Yeah, Cadet Milind got them. That's what must have given him the balls to go ahead with the colonel's suggestion. You see, he was there with me when the colonel split the lizard,' you say. 'The colonel, I felt sorry for him. I mean, doing Milind like that. It obviously broke his heart. I guess when you feel like that, all you can do is knock yourself off. What do you think?'

Cadet Rodriguez eyes you coldly. 'This camera of yours, can you lend it for a while? I have to check a couple of videos,' he says.

'Man, why do you want to borrow it? You can keep it, is what I am saying. All you have to do is take a couple more shots and knock thirty minutes into shape,' you say.

'OK,' says Cadet Rodriguez.

'Thanks, buddy. This thing was hanging around my neck,' you say.

Of course, you know which videos Rodriguez wants to check out. What you cannot understand is how he figured the whole thing out without seeing the video. Maybe, you thought, the colonel told him. Or he happened to see a portion of it with Shomali that crucial night when he escorted her home. And in a flush of anger decided to snuff Shomali out with the Amytal that the colonel kept to tranquillise himself before archery competitions. There were a lot of maybes.

'All you have to know is a couple of things with this shit out here. This takes the lenses forward and this backwards. After you get a grab on focus you get the thing rolling with this button here. Remember, when you pan the camera, you have to do it without any jerks. And flick on the mike switch when you are doing a talking shot. Another thing you guys will have to figure out is the background score.'

'That's more up my street,' says Cadet Kohli.

You zoomed the camera at Cadet Rodriguez's section of the room, your eyes glued to the eyepiece. You looked for something that could incriminate Cadet Rodriguez a bit more in your eyes.

'This zoom allows you to take a close-up shot from far. If you don't want the subject to know you are filming him this is the way to do it,' you say. You sit on Cadet Rodriguez's bunk. Rodriguez pulls his pillow out of the way to give you more space. What you see through the lenses gets the blood rushing up your face. You see Shomali's embroidered hand-kerchief on Cadet Rodriguez's bunk. Cadet Rodriguez pockets it with one fluid movement of his right hand.

'That's it. It's all yours, guys. Just remember to put me in the credits,' you say, leaving the camera.

'Hey, MM,' says Cadet Rodriguez as you are leaving. 'I never did know what your initials stood for.'

'Minty Mehta,' you say. Cadet Rodriguez had a very crude way of checking on facts, you think.

'Very unlucky initials to have around these parts,' says Rodriguez.

'Why do you think I am moving my ass?' you say. 'Milind Mohan gets knocked by an arrow through his chest. That guy Mong, I heard, slipped in Bombay and broke his fucking leg.'

Cadet Rodriguez blinks his eyes. He looks like he has just solved a crossword puzzle. 'Why, what was Mong's first name?'

'Myung,' you say. 'Fancy having a name like that. But he

was a deadly shot. I have seen him take out a flying pigeon at fifty yards at the Colonel's place.'

'He went there often?' asks Rodriguez. His voice is shaking with some kind of inner turmoil.

'The Colonel and he were like this,' you say, entwining two fingers. 'He cancelled his lecture tour at Bombay after he heard the news. Even the colonel's wife took to archery because of Mong. She didn't like it at the start.'

'Yeah,' says Rodriguez.

'Fancy her going like this. She had so much life left in her,' you say. You watch Cadet Rodriguez closely. But you see nothing. Cadet Rodriguez could gum his emotions successfully from the start of his motherfucking career.

'Here, MM,' he says, handing you a joint. 'Keep me posted wherever you are.'

Cadet Rodriguez even in those early days was a big fan of grass. You were too, and on a few occasions you rolled some joints together. That was the extent of your interaction.

That was the last you saw of him for more than a decade, but you didn't forget him. You kept a constant update on his whereabouts, waiting for something to come along that would allow you to even up. A simple hit wasn't what you were looking at. You wanted something theatrical.

Then one day, a month after you broke the nuclear submarine deal at *News Today*, you got a call from the RAW chief. You went and met him. He didn't beat around the bush.

'MM,' he asked, 'would you like to work with us?'

Of course, it didn't mean that you started at the top of the heap. They had you examined by a psychiatrist and gave you detailed questionnaires to fill in. They asked you everything possible, from your attitude towards killing someone for your country to what you thought about democracy. You had to take three months' leave without pay just to let them be able to pick and poke at your brain every four days. You went through four lie detector tests and had a two-month training session, a condensed version of the one they unplugged on their own regulars.

One of the first lessons you learnt about the trade was that paranoia was a plus in the spying business.

You learnt to construct covers. You learnt how to follow in groups and individually in 'busy' and 'slow' areas. You had to understand the strategic concepts of space and time. Learn to estimate the distance the subject you were following could cover in a certain period of time. You could lose sight of your subject at a street corner and by the time you arrived at the same spot he or she could have disappeared. You would then have to calculate whether in the time that you didn't have sight of your subject he or she could or could not have made it to the next crossing. If not, you examine the bus stops and the buildings on the street. Or simply wait for the subject to come out of one of the buildings.

Of course, once you had grasped the basics of following you were initiated into the technique of being able to tell when you yourself were being followed. It's a method the RAW calls 'road routine'.

You were assigned a particular route and at a fixed time of the day you left to do the route. At the end of it you were to write a report stating whether you were followed or not, and if so, by how many people and what they looked like.

You learned that in the business of espionage it's just as important to know that you weren't followed as it was to know that you were. In the paranoid profession you were embarking on, it was dangerous to know you were being followed for it then raised questions of who, why and where? One golden maxim you also learned was the thing never to do if you were being followed: you couldn't afford to lose your pursuer – for if you did, you wouldn't be able to verify whether indeed you were being followed and by whom and for what purpose.

You were also given to understand that in spite of the RAW chief's keenness to recruit you, it wasn't a *fait accompli*.

You had to pass the tests and the training session. You remember one particular torrid week. One in which they tried measuring your confidence levels and your presence of mind. Your instructor took you to Connaught Place and indicated the DLF building for you. 'There,' he said, pointing at the glass front of the third floor, which housed the British Airways ticketing office, 'I want you in that room with all the blinds drawn and standing next to a person in a suit for five minutes. I want you holding a glass of water.'

What you did was go to the business centre of the Park Hotel, which was opposite the DLF building. From there you made a telephone call to the corporate communications department of British Airways. You talked to a lady called Diana Pereira. You told her that you were from the Special Protection Group attached to the Prime Minister's Security and that the Prime Minister was due for a personal visit to the Park Hotel the next day. You had therefore to scout the neighbouring buildings and place some men for surveillance in one of them. You told her that you would need to look around the British Airways office for a site that served your purpose.

You were there within five minutes and she gave you a tour of the premises till you reached the area required. She was hospitable enough to provide you with a glass of Coke to slake your summer thirst. The problem of a man with a suit remained. You therefore asked specifically for one such specimen, as the area in question was full of women doing teleticketing. Diana's eyebrows shot up in curiosity. You explained. You said that there was equipment in place in the Park Hotel which was even then, as the person in a light blue suit came and stood beside us, measuring the refractive index of the coloured glass of the building so that it could tell us what colour suits the security men placed in the British Airways office would have to wear. They were suitably impressed. You told them to keep the entire thing hush-hush.

Of course, the next day you called to say that the Prime Minister's visit had been cancelled. You thanked them, nevertheless, for their co-operation.

Incidentally, you failed this particular test in the RAW manuals as your instructor for the day said that you were supposed to have water, not Coke. And that you were only supposed to stand next to a person with a suit and not a woman as well.

In another such session you were told by your handler to stop all traffic at the Ring Road near the Hyatt Regency Hotel for fifteen minutes. You stole a Maruti 800 from the hotel's parking lot and crashed it into the side of a Blue Line bus. You then got out groggily and lay convulsing on the tarmac with your mouth frothing. The driver of the bus got the thrashing of his life. The toughest part for you was keeping a record of the minutes even as you lay shaking with the hot tarmac burning your skin. Eventually, you got up and the crowd that had gathered around you cheered and a police Gypsy came around to transport you to the emergency ward of the All India Institute of Medical Sciences. From there you disappeared within five minutes.

You also learnt special methods of communication and underwent a weapons-training programme.

That was the start of your career at RAW. You joined for the fun of it. But the fun didn't last long. You were the first one to clue them on to Dinesh Patel, after he babbled to you the story about the Stingers over a drunken weekend at his Antwerp home. Patel was running a scam so simple and stupendous he had the Americans eating out of his fingers.

'How many Stingers do you think the US pumped into Afghanistan?' he asked you out of the blue. That was the way it started.

'Ronald Reagan didn't tell me,' you said. You were on your second Campari.

'Nearly two thousand. Now they want to buy them back,' said Patel. Typical American backasswardness. 'You know what the going price for a Stinger is?' You looked blankly at him.

'US$150,000. That's if you take one to the American consulate at Delhi. In the beginning you could even take a picture of a dismantled and destroyed system and claim your money but the Americans have stopped that now,' said Patel, winking at you. The softest route for getting Stingers out of Afghanistan was, in the words of Patel, through the Kashmir border. 'It's too hot at the Iran border. They want the Stingers badly but don't pay as much as the Americans. Same with the central Asian republics.'

This was hot news for you. Patel had so far got five dozen Stingers through to Delhi.

'What if one of them falls into the hands of the bad guys?' you asked him.

'Bad guys,' said Patel laughing. 'Those are the guys I buy from. The Americans don't deal directly with them.'

'What about the Indians?' you asked Patel.

He laughed. 'They sail right through at the border. US dollars can buy you passages anywhere,' he said.

'What about you?' you asked.

Patel's eyes widened. 'Yeah, what about me?'

'Nobody wised up?'

'I sail between the raindrops, partner. Dollars are the best raincoat you can have.'

It was Patel, incidentally, who locked you on to 5 Kumaon a month after your Stinger conversation. He wanted you to check out the unit.

'Some officer called Major Rodriguez', he said, 'contacted my man in Srinagar. They are talking big. Could you go and poke around?'

Ah, me, you thought, ah, me.

It didn't take long for RAW to understand the importance of the intelligence and you became their chief field officer in Operation Kalashnikov. It didn't take you long either to figure out that the guys who ran RAW were no better than the border Mossies the army went toe to toe with. They saw Operation Kalashnikov not as a chance to entrap and nail the army sonofabitches but as a way to skim some liquid funds for the agency.

'We are facing a resource crunch,' said the colonel. 'How much do you think you can net us?'

The dictum you gathered at RAW was that conscience doesn't have a place in intelligence agencies. 'It's the best thing that's happened to us in a decade,' the colonel confided in you one day. 'Mossie arms moving out of the country and the money coming to RAW.' The Wing, you figured, was still at loggerheads with the army after the Indian Peace Keeping Force debacle in Sri Lanka.

'What about the army? Personnel quality is going down the drain,' you said. 'The next you know they might let the Mossies smuggle in a nuke to South Block, punch the code under the PM's chair.'

'We skim first,' said Roy. 'We will nab the bastards after we are sitting on the bucks. You see, MM, arms remain in a region long after the conflict they were meant for. These are moving out. That's a plus. That they could be moving to Bosnia or Chechnya or wherever is also a plus. Any shit that happens elsewhere because of these arms is also a plus.'

You couldn't deny RAW's logic. The officially captured inventory of arms was sitting in ordnance armouries netting no foreign exchange and fucking no region. And RAW couldn't use it. You vibed well with RAW philosophy. It gave you an opening to make your own pile, unload some H on the world scene. It also let you have your little game with Major Rodriguez.

You have been silent for too long musing over these things.

'It's a crazy story,' says Karnam finally. Even she had to mull over in solitude the little that you told her.

'We live in crazy times.' Suddenly you are sleepy, but you

want to be awake for her, this island of sanity in the madness of your life. You lead her into your bedroom.

'I want you,' you say, 'like I have never wanted another woman.' Which is strictly a lie because there was Shomali, but she is dead and gone. In your mind she seems to have come again to you in Karnam. A second innings.

'I know. I can see,' says Karnam.

'No, you can't,' you say. 'Unless you have felt that way yourself.' You both lie on the bed. You draw her close to you. 'I want to only if you do, too.'

'Is there a choice?' she asks and laughs.

Karnam is made for you. She is woolly, and you like women who are that way. The blackness of her hair stands out in the high cream of her skin and swarms you with desire. The sweat and grime from your sun-up blitz envelops you in a strange aroma.

'I am dirty,' you say.

'It's OK,' she says. 'This way is better.'

A woman with a taste for salt. Her tongue moves over you. It checks the hollows of your armpits, first the left then the other. It rolls in circles over the aureoles of your nipples. She lingers there. And it's the first time you feel aroused through your nipples. She snakes down and your rod is like a mast, tall and full of direction. Her mouth goes down on you and for a long while it's as if you exist just there, as if the rest of you is fossilised. You note the skill with which she takes all of you and you know that she's done it before and instead of dampening your desire it works the other way.

Her fingers clamp on to the base, and her mouth goes up and down in soft slippery movements and the only noises out on the bed are your own sighs of delight. Your hands are holding the sides of her head slowing her down when your cock feels as if it could explode in a million fragments. Then she runs her teeth slightly, first on one side then the other, like little pin-pricks. You also take it as curtains for Act One. You pull her towards you, tilt her on her back. It's your turn now.

217

You work on her nipples first. Her bust is small, shapely and compact. As you suckle on her nipples she giggles but once you move down, her body tenses, she is electric with anticipation. You eat her as you have never eaten anything before, as if she were your last meal before doomsday.

'Oh, me,' she says. She is curving with pleasure. Her spine arches upwards. Her breath comes in short takes. Your tongue roves her clitoris and she's so oiled up the sheets go damp. Her hands encircle your neck. She can't take it any more. She wants you inside. She wants to be on top. Even you favour this beginning to the agenda. For you, that fuck is best that has you most at rest.

She's aching for you to enter, and she can't manipulate your cock fast enough. She feeds it into herself and it slides like a car piston. You place your hands on her hips. This way you can monitor her speed, keep the game from going beyond you. You are a perfect fit. You lift your hands off her hips and fold them behind your head and watch her work. You observe every movement she makes. The way she lifts up, the passion in her eyes, the hairs falling in front of her face, the ripples her breasts make at each sinking, the spread of her crotch hair and the angle she likes it best in. You pace yourself like a middle-distance runner. Your observation acts like so many brakes on your neurotransmitters, you delay going into the final lap.

As you feel your temperature going into the red band you lift her off you. It's time to try the dog now. This is your speciality. You can fuck so hard in this posture a woman's eyes can pop out. But you go gentle on Karnam. Soft thrusts that piston your dick into far-ranging crevices. You cup her breasts. You want to squeeze them till they burst. Karnam disengages from the clutter of limbs. She wants it on her back now. You usually have some entry hiccups in the missionary. You place a pillow below her hips, get the right gradient and she guides you in. Karnam wraps her legs around your back. Your legs stretch out behind you. You sweep the hair from her eyes. On the final stretch you like to look straight into the eyes, get obstacles out of the way. Your spunk shoots above the red band and as you come in the furnace of her belly you look deep into her eyes. Whatever else you might do you can never get closer than this.

She keeps you locked in after you have shot and the party's over. Even you like it this way.

'I love you,' you say and as thought becomes words and the words roll over your tongue you realise that you may have spoken the truth.

'Maybe you think you love me.'

'Maybe the sky isn't blue.'

'More than Shomali?'

'That was a long time back.'

'Why can't you answer straight?' she says.

'I don't know,' you say and that's as honest as you can get.

'What you are seeing is maybe what I am not,' she says.

'That could go for me, too,' you say.

And then you lock your palms behind her head and lift it till her eyes can't be any nearer to yours.

'Will you be mine? Will you marry me?' you ask.

Your doorbell rings at precisely this moment. It's strange. You rarely give people reason to come your way. You slip into your shorts. The door's unlatched. You open it to stare down the muzzle of a pistol.

You are familiar with the P7M8. The barrel has polygonal rifling, which reduces deformation of the bullet, and the eight-round magazine almost vertical to the barrel feed reduces the chances of jamming. But the unique feature of the pistol is its cocking, which can be achieved by squeezing the cocking lever that runs on the front side of the pistol grip. Another distinctive selling point is its sighting system, which consists of three white dots that can be picked up in all light conditions for a quick reaction shot. In short, it's an ideal personal weapon.

'Do I know you?' you ask. You face a Sikh in uniform with two nervous sidekicks in the background acting like a contingency reserve force.

'You know this?' asks the Sikh, waving the P7 in front of your face. That is as nice a way as any to begin on a strong note.

'Maybe you have the wrong house,' you suggest. Too much of your time these days is being taken up by pistol-waving military types.

'Maybe if you don't invite us in, we might feel like putting a hole in your head and making the place our own.' You step aside, a graceful host letting the execution squad in. You see the futility of an aggressive stand.

'What's this shit you have on the floor? Bamboo matting. A guy like you sitting on millions of dollars doesn't need bamboo to fuck up a place. These things burn like petrol, MM,' he says.

'You have a name?' you ask. You feel like you have seen him somewhere but you can't place him.

'Who sent you, asshole? Whose chicken-shit agenda are you carrying out?' you ask slowly, deliberately. He lines the P7 at your head. Your experience with fringe players is that they like to run the show on their own terms and the best way to baffle their radar is to derail them. A seasoned player like Rodriguez might, on the other hand, like to convey an impression of weakness till he got the chance to twist the screws on you.

But he goes red in the face and for a moment you think you might have taken a wrong read on the situation. You know he's going to press the trigger and you tense up, but he angles out at the last moment and takes out your ten-thousand-buck crystal vase on the sideboard. The glass shatters in a million fragments, some of the shard spray catching his sidekicks at the waist. The bullet goes clean through the wood.

'Jesus Christ,' you say, ducking involuntarily. 'You nuts?'

Karnam comes running out of the bedroom, a scenario you have been dreading. You had been hoping to settle the issue before it got out of hand or, alternatively, to raise your voice loud enough for Karnam to figure out that all was not well and exit out the back. With her in, you feel the odds tilt irrevocably.

'What happened? Is everything OK?' Karnam asks.

A saving grace, you feel, is that she has had time to get dressed.

'Ah me, what do we have here? Miss Universe herself,' says the Sikh officer.

'Leave her out of this,' you say.

'Now let me guess. 34–26–36. Am I right, beauty? You shack up with this cunt here. I could give you twenty big reasons I am better,' he says. He pokes her shoulders with the P7 barrel and starts tracing a line down her side. Karnam jerks his arm away.

'Keep your hands away from me,' she says. You tense for any opening you can get. The sidekicks are busy pinching out small shards from their uniforms. They aren't bleeding, a bad sign as far as you are concerned.

'What do you want?' you ask.

'I can see your vocabulary's taken an improvement,' he says.

One on one you feel you have a chance against him, but his back-up's behind you.

'You pulling this shit in uniform? The army's got this place wired. They don't like me very much. Your shot probably hooked some Military Police to come by, check out the new nutcase in my house.'

'The way I see it, if I sort you out, they are going to roll the President's Medal my way.'

'You have it all wrong. I have my arm so deep in their asshole, taking me out of the picture isn't going to take it out. What's it you want? Or is the best way you can socialise by blowing holes in people's homes?'

'You have something that belongs to us. Some little white powder which the 5 Kumaon stole from us. You know what it is, MM. All we want is what is ours. You do a friendly and we won't collect on interest.'

'I don't know what you are talking about.' But it's clear to you now whose agenda he is pulling. 'The 7 Sikh is barking up the wrong tree.'

'Bark. I haven't started barking yet, my friend. I am here to refresh your memory. I can see you believe in investing in quality. How much does this Hewlett Packard Vectra set you back? Is this the shit they advertise that has all these latest add-ons chipped in? Fax card, video interface, internet ready, CD-ROM. Does this wash your ass, too? Or you didn't sell enough of our stuff to go for that kind of superior model?'

'I think there's some tremendous misunderstanding. I think you are way off the mark,' you say.

He nods at his men. They start the search by opening the drawers to your sideboards, emptying the contents on to the floor.

'Where have you stashed the stuff? Or have you sold it already? In which case your time is at hand. All we will give you is a one-minute break to mumble your prayers.'

'You are wasting your time.'

'Not at all. It's giving me great pleasure fucking your place up. What's this? A dressing table in walnut wood. What kind of furniture you pick up, MM? A bachelor and all. Or did you buy it for our lady here to hook up her straps?'

'Keep her out of this. She just came by.'

'More bad luck for her. Going with a guy like you can cause a girl great harm. You should be more judicious, lady. Pick us sane types. This guy, Interpol's got a file on him a mile thick.'

A drawer's not opening. One of the men turns around.

'You have a key for this?' the Sikh asks.

'The stuff in there won't interest you.'

'Now I have to see it,' he says. 'Are you getting the key for it or do you want me to engage in some precision firing?' He aims the P7 at the drawer.

'I will get the key,' you say a little too fast. It's an opportunity for you to get the Glock, which is in the drawer of the study table in your bedroom. You walk to your bedroom. His footsteps ring behind you. One of the men stands guard behind Karnam. You keep your body between the drawer and the Sikh. Your hands reach out to pull the knob.

'Now there, MM. Not so fast. You are making me nervous. I am the guy that does any opening and closing that goes on out here,' he says. He presses the barrel point against your neck. You back off. He pulls the drawer. 'Now, now, now. What do we have here? A Glock.'

He picks it up, checks the magazine. 'This piece is something I have always wanted to own. You have put me in a very bad mood, MM. Very bad mood. You were going to pull this on me?' He weighs the piece in his hand. He looks at Karnam. 'This is some heavy artillery your boyfriend has here. Did he tell you how he got it?'

Karnam looks at you. You shrug your shoulders. 'I will explain,' you tell her, weakly.

'I can explain better,' he says. He latches the magazine out, springs the bullets on to his palms and hands the empty box to Karnam. 'If you see the inside, lady, you will see a name scratched out. Could you read it for me, please?'

Karnam angles it against the light. You don't know where the thing's heading.

'Captain Prakash,' says Karnam and your blood runs cold.

'Ah. As I had thought. You are a lousy player, MM. You can't even switch the magazines of the guns you steal.'

'I didn't steal it.'

'Prakash gifted it to you? Or did you sneak up to his room after you pushed him from the Cessna?'

'You know better than that,' you say. Rodriguez, you think, is either dumb in certain ways or an even bigger motherfucker than you thought.

'All I know is Captain Prakash was a buddy of mine. And now you happen to have a thing he was too fond of to give to a pimp like you.'

'Somebody presented it to me.'

'Who, Rodriguez? How a guy like you got mixed up with that asshole is what I cannot understand. Tell me, how did the two of you work Prakash in? I just want to know. I am curious.'

'His chute timer malfunctioned and pulled him out of the door.'

'Now, MM, even we know that. I was hoping you would tell me the real story. Earn yourself some points to make me go easy on your place.'

'If there was something else I am as much in the dark as you.'

'You chose the wrong side, MM. Rodriguez is going to dump you as soon as you have sprung the deal for him. Team with us and you might still have a future outside the crematorium.'

'Go fuck yourself.'

The men boot the drawer open.

'Now what do we have here? Floppies. What do you do with all these three-inchers? High-density Sony. What kind of data you store in here that makes you lock the drawer?'

'That's the entire *Britannica* in twenty floppies. You don't need to buy those big volumes,' you say.

'The way I see it I don't believe shit. I plan to have them checked out. There's more floppies in here than I have ever seen in my life. This kind of thing is way over my head,' he says.

The men come up with your shooting kit in the back of your wardrobe.

'What's this? You keep this shooter without any real stuff around. What do you shoot? Distilled water? The least you can do is get disposables for yourself instead of flushing your works with bleach. You better check in your local hospital whether this shooter of yours is boil-proof. Some of these needles collapse in the heat and you might crack them in a vein,' he says.

'Thanks for the advice.'

'The thing I have difficulty figuring out is how a grafter like you who doesn't want to spend a few rupees on throw-aways gets the mentality to buy this fashion stuff,' he says. He is fingering the trousers in your wardrobe. And the jackets. 'Armani. Gucci. Pierre Cardin. Versace. What is this Girodin? Never heard of it. But it doesn't stop me getting jealous. The only way guys like us get to see this stuff is in the magazines. And even the stupid magazines have become too expensive to buy. All you can do these days is flip through the pages till the guy tells you to fuck off. And here you are rolling in the stuff. Man, just feel the stuff. It's better than what a woman could give. You could fuck these things and not know the difference.'

'You are sick. You need some counselling,' you say.

He ignores you. He takes out a pair of your trousers and hangs them from his waist. 'Where did you get your height from, MM? This thing could hug a fucking giraffe,' he says. He tries on your jackets. 'What's this material your uppers are made of? They feel like fucking raincoats. Life sucks.'

He takes out a switchblade from his pocket and goes about making incisions in your pants at crotch level. 'Thing is with the kind of screwing you do in this room you should wear something that allows you to launch a quick shot. All these things with buttons they jam the action.'

'You can take them if you want, instead of doing it this way,' you say. You are pained to see your wardrobe hit dust. 'You mind leaving a few? I can't go to the office in shorts.'

'Shit. What's this in here? This looks like what the Eskimos must wear,' he says. It's your Everest kit he's discovered. You are grateful that your main equipment lies somewhere else. He throws the thermals on your bed. 'These things could fit a grizzly. What do you do with this stuff in Delhi? Hatch eggs?'

'Altitude gear. This is for the Himalayas. It's not mine either. It's David Breashear's, the American climber. He stores his kit with me,' you say. 'His name's stitched on the collar, in case you don't believe me.'

'The only David Breashear I heard of is this guy who hosts the breakfast show on Sky. For all I know this is a brand name. You might be packing some of the heroin in here. Always wanted to see what down looked like. I have this English sister-in-law that keeps these down pillows. They are so soft you could fold them in your pockets. Well, nearly,' he says. He rips a sleeve of your Gore-Tex. 'Man, this is like fridge packing. It smells like shit too. How can you sleep in this stuff? Jesus, what's this drum in here?'

'That's ice equipment.'

'I have to see it,' he says. 'Our mountain division doesn't get half this quality.' He rolls out your plastic barrel, pulls the lid out and hangs the drum in the air, letting your gear fall and scatter in a big heap on the floor.

'Now this is one hell of an ice axe. Look at the grip. Hell, adjustable glare snow goggles. This is like James Bond. You could even wear this to the Jazz Bar,' he says. He puts on the snow goggles and lifts the ice axe with his right hand. One of his men is holding the P7 for him now. 'You look like shit from in here,' he tells you. 'And you, lady, you look like you don't belong to this guy.'

Karnam's absorbing the whole thing with a cool head. You have been trying to make eye contact but she's following the Sikh.

Then he swings the ice axe as far as it can go and brings it down on the door of your wardrobe. It splits the door in two. 'Swell, man. Did you see that? This is one hell of a thing to haul around.' He throws the axe on your floor and it crashes against the side of your bed, hitting a hollow note. 'Jesus, what's this? You got a box bed. I thought it was out in the 1970s. This kind of tank design. What do you pack in here?'

'Why don't you see for yourself?' you say. You have given up.

He opens the side to one of them. 'Shit, shoes. What kind of place is this to keep your leg gear in? You will get the fungus on them. You have so much leather in here you could rig up a platoon. But what's your fucking size, MM? Looks like both my legs could fit in one and leave space for a bull to shit in.'

He looks out of your back window. There's an open drain hugging the houses your side of the road. He picks up your shoes and throws them in the drain one by one. He clears the backyard of your ground-floor neighbours with thirty-odd throws. 'Phew,' he says. 'You had some heavy soles in there. Didn't know Woodlands were like fucking dumbbells.'

Next, he crashes open the top of your other bed. That stores your booze. There's an array of Johnnie Walker, Bailey's, Drambuie, Jamaican rum, Smirnoff and some others. You haven't accessed your bar for a long time. You use the bottles to keep your sources in good humour.

'Man, you have enough alcohol in here to launch a polar satellite vehicle,' he says. 'Johnnie Walker Blue Label! The only time I have seen the bottle is in a Star TV ad, the one with that slinky blonde in it that blows her skirt in the ventilator. You seen that ad, MM?'

'I have better things to do.'

'This is amazing,' he says.

His men eye the bottles with considerable interest. 'Looks like this is the only interesting thing we can carry off from all your lousy stuff,' he says. 'You got some packing?'

'There are some plastic bags in the kitchen,' you say.

'This is what I hate about yuppie bastards. You guys are such stingy creatures. I can see those Samsonites stacked there on top of your cupboard and all you can offer me is some lousy cellulose. The thing would probably tear before we got to base,' he says.

The men pull down the suitcases. They are empty. They lay the bottles in neat rows, leaving you four bottles of Bailey's. 'This thing tastes like cold coffee,' says the Sikh and he opens the door to your bathroom to pour the Bailey's into the shit pot. 'What's this fancy shank you have in here, MM? How do you get the water going?'

You keep quiet. He kicks it on the side. 'The lever's on the side,' you say.

'What's inside? This is the first water pot I seen that's screwed on top. Maybe you have some stuff in there in waterproof,' he says. He comes back to your bedroom, picks up the ice axe and whacks it on the shank. It bursts like bloated plastic and the water runs all over the place.

'If I had anything I won't be stupid enough to keep it here,' you say. 'I am going to get you for all this, asshole.

Aggravated assault. The army's going to cook your goose within an hour of you getting out from this place. Your ass is going to be mine.'

'Well then, I guess I have to make the most of the time when your ass is mine,' he says, grinning.

'Can I leave now?' asks Karnam.

'Ah, lady. I just figured a new plan. I think you are going to make excellent collateral,' he says. 'What do you say, MM? Put yourself in my shoes.' The P7 is back in his hands and he's swinging it around with his forefinger in the trigger guard.

'You do that and I will kill you,' you say. And what you discover is that you mean it. 'I will talk to the army chief.'

There's a change in the Sikh's demeanour. His prancing goes. The lines on his face become taut and he steps up an inch from your face, the P7 hurting your ribs. 'You still haven't figured it, have you, MM? I am the army. This here is what the generals send me to do. How do you think the 7 Sikh shunted me into temporary Military Police duty? With the help of the generals. The generals, of course, don't know that I have two agendas. You can bomb your wheel questionnaire on Delhi for all I care, but we want the heroin and whatever else that thug Rodriguez has scrounged for you.'

It's now that you realise the deepness of the shit you are in. And this spark of reality ignites in you a memory that places for you the eyes of the intruder in another locale. You recognise the eyes. It was the turban putting you off all this while. You remember the locale now. The 7 Sikh officer at Kupwara on the day Captain Satish Warrier got sixty-sixed. That day he had no turban in place. He was a cut-serd.

'Major Raunaq Singh,' you say.

'You brain works slow, MM. You wouldn't last two weeks at the border,' says Raunaq. 'We will give you twenty-four hours. We want the hundred kilos that 5 Kumaon stole from us if you want to see your beauty again.'

With that he walks away with his two honchos and Karnam.

You don't bother to clear the mess after the departure of Major Raunaq. Events are moving out of orbit and you need time to dodge the debris coming your way, get your navigation racing full time. It's also time, you think, to set your own shit in motion. To slip in momentum now would be to lose your status as a player, let the likes of Raunaq and Rodriguez run the show. And right now, you have to use one to get the other. Somehow plan to bounce Karnam back into circulation. The nature of your profession trains you for all manner of contingencies. But the consequences of intertwining your romantic life with the business of espionage is something that no manual has answers to. Before pursuing Karnam, however, high on your immediate itinerary is to pick up some breathing space, boogy the army off your back. It's an opportune moment, you think, to use the tape.

You have had the foresight to prepare things in advance. You have taken the photographs from Jolly, the ones about the frolicking air marshals. You have also drafted a bogus VMA test report on a fake letterhead, facsimiled it to a friend in Phoenix, Arizona, who facsimiled it back to you. It confirms the voice on the tape as belonging to the defence minister. The original tape completes your blackmail kit along with a copy of an analysis of the wheel questionnaire. All these you kept in an envelope taped at the bottom of the gas cylinder in your kitchen, a precaution that came in handy in the face of Major Raunaq's armed intrusion. You remove the envelope from the bottom, pop two purple hearts, and hunt for something to wear that has escaped Raunaq's blade. You locate an Allen Solly. Then you hop in your Defender and drive to South Block.

You have direct access to Defence Minister Suresh Yadav. He is from your home town, Allahabad. The way you first met him was when he made his debut in parliament with the biggest winning margin in the history of the Indian electoral system and you were assistant editor at *Honey Bee*, your school magazine. Those were days just before you joined Academy and you took an interest in things literary and academic.

You went to interview Suresh Yadav and he indulged a schoolboy for ninety minutes. The encounter served you in good stead in later years, for the parliamentarian leapt ahead in his career because of emerging caste equations in Uttar Pradesh state politics and he learnt to play the formula to boost his ministerial ambitions in New Delhi. At suitable points along the route you got the opportunity to write up some goodwill stories, favours he remembered. The last time you cashed in on them was using his influence with the Haryana state government to allot you some prime real estate where Jumbo's and your entertainment complex now stands.

But dealing with the army is different. For all his political savvy Yadav is a little in awe of the brass button and stripe human species that he has to deal with daily from the forces. The first time he became defence minister, the story runs, he thought protocol demanded he pay a visit to the three force chiefs to get himself a briefing. But his personal secretary tipped him on convention and he avoided a *faux pas*. With great consternation he learnt that in a democracy the armed wing was subservient to the executive and all he had to do was pick up some fancy hotline and the generals and admirals and air chiefs would come wagging their tails, give him a blow job.

You bump into the army chief's ADC, Major Rishi Bhatnagar, in the minister's anteroom. You haven't met him since you submitted your application to train with the paras. He is surprised to see you.

'What are you doing here?' asks Major Bhatnagar.

In the present state of affairs the question assumes the proportions of a physical assault.

'Can't see that it's any of your business,' you say.

'It already is. We are cracking into you after the minister signs this,' he says, waving a file. 'We have filed a First Information Report with the Delhi police and are having the case transferred to the Central Bureau of Investigation.'

'What's this, a frame-up?' you ask. With this one, you feel, the generals could be caught in overreach. 'This morning I get a bunch of goons smashing up my place and now you tell me the army's cranking a case up my ass. Even a set-up hasn't got to look like one.'

'I guess they are just pissed about the poll you pulled on the troops.'

Bhatnagar, you judge, doesn't know white from black. It was not like generals to get so worked up over a questionnaire. A whole regiment on the move with arms for export could, however, work them into a heavy sweat, commit them to an indiscretion. What you wonder is how they got the stink. You look afresh at Bhatnagar. There was no need to lose your cool with a duty boy. Bhatnagar, you remember, is an ex-para. Someone who once mentioned to you that he hates not owning a parachute himself. That would provide him the opportunity to do a bit of sports jumping. A free-fall top from Pioneer costs in excess of $8,ooo. You have one to spare. You diversify your conversation.

'Thanks for the help in getting me through to the Pathfinders. The jumps were good. I loved them. Thanks. I got a spare chute in case you want to keep it,' you say.

Bhatnagar's eyes light up. 'I would love to.'

'You are lucky those assholes didn't come on it today or they would have ripped the webbing.'

'Now who would do that?'

'You bump into this Military Police asshole yet? Goes by the name of Major Raunaq Singh. He was in Sikh 7. How come he's on MP duty now?'

'Yeah,' he says. 'Normal infantry doesn't ever go MP. He got floated in from above ten days back. Temporary assignment.'

The 7 Sikh, you deduce, is on a dangerous squealing mission. It's important for you to sing a melody that warms Bhatnagar's heart, sets him up on a kindred pitch. He's tuning to your megahertz.

'All this is nothing personal, buddy,' he says. 'I heard you did real well up in basic course. For me you are para. And I never made it to the Pathfinders. I heard they took you up for a while.'

'Yeah. It was tough. I dropped out. It was a motherfucker.'

'So it is.'

'Listen, you better tell me what's in that file. They get me here they might move to confiscate my properties. Seal my flat and some MP asshole might disappear with my spare chute,' you say. 'Know what I mean?' You wink.

'I tell you what. You go in there before me. All I have in here is a copy of the FIR that army HQ has filed against you and your editor Ashok Mehra. There's also a copy of the notification transferring your case to the CBI. The chief, he wants to hide his ass behind the minister,' says Bhatnagar. 'He's worried about something. I don't quite know what.'

Army Chief General Subhas Rampal, you think, has reason to worry about his goose getting cooked. Corruption makes banner headlines and the kind that you were helping personnel from the 5 Kumaon practise would roll many heads should it become public knowledge.

'He surely should have more things to worry about than me,' you say.

'Right now it's you. He rang me up at eight in the morning to get copies of all this and have them delivered to the minister. I didn't meet you, right?'

'Right.'

You walk the hallway to the minister's room. You don't plan to let Yadav's secretary, Yashpal Ande, buzz you in.

The minister might avoid you or slot you for later in the day.

But you can't bypass Ande. He chooses this moment to step out of his room. He has a cigarette in his lips and you have no doorway to slouch in.

'MM,' he says. He's lighting the end. But the lighter slips from his hands and clatters to the ground. You pick it up and light his Wills for him.

'The minister in?' you ask.

Ande blows some smoke in your face. Yadav is asthmatic. He's into smoke-free zones. Ande has therefore to indulge in his vice outside his room, since the minister often comes by with personal instructions instead of buzzing on the phone and calling him. Ande isn't part of the government steno force. He's Yadav's trusted aide, his go-between and henchman. It was he who ironed out the kinks when you were trying to push through your documentary on Siachen. In return you remembered to get him a carton of Rothman Kings, his favourite brand, the next time you passed through duty free. That, and a Toshiba laptop for his son, paid for by selling part of the Siachen footage to a French company. Clearly, the Toshiba had regressed into dim memory.

'He's in a meeting,' says Ande.

'It's an emergency.'

'I will have to check.'

Ande has taken four puffs so far and you wait patiently for him to run through his stick.

'We have to discuss things,' you tell him. 'I might have something to buy from your nephew.' To dial Ande right you have to keep up his expectation levels. Ande's nephew has an interior decoration outfit. Ande wants him to spruce up your Gurgaon drug retreat.

'Not here,' says Ande. 'What are you up to anyway? The army chief's been calling the minister about you.'

'Yeah? When?'

'Four days back.'

'The chief is paranoid. He's cracking.'

'What's in that envelope?'

'Heroin,' you say. 'The minister needs it for his asthma.'

Ande chews your answer over. He is having a hard time chewing the intelligence you seem to have provided him with. You can almost hear him shifting it backwards and forwards and sideways in the various compartments of his brain. Yadav's tried many cures to contain his asthma. Once he swallowed live fish.

'You can go in,' Ande says. 'He is having his juice.'

Yadav has an elaborate morning routine involving carrot and orange juice. Orange for his calories and carrot for his weak eye muscles. Both for his late-morning shit, which is vital to his mental equilibrium. Then he does his eye exercises. If you didn't know about them you'd be in for a shock. He'll drop off right in the middle of a sentence and squint at the tip of his nose or rotate his pupils clockwise and then the other way. He finishes off by drawing one finger slowly towards his face till he sees it double and keeping it there for a count of ten seconds.

You know his habits in detail because you have travelled with him on campaign trails, watching his personal assistants lug carrots and oranges over the countryside and pack a battery juicer in the car. Once, when the juicer's battery died, the Exide battery pack under the car's bonnet was pressed into service. It burnt the juicer's coil and Yadav cancelled his speeches till late afternoon.

Yadav looks at you over his spectacles as you enter his office, the corner of his lips wet with carrot juice. He smiles and waves you in from the door, belching, 'Aghm. I have been wanting to get in touch with you, MM. What trouble are you up to?'

'Sir,' you say, 'things are not looking good.'

Yadav muses over this. He takes a sip from his glass.

'The army chief's been ringing me about you. He's saying your magazine is about to publish an illegal poll on troops in

Kashmir. That you conducted that poll. They have also registered an FIR under the Official Secrets Act and the NSA. Then two hours back he rang me up again to say that you assaulted an army officer in the morning at your house. It's troubling. What is all this?' asks Yadav.

Part of how you went to Kashmir was by getting Ande to call the army chief's office. The chief was now attempting to smear responsibility on Yadav too, make a merry party if his ship sprang a leak. He has precedent to warn him. One of his predecessors nearly got yanked out of his chief generalship by giving an interview to a paper that called a neighbouring country a nation of 'bandicoots'. The then chief had great problems wriggling out of that one. He got away by mudding the reporter and later sacking the defence PRO who had set up the interview.

'Sir, I think you should know what really happened. That's why I am here. It's General Rampal who's having all this done to me.'

'What?'

'He sent over three MPs to my place. They tore my clothes, broke my desks and cupboards and took my liquor away in suitcases. Next I'll be charged with bribery.'

'MPs?' says Yadav.

'Military Police, sir. Not Members of Parliament.'

'Yes.'

'They left this packet with me. They know about our relations and knew I would come straight to you. I think you should have a look at what's inside,' you say. 'They are trying to get at you through me. They are framing you. You have to be careful.'

There's nothing that spokes Yadav's antennae into hyperactivity than the mention of trouble headed his way. You tear open the envelope and heap the contents next to the teapot that holds his orange juice. Yadav stares. When he concentrates on things at hand his specs slip on his nose. He has to keep pushing them up.

'How?' he asks. He buzzes Ande on the intercom. 'No calls. No visitors.' He motions you to sit next to him.

In the murky politics that Yadav is used to dwelling in, the easiest thing to sell is a conspiracy theory. That said, Yadav is unusually paranoid.

'The Intelligence Bureau and Military Intelligence have had you under surveillance for six months. They gave me a tape,' you say. You place the tape in your pocket-size Sony transcriber and play it for him.

'We regret the mistake,' the Korean says. 'We confuse between bank. I get information you call, I call you immediately. We rectify mistake tomorrow. OK, sir. *Gam sa nida.*'

A short lull.

'Yes, yes,' says Yadav. 'Could you repeat the number, please?'

'78910123,' says the Korean.

'That's right. Please do the needful. I need two million dollars immediately,' instructs Yadav.

'OK, sir. *Gam sa nida,*' says the Korean and the line goes dead.

'*What is this?*' asks Yadav. He has some trouble placing the context but memory sweeps his eyes for one brief second and that's your confirmation.

'They are saying it's you and a representative from Korea Power,' you say. 'They faxed me a copy of the report of a voice match analysis. It's 100 per cent identification.' You hand him over your fabrication and though he takes it from your fingers he doesn't read it. Of course, while you are on your game, you have to provide Yadav a hole to save his face. 'I think what they have done, sir, is patch together the tape from your conversations. It's very easy.'

Yadav nods his head. 'But why?'

'Sir, your juice will go sour,' you say.

'Huh,' says Yadav.

'The three chiefs are after you, sir,' you say. 'You see, our magazine is on to the MiG-21 upgrade scam. The air force is worried once the story breaks you might go for a scrub at the top. The army is . . .'

'What's the MiG-21 scam?' interrupts Yadav.

You look at Yadav with shock. 'I thought intelligence would have briefed you by now.' You hand over the pictures to Yadav. 'These are Indian air force officers in Russia while they were striking a deal with the Mikhoyan design bureau, the agency that designed and developed the MiGs.'

'How do you know?' asks Yadav. Of the dozen-odd snaps he's riveted most by the air marshal giving it to a woman with her palms clenching a bike's handlebars and her knees on the single, padded seat. So enthralled is he by the snap he places it apart from the rest. It sticks out between you like a third presence.

'We know. A few officers squealed.'

'And the army?'

'You wouldn't believe what they are up to, sir. First, there's the IED detectors . . .'

'IED?'

'Improved Explosive Devices. What the Kashmir militants use. Remote-controlled things that can blow your shit out from a couple of hundred yards away. On paper the army owns several million dollars' worth of IED detectors and jammers to block the frequency of these things. Shipped in from Germany, Belgium and Canada. But the equipment, except for a few samples, never came in. All the IED detection team does is give demos to journalists about the sophisticated stuff they have,' you say.

This all comes from Major Rodriguez. Army Command in its foolishness kept passing the non-existent equipment to 5 Kumaon for trial and evaluation, and 5 Kumaon duly reported high attrition levels, equipment breakages and losses to militants, and inventoried the phantom gear out of stock. Colonel Sangma and Major Rodriguez were only too happy to oblige. This is part of the discomfiture burdening the army chief: the top brass in a regiment going solo and having the gunpowder to blow the lid on the IED deal. Robber against robber.

'Who told you about this?'

'Army sources,' you say. There's a spare glass on the table. You pour yourself some orange juice. 'This is not all. What the chief is worried about right now is the 7 Sikh. He is planning to swap the blame on you.'

'*What blame?*'

'The regiment is exporting the arms it captured from militants. To terrorists. It's not only AK-47s. They have detonators, explosives, walkie-talkies, the works. Even a few of the IED detectors. I think the chief's involved too. And they know that I know. They plan to get you through me.'

'How?' asks Yadav. He is functioning on basic vocabulary.

The orange juice tastes good. The problem with politicians like Yadav is that you have to spell everything out for them, number each piece like the back of a jigsaw puzzle. And since you are inventing most of the cut-outs you have to make sure they fit snugly.

'They are building a smokescreen.' Yadav has trouble with big words. They make him acutely aware of his small-town upbringing. (And Bahraich, his ancestral town, is as small as they come.)

'Smokescreen?'

'Diversion, sir,' you say. 'They are setting 5 Kumaon up. They are going to claim that *I* am the conduit and I was acting under *your* instructions. They will shovel all the blame on to 5 Kumaon, and since Yashpal Ande helped organise my stay with 5 Kumaon when I was filming this border documentary film a few weeks back, fingers are going to be pointed at you. Big numbers are involved, sir. The chief, he was the commanding officer of the 7 Sikh twenty years back. That's how he has his finger in the pie.'

'How big is the consignment?' asks Yadav.

This is a sign that you are at last beginning to align him on the field. A big bastard like Yadav sees the implications of the tangle first in terms of green packs and then national security, if at all. That is how he got this far.

'Forty million dollars. Maybe more.' You sit in the sofa. You make him an offer. 'They told me to make you an offer, sir,' you say. 'Actually, they made me the offer so I could work on you. They said it came straight from the general.'

Yadav's squinting his eyes now. He wants to work on his vision as he listens to you. A two-in-one approach. Debutants witnessing the phenomenon might think he was about to faint but you know better.

'How much?' he asks. At least Yadav always takes the shortest distance between two points.

'Twenty per cent,' you say. You're acting out of authority here, speaking on behalf of the 5 Kumaon brotherhood. It might make Rodriguez, Kohli and Sangma squirm, but with the 7 Sikh and the army chief on your ass you have to buy some cover, go for some overheads, instead of filing for bankruptcy.

'What does that mean?' asks Yadav.

You have cut deals for Yadav before. The last one involved container-loads of rotten cashew nuts that you had shipped to Antwerp, over-invoicing them heavily. The cashews were incinerated at destination, the commission came in laundered and you used one of Jumbo's many front companies to siphon cash to Yadav's constituents.

'Payment for neutrality. Passage money.'

'What do you say?' asks Yadav.

'We could play along,' you say.

'No problems with your magazine?'

'Even if there is I will take care of that.'

'The chief?'

'He's an amateur. We will outflank him,' you say. 'But I need you to sit on him for a while. Get him off my chest.

Also, call the CBI director and tell him to go slow. Tell him I am on a special mission.'

'Why is that?' asks Yadav.

'General Rampal might call the CBI director and feed him some bullshit. He's itching to smoke me out. Tell him I have special clearance, I am your mole in the hole.'

'If they jump the gun?'

'We will jump it before them. We have enough dirt on them to blow their shit out of army HQ.'

Of course, your main purpose is to buy time. If you go under, Karnam goes under. If you are afloat and fighting, she has a chance. The last thing you wanted was the CBI to crack a non-bailable arrest warrant for you, fuck up your hectic schedule.

Events are coming to a head and for you now speed is the essence of war.

Your next stop is the office. The time will come when you will clear your head and concentrate on your love life but before that certain logistics have to be smoothed out. You have to whittle the MiG story to size, lash together a pager on the IED scoop, keep in readiness the Yadav tape and write, in record time, your fabrication of the doings of border regiments. This should be your lead piece if you use them all at one shot.

As things are you don't stand to gain a lot by letting these stories through the gate right now, but in the eventuality that you have to use them you have to keep them in the system like loaded and cocked weaponry.

It's when you are scanning the pictures that you have a brush with Digs. His antennae have sensed your presence. He catches you alone in the design alcove.

'Where's Karnam?' he barks.

You shrug your shoulders. 'I don't know,' you say. And, for once, there's some truth to what you say.

'Her car's parked over at your place,' says Digs.

'She spent the night with me,' you explain.

'Damn you,' he hisses. For a moment you think he's about to hit you. But he's delivering a warning. 'Stay clear of my daughter, MM.'

'She has her own mind.'

'See me in my office,' says Digs and walks off. Unfortunately, you need him: the magazine is one of your most important tools of war. Today, while coming up the stairs you stuck your head through the door to the mezzanine floor but Gulab Chand wasn't there manning the ducts. Though he could have stepped out momentarily for a cup of tea you have forbidden him to do so. One of the dangers inherent in that act which would give the game away was if he was spotted by some 7 Sikh asshole keeping tabs on you.

You enter Digs's room with great apprehension. Others too have collected there. What's this, you think, a public sacking? But Mukherjee has a wire printout in his hands. You come to know that your dawn raid on Delhi police HQ has been picked up and flashed by the Press Trust of India.

There's a transformation in Digs. Like a good CEO he has put his personal problems behind him. He's also putting into application Robert Fritz's creative curriculum. A few weeks back he spent ten thousand per head to herd editorial staff into one of Fritz's seminars, where you were told over two days that creativity was a skill to be mastered the way you learnt to drive a car. It's Digs's philosophy that creativity should be an inherent factor in a journalist's make-up. It makes him write better copy, apply the right syntax while editing. Part of Digs's enhanced creativity after applying Fritz's formula has resulted in him clubbing some yoga relaxation techniques with Fritz's step-by-step goal realisation scheme. What has become disconcerting is Digs's attempt to introduce Fritz's formula into editorial meetings, which is what this gathering seems to be.

'When dealing with the unknown, any thought about it is pure speculation,' says Digs. 'Your starting point has always to be current reality.' It was Mukherjee's good fortune that he was on sick leave during Fritz's seminar, but now he has to contend with Digs's version of Fritz without adequate background.

'What we know is that there was a successful commando type of operation and an inspector got injured because of firing from military personnel,' says Mukherjee. 'These army–police skirmishes always make interesting reading. I think we should slip a pager in. We still have time before the issue closes for the week.'

'There's more to the story than that,' says Digs. 'The army has officially denied any involvement. For all we know the raiders could be civilians disguised in uniform. Assuming the person rescued by the raiders was from the army, we don't know why it was so important to rescue him.'

With Digs speaking your mind you don't feel the need to join the fray. You avoid looking at Mukherjee. You feel it best not to pick up any imploring eye signals. In normal circumstances you might have thought his case had some merit.

'We will be the first magazine with the news,' argues Mukherjee.

But Digs is wallowing in vintage Fritz. 'It's important, Mukherjee,' he says, 'to distinguish between what can be known and what you cannot possibly know within the time frame you have. If you can answer the unknowable within the next hour you are welcome to do the story.' Out of the corner of your eyes you can see Mukherjee look at you with some bewilderment. Leslie chips in with a weak, 'I will tell Photo to click police HQ and the injured inspector just in case.'

Digs treats the matter as dismissed. He swivels his chair around to face you. You are the only person who can see the lipstick imprint underneath his shirt collar on the right side of his neck. Nonita, you feel, is leaving her signature in rather conspicuous ways.

'MM,' begins Digs, 'I want to carry your para story this issue. I don't want the issue after the anniversary issue to be a total let-down. But I want you to add a box to that. The human-interest angle. The death of the jumper you told us about.'

You nod your head. This, you can see, is the beginning of Digs's fucking with you. He isn't finished either. 'I would also like to see the edited version of your border documentary by next week. It's to be forwarded to the army for screening before Doordarshan can telecast it.'

You nod your head once again. A week is a long time in your current situation. Even to tuck in a human-interest, journalistic obit on Captain Prakash is going to put a strain on your energies. But annoying Digs is out of the question. He dismisses the others. He motions you to stay on. You know what's coming.

'I don't want you socialising with Karnam,' he says.

You listen peacefully. Under an artillery barrage it's better to wait things out in a bunker.

'She's impressionable and I don't trust you.'

You cough. 'It's not what you are thinking, Mr Mehra,' you say.

'Don't even begin to think what I am thinking or you will shit in your pants,' he says. 'I have seen climbers like you, MM. All you can see are footholds on the way to the top. I don't want my daughter to end up as a foothold.' If Digs keeps holding you from business at hand, you think, Karnam might end up being worse than a foothold. But what you say is what you want Digs to believe.

'I think, Mr Mehra, in being harsh on me you are being harsh on your daughter. All she wants to do is surprise you with this investigative story she is working on. She wanted a little help from me because she was afraid of the kind of people she was having to mingle with. I was just her bodyguard.'

Digs is starting to look confused. 'What do you mean?' he asks.

'Karnam is on to the hottest story this magazine will ever have. She is her dad's girl. She wanted to prove herself to you, to make you proud,' you say. You slow down. You don't want to lay the poetry too thick.

'What story?' Digs asks suspiciously.

'She told me to leave it for her to tell you.'

'Where is she?'

'I wish I knew.'

'She is not in any danger, MM, is she?'

'I hope not.'

Digs appraises you with a new look. 'I hope you haven't got her into some jam, MM?'

'Not me, Mr Mehra. I admire your daughter,' you say. There's truth in that too.

Digs mellows a bit. He seems to be coming to a decision. 'I hope you are coming to the anniversary party I am throwing at my house tonight. I have invited five hundred people. The politicians are going to be there and some bureaucrats. Some cabinet ministers might also turn up.'

'Certainly, Mr Mehra. Wouldn't miss it for all the world,' you say. 'Now I think I had better work on the human-interest box, Mr Mehra, if you want the story to go this issue.' You have half a mind to scare him with the FIR the army has filed but you don't want to raise his temperature too much.

'Yes,' says Digs. He throws another peculiar look at you. And it floats in your brain as you give Captain Prakash some evocative treatment. This is how you begin in your cube:

> Captain Prakash was a friend. He was part of the élitist force in the Indian army. The Pathfinders. A force so élite it has just a hundred men on its rolls. They specialise in jumping from aircraft at heights upwards of thirty thousand feet and gliding towards their target. They are the advance party that secures the landing zone of paratroop forces behind enemy lines. They jump from high up and open their parachutes low. This is so they can avoid enemy fire for as long as possible. In February of this year, as he was going on a practice run, Captain Prakash . . .

The rest was easy. Of course, while you're on the job you also write up your lead piece. Mixing truths with half-truths you plan to sling a few convoy-loads of mud on to the 7 Sikh and the army top brass. This is how you start with your *coup de grâce*:

It's possibly the most ominous development India has seen since independence in 1947. Evidence available to *The Post* incriminates an army unit in Kashmir in arms dealing and heroin smuggling over a period of two years. Though the army top brass haven't yet launched thorough investigations of their own, highly placed army sources indicate that it would be highly optimistic to believe that the rot would be limited to just one unit.

The rogue army battalion in question happens to be the 7 Sikh. Based in Kashmir for the last two years and led by Commanding Officer Colonel Sukhvinder Singh, who is in detention, the unit reportedly amassed a huge fortune for its officers and select men by selling arms and ammunition confiscated from militants. Over a two-year period the unit, according to a conservative estimate, amassed a sum close to $10 million. The sum also included profit from selling heroin at market prices. Says a top Defence Ministry official, 'We can no longer say that the army is the one institution in the country that's by and large been able to remain untainted.'

What is even more alarming is that most of the arms and ammunition made their way to anti-India terrorist outfits. For instance, the NSCN in Nagaland, the LTTE and BODO and ULFA activists. Sources indicate that the recent spurt in railway track bombings in the north-east could owe a lot to the sophisticated arms and ammunition sold to the outfits by 7 Sikh. Apart from state-of-art assault rifles, big quantities of RDX, Semtex, detonators, IEDs and walkie-talkie sets were also sold. Right now it is not yet known whether training was imparted by army personnel.

What's ironic is that the same unit or any of its sister outfits could be posted in the north-east to face the same militant organisations they sold the arms to.

Cause for even more alarm, however, are reports from highly placed sources that army chief General Subhash

Rampal himself may be involved. (General Rampal's parent unit is the 7 Sikh and he is the brother-in-law of 7 Sikh Commanding Officer Sukhvinder Singh). Though it's still too preliminary to know the exact extent of his complicity in the selling of arms, what's beyond doubt is his involvement in the Improved Explosive Devices (IED) deal which he signed one year ago. Worth US$5 million, it involved the purchase of detectors, jammers and other related equipment to detect and disable IEDs, which have emerged as the second largest casualty factor of Indian armed forces involved in counter-insurgency operations.

What's also been intriguing has been the manner in which the army and air force top brass have combined to falsely incriminate Defence Minister Suresh Yadav in this matter. According to sources, in the preliminary investigation by the Central Vigilance Commission the entire blame has fallen on Yadav . . .

You continue in this vein. You entangle Rampal and the 7 Sikh in webs so complex no press conference could unravel them. Then you crown your effort with a stroke of genius. You attach Digs's by-line to the story. You figure it will be tough for the bastard to get out of this one. You then access systems with Jain's password. You don't want a trail leading right to you.

You retrieve Jolly's MiG story from Digs's file folder. You give it some sheen and direction. Next, to add greater lustre and background to the whole package, you retrieve your sizzler, the ace in the hole, the wheel questionnaire. This completes the package. Your first spread is all photo and headline. You go for 'Dangerous Exposures'. The lead photograph is of 7 Sikh CO Sukhvinder Singh addressing his men. You punch the caption: 'Sukhvinder with his men: how many rotten apples?'

After you have chopped and fitted copy to size for the ten pages in your package you convert your Quark file into a

PostScript (PS) file. The way the publishing and printing mechanics of *The Post* work is that the magazine files are sent by telephone lines directly to the Data Printing Press in Mumbai. The PS file which carries the data cannot be opened or seen. The file can only be downloaded by the shit-heads at the Data Press on to an image setter and seen on the screen as positives.

To cross-check whether the positives are coming right or not, a PDF file is sent. It has low memory bytes and you can chuck it along as e-mail. You can open and print a PDF file but you cannot edit it. Its primary function is to serve as a quality meter of the PS file.

What you have already done, unknown to Dilip, the sys-tems guy at *The Post*, is install software in the server that intercepts all *The Post*'s outgoing PS and PDF files for you, if you so wish. You can therefore by a few strokes of the keyboard delete the regular PS file and piggy-back your package on to it. Along with this, of course, you also have to delete all the relevant PDF files and manufacture your own.

To cut down on costs, Digs has stopped the policy of checking last-minute proofs of what's going in the maga-zine. You intend to exploit this single loophole to your advantage should you feel the need to. What it therefore means is that you could even in the running issue substitute the sex survey cover with your own defence special. Replace the current cover visual of a supine model with the army and air force chiefs in Hindon airbase. In the background you can see a row of six MiG-21s lined up.

In what you were planning to do, as in other things in life, it was good policy to have your weaponry greased at all times. For what good is a weapon if it's not a breath away from flashing its venom?

There's an art to drawing a gun. The way you have learnt it at RAW is to twist and bend down at the same time to make yourself a smaller target. You leave your jacket open – the time taken to unbutton it might cost you a hole in your heart. You pack a Beretta because it's small. Your other colleagues at RAW prefer the Browning, the favourite of Scotland Yard.

Your weapons training took place in Manesar, where the National Security Guards have their training base. You checked in as police personnel. You learned to shoot in 'extreme static', the term RAW has for impossible circumstances. You would be walking in the gallery and cardboard targets would spring up all around you. You have also put in time shooting targets in strobe lights. Some day, your instructor told you, you may have to plug a Lashkar-e-Toiba Mossie in a discotheque.

You learned that survival is an end in itself. To live is to fight another day. You were told in plain language that in a shooting mêlée there is no such thing as an innocent civilian. Your responsibility, RAW explained, is to protect the assets of RAW – that is, you.

You learned how to pull a gun when sitting in a restaurant. You were supposed to fall back in your chair and kick the table over as you were falling or just fall back and take aim from under the table. All this in one fluid motion. They also told you to lift your head as you were hitting the ground so that you took the weight of the fall on your shoulders. What they didn't sort out for you in their manual was that often in a disjointed fall like this you had your head up your ass and the real danger in shooting your metal piece in such a situation was saying goodbye to your balls.

For all of Major Raunaq Singh's bluster in your house you have him listed in the amateur book. Your kitchen cupboard has a false back, an inch and a half from the wall. Behind it you've stashed the Beretta and five kilos of heroin, a little cut to cover your overhead expenses for the 5 Kumaon deal.

Your dealings with Akramov have reached combustion phase. In two days' time you are airlifting your container-load of heroin to Moscow in the cargo hold of a Russian charter plane, concealed within tonnes of furniture: a dismantled oak sitting room (part of an executive ranch house), cowboy-style. A rage among Moscow *rekitry*, office furniture is always easy to unload in Russia where businesses start and disappear daily. This background of instability has made the Russian citizen hesitant to do business with any company that looks down-at-the-heels. People like Jumbo have made a killing selling the con-man's show of prosperity.

Of course, you yourself aren't turning Chippendale. Most of your furniture pieces have secret cavities. Little hollows you will soon be filling with heroin. To throw the dogs off, you spray concentrated lacquer on the wood. Lacquer throws a spanner in the canine sense of smell. There is a neat pile of money to be made even in the furniture and since you had over-invoiced it, part of Akramov's payment was to be overboard. The rest, of course, you plan to take in old hundred-dollar bills when you prime the furniture and shut the container in the presence of Akramov's lieutenants.

What Akramov does at his end is his business. But you know of the stateless nations employed by Akramov and his kind. The Ibos and Ogoni of Nigeria, the Kosovan Albanians, Kurds in Turkey and Iraq, Chechens in Russia and your very own Tamils in Sri Lanka. The politically fucked of the world make excellent narcotic runners. They carry the mob's powder in one direction and return with its dollar stash from the other. In the late 1980s, you have learnt, 90 per cent of the heroin in Spain was carried by Liberation Tamil Tigers for Eelam guerrillas working with Pakistanis in Barcelona,

Madrid and Seville. After the cops destroyed the network, they were soon replaced by Kurds. At the end of the century it's the Kosovans and the Africans who run the show. The desperation of the Kosovan Albanians makes them ideal recruits for the mafiosi. Till NATO wrought havoc, the nerve centre of deal-making was the lounge of the Grand Hotel in Pristina, where you could sell napalm, grenades, detonators, missiles or assault rifles for shipment to all corners of the globe. Discretion in a place like The Grand was pointless.

The bulk of Akramov's narcotics goes in plastic sachets at the bottom of his gasoline trucks. Very early during the Yeltsin years, the *rekitry* learnt the supply-and-demand mechanics of state-subsidised gasoline. Tanked up at 65 cents a gallon, the trucks are driven to the Polish border where a network of contacts ushers them into Poland and then to Germany, where a 65-cent gallon of Russian petrol trades for up to $6. In this manner and with similar margins the mafia have drained coal in millions of tons, Uzbekistan cotton in wagon-loads, gasoline from Kazakhstan and Chechnya by the lakeful and acres of Siberian timber. None of the money going to the various government treasuries involved.

You know all this because in one of your trips to Moscow, when you went on behalf of RAW to recruit Russian naval engineers for the Indian navy's nuclear submarine project, you had to tap the resources of the mafia for quality personnel. It was then that you had first heard of Akramov. You have had a brush with his henchmen but at that stage in the break-up of the Soviet Union it was too unimportant for him to notice personally, his underlings doing the job. But you have remembered. It was only as a safety measure that, for your current transaction, you contacted him through the help of Patel.

Your search for personnel took you far and wide. It involved locating former employees of the Central Design Bureau for Marine Engineering (RUBIN) and ballistic missile experts. The Indian navy, you learn, was having problems launching a ballistic missile from submarines. The main trouble was the effect of water in the nozzle on motor ignition. The US Trident 11 system faced similar setbacks. What you have also learnt is that the submarine-launched Sagarika was not a cruise missile as reported but the 'big one', with a range of 5,000 kilometres.

Since then you have kept close tabs on the Advanced Technology Vehicle programme, navy jargon for a nuclear-powered submarine. You know, for instance, that even though the diplomatic line is deterrence against China, the main perceived threat is the US military presence in the Indian Ocean. The job of your employers in RAW has been to acquire, steal or buy whatever has been essential to the ATV project. The mission has also been to spread disinformation. This was where you came in handy. You planted stories about problems in the development of the 190 MW power reactor. It wasn't only the media you were trying to con, but foreign intelligence agencies as well. This necessitated some time and expense. It led to the purchase of low enriched uranium from China, essentially to suggest that the capability to separate large amounts of highly enriched uranium didn't quite exist in the country.

You know, although you shouldn't, that of the five nuclear-powered submarines planned, two have already been tested and are operational: the people you recruited for the project have got back to you time and again. Although that's something RAW wouldn't have you indulge in, you firmly believe that in the theatre you had chosen for yourself, battlefield awareness is a vital tool for your own survival and that of those who depended on you.

Digs has strung up helium balloons on the roof for *The Post*'s first anniversary, which thanks to you might turn out to be its last. You spot your gang of Dravid, Karim, Dilip, Jolly and Matthew. You tap out a Marlboro and try to put Karnam out of your mind.

But there was the need to watch your back. Though you have been more than useful to RAW, you aren't, so to say, an insider. You don't exist in the personnel files, and loyalty in intelligence outfits, your own experience tells you, largely boils down to the principle of immediate exigency. In the manoeuvres coming ahead you are going to be playing for high stakes and the fall-outs involved could make you an ideal candidate for emerging as the *numero uno* fall guy. The Lee Harvey Oswald kind of situation. Eventually, that leads to you being worth more dead than alive.

You have since morning thought it best not to dwell on what the 7 Sikh could be doing to Karnam. There are other pressing matters to attend to. So long as you have the white powder the controlling lever is in your hands. And when the time comes, you have what it takes to bring them to the table, or so you think.

You spot a triumvirate of defence correspondents. You will soon have need of them. Ashish Massey of *The Nation*, Vikas Khanduja of *The Times of India* and Brajesh Gupta of *The Indian Express*. You decide that the time is propitious to do a little advanced public relations drill with the defence caucus. You insert yourself into the group. You know them well and have travelled together on many occasions. You come in when, arms waving like copter blades, Khanduja is directing his artillery fire at army policy.

'They said in 1987 during the war in Siachen that they would raise an alpine division. After the victory it went on the back burner,' says Khanduja.

Gupta chews Khanduja's salvo left and right, up and down.

'Costs, costs,' mutters Gupta. 'Seventy per cent of the budget is going in wages. Some artillery officers were telling me the last time they fired their guns was two years back. Half the units have netted their field guns to conserve on ammunition and spares.'

What you would like to know is which ones. But Massey is opening his mouth.

'I shouldn't be talking about it, guys. It doesn't go beyond here, right?' implores Massey. His itching to be the first with the information militates and wins against his desire to be prudent.

'The MiG-21s,' Massey begins.

You tense involuntarily. Sensing that Massey is on the brink of some big news, Gupta and Khanduja bank towards him, drinks forgotten. Massey goes into a whisper.

'Ninety per cent of them were grounded till two weeks back. Engine problems. Best-kept secret in the fucking air force since God knows when,' finishes Massey.

It's your turn to chew on something now. This, you admit to yourself, is news to you as well. Gupta recovers. His tongue swipes his lips. A predator eyeing a tip.

'Yeah, I had heard of something like that. But I doubt it was on this scale. I think it was just some routine maintenance snags. A little more than usual,' says Gupta.

Massey's face contorts with agony, his master scoop of the evening dismissed as 'routine maintenance snags'. 'What do you mean, routine? Half your force goes into coma and you call it *routine.*'

You give more credence to Massey, for it plugs with your own assessment of what you think could have happened. The Russians blowing up the MiG-21 upgrading scheme.

But the problem, you figure, could have been more on the avionics side of things. Khanduja looks for an opening to regain the momentum.

'The Mirage 2000, man, it flies with no bombs,' says Khanduja. He looks around at the three of you, scanning your faces for effect. 'It's a gun with no bullets. The French delivery schedule is all screwed up.'

'This is scary, boys. An air force with planes that cannot fly and no bombs to chuck,' you say.

'And a navy with a submarine that doesn't sink,' says Gupta. His ace in the hole for the evening.

'You are joking,' says Massey.

'Serious,' says Gupta. 'I heard the Mazagon docks just made an on-scale prototype for their ATV – minus the power reactor, of course – and it wouldn't sink off Vizag.'

This, of course, you recognise as a bit of propaganda from your own outfit. You decide to add some fuel to it.

'Yeah, it's true,' you say. 'The hull also leaked at a depth of three hundred metres. It was designed for seven hundred metres plus. Turned out they have some major complications with the HY-80 steel they are using in the hull.'

'Yeah?' says Massey.

'That's incredible,' says Khanduja. 'They should have the entire ATV project audited. It's a scam.'

You decide it is time to go into battle with your hooks and tackle.

'Are you guys free for the whole of July?' you ask.

'Why?' asks Gupta. You figure he is the key for the two others also to say yes.

'There's a project of the Indian Defence Initiative coming. It's an NGO with Carnegie Foundation links. It wants some research work done in Russia and the central Asian republics. Map out the Indian army's supply line, the T-72 assembly in Ukraine, the MiG factories, the works. It's part of a long-term project. They don't want academics. They want solid, investigative guys. All of you would be on a fellowship,' you say. You take a pause. Let the hooks settle in. Then reel it all in. 'They are willing to dish a per diem of US $300. That's $12,000 for the month plus research and travel costs of $2,000. Any of you guys interested? I have to tell them by next week.'

Gupta's lips are going dry. Khanduja draws closer to you, body language of a supplicant. Massey's pupils are dilating.

'I have been to Moscow,' says Khanduja, laying the foundation for his credentials. 'They have whores falling at you from the hotel walls.'

'I know this army colonel, he was the Soviet defence attaché to France. Met him in Paris on an Airbus trip,' Gupta squeaks, throwing his jack of clubs.

'I think you need the mafia pitching in on this. You can't take a leak there without a Chechen asking for his cut. My brother, he works with IBM Moscow. His job is to know which mafia to send the monthly to,' says Massey.

You throw some competition in to quicken the pulse.

'They might just go with two,' you say. 'But let's see, I might be able to work out something.' It's been your policy now and then to grease up the defence correspondents at RAW's expense. But here you are playing solo, lubricating the media with your own hard-earned cash.

Khanduja feels his gambit hasn't been quite as decisive. He makes amends. 'I was on this Aeroflot fight to New York and got spooked in Moscow for a week. No flights. Fucking airline strike. They didn't even put us up in a decent hotel. But I used the time to do a few interviews. I met Zhirinovsky, that nationalist guy. He said if he was in power he would swing a couple of dozen nukes India's way instead of putting them in the grinder because of these SALT treaties. That's your ICBM problem solved right there,' he says.

Gupta senses the temperature variations. He goes for the kill.

'This colonel I told you about, he retired. He went into defence consultancy. He's been to India about a dozen times.

His mind, it's like a computer. He could reel you out the dimensions of the T-72 turret. Every time he meets me he wants me to do some liaison for him. I told him no. The guy ultimately went for this retired deputy naval chief. But he's got a dacha outside Moscow the size of a football field. He's sent me about a dozen invitations to spend time there over New Year,' says Gupta.

You are in the mood to check out any prospects of interference at the starting block itself. Get your early warning system in the air to detect any circuitry quandaries.

'By the way,' you begin, 'I might be cruising some hard news by your noses in the next few days. I will make sure to send you an advance press release of the scoop we will be carrying in our magazine.'

'On what?' asks Gupta. His antenna's on full alert.

'You will know when you see,' you say.

'Will the shit hit the ceiling?' asks Massey.

'And more. We will need some six-column front-page preview on that. We need to get some power under our hood. A steroid boost to circulation. Give the competition a scare,' you say.

'It won't cost us our jobs, will it?' asks Gupta.

'The thing I like about you, Brajesh, is that you come to the crux of the matter,' you say. 'I think you will be chasing the story for the rest of your goddamn career.'

'Can't you give us a hint?' asks Khanduja.

To give a hint now, you think, would be inappropriate. If things leaked it might put a snarl in your kismet.

'Well, let's say that people will be going down. There will be carnage and mayhem. It will be happy times for our breed,' you say.

In the distance you see Digs heading your way. A cruise missile with a purpose. You are not in the mood to take him on without your mental supplementaries. Your Marlboros, too, have run out. With his heart condition he doesn't like smoke wafting his way. You look for background you can disappear into. You say bye to your peers and disappear behind the bar. It's a saloon construction, complete with Western motifs and guys with leather boots and cowboy hats. One of Digs's literary heroes is Oliver Strange. You, too, have grown up on Jim Green alias 'Sudden'. Times, you muse, haven't changed much since the days when being the fastest draw made you king of the dung pile. Of course, in the age of atoms, you figure, it doesn't make much difference who pulls the rod first. Now, whether you score first or later, it's immaterial, for you still end up not being in the frame.

As you walk behind and past the bar, your radar scope on battlefield alert, you spot intrusion.

Colonel Ray Chowdhary eyes you with carnivorous appetite. You have spent a big part of yesterday afternoon planning the Akramov end of the operation at the RAW HQ off Lodi Road. You are rarely invited to HQ: they don't want you bumping into anyone you might know.

But rules were given a detour in this case, as the chiefs in RAW were salivating at the prospect of netting close to $40 million, money they wouldn't have to account for even in internal audits. Money, some of which at least could go and line their own pockets. You are hot property at the moment, a fucking pioneer. A Vasco da Gama establishing the Asian spice route.

'I didn't know you were coming,' you say.

'It's best to keep the cavalry on the hoof.'

You notice he sticks close to the hum of one of the many lawn fans Digs has sprayed over his property to keep the breeze in circulation. A creature of habit, Chowdhary is making it as hard as possible for any potential eavesdroppers. He was on deputation for a while to the Indo-Tibet border police, having cut his teeth going toe to toe with the Chinese in Tibet. You know for a fact that he masterminded SSB forces, Tibetan irregulars, to blueprint the Chinese nuclear capability stationed in Tibet. It was courtesy of the SSB that the rest of the world came to know of the three nuclear sites in Da Qaidam, Delingha and Xiao Qaidam. The Chinese house their Dong Fieng ICBMs there. They have a range of 7,000 kilometres. The Chinese are also developing a fourth site 200 kilometres north of Lhasa, in Nagchuka. It was largely the Chowdhary investigation that forced the Indian government to go for its three nuclear tests in Pokhran in 1998. But ballooning over the Himalayas hasn't really spiffed Chowdhary up with the demands of urban espionage.

'There was some trouble in the morning at police HQ. Were you involved?' Chowdhary asks.

'A piece of cake. Nothing that we didn't have the enzymes for,' you say. You wonder too late whether Chowdhary might mistake enzymes for a new kind of assault rifle.

'We don't want any incidents. The press starts making some links and we are dead,' says Chowdhary.

'The press will think what you lead them to think. They are sheep you can lead to slaughter,' you say. You believe it. You have an insider's view. Chowdhary, for all his slant-eyed experience, was a little less equipped to operate at your level of subtlety.

'What's getting me worried is whose slaughter you are planning,' says Chowdhary. 'Ours, yours or some people we don't know about? We are getting nervous, MM,' says the colonel.

For all his Chinese CV, you admit to yourself, Chowdhary wasn't totally without weight. You hadn't quite made the whole of your plans legible to Chowdhary and company. Also, the 7 Sikh escapades of the morning and your meeting with the defence minister have made it clear that, for you to survive, the first salvo has to be fired at the army. Somebody there had to go down. The bigger the better. These aren't plans that you are anxious to get approved by RAW.

One, they might get nervous at your audacity and forbid it. That would complicate your life. You might still have to go through with your plan for want of any better and earn their disapproval. Censure in the intelligence agency lexicon often meant a bullet in your head. Two – and this was your premise – once the shit started it would be difficult for RAW to back down, as that would only encourage the cycle of shit to get bigger. So to step on the shit was, ironically, your best bet of pulling your scams off. Of course, with Karnam coming in the frame, something which RAW wasn't tuned to yet, you figure the complications, and therefore the shit, would amplify in proportion.

'Nervous at this chicken-shit operation? Save your fuel for bigger contingencies, sir,' you say. You are not normally obsequious to the likes of Chowdhary, but you don't want to raise his hackles, give him cause for alarm, get the RAW artillery on your case. That would mean the opening of another front, a stretching of your resources.

'I think your paranoia is derailing you, sir,' you say. There was no point in omitting your flattery after once giving him a taste of it. That would be another glitch. 'Things are under control.'

'They had better be,' says the colonel.

You savour an ominous echo in his parting words. But, in your game, if you were jostled by the likes of Chowdhary, it meant it was time for you to go AWOL. It would be more dangerous to tell him your plans than to act and draw him in, whether he likes it or not.

Chowdhary takes off when he sees Digs head your way. Digs is in a rugby charge, a Tomahawk on lock. You have no option but to weather the storm. Your life, you feel, is a dossier on tangling with the Digses and Chowdharys of the planet.

'The party's going great,' you say. 'Is the Prime Minister coming?'

Digs glares at you. He's not frothing at the mouth, but he's pretty close.

'Listen, where's my daughter? You'd better tell me before I file a complaint with the police.'

You take Digs aside. His posture is rigid. He's eyeing you like you are about to drizzle him with your spit. You have to buy some time. Think of some outlandish bull extempore. Plausibility, you have always felt, has to have in it elements of the truth.

'Mr Mehra, this is no way to lose your cool. You remember after the nuclear blasts there was this big talk about some of India's retaliatory nukes being mobile on the rails? Karnam's working on an exclusive on that. A contact's taking her right to the secret depot. We are getting the works, photos, everything but a test firing.'

'What?' says Digs.

'I didn't want to load you on it from the start. If she scored a zero it would mean booting you up for nothing. She told me not to tell you. I am sorry. I think in something this important we should have pulled you in from the start,' you say.

Digs is sweating. He is pulling his trousers up. His mouth is opening and closing. 'Huh,' he says. 'Are you monitoring the whole thing? Is she safe?'

'I think once we get the story we will have to think in terms of a print overrun of at least thirty thousand copies. We could look to sell an advertising logo for the pages. Give *News Today* some ulcers,' you say. The logo, you feel, could be a clincher. 'Some defence companies might give it a bite. Bofors, for instance. They are looking to mend their fences with the Indian set-up. Even these German wagon makers. I believe the Indians blew the top off to fit the missiles in. Next time around, they might send some that fit the Agni 3 just perfect.'

You don't know whether Digs has really bought your story. Either he is a very good actor or plain dumb. As you await his comeback to your advertising logo brainwave, you are joined by Tapash Mitra, editor of *News Today*.

'Congratulations,' says Mitra. 'But you have a lot of catching up to do.' Mitra, of course, is rubbing in the fact that his magazine had a superior circulation. A prig in the office and a prig out, Mitra, you cannot but believe, is vying with Digs for the crown of the gilt-edged asshole. There's a transformation in Digs. He's back to his garrulous self. The perfect host. He starts subpoenaing his waiters and Mitra gets inundated with Scotch.

'We sure do,' says Digs. 'But I believe there's a place for both. Ultimately, it's to the reader's benefit. Previously there was one, now he gets two.'

'It's good for the information highway,' you say. Mitra now deigns to notice you.

'Hello, MM,' he says. 'Read your piece on the Narmada agitation. The business behind anti-dam agitations. Good stuff.'

'That was Jain,' you say.

'Yeah, sorry, I always get confused between the two of you,' says Mitra.

That, you think, was highly illogical. But you let Digs come to his rescue.

'Let me introduce you to our designer, Leslie,' says Digs, sweeping Mitra away. 'He's got some fancy ideas.'

You take a breather. You notice Karim signalling you from the first floor of Digs's house. You trespass in Digs's house. In your absence your fraternity has been venturesome. Dravid's fiddling around in Digs's study, going through the book titles in the shelves.

'Look here what I found, *Camp 6*. The book has been out of print for sixty years. Shall I ask Digs for a read?' says Dravid.

'I doubt he knows he has it. Keep what you see. It's on the house,' you say.

'What's with Digs's wife? Are they divorced or what?' asks Jolly.

'Who's surprised?' says Dilip. 'Look what I have here. A *Playboy* collector's edition. They were in this drawer here.'

There's a scramble. Karim, Dravid, Siddy and Matthew make their way to Dilip's electric haul. There's *Hustler* as well and a French porn magazine that has a lengthy photo feature of women doing dogs.

'This is sick,' says Jolly.

'It's fucking art,' says Karim. 'Look at the layouts. We should get Leslie to copy one of these.'

'Where do these women come from, man?' Siddy asks of no one in particular. 'The only time you get to see this quality is in hotel lobbies and fashion shows.'

'Consider yourself lucky you don't have any of them in your life,' you say.

'Why's that?' asks Karim.

'Women like them, they skin off a man's defences. First they will suck your romantic side in about two days. Another half a day perhaps for your masculine self. And then you will be left all exposed like a peeled banana. You will soon discover she's cut your cock in her cornflakes,' you say.

Everybody laughs.

It's at this moment that Digs enters the study, a look of maximum alarm on his face.

'MM,' he says. 'We have a murder in the office. Somebody killed this electrician on the mezzanine.'

The Beretta digging into your flesh is alive, once again.

Gulab Chand has a tiny bullet hole above his heart. The exit hole in his back is the size of a rhino's head. This you and others notice after the rope tying him to his chair is unwound and they lean him on the table for a few minutes. There is blood splattered on the walls, on the floor and on the ceiling. On Chand's work table lies a copy of *Debonair* and a tiffin box, undamaged, with the dinner uneaten. Chand obviously had slipped in his sentinel routine, left the mezzanine door unlocked and made it easy for 7 Sikh powder-explorers to punch him a one-way ticket ahead of the millennium. You look for signs of torture. You notice the toes are squashed, the nails turned and burn marks on the chest. Chand, you realise, hadn't given his secrets easily.

The guards didn't hear any gunshots. But Chand had two visitors at 8 p.m. They made a few trips with duffel bags to a parked jeep. You know why. But you hope. The guards got nervous during the duo's last trip to the jeep and asked to look in the bag. One of them got a bullet in the shin for his challenge. That alerted the neighbourhood, but the damage had been done.

Of course, there's also the lettering on the wall in Chand's blood. 'Ha ha ha we found out.' That's intended for you. Only one part of the scene remains to be checked out further. But you have reached the mezzanine about the same time as the local police. Digs was too nervous to be able to take the drive. A Delhi police DCP is poking his forefinger in and around the scene of the crime.

You don't want to stay longer than necessary. The forensics don't interest you. You just want to confirm your worst fears. You look closely at the grille that guarded the air-conditioning vent, for signs of an entry. You find scratches all around the frame and the top end bent, as if with a crowbar. The vent hadn't been a good idea after all.

The photographer has come now. You notice that Chand's Glock is missing, a value-adding manoeuvre for the 7 Sikh armament acquisitions. Chand, you know, didn't carry around his army ID, specifically to avoid trouble for his 5 Kumaon brotherhood in case of disasters like this.

You go to your office on the first floor. You draw the blinds on the windows and the door as well. You lock the door and switch off the lights, so nobody knows you are inside.

You take off your shoes, jacket, shirt and trousers. The Beretta you lock in your drawer. You stand only in your VIP briefs for your commando assignment.

You push your table till it's underneath the vent, remove the grilling and pull yourself up into the aluminium tunnel. Your legs thrash under you, hitting thin air for a second, as you heave your torso through. Once inside, you navigate your way using light from your wristwatch, its glow pattern as powerful as a pencil light. The duct leads to the library. There another duct will take you to the mezzanine.

In the dark of the library you work hastily on the grille. You don't want somebody taking it into his head to include the library in the investigation. Discovery would involve more than a little explanation on your part.

You work your way into the mezzanine, dragging yourself as softly as you can, for part of the way takes you over the landing where dozens of police personnel jab and peck at would-be evidence. You don't want any metal-to-metal clank and your watch has a metallic strap. Progress is slow: it takes you close to fifteen minutes to reach the turn that gives you a clear look at the mezzanine vent where you had stashed the heroin. The light in your watch has been faltering for the last two minutes. It's flickering on and off, the battery packing up. The vents are, as you knew they would be, empty.

What you had come for were any tell-tale signs the bastards might have inadvertently left behind. Signs that you could use to zipper down on their tracks. Scraps of paper or maybe even a necklace that had come loose.

You have to return fast for your light is nearly gone and the way back slower, since you have no place to turn around. But you feel you have to go forward one more yard to get a look at the mezzanine grille, the hole that looked directly over Chand's desk, five yards away. Your light flickers off and on, and then off. Your eyes adjust to the darkness, illuminated only by the spill from Chand's vent hole. It's not enough for you to see the trip wire.

It's a trip mechanism with a difference. Instead of blowing up the grenade directly it loosens the grenade inside the vent, rolling it down the incline to where you are squeezed in aluminium, a coffin in the making.

You know what's coming. You can hear the special rattle that, in your ears, can only be the sound of death spinning your way. Your right hand is stretched in front to probe for the grenade. It's too dark for you to see.

All at once the light in your watch comes back to life and bounces off the grenade, allowing you to make the catch of your life. You hurl the grenade towards the vent. You know you have four seconds before the chemicals mix and match, and you hope the grenade will catch the vent where its energy would be directed downwards instead of at you. You bury your face in your arms.

The explosion fills your hole with light and smoke. Even as the acrid smoke fills your nostrils you realise it's just a stun grenade, a light and sound show to unnerve the enemy. The assholes, you figure, had a sense of humour.

You take your own sweet time back, making all the racket you want. You could hear the stampede that cleared the building.

In the silence and dark of your room you get back into your clothes. Though your heartbeat has slowed your central nervous system is still disorderly, the neural pathways clogged with traffic. You feel the need for a hit to improve the aerodynamics of your mind.

In your drawer you keep enough for a couple of lines. Within a couple of minutes of snorting them your belly warms up and calm flows through your veins. You return to what it must have felt like when you were in your mother's womb. Today, you take more than your normal dose.

The world, you feel, owes more than it thinks to the Germans. Perhaps even the Renaissance. It was during that period in the sixteenth century that the Swiss-German physician Bombastus von Hohenheim accomplished the pharmacological breakthrough of producing a tincture of opium by mixing it with alcohol and calling it laudanum. The concoction saturated Europe and civilisation was on track for sedation on a mass scale. The following generations fiddled with Hohenheim's pharmacological forerunner, which became the indispensable tool of medicine in the eighteenth century.

In 1805, however, it was left to another German, Frederick Serturner, to isolate the alkaloid of morphine from opium. This separation of the principal ingredient from the parent compound was a dazzling feat. It unleashed into the market a drug ten times more powerful than opium. There was another first for Germany when Bayer Company started the commercial production of heroin in 1898.

Heroin wasn't Germany's only area of chemical triumph. In 1855 the German physicist Friedrich Gaedcke isolated the 'active principle' of cocaine. World War Two also saw the invention of methadone as a substitute for heroin in Germany.

Half an hour later, your system at peak efficiency, you make a call to Major Kohli.

You are in battle gear for the second day in succession. Major Kohli's army networking has got him the intelligence all of you need. You have the precise location of the 7 Sikh hideout where Karnam in all probability is too. It's a farm-house on the outskirts of Delhi, in Chattarpur.

To your surprise, you receive a call from Major Raunaq Singh on your mobile. You don't normally like to carry one, for in your business the instrument could be pinpointed and your location given away by Airtel software. But in predicaments like the one you find yourself in, it becomes a sterling device.

'Asshole,' says Major Raunaq, 'are you feeling a little less cocky?'

You recognise the voice. That he was able to trace your number increases your estimate of his ingenuity, for your office doesn't list your digits.

'Maybe,' you say.

'How about we do some business?'

'Depends on what you want.'

'What I want is what I already have and more. Your balls are here too. They are worth maybe something extra,' he says.

It's easy to digest the general theme of proceedings if you are at the butt end of things. In the overall blueprint, Major Raunaq was now aiming for a wholesale conquest. 5 Kumaon's arsenal of weapons, though loose change compared to the haul in heroin, was still a tempting acquisition. But you feel a little combativeness is in order.

'Maybe we are already drying our gunpowder. Getting ready to fry your nuts,' you say.

'That would be a mistake,' says Major Raunaq. 'We have already drilled a hole in one of your heroes. If we have to do that to you and some of your other friends from 5 Kumaon it would put me into a depression. Besides, in case you are forgetting, we hold the cards. You try something funny and your whore might end up as our evening recreation.'

You grimace. Your life, you feel, is getting too entangled with all the fucked-up majors of the world.

'Keep her out of this,' you say. 'It's not her fight.'

'That may be, but she stays. You see I have got used to her presence. It takes a while to break a habit.'

'What do you want?'

'Ah. The thing I admire about you, MM, is that you have brains enough to see that the shortest distance between two points is a straight line,' says Major Raunaq.

'That's also the way of a bullet.'

The major ignores you. 'How about letting us lift your little booty from your warehouse?' he asks. 'I will see that you get a cut and the army gives you a certificate of merit.'

'It isn't mine.'

'All the better. That way you wouldn't lose sleep over it, would you?' says Major Raunaq.

'I haven't seen the place.'

'Aha, now you disappoint me, MM. All I want is an address.'

'All you need is a bullet up your arse, Major. You are a thief and murderer,' you say.

'So are you, MM. We are quits now. Captain Prakash can feel easy in his next life now.'

'How about a partnership? That would be more up my street. I could get a price for you guys that would double whatever you are selling at,' you offer.

You get a little quiet at the other end.

'Interesting,' says Major Raunaq.

'Let's meet,' you offer. 'The Jazz Bar in the Maurya at five. If you want a change of plans you have my mobile number and I yours. And, please, no grenades this time. I don't want you strapping one to my chair.'

The major laughs. 'That was a little present to bring you up to date with reality. I didn't think you would fall for it, though, MM.'

The line goes dead.

Major Raunaq takes your enticement. The major, you feel, would chime an SOS if he knew you were taking his call outside his burrow. He isn't up to date with cellular technology. With Dilip, your resident computer expert, who has access to Airtel software, you confirm the location of the major's call. You are on the right track. Your plan is to wait till the major leaves for his appointment with you. You have a feeling Major Raunaq will leave with a few of his gang members, insurance in case you are pulling a fraud. That would leave 7 Sikh with a major personnel depletion.

In your reconnaissance you have photographed the building from as many sides as possible with Polaroids. It's a sprawling double-storey structure with a swimming pool thrown in. At a corner and attached to the main house is a huge garage: likely the 7 Sikh armament warehouse. Though you have no way of knowing for sure where the heroin is, the only way to find out is to get in the game. The same goes for Karnam as well.

It's your belief that your opposition has between eight and ten hardcore 7 Sikh faculty. You are three. But you have roped in Jumbo as your ace-in-waiting. He sits a hundred yards away in a white Sierra wearing dark glasses. His job is the getaway if you have the 7 Sikh chasing you in vehicles they have hidden away from your prying eyes. If you located any such vehicles Kohli's planning included smashing their distributor caps. Since you didn't recognise a distributor cap, you would be concentrating on the wheels. It was less messy and it didn't involve opening the bonnet.

Ideally, you would have waited for Major Rodriguez to come and boost your manpower. But you have no time. If the current section split, you could say goodbye to your heroin and that will create an obstacle course for you that you have no mood to attempt. And for you to tap into RAW's resources would make them privy to the picture, which eventuality you wanted to detour too.

Besides, you take comfort in Kohli's antecedents. You know he is on deputation to the National Security Guards for three years. He has also trained with the Gourmet d'Intervention de la Gendarmerie National, the low-profile French anti-terrorist outfit where soldiers learn to hit a moving target at a range of twenty-five yards within two seconds and, subsequently, graduate to hitting the 'vital' spots on six moving targets at twenty-five yards within five seconds. You have been on courses like these yourself and know what it takes. Hence your confidence in Major Kohli's abilities. Indramani was hardcore infantry and stable.

Your raid arsenal is formidable. All three of you have MP5 machine pistols with silencers. Indramani's weapon of choice is the AK-47 but you have forbidden it because you don't trust anybody with it on auto. The major oscillates to your viewpoint. Besides, your inventory doesn't have a silencer for the AK.

The three of you sit lined up in an Ashok Leyland truck. This you have brought along to haul the 7 Sikh arsenal. Major Kohli's at the wheel. You sit beside him while Indramani lines up the 7 Sikh bungalow in his binoculars from behind. Major Kohli has already identified your team's approach route once Major Raunaq leaves. The truck sits on top of the manhole cover which, in fact, is the main service outlet for the drainage channel that empties the swimming pool in the 7 Sikh compound. The three of you plan to follow the channel to the swimming pool at the back of the house, which is nearly empty. From there you split three ways. Major Kohli takes the ground floor from the east side and you take the balcony route from the roof while Indramani remains your principal reserve, cutting off exit routes from the rear of the house. Though you stand to wet your legs, it's less risky than a frontal entry through the main gates or over the boundary walls.

Jumbo's lined up your local pizza boy to go and ring the bell two minutes after Major Raunaq's exit.

You have planned this diversion to allow you the minute you need to get out of the swimming pool and rush for the roof and for Major Kohli to make a breach through one of the bedrooms. The pizza ploy would necessarily draw at least two of Major Raunaq's thugs to the open in the porch. It would also give you a clue to the numbers you have to deal with. Of course, your pizza boy is under instructions to say, 'Sorry, wrong address,' and beat it the hell out of there.

You have a long wait ahead before Major Raunaq leaves for the Jazz Bar. You listen to Major Kohli's tale of how it first started out with 7 Sikh on the border.

'Rodriguez came up with the idea of LRRPs. Long Range Reconnaissance Patrols. Four guys slogging it for a week or more. We used to cross the LoC and make underground shelters right under the noses of their border outposts. Sometimes as close as fifty yards,' says Major Kohli.

'You were allowed to do that? Cross the LoC?' you ask, incredulous.

'The fuck we were. We never let out. At first we didn't even tell the boys. Didn't want to make them nervous. We did it to gather intelligence. Check out the Mossie movement. The moment we spotted them preparing to go across we would alert our boys on the other side by radio. Sometimes we would even radio down mortar fire on them when they were near the border but on their side of the hill. This way it was less messy. They would ditch their equipment and heroin and if it was a big catch we would just pick it up and return. That saved us some firefights. We rarely called for artillery fire since then the news would get to brigade HQ and they would start poking in their noses,' says Major Kohli.

He unwraps a packet of Wrigleys and cuts himself half a band. You take the other half.

'The first time we did a hide, we didn't know what we were getting into. It was Rodriguez, me and two of the men. We wanted to check out the concept. It gets incredibly boring. You are sitting here in this underground six-by-four thing, if you are lucky, and waiting. That's the worst part. Not even the shitting is that bad. You shit in polythene. The first time we mixed our shit and piss together and the packet burst. We had to stay two more days in that as some fifteen Mossies came and parked themselves forty yards from us. We couldn't even call for some shelling as we were too damn close. We used to take turns sleeping. One sleeping bag for four people. Every time a patrol returned they would be smelling like pigs.

'We would only move in the dark if we needed to; otherwise we had fashioned our bionics into periscopes. We had night-vision equipment. Sometimes in daylight we even took pot shots with a sniper rifle we had captured from four Mujahedin. A Barrett M82A2. It's a 12.7 mm calibre thing. It's a fucking monster. It weighs 12.4 kilos and the best part is it cuts a guy in two even if he's got steel plates on. This way they never got to know where the shots were coming from. We used silencers and flash suppressers. Things got bad when one of our LRRPs bumped into a 7 Sikh patrol in the night as they were returning from a mission. They bumped off three of our men. One escaped to tell the tale.'

'Can't say I blame them. How were they to know you weren't Mossies?'

'Funny thing is, they were waiting for us. How they came to know about our patrols we don't know. But they wanted a piece of the cake. And the guy that was leading the 7 Sikh patrol that night was Captain Prakash,' says Major Kohli.

'Hmm,' you say, things beginning to fall in place. 'No inquiry?'

'They never claimed any kills and we wrote our three off in a terrorist encounter. Nobody did a post-mortem to check on the slugs,' says Major Kohli.

You figure it was time to put a brake on the major's

monologue. You know about the major's not-too-recent attachment to an élite unit and you don't think he knows you know.

'What if you were captured? What uniform did you have on?' you ask.

'We always had our own. That way we could say we strayed and maybe return as POWs. But luckily nothing like that ever happened,' says Major Kohli.

'There's some talk about mining the passes with TNMs,' you say. 'You guys try any long-range patrols after that and it's going to be tata, goodbye. Your balls will land on the moon.'

'TNMs?'

'Tactical Nuclear Mines. Five hundred yards total kill radius. No radiation detected after one hour,' you say.

'Where did you get that?'

You can almost hear Major Kohli's antenna oiling into fifth gear.

'Ministry. Top secret,' you say. You tap out a Marlboro and offer the major one. Of course, you are indulging in your speciality here. The MM gas discharge.

'You know what, that cannot be,' says Major Kohli. There's a sly look in his eyes.

'And why not?' you ask. You can see the climax coming.

'We have this Mahatma Gandhi syndrome munching on our system. Fucking politicians want to go for a second-strike option. Want the Mossies to vaporise our own nuts first before launching the big ones. The TNMs would be first strike,' explains Major Kohli.

'If at all. I doubt they have weaponised,' you say.

Through the smoke of the Marlboros you can see the major smile.

'I was wondering when you would come to that, MM. It took you a long time, didn't it? Rodriguez had fucking warned me,' says Major Kohli. He lets loose a string of smoke rings on your face. Tracer bullets hitting your nose.

You freeze at first, but then you say, what the hell, you can't win all your PsyOps.

'Rodriguez is a motherfucker,' you say, smiling.

'Well, MM, he isn't the only one,' says Major Kohli.

The major is holding the cigarette with his thumb and forefinger. You don't see any mirth in his eyes. But the thing that keeps your spirits up is the fact that you don't see any hostility either.

'Never lose sight of that fact. I was just wondering what kind of rail system they have going to keep our nukes on the toes,' you say. You are, of course, referring to the sixteen Agni 2 missiles that you know are temporarily the responsibility of the NSG till the army raises two battalions of its own on line with the special forces. You have known for a while, courtesy of RAW, that Major Kohli was part of the initial deployment till his deputation term in the NSG expired and he reverted to his parent unit, 5 Kumaon. Technically, that is. Otherwise, the major these days is squeezing all the sick and study leave he can take from the NSG to be with his parent unit. He doesn't want the riches to be bypassing him.

'They put us on dummy runs for a month trying to identify the security kinks. It's a fourteen-wagon train, eight for the missiles and the rest for the troops to bunk in. The missiles are in these special wagons. They dip in the middle to get bigger clearance at the top. The command wagon from where you can launch the lot is right in the middle. It has about twenty different kinds of radio sets. I went in just once,' says Major Kohli. He drops his cigarette stub on the truck floor and crushes it with his black sneakers.

You promptly offer the major another and light it for him. It's in your interest to keep his train of thought going.

'Because of the special wagons the train can't go faster than seventy-five kilometres an hour. But the average speed is just twenty-two kilometres an hour. That used to give all of us a lot of sleepless nights. At those speeds even bloody dogs can jump on and off.'

'Traffic?' you say. Your own Marlboro has run out. You spin it outside the window.

'The bloody Indian railway's got 80 per cent of its traffic on 20 per cent of its tracks. On the Delhi–Mumbai sector you have fifty trains going up and down each way. Your freight train priority shunts you at the bottom of the list. You have to watch every sonofabitch on wheels overtake you. Every time the shit halts your blood pressure goes up. It takes about three minutes for the piece to stop even if it's going at just forty kilometres an hour. I don't know whose dumb idea it was to stick it up in the Indian railways. Twenty guys could take the shit down and roll with the rockets.'

You log on to what the major has just told you.

'Say, Major, will six men do?' you ask. You have a twisted smile on your face. You don't know which way it will play. A leap in instinct is what you are taking. If things went bad the major would have to be taken out and fast.

But the major's got a big grin on his face.

'Why go for six when you can raise all the men you want? Policy of my entire life. Where you can grab a chocolate fudge, who wants a Diet Coke?' says Major Kohli.

The 5 Kumaon, you feel, had its wisdom all cut out and dried to keep the airwaves free from chaos. You are smiling too. But the major's smile is thinning out. There's more coming.

'Of course, it depends on whose funeral you are planning,' he says.

'Nobody's,' you say. For a change you mean it, too. 'Some missile doctors just want to glue their ears to the ends of their stethoscopes. Find out the kind of circuitry our chips have going in the cone. Your folks on the train can have the gadgetry back once the surgeons are through.'

'What's this? Hire purchase? You play for keeps in this business, MM. Also, what species of diagnosticians are you playing out the rope for?' asks Major Kohli.

'Well, let's say from the developed world,' you say.

'We are having no Mossies,' says Major Kohli.

'Who wants them?' you say.

'Of course, it all depends on what Rodriguez thinks,' says Major Kohli.

'Of course,' you say. But you don't quite want Rodriguez to hop on to this if you can avoid it. Major Rodriguez brought with him his own set of complexities that drove your hypertension. Besides, you want to drive a little wedge between the two 5 Kumaon gunslingers. You want to start by giving Major Kohli a little food for thought. 'There are a lot of zeros in there for you, Major, if you can pull it off. But the more lads you get in on this, by the time your turn comes to lift your bag of cash you would find it quite a bit lighter. There's the security aspect as well.'

'What you are telling me, MM, is that you don't want Rodriguez in on this,' says Major Kohli.

'That's not what I said,' you say. You didn't want any mis-understandings with a beast like Rodriguez at this stage.

'Now you are telling me I don't know my English,' says Major Kohli.

Major Kohli is a difficult customer.

'No. What I am telling you is that Major Raunaq's Gypsy is just moving out of the gates,' you say. The major, how-ever, is moving alone. But that doesn't make your team change its operational plan.

Surprise, as always, is the key factor. As you elbow your way in through the swimming-pool channel, you convey last-minute reminders to Kohli.

'Nothing happens to the girl,' you say. 'Or you are dead meat.' You have already described Karnam in detail to your team.

In the end, that doesn't prove to be necessary. Even before the pizza boy has left you have found Karnam in an upstairs bedroom. The windows have been pasted with brown paper and the curtains all drawn but the door is open. It's the second door you check. She is lying on the bed, the same clothes that you last saw her in. She is surprised to see you. You raise your finger to your lips. She motions to the end of the hallway, quick to the game.

'How many?' you ask her softly.

'Four,' says Karnam.

With Major Raunaq gone, that is three your team has to face. The 7 Sikh, contrary to your expectation, is impoverished in the employee department. With nearly a one-on-one ratio, the battle, you feel, is going to be a cakewalk. You signal Karnam to get under the bed.

You can hear the engine of a Kinetic Honda starting and picking up power. That, you infer, would be the pizza boy leaving. Time for you to step on your artillery. Your upstairs approach gives you an advantage over any 7 Sikh gentry breaking ground to come after Karnam. Your weapon is at your shoulder and you are seeing things through your sights. Your training has taken over.

Already, from downstairs, you can hear the soft spits of an MP5 riding a silencer. But some of the bullets are hitting glass, furniture, whatever and now, to any professional on the first floor, things would be unmistakable. The first shouts and yells follow.

The door at the end of the hallway bursts open and you eye a soldier in your sights. He has on the trousers of his uniform. His upper body is bare. He, you figure, has just been raised from his sleep. You go for some precision shots here. You aim for the left shin. You hear the bone crack and the man scream. Like your team below, you don't want to take any chances. You don't want to go for any 'hands-up' routine. You have only inflicted an injury that will make your man incapable of any surprises but which will eventually heal. Your man is down on the ground holding his shin.

You check out the two other rooms on your floor. Quick sweeps of your vision with weapon on alert. Your floor is clear and the shooting downstairs has also stopped. But your training won't let you relax. At the NSG 'killer range' where you have whetted your bag of tricks, they had electrodes attached to your various muscle groups for measuring your relaxation levels. If your adrenaline dipped, gun barrels would whizz up on hydraulics thirty yards from you and riddle you with airgun pellets. They wouldn't make you bleed, but had a sting you wouldn't forget in a hurry.

Major Kohli and Indramani race up the steps, two at a time. The major's holding a thumbs-up sign for you. Your own thumb is up as well and your weapon falls at your side.

'How many?' you ask Major Kohli.

'Two,' says Major Kohli.

'There's one here. I picked his shins,' you say. Seeing Indramani, though, his groans have abruptly ceased. There's a panic in his eyes. And before you can quite read the situation, Indramani has levelled the barrel four inches from the man's face and pulled the trigger. His head bounces twice against the floor. His mouth opens to ooze a dribble of blood down his chin and his eyes roll to the back of his head. His hands have already released his shin and now they lie by his side as a low whistle of air escapes from his mouth. A spray of blood follows.

'Payback time,' explains Major Kohli.

'What the fuck for?' you say, aghast. 'It wasn't essential.'

'You found your girl?' asks Major Kohli.

'Yes,' you say. You indicate the room she is in. Indramani has taken an amulet hanging from his breast. He is kissing it. He is kneeling down in prayer now. Elaborate 5 Kumaon post-murder ritual, you think. But the major explains.

'You see, MM, Indramani was the sole survivor from that LRRP that ran into the 7 Sikh. These three here were part of Captain Prakash's patrol. They killed his mates. He has waited a long time for this.'

On your way to keep your appointment with Major Raunaq, you drop off Karnam and change clothes at Jumbo's place. You have two reasons for keeping your date. One, you want to hold the major there long enough for your team to clean out his warehouse. Two, you need to know who his buyers are and avoid them, or word will also get back to Major Raunaq about who was floating around the 7 Sikh inventory. They might try to get it back. Also, right now, though you and 5 Kumaon will naturally be suspected of the mayhem and the rip-off, you will have a partial alibi in the major himself. As a diversionary tactic you have told Major Kohli to take out the 7 Sikh hideout with a few anti-tank missiles. Get the police working overtime. You have also told him to leave some of the hardware in the garage for the police to recover. Among them a MILAN anti-tank system and a few crates of RDX. Not counting, of course, the trail of bodies along with their IDs.

You spot Major Raunaq in the corner near the entrance of the Jazz Bar at Hotel Maurya Sheraton. He has half his eye on an escape route.

'Hello, Major,' you say. 'I hope I haven't kept you waiting too long. The traffic's a killer at this time.' The major, you notice, doesn't shake your proffered hand. You smile at him. 'How come you are alone? Your goons have abandoned you?'

'For you I am enough. Two more minutes and I would have been away.'

You think the major's been nursing a Bacardi. You order more of the same for yourself.

'How's Karnam?' you ask.

'Well, I haven't come here for some social chit-chat, MM. If you have things on your mind, spell them out.'

'I have some contacts. Together we could go places with this,' you say. 'In this game if you don't know the right people you could end up taking a hit. All your sweat on the border chasing the Mossies could go down the drain.'

'What I am wondering is why you should be so helpful.'

'You hold my girl. You have the powder. I already have overheads. I figure I have to make good on my investment,' you say. 'Besides, in my line of business, we stick with the players. You seem to be holding the aces right now.' You offer a Marlboro to Major Raunaq. He refuses it. You light one up yourself. The waiter comes with your Bacardi. 'You need another drink, Major? Try a pineapple colada, it will smooth your wrinkles. Stop your hair from greying.'

'Black or grey, my hair's taking me nowhere. I got a turban to pack it all in. But you, MM, with your kind of lifestyle, you need all the black you can keep. You have this fancy girl lined up. She might ditch you for some other asshole if your hair turns light,' says Major Raunaq.

You tap the ash of your first three drags. You need to pump the major a bit more tight.

'I know these Italians. They will give you door-to-door service. Cash at your doorstep and you don't need to bother about packing your stuff. That's a turnkey approach,' you say.

'I am happy shaking a leg or two. Keeps my muscles in shape,' says Major Raunaq.

'That's not the point. The Italians will take your hardware as well. They will dump it on the Kosovans. Save you the bother of looking up the Red Brigade's number for selling your MILANs. They have all their works under one roof. It's a clearing house,' you say. You can hear the major's mind whirring and buzzing, a killer bee on a race flight. You can see 7 Sikh is having problems vending its goods. Of course, in about ten more minutes they won't have any more goods left to vend.

'We don't want to hold our stuff too long. The boys have to go back to their units,' says Major Raunaq. 'We also have these 5 Kumaon dogs sniffing at our asses.'

'No problem. I could have your shit lifted out in two weeks. In fifteen days you could be sitting in Lausanne looking at the boats sailing on the lake.'

'Lausanne. Where's that?' says Major Raunaq.

'You come with me, Major, and I will give you a world geography tour free of cost. Lausanne, it's in Switzerland. That's where Bill Gates has his flat.'

'My problem is the LTTE's already paid me an advance. The last thing I want are some Tamil assholes chasing me with bombs strapped on their chests,' says Major Raunaq.

You hadn't thought that the major would reveal his card so easily. 'That can be taken care of, Major. I can pay them back with interest. All you have to do is give a nod and I can start things rolling. Of course, I would want you to free Karnam first and it would be great if you could take the generals off my case. Tell them nobody is going to squeal,' you say. You have the major in your sonar, no obstruction. You look at your watch. By now, you estimate, you could start a zoo in the 7 Sikh warehouse.

Digs is in observation at the Escorts Heart Institute. The attendant publicity that Gulab Chand's murder in *The Post*'s premises brought has freaked his metabolism. His heartbeat has gone irregular. The newspapers are doing their bit to aggravate Digs's condition.

The stun-grenade prank of Major Raunaq has widely been interpreted as an unsuccessful bomb attack. Your normal stun grenade contains a mixture of magnesium powder and mercury fulminate. The fulminate is a percussion explosive and detonates with near eardrum-shattering intensity, igniting the magnesium, which generates a sixty-thousand-candle-power flash, disorientating a room's occupants for up to sixty seconds.

In the library the magnesium had set a blaze going and it had consumed all the building's fire extinguishers before gasping its last breath. You were in your own office snorting on heaven while everybody was panicking downstairs. Then you simply went up to the roof, crossed over to another building and walked down the stairwell to the street.

Naturally, you added your own spin to the incident when crime reporters called you on your mobile for inside dope. You spoke reluctantly and off the record. You spoke about it as an 'attack on democracy' and a 'sinister government conspiracy'. You let it be known to selected reporters that you suspected the attack was meant for one of the reporters working late-night on a hot story but the assassins 'goofed'. They were so happy about your precious comments – since Digs was unreachable and the other staffers too scared to open their mouths – that even though you offered no facts supporting your theory, they ran with the story.

The murder has knocked your assault on police HQ right off the front page.

Fortunately for you also, the office network has emerged undamaged from the fire. It's late in the evening when you reach the office. You are on the soot-blackened correspondents' floor when you bump into Leslie.

'Hi, MM,' says Leslie. 'You heard the news?'

It has been a hectic day and you have had no time to scan the wire. 'Why?' you say.

'The MiGs thing,' he says.

You freeze. What could Leslie have come to know now, you wonder. 'Yes, what about them?'

'Oh, you don't know? The Mossies picked two of ours from the skies. Boom. Boom. Missile hits. One pilot's in their custody. The other's got a ticket to Abracadabra,' says Leslie. 'Buddy, we have war on our hands with Pakistan. What fun.'

You stop in your tracks. You have known the push was imminent. Since early May reports have been trickling in from the border. But you were expecting the fun to begin a few weeks later.

The fresh dimension calls for some emergency stocktaking. Your sex survey went to bed this morning. You had planned your spurious defence cover for the following week, but by then it will be too late. You figure, as war escalates, nationalistic sentiments won't take kindly to an anti-defence forces cover. It will have to be now or never. You check the printing schedule, which gives you an idea of how to juggle the pagination of the issue. You give your questionnaire a new slant. First among the many questions you raise is the capability of the Indian armed forces to fight a war with Pakistan in light of the findings of your survey. War that is imminent. You also find some space for the reported cache discovered at a 'destroyed' 7 Sikh armament warehouse and give hints about a battle which seemed to have taken place before the building was blown up. A call to Major Kohli gives you the names of the three dead 7 Sikh soldiers. Even though crime reporters will have reached the site of your battle in Chattarpur, information would leak in little dribs and drabs while the rubble is sorted out and the police decide on a course of action. As a magazine man you want to be on the ball with your story when it hits the stands on Monday. There is some risk that the police might decide to hold back the identity of the bodies and might give a different spin to the incident altogether, but such risks you're prepared to take. What you have done, however, is plaster the story with Jain the motherfucker's by-line. It will buy you time.

You then access from the system the PS and PDF files on the sex survey, which haven't been sent yet. You substitute your bumper issue with the contents of the sex survey and flash the whole thing on its way using Jain's system ID. He is in the office too, the asshole. Thursday is a big load day for the business section.

Next, you prepare your press release on the cover story, which, however, will be special-delivered to your three select defence correspondents only on Sunday. This on Digs's letterhead and with his fake signature. You don't want the shit to break a day earlier, when magazines usually allow newspapers a sneak preview. On Sunday you'll have other pressing matters to attend to. Most significantly, your container-loads to Akramov. Major Rodriguez too is landing up early morning with the rest of the heroin, just a day before the transaction. From then on Jumbo along with the rest of your men will be busy packing the heroin in the furniture. Though the 5 Kumaon have got their marching orders from Kashmir they haven't packed their bags yet. With war looming, you feel, their peace posting could be delayed by Northern Command HQ.

A few unsolved blips remain on your radar. But you have plans for them, too. Digs has planned a blitz of advertising for his sex survey issue, labelling it the Anniversary Special. Leslie has designed the layouts to be released to newspaper offices directly on Monday. They were to run on Tuesday, a day after the issue would hit the stands. It would be a goof-up of a phenomenal quality if the issue itself was a defence cover and the advertising of it that of a sex survey.

You design your own layout in the same size. Nothing fancy. You simply substitute the picture with new text. 'Is India prepared for war?' is your headline. Under a second headline, 'Wrong timing', you run three strap lines: 'CVC report nails Defence Minister Suresh Yadav', 'The Indian air force in the dock for MiG upgrading scheme' and 'Army Chief Subhas Rampal under cloud because of suspicious IED deal'.

The negatives you get developed outside the office. What you plan to do is substitute the packet that left for the newspaper offices with your own. In the whole operation just one uncontrolled factor remains. On Monday, when Digs comes to know about the fiasco, he could order a recall of the copies from the stand. But that's easier said than done. The damage will have been done. Packing a genie back into a bottle is not as easy as letting it out.

Later, you catch up with Karnam. Digs being in hospital gives you a free run of his place. You are tired.

'Hello,' you say.

'Hello, sweetheart,' says Karnam.

She kisses you on the lips then leads you to her room where a leather couch awaits. You slump in it. She adjusts your posture. You now lie with your head on her lap. You kick your shoes off. Your Beretta is digging into your flesh. You take it out and keep it on a side table. Your jacket you hang on a chair.

'You still haven't answered me,' you say.

'About what?' asks Karnam.

'Well, what was it that I last asked you about?' You look hurt.

'Oh, marriage. MM, you are really weird. Bringing up marriage amidst all this. I was a nervous wreck with them,' she says.

'This is nothing. This is routine,' you say.

'Maybe for you. But not for me. Being kidnapped, then shootouts. What happened to them, anyway? I didn't see any of them coming out.'

Major Kohli and Indramani had dragged the bodies of the 7 Sikh soldiers to adjacent rooms before letting Karnam out. You had shepherded her outside the house as quickly as possible.

'You don't see dead people,' you say. A silence hangs over both of you.

'MM, I don't understand. I am not used to this,' she says.

'It's a phase,' you console her. 'It will soon be over. Trust me.' You nestle your nose against her belly. Her smell is setting you off. She unbuttons your shirt and you help her take it off.

'You haven't told me of this,' she says. She traces an eight-inch-long suture on the side of your ribs. 'What story does it have?' Her fingers knead softly your neck and shoulders.

It was a long story and you set about telling her.

It all began when the then USSR withdrew from circulation fifty- and hundred-rouble notes in January 1991. You were stranded in Poland after crossing over at Brest-Terespol. Along with you were four Russian scientists that you had hired for the submarine project from Jupiter Z, a scientific institute in St Petersburg that was part of the Russian Academy of Natural Sciences. Apart from individual contracts that you had negotiated with each of the scientists, who were to lend their expertise in the area of submarine communications at ocean depths of six hundred yards and more, you had to pay off the Russian 'defence mafia' for having located the personnel you wanted and helping you arrange their passage to Poland, where you waited with Canadian passports for them to aid their onward, zigzag travel to India.

In short, you owed five million roubles to Akramov's men. You were not part of the main negotiation, which was conducted by an RAW agent, Sishir Datta. Datta had been one of your instructors in your training interludes with RAW. With the rouble notes being outlawed, an unforeseen hitch, the Russian mafia was trading in its currency stash at discounts of up to 25 per cent. Caught in no man's land, the two of you suddenly found that you were half a million roubles short of your facilitators' fee. You asked for credit. Which was denied. So you went for the next step you were trained for. You decided to jump the mafia. You and Datta sped with your scientists to Germany instead of boarding a plane from Warsaw.

Though you could have waited for money to arrive, Datta was harried by the fact that the Pakistani ISI was hot on your trail. Colluding with the CIA, it had already sabotaged two personnel deals, in one case having a scientist liquidated. Two of your present catch were known authorities in the blue-green laser field whose further development was vital for the ATV's communications set-up. The Laser Communication Laboratory in the Indian Institute of Technology (IIT), Madras, was producing laser beams that couldn't penetrate the ocean waves. With hired brains they hoped to rectify this.

The 430-kilometre-long Oder–Neisse line separating Germany from Poland was hardly anything that could be called a frontier in 1991. You crossed the border at Frankfurt-an-der-Oder, the chief German checkpoint (the Polish wasn't manned at all), and fled to Frankfurt, where Indian embassy people waited for you with papers for your Russian friends. They made it out safely. They, of course, didn't know anything was the matter.

Datta and you stuck on in Frankfurt. You were working on a deal to get blueprints of the acoustic system used in the top-of-the-line Russian Lada-class nuclear submarines. A Ukrainian naval officer was helping you.

But Datta was spotted one fine morning by the Russians. They had an alert going out for him. They didn't know about you. They trailed him to the apartment you were using and followed him in. Amongst other things that they did to him was nail his scrotum to the planks of his bed and cut the skin of his legs and peel it off like a stocking down to his knees. The killers were on the way out when you abruptly entered the slaughterhouse. There was blood everywhere and you had a tough time keeping your feet on the floor. Even now, when you remember the way you fought for your life, a shudder passes through your spine. The first of the Vorovskoy Mir killers swung his serrated knife at you, opening a long gash at your ribs. You butted his face with your head using all your strength. It broke his nose. His knife clattered to the floor and the best luck you had was getting hold of it, even as the second Russian was on you and you grappled on the floor.

Amongst the techniques that you learnt at RAW the one that saved your life was pushing the knife through the killer's eye into his brain. Least resistance, maximum effect, you were told at RAW. You can still see the shock on his face, hear the yell of pain that suffocated as soon as it came up, and see the fading of life from his left eye. The long-distance look that glazed over his other pupil. That, and the soft quivering of the limbs even after his breathing stopped.

The other killer ran. To this day you don't know why. The contact was too violent, sudden and short for him to have carried memories of how you looked. That's why you took your studied risk in walking unprotected into Akramov's lair. But you have planned on getting even with Akramov for a long time and Sunday will give you that opportunity. Datta had taught you many things and even though loyalty to him or RAW didn't fit in with your larger agenda, it was a luxury that you were permitting yourself, a small game within the many big ones.

Karnam's mouth is still open when you pull up. You have clearly been around and seen a lot. This no one would grudge you. But your life has strung you up like a bow for too long. It is time you fired your last few arrows and dropped out from the scene. In your calling, things catch up with everyone without exception. The trick is to know when to retire. Too early and you won't have learnt anything. Too late and you die a dog's death.

You don't know what moment of weakness makes you confide your RAW background to Karnam, but in the insanity that you swim in you want to tell her everything.

Karnam's lips are finding yours. Her hair is falling over your face like a shield. She jerks her hair back and brings the bundle back again with a toss. You find it superhumanly sensual. You get up and lead her to the bed. She does the hard work of undressing you. Your cock is still not straight and high like Mount Everest. It needs some work along the fault lines, the crevices where desire rests.

She's taking off her blouse. It's on the floor. Her breasts are placards for the endomorphically endowed. In spite of yourself a soft whistle of air escapes you. She's taking off her trousers now. They are a heap on the floor. Her panties are white and translucent. You can see the dark hair sticking to them inside. There's a design as well. You gasp.

'What's that?' you ask. You see a designer pussy. Hair razored and ordered in the shape of a swastika. The Aryan denominator.

'I did it for you,' she says. 'A treat for rescuing me. It took me a full hour.'

You smile. Every day you live and learn, you think. Today you learnt the ways of a girl feeling indebted. But the motif has done wonders for your arousal, specially the thought behind it – a lover's special stencil. As your hands roam her back, her breasts, and trace the swastika on her mound you start feeling like an ancient Aryan warlord yourself. A chieftain in communion with his power source.

You are kissing her now. Her cheeks, her ears, her neck, the middle of her breasts, her breasts themselves and the nipples which stand like two twin peaks of pink. She is arching her back. With pleasure, you think. She's on to you now. She starts with your nipples. It tickles you. She has moved to the base of your mountain, her tongue tasting your sac. She looks at it with the fascination and desire of the newly initiated.

She sandwiches your nozzle between her tits, massaging it with a slow rhythm. A trailer to bookmark the events ahead. For now she has taken you in her lovely mouth. Your palms are holding her neck and thumbs are at her ears regulating the speed of her head as she swallows and then sucks up your machinery.

She is topping up your engine oil for the cross-country coming up. Your RPM is hitting a new high. To wait any longer would be to lose prime time.

'Yes,' you say. And she mounts you. The first insertion, you say with experience, has always been your most delightful. You try a novelty here. You protect three-fourths of your cock with a closed fist. You limit your area of operations for the time being to the top of your cone. You let her raise her steam to a new desperation level. You can see droplets of sweat building on her forehead, she pleads with her eyes first and then moans for you to relent. But you wait. You exercise an iron restraint, building your own cubic feet of pressure, till you can hold on no longer and she slides all the way down to the base of your cock. You feel the heat, the viscousness of molten metal.

She picks up a Bugatti's momentum. You want her more at a Volkswagen's steady trot. Squeeze the maximum mileage out of your gallon of gas. But she's eating up the road with all cylinders blazing. You lift her out. You want to try different kinds of fusion.

You turn her around. You are looking at her back now.

'What's this?' she says.

You don't need to explain for she is inducted easily. She starts fucking you looking at the ceiling, your hands pressing on her breasts. This way, somehow, you feel closer.

'I didn't know you could do it this way,' she says.

But you tire of the oddity. For your final moments you return to tried and trusted postures.

The missionary for all its drawbacks still works for you. In it alone you get the melting feeling when you are nearing apogee and your eyes are padlocked with one whom you wish to possess and own. You look at each other in your moments that burst in your brains and down below and you, at least, after a long time feel this is heaven and the rest is but waiting.

You lie on her for a long time, breathing her own breathing and inhaling the air she inhaled. Then you break up and lie alongside. Things are quiet till you hear a rush of steps coming to the door of your room. There is something abnormal here, you feel. Your Beretta is still at the table many yards away. The door opens and in bursts Digs. His mouth opens in surprise. The ambush is the other way around. His face is going red. He is taking too long to take in the spectacle, you feel. But you can almost see him gather his reserves. He straightens his spine.

'Out, you two,' he says. '*Now.*' He then walks out.

Karnam is also jolted with embarrassment. Though you recognise the feeling you are beyond that sentiment yourself. You wonder with amusement whether Digs had had enough time to take in the swastika that his daughter had tooled with such care.

It's dawn. Sunday. And one of the amusements that you are still savouring from the day before is the knowledge that Akramov's man in India is Colonel Anatoly Grupov, defence attaché in the Russian embassy. Such mafia–state collaboration is not unknown to you. Hence the amusement rather than the surprise.

You are planning a con so simple in nature as to be almost childish. You have rented a warehouse in the Gurgaon Export Promotion Zone on Haryana Urban Development Authority land, 20 kilometres from the Indira Gandhi International Airport. It has a high-security wall all around it and fifteen concrete sheds of considerable dimension. They stand in a single line. For a decent pile of money you have rented the entire premises for two weeks. You don't need all that huge space or time. For you, just two sheds and three days will do but you don't want to bump into other civilian traffic at the site. Besides, with the array of numbered sheds you plan a little confusion for Colonel Grupov and his band of chemists with their little portable laboratory to test your H.

For purposes central to your deception, you have rented six dozen empty containers of aircraft specifications and unloaded them at your shed. In work that has taken a full month, a team of twenty carpenters working round the clock under Jumbo's supervision has scraped, hammered, peeled and varnished two identical sets of furniture, possession of one of which Colonel Grupov will be taking later in the day. In the presence of Colonel Grupov and his lieutenants, Jumbo's men will kit the hollows of the special furniture with heroin and pack them in four containers. Then Jumbo will seal them all in his own very special and irrevocable way. All this you have discussed with Colonel Grupov in minute detail.

Then you will use the locks that Colonel Grupov will provide and secure the shed. The containers will stay at the site overnight. In the early morning the Russians will come with their handlers and truck the load to Aeroflot.

Of course, here's where your special execution plans are to fall into place. You are not going to tamper with the locks. That would be amateurish. Instead, fresh numbers will be painted on the doors. In the shed everything will be organised the same way and the four other identical containers placed in precise locations. These will, obviously, contain the matching set of furniture, packed and sealed in a similar fashion. You have divided your load of empty containers in both sheds for background effect, to make the whole thing realistic.

To cook Akramov's goose in full measure you are filling the hollows with white distemper. Provide them with the arsenal to spick their set-up, whitewash their dreary Moscow abode. In the morning the Russians will be led to the dummy consignment.

Needless to say, you have exempted 5 Kumaon from this bit of chess play on your part. You have, however, chosen a calculated hazard by opening a channel with the LTTE. You have the numbers of one-eyed Srinivasan, who you know is the LTTE's point man in Delhi, their liaison with mafia don Dawood Ibrahim. You have met him in the past in Singapore and discussed matters of mutual interest. You have conveyed to Srinivasan that his advance to 7 Sikh would be honoured by you as well. You also convey to him the enormous volume of arms you are seeking to unload. Over a cup of coffee and a set dosa at Kovil restaurant in Connaught Place you have sung an exquisite melody to him, a 15 per cent discount over the prevailing market rates. The Stingers, you feel, have clinched the deal.

The LTTE's mode of payment, however, will not be cash. This much you have known before you initiated contact. It will be a barter with heroin. The Tamil troupe will be delivering you a tonne of heroin. You know where that will come from. It will come to you from the Malwa-Mewar region of Madhya Pradesh and Rajasthan which has nearly twenty-five thousand hectares of land engaged in legal cultivation of opium. The districts of Ratlam, Mandsaur and Neemuch in western Madhya Pradesh supply 50 per cent of the world's pharmaceutical demand for morphine. Its yellowish-cream powder is higher in quality than the neon-pink variety that comes out of Pakistan and Afghanistan.

You have nothing against the swap. In the long run it increases your profitability. The heroin you intend to dispose of without too many intermediaries in the lucrative markets of Europe and America.

The way you are going to do it is dissolve the heroin in bottles of solvent. It's going to take one million bottles of solvent to dissolve a tonne of heroin. The solvent will then be vaporised to get back the heroin in temporary laboratories set up for this very purpose and spread over many countries. The way you and your Sicilian contacts – you have sought Dipak Patel's help here, for whose efforts you have set aside 2 per cent of the net profits – have planned the shipments is for the containers to be shipped to Amsterdam from India.

The Dutch, you think, are amongst the most civilised of modern states. While marijuana is outlawed in all EU states it's a commercial crop in Holland worth $200 million and distributed legally through four hundred licensed coffee shops. The Dutch policy of dissuasion rather than prohibition has paid rich dividends in the controlled consumption of soft drugs by its own civilian population. Its laws are also custom made for the goons of the planet. Holland doesn't believe in sending anybody to jail for more than six years. And those who escape are not tailed, on the grounds that 'wanting to regain freedom is a natural tendency in human beings'. As a result drugs in transit through Holland are 'not a priority for the Dutch police'. The forty thousand ships docking in Rotterdam annually offload 7,500 containers every single day. The Dutch have allocated ten customs agents to go through the manifests of all the ships. You have it on mafia authority that, on an average, the agents manage to check just twenty containers a day.

From Holland your containers will move on Transports Internationaux Routier trucks to various ultimate destinations. The Customs Convention on the International Transport of Goods under the cover of TIR is customised for the Cosa Nostra. The EU now saves half a trillion dollars a year just by cutting the time a truck needs to cross its territory, the time and expense of checking cars and baggage at the dozen internal borders. TIR is an essential component of the narcotics movement. It eliminates the necessity of customs examination of road vehicles as well as containers carried on road vehicles at each international border. Containers which have been approved for transport under customs seal are inspected again only at the end of the journey. You observe, cynically, that with the forming of the EU the inner borders have gone down for the thieves united but not for the cops.

Part of your consignment will also move within traps built into the TIR trucks themselves. Traps built into the gas tanks are favourite methods.

Your defrauding of Akramov and cuts from the arms consignment will garner RAW a profit of $40 million. This you are stashing away in many different forms. It has been your procedure to spread your illicit gains around. A significant percentage of your money is going to Austrian banks. The Swiss no longer offer ideal protection for laundered funds. The crown now belongs to Austria, western Europe's number-one laundry state. The Austrian enclave of Oberstdorf has a network of banks where you can open an account by just flashing the colour of your passport.

The bulk of your greenbacks will, however, be deposited in the Commercial Bank of Aruba. Aruba, after gaining independence from the Dutch Antilles in 1986, has blossomed in financial skulduggery. The beauty of the operation is that you are not an account holder in the bank. You *own* the bank. You have bought the fully chartered private international bank with no assets or liabilities, with a Class A licence, bearer shares and a professional management service thrown in for all of US$20,000. The hard part, as is well known in banking circles, is to get the suspect cash into the banking system. Once in, you can wire-transfer millions of dollars anywhere you want, a concept that goes by the name of layering. Soon, after a dozen-odd transactions, the cash is untraceable.

Aruba also gives you the facility of establishing AECs or Aruban Exempt Corporations, which can be controlled through anonymous bearer shares and are exempt from taxation of all kinds. You will form these corporations to deposit money into your own bank and then loan them more of your laundered money. The loan, now legitimate, you will never pay back but use to invest through further dummy corporations wherever your fancy takes you.

The 5 Kumaon dollars, which Colonel Grupov will be disseminating later in the day, you plan to get converted through the *havala* (unofficial) route. Not all of it, but a big chunk. For officers Rodriguez, Kohli, Colonel Sangma and others you have offered a financial consultancy in the Caribbean free of cost. For the soldiers you are opening many chit-fund companies in India where, gradually, their share of the hard work at the border will be made available to them in currency that they will understand.

Things, however, rarely work to plan. Colonel Grupov has come to your den with his own set of ideas. He is also flanked by four plainclothes Russians, from the embassy or otherwise you don't know and don't ask. The various bulges in their suits speak of concealed weapons. Akramov's bewildering crew has come well prepared.

'Shall we take them on, MM?' Major Rodriguez asks you.

You smile. Major Rodriguez has joined you on that very day. He drove non-stop in an army Jonga jeep followed by a

Shaktiman with the remaining portion of the heroin from Kupwara. The 5 Kumaon, you learn, is under orders to proceed to Kargil from the valley to take on the six-hundred-odd Pakistani intruders atop different heights. And the deal with Akramov has come at just the right time for the unit to jettison its extra load and become fighting fit. Majors Rodriguez and Kohli have, of course, to return as fast as possible to begin their height acclimatisation at Drass, which stands at 10,500 feet, before fanning out in the Mushkoh valley to take on the Mossies. You plan on joining the major and his unit soon. You have reasons for covering the war as a journalist. But first you have a few more scores to settle.

'Major, they are giving us just 50 per cent of the money right now. The rest they will release in our numbered accounts abroad tomorrow, after I deliver to them the relevant banking papers. Of course, if you want to give them a 50 per cent discount, we can take them now,' you say. You forget to add that your little background check on Colonel Grupov has disclosed to you his Spetsnaz breeding, the élite Russian force. That is an added complication.

Major Rodriguez smiles back. 'Just nervous,' he says.

The major, you reckon, has reason to be. His own share is coming to a couple of million dollars. In a few days' time he is also going to be fighting a war. You send the major to the office you have set up at the back of the sheds to organise a power point for a currency counting machine and some laser equipment to do random checks for counterfeit notes. Better to keep the major busy than have him come up to you with bizarre whims.

Colonel Grupov's gang is doing a lot of random sampling from the containers. They have brought their test tubes and burners. The purity of your cargo is too high to lend to analysis by snorting. You would need an elephant. It takes Grupov's crew two hours to sort the integrity of your operation. Jumbo seals the containers. He nods his head. And then Grupov drops his bombshell.

'My men will be sleeping here in the shed for the night,' says Colonel Grupov.

You haven't been prepared for this. This uncalled-for eventuality could burn your pocket out of many millions of dollars. There is the possibility of bribing the men but you discount it as too remote to work.

'Of course, Colonel. With pleasure. Anything you say goes,' you say. You can see Jumbo raising his eyebrows. 'But first let us celebrate, Colonel. I have a case of champagne ready just for this moment.' It's imperative that you lead the colonel and his men outside the shed. You lead the colonel and his men to your office where Major Rodriguez does the honours. You can see everybody relaxing. Colonel Grupov has handed you over three trunk-loads of cash. You have started the process of counting the greenbacks.

Elsewhere, you can hear the double siding cranes start up. You'll need something to cover the noise of Jumbo's operation. The container forks are busy switching containers.

You lead your group to the main gate where Major Kohli keeps vigil with a platoon of 5 Kumaon men. You can discount the 7 Sikh only at your own peril. You are huddling with Colonel Grupov.

'Colonel,' you are saying, 'I want your opinion.' You take the INSAS from one of the soldiers. 'This is the new Indian infantry rifle. Could you give us an opinion? The Pakis up in the mountains have the AK. Will the INSAS hold?' You collect ten magazines from the soldiers, two each for the Russians, and lead your group to the edge of the boundary fencing. For the next fifteen minutes, you intend to convert it into a firing range.

Jumbo comes to your shooting party after ten minutes. Fast work, you think. You lead the colonel back to the shed. He is spraying you with his opinion on the INSAS but you have other things on your mind.

'Colonel, do your men have sleeping bags or should I send some over?' you ask.

You are with Major Kohli at Khachar, 20 kilometres as the crow flies from Mughal Sarai, the biggest railway junction in India. Kohli has taken your bait. Your experience in human affairs has taught you that once you have the key to a guy only the price remains to be negotiated. The key to Kohli is his desire to become rich. You have already, unknown to Rodriguez, passed Kohli a sum of $250,000 as advance incentive to help you make off with the Indian nuclear warheads moving on the rails. Kohli is a dog on a leash as far as you are concerned.

The price you offered him is chickenfeed compared to what you stand to make. You could have a bidding war going amongst the Americans, the Pakistanis and the Chinese. You might also consider keeping some of the warheads as mementoes. Part of the reason you are in this, after all, is to test your own motherfucker potential. Apart from earning bonus points from your handlers if you deliver a coup of this magnitude. That will ensure your making the leap from triple agent to legend.

Of course, if RAW got wind of where you are or what you are planning to do, the game would be up.

But you are planning this to be your swan-song. Not only does the size of your retirement kitty hinge on this operation, but you have dreams that your many days of hard work might in due course form a case study in the annals of espionage. Maybe some day a professor at Harvard University will lecture about your work in the subcontinent and you will listen to his words of wisdom sitting in the audience. Of course, there would be an aura of mystery about your real identity which, in more ways than one, was equally confusing for you.

You have roped Karnam into the operation. You trust her. Or hope that in showing this trust you will make her more a part of you than she was. You have prepared the logistics of it with Kohli. Though Karnam doesn't know what the operation is about, she helps you hire Dauphin helicopters from the Oil and Natural Gas Commission. The Dauphin AS 365, with a range of 830 kilometres, maximum speed of 280 kilometres per hour and a carrying capacity of eight people. You are wearing freshly starched Strategic Forces Command uniforms, the newly created unit that has been given the weighty task of guarding the Indian second-strike capability.

You have learnt from Major Kohli that in exercises to check the state of alertness of the company guarding the rail, nuclear arsenal headquarter inspection parties have flown themselves, without notice, in Dauphins to the train.

To exploit this accepted tradition is your main game plan. You plan to fly to your target with six battle-hardened 5 Kumaon veterans including Major Kohli and a captured scientist whose expertise may be called upon. You yourself are dressed in the uniform of a LT Colonel from the SFC.

Of course, you are not taking Karnam to the battlefield. But you have also utilised her services to organise ground transport at Khachar, possibly in Tata Mercedes trucks parked near the expected rendezvous. You have explained to her that it was an Indian government exercise to check the security apparatus in charge of the nuclear arsenal.

And how are you going to ensure the stoppage of the train at Khachar? You might think that elaborate planning would go to managing the Indian railway signalling system. Blinking certain red and green lights at crucial points to fool the engine driver and make him switch tracks, but that would have required a company-level engagement, besides the co-opting of railway personnel. And no way are you planning a commando-type operation on a moving train. It would be suicidal to take on the skills of the NSG, whose job it was to take care of the nukes till the SFC raised its own cadres. You see those riveting engagements only on celluloid. You have trained with the NSG and have made sure that the detachment under Colonel Kothari, the CO of the nuke train, is not one you trained with. Nor for that matter have you bumped into Kothari.

But Major Kohli works under his command now since his deputation to the NSG from 5 Kumaon. He has knowledge of the communication codes that the SFC has formulated – the highly secure communication set-up that is lodged in the central wagon of the nuke train. He has the authority to access the set-up through the SFC's temporary offices at Manesar, which also headquarters the NSG. And he has accessed the network for you.

You know for instance that Khachar is one of only three places that the SFC uses to rotate its staff on the train. They avoid the big stations for they want to keep their movements under wraps. And their staff is flown in on Dauphins from the SFC's support base at Lucknow.

Like all things Indian, the Ministry of Defence has left scope for confusion. While the SFC's writ runs in the central communication wagon housed in the middle of the nuke train and in the wagons that hold the Agni missiles, elsewhere on the train the NSG rules.

You learn through Major Kohli that there has already been huge friction between the staff of the two agencies over the rotation policy of the staff on the train. While the SFC rotates its communication experts and the missile maintenance personnel by choppers once a week at Khachar, the NSG sharpshooters and officers have to lug it by road to Bamrauli station, near Allahabad where the Central Air Command is based. There they relieve their staffers once in ten days. Ten days on rail can be quite a desultory and perhaps a shaking experience, even for special forces.

There is also the question of the daily hardship allowance. The SFC has sanctioned Rs 500 per diem for its non-commissioned staff for the time they spent shitting on railway tracks, while the NSG had budgeted a measly Rs 100 per diem. Such five-star treatment of the SFC had given the NSG gunslingers cause for bellyaching.

Though Major Kohli's chumming up with you had little to do with this disparity in allowance structure, it opened up avenues for information to be gathered through disaffected personnel. You learnt of passwords, missile drills and other such titbits of information. But you are still unhappy with your planning. Then a piece of luck heads your way.

You learn that a missile crane on one of the wagons has malfunctioned and damaged the fins of a pair of missiles. Needless to say, this provides you a window of opportunity for a rather ingenious intervention. The warheads have already been separated from the missiles by the maintenance crew on the train, and while the missiles themselves will be unloaded at Khachar into waiting army trucks – amongst which your civilian trucks will wait too, courtesy of Karnam – the warheads are going to be flown by helicopter to the SFC headquarters at Manesar.

Flying in warheads for repairs on choppers is a rather unusual and dangerous procedure, but you assume that the border skirmish at Kargil has something to do with the haste.

Your trucks waiting at Khachar are also carrying three platoons of the 5 Kumaon, your contingency plan in case the SFC decides to abandon the chopper option and relies on wheels on the road to see the warheads through to DRDO labs. That will shift the theatre of war to the Grand Trunk Road or National Highway 24 and necessarily force you to engage in a firefight with the NSG, a scenario you don't relish. While you rate the skills of 5 Kumaon high, the NSG are a pain in the ass. You might have given yourself some healthy odds, seeing that the element of surprise was on your side, but you realise that you lacked leadership. Keeping Major Rodriguez out of the picture has meant avoiding any risk with other officers of the errant Indian unit. If your sonar hit an officer at a deep end it would alert Rodriguez.

Even Major Kohli won't be on the road. He's going to relieve Colonel Kothari's second in command and stay on at the nuke train, just long enough to give your Dauphin enough flying time to reach Delhi. Then, before the shit hits the ceiling, Kohli will slip off the train and go AWOL. You have provided him with the necessary papers to slip into Europe where you will take care of him in peace. Part of your plan is to break up the bastard team of Rodriguez and Kohli. Together they are a nuisance that you can do without.

Your plan is simple. Almost too simple. You will be impersonating the SFC crew that is supposed to get the war-heads back to base. A simple matter of loading the cones into lead containers and flying them back to Delhi. This time you won't be returning to the Manesar helipad but will detour to the Safdarjung airport in New Delhi where your army of helpers are waiting to protect and escort you to your muni-tions warehouse. Jumbo is oiling the logistics at this end.

At Manesar, Kohli and his gang of mercenaries have taken out the SFC missile crew – four scientists from the Bhaba Atomic Research Centre at Mumbai and two from the Defence Research Development Organisation. All six are on deputation to the SFC. The substitution involved a complex manoeuvre. It was facilitated by the fact that the SFC still hasn't managed to raise a captive fleet of choppers for its use. Although the helicopters have been sanctioned by the Ministry of Defence, Bell and Dauphin haven't delivered the initial lot of ten.

The SFC therefore has had to make do with hiring the spare capacity of the ONGC fleet and, of course, occasional SOS calls to the army and air force. The SFC's favoured heli-copter because of its night-vision capability and reliability is, of course, the Dauphin. Which is where Major Kohli tells you to pitch in. It was your job, through your contacts and Karnam to hire, for miscellaneous purposes, all the available Dauphins in the ONGC fleet for a whole week. There are four of them. You used the good services of an aviation correspondent at *The Times of India*. You paid money in advance through one of Jumbo's front companies.

You have gone through all this labour and paperwork so as to replace the ONGC pilots with your own. You have flown in four pilots from Mauritius. They aren't participating in the ruse, but think they are making good money for a week's work. It would have been dangerous for you to have hired pilots from Europe. White skin for such an operation would be a risky proposition. You have made the jobs of the pilots easier by supplying them with an abundance of navigation data.

The original ONGC pilots you have kept captive at a secret location in south Delhi along with five of the scientists. Jumbo is moving them around in safe houses. They will be released two days after your operation.

The initial stages have gone off without a hitch. The SFC, as expected, send in an SOS to the ONGC requisitioning two Dauphins. The ONGC, in panic, as expected, call Jumbo's front company to cancel leasing arrangements for two of the four choppers. Of course, since the helicopters are in your possession by then their pilots have already been safely relieved of their duties. Your crew are in place. At Manesar, Major Kohli performs another sleight of hand. He has an NSG supply truck full of coal tar break an axle and veer into the helipad at full tilt. A stunt of high magnitude, it forces the SFC scientists to catch the choppers at Palam airport. It is while they are on their way to Palam that Jumbo hijacks them.

One scientist you are flying in your party for any nuclear emergency that might develop. You foresee none, but you don't plan to get a dose of lethal radiation either. The scientist has been blindfolded and then had cakes of soap strapped to his thigh, which he has been told are plastic explosives. He's sweating and pleading with you. You calm him down periodically.

Colonel Kothari and his men have been expecting you. With Major Kohli in your flying party you feel your bona fides will be apparent to Kothari. You are a little worried about the rest of your six-man crew passing themselves off as scientists, but they are in SFC uniforms with fake IDs and you will do your best to keep them in the background hum. They have borrowed their outfits from the abducted scientists so they look genuine, at least. That's how you convince yourself. For you to have roped in actual nuclear personnel would have been even riskier.

Besides, you have travelled here in two choppers. It's late evening and by the time the dust settles and the rotors stop their racket, night has set in and you feel more confident. More significantly, perhaps, the clinching point in your favour, are the sonic booms coming your way from a pair of Mirage 2000s flying overhead. The slick flying machines are there to escort your choppers back unscathed to New Delhi.

You are walking the whole length of the train. Your main purpose has been to attach sensitive transmitters to the train wagons. A purpose that even Major Kohli doesn't know about. These are third-generation pulse transmitters that have a battery life of five years. Rust coloured and the size of pencil erasers, they attach themselves magnetically to targets. You are flashing your torch ahead of you. And as you cross three wagons that you know house the Agnis you stoop, as if your boots are bothering you, and stick your gear in the undercarriage.

Of the six personnel accompanying you, three you have instructed to walk on ahead and full beam their torch-lights. You want light in the eyes of the NSG personnel watching you walk up to the communications wagon. Your twin Dauphins too are lighting up the area with their landing lights. Behind you, towards the tail of the train, NSG personnel are walking Alsatians. Major Kohli has omitted to tell you about the dogs. But, you figure, dogs or no dogs, the satellites will take over and programme the transmitters.

Colonel Kothari meets you at the steps of the communication wagon. He cracks a smile at you. Your eyes crinkle. You nod. Major Kohli does the introductions.

'We have a situation here,' Colonel Kothari gesticulates.

'What?' you ask. Your neck muscles tense.

'The Rajdhani to Calcutta is speeding up on this track. We can't stop long,' he says.

'I am told it will just take ten to fifteen minutes,' you say.

'We haven't done it before so we don't know. But are your boys all prepared?' asks Colonel Kothari. He sizes up your contingent.

You feel the cold metal tucked away in the small of your back. Your six-man crew too is all loaded and primed.

'Raring to go,' you say.

'How come you got a deputation to the SFC, colonel?' asks Colonel Kothari.

'The 2nd Rajput Rifles didn't like my face,' you joke. 'Besides, I wanted a posting to New Delhi. Also, I have a degree in nuclear physics. They figured it could come in handy, though I can't see how,' you say.

'Major, why don't you lead the men to Wagon Two? That's where the action is. I will show the colonel around,' says Colonel Kothari.

While you are happy that Kohli's taken your six goons out of the way before Kothari's antennae started crackling with suspicion, it makes you nervous to see your party split up.

'Come let me show you our communication set-up,' offers Colonel Kothari.

'Shouldn't we oversee Wagon Two?' you suggest. You want to keep your army together.

'Don't worry, Colonel. The guys are lining up the Caterpillar we have on Wagon Three. It will take the cranes some time to load the Caterpillar with the missiles. The trucks are a hundred yards away. We will join them once the cartage starts,' says Colonel Kothari. 'The warheads are more important. We will oversee that personally.'

You can't see how you could suggest having problems with that. What's worrying you is that your troops have moved out of line of sight. Also, four NSG personnel have come in behind you. Presumably, you think, Colonel Kothari's personal ensemble.

'You see that dish going up there? That can send a signal to Andromeda and back . . .' boasts Colonel Kothari.

'What?' you ask. The jets drown out the colonel.

'Retractable housing. Israeli technology. We can track our babies right to the point of impact,' educates Colonel Kothari, his hands moving like rotor blades till he smashes his right fist into his left palm.

'Deadly stuff,' you agree.

The two of you enter the communications wagon. Cool air surrounds you. You have people sitting around computer screens with earphones. There's also the crackle of walkie-talkies.

'A bit like ATC,' you comment drily. Colonel Kothari looks blankly at you. You feel you have to expand on the initials. 'Air Traffic Control.'

'Yes,' nods Colonel Kothari. 'Come, let me show you the command centre.' Kothari punches codes on the door and then puts his five fingers on a fingerprint scanner. The door whirrs and opens. The SFC, you summarise, has organised a five-star nuke train for itself.

As you follow the colonel the door shuts on you. You baulk. Colonel Kothari comes out. 'No weapons allowed inside,' says he. 'The door has an in-built metal detector.'

'Oh,' you say. You would rather not go inside than part with your Beretta. But SFC sidekicks on the train join you and you have little option but to deposit your weapon. You feel naked as you enter the room.

You realise a little too late that you have committed a blunder.

A chair swivels and you see the visage of Colonel Ray Chowdhary, your RAW handler, rise to greet you.

'Hello, MM. Fancy seeing you here,' he says. There is no mirth in his eyes. You realise the immense complications you have inserted yourself into. You feel the barrels of two guns, one an MP5, poked against your ribs.

'The surprise is all mine. I didn't know they had recruited you as well for the STO,' you say. You even manage a grin. You're busy figuring the mole in your pack. To give yourself a chance in what you now know will happen, this piece of information is vital.

'You see, MM, you aren't the only smart guy around. And this isn't a Standard Training Operation,' explains Colonel Ray Chowdhary.

Colonel Kothari is eyeing you like a viper.

'Good acting, Colonel,' you compliment Kothari. 'What's next, Ray? I can explain. Things may not be what you think.'

'Depends on what you think I am thinking, MM,' responds the colonel. 'Right now you may be interested in seeing a little closed-circuit television.'

Colonel Kothari flicks a switch on and the television lights up. You know what's coming next. You see images of your six men lined up against Wagon Two. Hands on their heads, knees on the gravel, searchlights on their faces. For a moment you begin to curse Major Kohli, but he too comes into the frame with three gun barrels pointing at his head. Two dogs are chasing your pilots out of the Dauphins. Even though you are sinking in shit you can't help but smile at the plight that faces your Mauritian pilots.

'Ray, you are playing beyond your league. Cool down. This is coming straight from the office of the National Security Adviser,' you say lamely. Anything to gain time while you think.

Colonel Ray Chowdhary ignores you.

'I am disappointed I ever let you in the game. The question is, whose game are you playing, MM? This is as serious as it gets,' he says.

'Ray, be a hero for a while. Tomorrow your ass is mine. I am going to blow the shenanigans of RAW sky-high,' you say.

'Let me take the smirk off your face, you piece of shit. You don't know what's headed your way,' says Colonel Ray Chowdhary. 'Officer, could you enter now, please?' he roars into the intercom.

The colonels are in the mood for a party in the command centre, you figure. You hear new steps coming in through the door.

'MM, I figure this officer might be after your own heart,' says the colonel. 'Meet Captain Rekha Satpathy, Military Intelligence. You may stand at ease, captain.'

Your head turns and you go numb. Whatever it was you thought had given you away, this was one thing that you never doubted. But then you think of when you flipped through Digs's family album in his sitting room. Which contained no snaps of Karnam as a child – Karnam, who didn't resemble Digs's wife at all. The flaw in memorabilia that should have tipped you off.

You are trembling. Emotions are running through you. Your voice has deserted you. You know that after this you may not have a ticket out.

'I loved you,' you say.

'I love my country,' says Karnam.

She doesn't look at you, though. Elsewhere you can catch faint noises of a firefight. That would be the NSG mopping up your 5 Kumaon brothers waiting in the Tata Mercedes trucks.

'Well, Ray, since you seem to be flashing all the cards, you might educate me as to what's happening next,' you say.

'Captain here has been our double ace, MM. You have been forgetting your training,' explains the colonel.

You ignore him. You turn to Karnam. Your confidence is coming back. 'What about the Syrian?' you ask.

'That was for real,' says Karnam. 'I joined the forces soon after.'

'Well, baby, that was good work,' you say. 'I hope you maintain the swastika in my memory.'

Karnam blushes.

311

Your body is suspended in a tank of slowly flowing water. Your head remains above, enclosed in a black mask. You can hear the monotonous rhythm of your breathing and sometimes the imperceptible sound of water gurgling in the pipes. You know the routine, and your only slim advantage lies in the fact that your interrogators may think you are unfamiliar with contemporary regression techniques.

They are depriving you of sensory stimuli and feeding in you a hunger for more. Isolation serves as a powerful stress factor for the mind and, deprived of its usual diet from the senses, it soon starts projecting its fears and memories outward. This is the theory at any rate. The final aim is, of course, to induce regression of your personality to a level that dissolves your resistance, breaks down the many interrogation roadblocks you are creating and ultimately snaps your mental autonomy.

You are being interrogated by officials from Military Intelligence, though occasionally Colonel Ray Chowdhary from RAW makes an appearance. The authorities have slapped the National Security Act on you and even though your case would go to the CBI eventually, right now you are being given a combing-over in the premises that house the offices of the Directorate General of Military Operations. They have a basement set aside for cases like yours. You can sense their fight against time. A war with the Mossies is on and the Indian nuclear arsenal has nearly been compromised. Besides, there is the matter of the two deviant army units. There might also be other unknown threats. They want to crack you as quickly as possible to avoid future surprises. To know whom you really work for. They also want to keep you quiet.

What would also be important for RAW and gang would be to ensure that you don't damage them inordinately. For if you started speaking the truth it would cause upheavals in the intelligence set-up of the nation.

You know you cannot last indefinitely. Nobody can. But you will stretch the game as long as you can till you buckle. In the first few hours you have already gone through the detention rigmarole. Your clothes were taken away and you were given prison garb. You know the psychological imperatives working behind those moves. The circumstances of detention are supposed to amplify your feelings of isolation. You have not been given a belt and your pants are four sizes too large.

You know what is coming next. Even as the drug flows through your veins you know from the initial creep in your arms that you have just been injected with BZ, or quinuclidnyl benzilate. An LSD variant, its psychotic properties are more potent after an immersion in a sensory deprivation chamber. You know monsters are soon going to fly in your brain. The BZ is a brain bomb. Though you don't have immunity, you have built up considerable resistance against the drug.

A large part of your training has been devoted to weathering coercive interrogation methods, specially chemical. That, in fact, has been your speciality. You have been injected with mind-boggling toxic substances to evolve your chemical safeguards. The mind, you have been told in training, is above the body. This much you knew. But they took you a step further.

They put you through an extended course in audio-visual desensitisation. They gunned you with disturbing images till you became tired of them and your distress meter flickered at zero levels. Then they graduated you to more extreme images and repeated the process again till your anxiety levels hit a new low. They started you off with films of heart surgery and then graduated to amputation before

313

progressing further to show videos of people accidentally cutting limbs and severing toes and capping it still further with films of torture. To make you overcome your initial nauseated responses they clamped a device on your eyes to prevent blinking.

It was thought that the desensitisation would work to your advantage when psychotic drugs started playing havoc with your mind.

You did, in fact, benefit enormously. You passed a test run with Haldol at a high dosage. This was a drug that nearly killed you with hypothermia when you took a low hit before your desensitisation drill. Haldol, of course, first gained notoriety in Vietnam where it was administered to unsuspecting troops as a cure for shellshock.

But BZ otherwise is a big bastard. In your course a team mate was found pissing his pants and taking a shower in his uniform. These effects were considered mild.

They haul you to the interrogation chamber while you are still combating BZ. This you see as a big flaw in their routine. The interrogation drill should follow the SDC directly. The calculated provision of stimuli during interrogation makes the subject view the interrogator as a father figure and strengthens feelings of compliance. But with the BZ in your bloodstream you have a licence to act like a psychopath.

You stand up from your chair. Your pants fall to your ankles. You make no effort to pull them up. You start urinating in front of your interrogators. This is a high-degree provocation from your side. You intend to extract a violent response. One of your other specialities is to be able to bear intense pain for long periods of time. Your strategy is to break up the interrogation assault into two modes, chemical and physical. That way, because of the time constraints faced by your interrogators, neither mode will gain enough momentum to make you talk.

But the physical response doesn't come your way. Your two interrogators react as if pissing is quite normal on your part. You are not rattled by this response, but impressed.

Your interrogators have been successful in disrupting your sense of time. There has been no light in your room and the sound-proofing has been uncanny. Your meals and sleep periods have been highly irregular and you can't tell with certainty how many hours or days have elapsed since the BZ first flowed in your veins.

The questions are coming at you through a haze.

'How did you come to know about the rail deployment?' asks the interrogator to your left. Though he is in uniform he's sitting in a shadow so you can't make out his stripes. The other is in civvies. His armpits are damp with perspiration. Both bastards, you notice, have come in without wristwatches. Part of the plotting to give you permanent jet lag.

'There was an advertisement in *The Times of India*,' you say.

'Who were your partners in this project apart from Major Rodriguez and Major Kohli from 5 Kumaon?' asks your uniformed friend.

'There was ADC Bhatnagar from the office of the army chief. There was the PA to the defence minister. There was Colonel Antony Howard, defence attaché at the American embassy,' you say. You want to delay the next round of chemical intervention as long as possible. Even though your interrogators are eyeing you with maximum scepticism you have to keep the routine up. You have to think up new and complex admissions that will take them longer to disprove and discredit. You are exploiting one of the fatal flaws in counter-intelligence interrogations – because your sessions are being conducted for the purpose of information and not for prosecuting reasons, as long as you talk you will be less vulnerable to your second bout with chemicals.

'Could you describe Colonel Howard to us?' asks the guy in civvies.

'Tall guy. Black hair. Wears his uniform. Age forty-plus. He's got a herpes situation,' you say. 'Can I get a smoke?'

You are trying to figure out their routine. You aren't quite sure which one of the interrogators is planning to play the good cop. Or maybe the situation is so fluid they'll decide along the way. They ignore your request.

'Have you any friends in 7 Sikh?' asks the guy in civvies.

'You aren't believing me, are you? I mean, I was told there was a mock exercise on the rail arsenal and I could come along as a journalist. I didn't have any hand in planning or anything,' you say.

'How long do you know Major Rodriguez?' asks your uniformed questioner.

'How long would you have me know him?' you say. 'I really do need a smoke.'

'What's your height?' asks the guy in civvies.

'You want to stitch me a coat?' you say.

'How many times have you been to Europe?' asks your uniformed interrogator.

'Did you have sex with Karnam?' asks the guy in civvies before you can answer the last question.

'How many bank accounts do you have?' asks the guy in uniform.

You are now wising up to the tactics. The Alice in Wonderland routine, part of the CIA manual. A confusion-inducing technique, its motive is to confound your conditioned responses. The questions, you notice, are following illogical patterns, and pitch and tone are unrelated to the importance of the questions themselves.

Your interrogators are soon replaced by two others. A fucking relay they're throwing at you. They are systematically thwarting your attempts to establish a rapport. You are a little unfamiliar with this babble procedure and the logic behind it. But they soon move you to familiar territory.

You have been patched up with electrodes on your chest. You are getting an intra-muscular shot of something. You don't yet know what it is. Then when the ants start climbing up your spine you get your first clue. Prolixin. The beauty of this drug lies in the fact that your nerves don't remain your own. It grinds in your sinews and synapses till you ache with a disquietude that you don't want to downgrade by calling it an advanced form of restlessness. You get up and pace your cell, which is a ten-by-ten proposition where you can't see your own hands. You think your vision is blurring but you can't really be sure as there's no light to check on the fact. After ten paces you think you are increasing your pain by pacing so you sit on the floor, but then you think you are better off walking. So you get up again and this goes on in swift cycles. You are finding it difficult to locate the source of your pain. It's everywhere and nowhere in particular. You can hear yourself hitting the walls.

And then they come in again and lead you to a different room where they poke something into you again. Your restlessness subsides a bit. You think they have given you a tranquilliser, maybe Sinequan, to calm you down, but you soon change your opinion. And in spite of a tranquilliser coursing through your system, you are beginning to panic. The muscles of your fingertips are dying. You feel the special panic that comes when you start losing control over your eyes. You recognise the early warning system of the drug Anectine, a variant of the drug tubocurarine, which raids your respiratory system within two minutes of being injected. You feel the dosage is still symbolic, since you are still breathing. But they have been smart enough to place a lung machine alongside where they have strapped you and even though your vision is not normal it's good enough for you to identify it.

Anectine, you know, specialises in providing a sensation worse than dying. In minute quantities it can run as a muscle relaxant, but in high doses it collapses your respiratory set-up by arresting your intercostal muscles and diaphragm. Your heart rate nosedives to fifty beats a minute and your lungs could collapse in two to four minutes. In terms of sheer torture you rate the drug at the top of the horror list.

You have never been apportioned a combination of Pro-lixin and Anectine. But as the chemicals attack from deep inside you, and before your ability to concentrate is decimated, you realise the complementary nature of the drugs. Prolixin is panicking you like never before and Anectine, because of the way it has relaxed your muscle groups, is denying you the mechanism to provide an outlet for your panic. You are in semi-paralysis and the flood waters are rising. You don't think you can hold out to a full dose of Anectine if and when it eventually comes. You are in uncharted waters. Your training has never thrust you to such an edge of chemical endurance.

Some small feelings of guilt are beginning to rise in you. The people you work for had trusted the potential you once showed and now you are feeling yourself to be a big let-down in their hour of dire need. Your capture couldn't have come at a worse moment. You don't have much to give by way of spoils if you crack, for Jumbo will have taken the expected precautions. He will have moved the money around and hidden other critical trails.

But you are the spearhead. The anointed leader of the Alk-ifa. You have a lot to give if the Indians know what to look for. For you the victory is in not lending them the key to what you really are. What they think you are is none of your concern.

Even as you begin to slip into unconsciousness and see them monitoring your vital signs, you feel a big rumble and then a roar. You are thrown from the stretcher that holds you on to the floor. You are already hoping against hope. And as you fade out there's a smile on your face.

Your real name is Arbaz Khan. You are the new face of Jihad. For you Islam without Jihad doesn't exist and the best of all Jihads is the word of truth in the presence of the unjust ruler. In the emancipation of the oppressed people of Kashmir lies your own deliverance. The Hindu *kafirs* have to go or die. Such is Allah's will and so you have been taught.

For you, it's been a long journey and it began just after you left Academy and your father Colonel Om Mehta was given a voluntary discharge from the Indian army for health reasons. As your family adjusted to civilian life after the orderliness of a cantonment, the two of you spent many days alone together. You sensed a preparation for something. One fine day, the waiting ended. He took you for a drive to the tomb of Nizamuddin Chisthi.

You were perplexed. The destination wasn't unusual, though. You had done this sort of thing with your father in more places and times than could have come about purely from secular dictates. In the past you had put it down to his Sufi mindset. As a child you had been taken innumerable times to the shrine at Ajmer Shariff. You love the place. And you paid regular visits to the Baba Haider Sheikh shrine at Maler Kotla in the Punjab.

In the early years these things inculcated in you a tolerance for all things religious. Later, of course, to your father's chagrin you devoted yourself to the pursuit of pleasure. Even in those days, as now, the Muslim call to prayers, the *azan*, struck a chord in you that you were never able to explain rationally. It always calmed you.

Later, the drugs took over. But that day there was something in his eyes that warned you that whatever was coming was going to leave an indelible imprint upon your life. He held your hand and with his eyes far away he made you familiar with your roots.

He started with a bang. He told you in so many words that he wasn't your biological father. Even as you mulled over this piece of news he spun a story so astounding that you immediately sensed it was too tangled for imagination to have played a part in its origin.

He told you that you were a child marked for the Alkifa or struggle. That you were the first-born of parents who had the courage and the spirit of sacrifice to bequeath you to Jihad. He himself didn't know who they were, for you came bundled in the laps of a courier couple who flew in one night in December on Pakistan International Airlines and left you in the custody of your father. They left a week later. You were then a month old.

You learned that the man you knew as your father came to India at the age of seventeen in 1965. He enrolled at Allahabad University. Of course, new papers were provided and a Hindu identity assiduously built. Your father was one of an élite. One of an exclusive band of sixteen who came to India with the single-minded purpose of infiltrating key areas of functioning of the Indian government.

You ask anxiously about your mother. You want to know whether she too was a part of this cold-war subterfuge. You remember even at that moment hoping she was Indian, a Hindu. That would provide some reason to veto the existence that you could see coiling towards you. But you had no such luck. She was very much part and parcel of the operation. Smuggled into India in 1970, she was a bride carefully designated and assigned for your father. You were adopted only because early on your father suffered from impotence.

Your father, you learn, kept his part of the promise in the 1987 Indian army battlefield exercise Operation Brass Tack. Held under General Sunderji's command, the salient features of the armour show were documented in detail by your father. Apart from alerting Pakistan in case the exercise suddenly developed into an armoured thrust into Sindh, your father was able, later, to pinpoint the weak points of the Indian effort and relay to the ISI chief such engagement minutiae as the sand attrition effects on the tracks of the T-72.

That was the apex of his career. At the point of his retirement he realised he could travel no further in the army hierarchy and was advised not to compromise himself for fear of endangering the future that you, MM, might harvest for Pakistan. Your family moments suddenly began to fall into place. How happy your father was when you joined the Academy and how aghast he was – something you didn't understand then – when you left.

That night you couldn't sleep. Or, for that matter, many nights after that. Initially, you sought in your mother something that would oppose the perplexities your father had just introduced into your life. But in her eyes was all the confirmation you would ever need. You wanted desperately an ally to strengthen your initial, mutinous desire to sever ties with a past you had had no hand in shaping. But to deny a future for their lifetime of work would be to reject them. Out of guilt grew a sense of duty. Theirs wasn't a story of three decades of deceit. It was instead a cocktail of duty, sacrifice and competence. Above all, you simply loved your old man. After the rebellion of your teens it wasn't in you to refuse him anything.

Your father hadn't met or seen his family since he'd come to India. For pragmatic purposes his death was staged in a 1965 fire in Islamabad's Gulshan enclave. Your mother was an orphan. Over the years she tried her best to invent a Hindu motherhood for herself. You are reminded once again of the small routines that your family never had but which you observed in full flow in neighbours. Daily rituals for the gods were, of course, absent in your house. The deities were there in a symbolic concession to popular perception but they often lay in layers of dust. You have on numerous occasions felt the absence of aunts and uncles. Of the band of sixteen that came to India in 1965, your father knew just one.

Of course, you knew who that was before your father had to unravel the mystery. He was the head of the only extended family you ever had. Jumbo's father went on to join the Indian Railway Service. You might ask what good that would do for the Pakistan establishment. But he systematically rose, plotted and gained for himself a position in Military Rail, the exclusive All India cell that co-ordinates all military traffic in India. He sat in the chair that the military approaches for requisition of wagons and locomotives to move their battalions. At any given point he had with him the location of India's strike formations.

It comforted you to know that Jumbo too was in the same boat. You had an ally to share your trials and tribulations.

But you didn't train together. For you they arranged a fellowship in the UK. From there you flew on a Singapore passport to Pakistan. You stayed there a year before going back to England and then you returned to the land you knew first but which now you had to plot against. You have returned subsequently for more bouts of training. Your inventory of motherfucker skills has grown by leaps and bounds. Specially after your biggest coup, the infiltration of RAW that you achieved in the early 1990s. There your annexure of talents grew and you are one of the rare breed who have been schooled by two intelligence agencies.

Now, of course, you stand exposed. The whole breach is not yet visible but there will be questions. And with questions come suspicions.

As you are making your way to Kargil you are going with the full knowledge that the final chapter of your life is possibly unfolding. With Karnam you might have had a reason to begin anew. But your antennae had short-circuited there. You still believe that she really felt for you, but you don't know for sure now. You can only laugh at your own indiscretion. The one saving grace is that your confidences never crossed the line where all would have been irrevocable.

In Kargil you intend to bow out with a bang. You have not come with suicidal focus, but as a professional you understand the inherent risks. The task you have been assigned is to recover something of what was soon turning out to be another embarrassment for your brothers from across the border.

Though you had intended to be in the war zone from the start under the pretext of covering the war, now, with the devaluation of your status, you have to sneak in as a civilian truck driver carrying relief material for the civilian population of Kargil. Jumbo is your cleaner. You are a month late, thanks to your nuclear expedition – which wasn't totally unsuccessful, since the direction finders you installed on two of the wagons are transmitting loud and clear – and to your brief capture and subsequent recovery period.

It had been a simple operation to flush you out. The surprise was all on Jumbo's side. Your handlers in Islamabad had assigned four personnel to Jumbo for the purpose. You were too valuable to spend more time than necessary under the MI's scalpel.

They parked a civilian vehicle right next to the DGMO building and before the flimsy security could come and raise a few questions the two hundred kilos of Semtex it held had blown half the annexe away. Of course, you weren't in the annexe. In the resultant confusion they extricated you from the basement without any opposition. Before departing they blew up the basement as well, so for a time, at least, the Indians wouldn't know whether you were alive or dead. That gave you some space for a breather and time for a detoxification course.

You used it to catch up on events. Your manipulated issue of *The Post* taking on Defence Minister Yadav, General

Rampal, the air force and 7 Sikh amongst others had been a sell-out the day it hit the stands. Jain the motherfucker, whose by-line you plastered on big chunks of copy, has disappeared. There has been much talk about the wheel questionnaire. And Digs, you learn with great amusement, had a mild stroke the day he saw it. He has since then been under strict observation at the Escort Heart Institute's ICU ward. Your three defence correspondent friends had previewed *The Post*'s story as front-page leads. Innumerable follow-ups have ensued and television chat shows have devoted entire evenings to Digs's scoop.

With war at full tilt, criticism of the forces was muted. Right now patriotism swayed more in the media. Calls for heads to roll, specially those of Defence Minister Suresh Yadav and the army chief General Subhas Rampal, have begun in a small way but will pick up after the war reaches some sort of conclusion and the monsoon session of parliament begins. But again, if the Indians win all will be forgotten. The characters at the top might make the leap from the dung-heap to the list of heroes. Expectedly, General Subhas Rampal has given a clean chit to the 7 Sikh, his parent unit, now attached to the Drass brigade.

Interestingly, however, there has been no mention in the media of the attempted nuke train heist. Though news has leaked about your arrest it has to do with a red herring: the wheel questionnaire. After your escape from the DGMO HQ, you have been declared dead in the bomb explosion. At first you credited the genuine confusion and the profusion of unidentifiable bodies. Now you know they want you dead. Their blunder in declaring you dead has hindered their search for you on a war footing. What reason could you possibly give to flash a dead man's snap on television with rewards leading to his capture?

For a while you tinkered with the idea of an under-cover press conference with a select few to embarrass the Indian army, but that wouldn't contribute to your overall scheme.

Instead it could provide them clues to your whereabouts. It has taken you many weeks to recover from their chemical barrage. Jumbo has nursed you back with great care and concern. The whole of June you have been bedridden and building up your strength for the final lap.

You think about Karnam as little as possible. You are still baffled by Digs's co-operation with RAW, planting her on you. Fucking Ray Chowdhary, you think. You have under-estimated the bastard.

There have been reasons, though, to feel pleased with yourself. You are sitting on $80 million in your bank account in Europe, the bulk of which you will soon pass on to Pakistan's ISI. Sixty per cent of that money having come from Akramov. The rest from the heroin that the LTTE headed your way as payment for the arms and armament you channelled into Jaffna via Vedaranyam in Tamil Nadu. Jumbo oversaw the logistics of that while you recuperated. You are pleased that you have all but wiped Akramov out of business. You hear that he has taken out a contract for you. A worry for another day – if you survive what you have set out to do in Kargil.

If Shomali were around you wouldn't think twice before splitting, but if Shomali were around you perhaps wouldn't be what you are. Maybe if Karnam hadn't been what she turned out to be, you may have considered absconding, but you hope your sense of pride in what you do is too over-whelming to be overridden by romantic considerations.

What you know is that if you survive July you can take Jihad to new heights.

But June has seen many reverses for Pakistan.

Tololing Ridge fell on 12 June. Peak 5100 fell on 28 June and 4700 fell a day later. Now Tiger Hill alone remains and Point 4875 which rose from Mushkoh. There was hope as long as Tiger Hill remained. It was possible then to rally troops and go for a fresh offensive. Your job in two days is to see that Tiger Hill remains in the hands of the Jihad.

The Iridium satellite phone that you and Jumbo carry can provide you with GPS data. Your immediate task is to get a fix on all the artillery positions on the Indian side, especially the Bofors batteries. The Indian success at Tololing had to do with the direct firing from the Bofors guns, something which artillery manuals don't teach you. You want to nullify that advantage when the Indian troops push for Tiger Hill.

In the gunnysacks of relief material that you are ostensibly carrying for the civilian population of Drass and Kargil you have considerable quantities of explosives. You have come prepared for all eventualities. Opportunities, rather. Of the many acts of sabotage you could enact, blowing up a bridge or two on the Drass–Kargil highway is high on your list of priorities. Of course, though the Drass ammunition dump had been taken out by your brothers just a few days into battle you plan to get a fix on the new location. All this in addition to your general brief of placing IEDs at strategic checkpoints and unit camps.

Jumbo has already pulled off a coup. At Sonmarg, the first stop on the Srinagar–Drass–Kargil–Leh highway and a halt for the civilian truck convoys, Jumbo pushed IEDs wrapped in special polythene and timed to explode after forty-eight hours into the gas tanks of fifteen-odd trucks. The trucks will soon spread out on the highway. Who knows where they will be in forty-eight hours? But they would necessarily block out huge stretches of narrow mountainous road.

Once you reach Kargil, you plan to switch to a Maruti Gypsy complete with army uniform and rank. You have one waiting there for you in army green with identity marks of the 15th Corps, which is headquartered at Batwara Gate in Srinagar. Though the local population at Kargil is Shia, their sympathies are with their Sunni brothers in this conflict with the Hindu *kafirs*, and it wasn't tough to organise the logistics of this conversion in Kargil. Besides, the network has come good in the early days of the war. They had radioed in exact positions of the TV tower at Kargil and the huge ammunition dump at Drass. Both are smouldering remains now.

At Sonmarg they hold up all upgoing traffic till 1 p.m. to make way for the convoys coming down. They don't want the convoys to cross each other on the mountains, since that would slow them down and create pile-ups which Pakistan artillery spotters would be quick to exploit. Particularly in the 12-kilometre stretch between Kharbu and Zero Point beyond Drass where our hills look down on the Indian high-way. Spotters have been told to give the green for shelling at the slightest bit of traffic movement and the treacherous Indus riverbed skirting the highway holds many burnt-out, skeletal remains of Tata trucks.

The way up to Zojilla Pass where the climb bottoms out is muddy because of rain. No matter how many times you cross the Zojilla Pass it never prepares you for the next time. At 10,500 feet it's one of the highest motorable mountain passes in the world. And today your crossing is met by the roar of the Bofors guns. At a hundred yards nothing can prepare you for that as well.

It's a battery of four guns packed at the side of the moun-tains where our shells would find it difficult to loop and zero on unless the exact quadrants are known. It is your job to find out.

A press briefing is in progress. You see Major Purshottam, PRO of the 15th Corps, with a minibus-load of journalists. You don't want to complicate matters at the outset by taking the risk of going yourself. You pull up and spring open the bonnet of your Tata truck. Jumbo goes with a jerry-can to fill up on water from a nearby waterfall. Of course, Jumbo's also got the Iridium under his loose *salwar kameez* to get a fix on the Bofors. You recognise a few of the journalists.

'Let's have some fun,' says Jumbo once he gets back.

You know what he's up to, and you give your smile of approval. You move up five hundred yards and park again, this time behind rocky protection. Jumbo dials the necessary numbers. The quadrants travel to Delhi and then by e-mail to a web-based encryption service which is then reforwarded by fax to Karachi and from there it travels to Skardu, the concerned brigade HQ for the Pakistan Northern Light Infantry. It takes ten minutes for the information to reach Skardu. From there, the artillery units can have their music going in five minutes. You watch the briefing going on through your binoculars. Jumbo is waving the other trucks on.

The likelihood of a direct strike is slim because of the height of the hill that the shells will have to loop over. But they can definitely land fifty yards away and close in the perimeter by a few yards in every round. It's too risky to stay on and correct the fire. And you don't want some jagged lead flying your way.

You wait for the first few rounds to land just so you can watch the scattering of the assembly. You hear the whistles first and then the thuds. If you hear the whistle and hit the ground, they say you are probably safe. Of course, if it's an aerial burst then you have the odds stacked against you.

The first few land after twenty minutes. You are beginning to think your side isn't in the mood when the barrage finally comes. The first shell gets the bus. It explodes in a ball of fire. Some shells fall on army tents. But they perk up the assembly and send the journalists scrambling.

You move off with relish. Your first kill. The war is an adventure for you, though you are hopping on late. You travel at a leisurely pace, stopping off at various places to talk to the troops, finding the location of their units and mapping the quadrants off the artillery guns. At times you are even giving lifts to stranded troops. They prove a valuable source of information. For instance, a 5 Para commando tells you of his Dhatak company which was operating behind the LoC, trying to cut the supply lines leading to Mushkoh valley. They had suffered some losses at Kala Patthar.

Jumbo's dialling up a continuous relay of information. You don't call in the hits. That would be a sure give-away. You are saving up the information for tomorrow, when, your network tells you, the Indians will be making a push for Tiger Hill.

You plan to reel in the strikes then. Hit the guns or whatever can be hit at one go. This will leave the 18 Grenadiers, the unit charged with leading the assault to the top of the 16,000-foot peak, with little artillery support. It would expose your friends at 7 Sikh as well who had been charged with encircling Tiger Hill at the base. The western ridge is still in your hands and the sole supply route to your men at the top. Lack of artillery support for the 7 Sikh will make it difficult for them to assault the western ridge and threaten your supply lines. Tiger Hill, incidentally, is your escape route as well.

The dragnet is closing around you: using the airports would be suicidal. The choices for you are Kathmandu and Dhaka, both of which you have ruled out. Your minders across the border would be sending a detachment of the élite Special Guards to Tiger Hill to assist you in switching sides. That is the plan, anyway.

Of course, for that you need to tune in Major Raunaq Singh who no doubt is nursing his wounds in the combat zone. The 7 Sikh has been sucked into the war along with 5 Kumaon because they happened to be in Kashmir when the shit first hit the ceiling.

You hit Kharbu at eight in the evening. You are the fortieth truck in the queue. All of you are waiting for the convoy from Kargil to cross you. Kharbu to Zero Point is a high-risk area. Trucks drive in the night with their headlights switched off. If the shells don't get you the drop to the Indus will. The river roars and swirls ten to fifty yards below the road.

Between these points the drivers drive with a fear that you can smell from afar. The convoy you are part of leaves in total darkness. Just yesterday three trucks were knocked off,

329

an Indian oil gas tanker taking a direct hit. The tanker burst and then rolled down the slopes into the river and disappeared.

All is silent till you reach the halfway mark and then you hit a road jam. Five trucks ahead a Sumo with a flat is holding up the traffic. Drivers start honking horns. At Kharbu there are stories of truck drivers bulldozing cars and knocking them into the Indus if they block their way in the shelling zone.

Jumbo's nervous. You are too. Not so much for yourself as for your cargo. A stray splinter is enough to blow everybody within fifty yards to kingdom come. You climb down and watch the Sumo driver work his jack. He is feeling his way around the screws. There isn't enough light to work the wheels at normal speed.

And then with the pressure getting on him he does something that nobody thinks he would ever be dumb enough to do. He dives into his dashboard and pulls out a torch. His co-passenger in the front seat holds the beam in place as he attacks the wheel with renewed haste.

The convoy is aghast. You can feel a wave of terror pass from the front to the back.

'Incoming,' says Jumbo.

'We have five minutes,' you say. 'Any chance of calling in a negative?' By the time your message reaches Skardu the shelling will be over. You figure you will have to take it with the rest of them.

'No,' says Jumbo.

He's already in the back of the truck selecting stuff you couldn't afford to have destroyed. The MP5s and Glocks and some special flares. Your pre-decided signature tunes for the Special Guards waiting to flush you out. The Sumo's right on the edge of the kerb and falls short of letting the rest of the traffic go by on the road by a matter of a couple of inches.

In the night you first see the green and yellow trails of light the shells make as they travel across the cold summer evening. The first few hit your side of the mountain fifty yards up. It starts a gravel shower in your direction. You knew the next few rounds would travel down systematically till the gunners figured the right trajectory to land the shells on the road. The Sumo driver is panicking. He hasn't had time to unwind all the screws in his flat tyre. Three are still on. He decides to risk the mountain terrain on his hobbling wheel.

In your truck Jumbo takes the wheel and shifts into gear. You have packed all your gear along with the satellite phone into a waterproof army haversack. If you have to jump off your truck you'd better have all your workings in one bag. You watch the Sumo career off into the first bend. The sonofabitch, you mutter.

The drivers are going berserk now.

'Switch on the lights,' you instruct Jumbo. You don't want the Indus to have you for dinner even if the shells miss you. The chances of a shell hitting you in the zone you calculate as one in a thousand even if you are a dead give-away because of your halogen lamps.

The others follow the logic. Tonight the shells have no luck. Your gunners aren't getting the range right: within ten minutes the quarry has cleared the danger zone.

You hit Kargil three hours behind schedule. On your previous trips you have put up at Hotel Siachen, the designated media spot. But times have changed and you push straight for the plateau, five kilometres from the main town and en route to Leh. There your Gypsy awaits you and you get a briefing from the network. Tomorrow you have a climb ahead of you and you are worried for Jumbo. Neither of you has time to acclimatise and although your body has withstood such abuse in the past, Jumbo already has a headache.

You are up at six in the morning. The coffee brings with it a phone call. Your Iridium shakes and shudders, its vibrator battery in overdrive. Both you and Jumbo freeze. You know it can't be glad tidings. You press Receive with great trepidation.

'Arbaz Khan, your time is up. You Mossie piece of shit.'

You recognise the voice. Major Rodriguez has sourced your number and he knows your name.

'You bastard. Why don't you go to the nearest checkpoint and surrender yourself? It would save all of us a lot of running around,' says Major Rodriguez.

Jumbo is listening in on an improvised headphone.

'Aha, Major,' you begin. 'I am glad . . .'

'Glad my ass. You just listen now and listen hard. Your game's over. You can't come off the hills.'

Major Rodriguez, you observe, is giving you more than he should. He is, for instance, implying that he knows you are in Kargil. Or he thinks you are and wants to confirm.

'Major, whose side are you on anyway? I thought you were content with the money coming your way,' you say.

'MM, you piece of shit. It never was the money and you know that,' says Major Rodriguez.

'Then what was it, Major?' you ask. You want to push him, to get to the bottom of the affair. You want to know the source of the leak.

'MM, you piece of turd. Here, listen to your old man,' says Major Rodriguez.

You stiffen. So does Jumbo. You aren't prepared for this. You hear the scratch of a chair and then the voice of your father.

'Sorry, son,' he says. 'They nearly killed your mother . . .'

You want to ask him more. Find out about your mother. But Rodriguez isn't finished with his games.

'Happy, you Mossie asshole?' he asks. 'Finished with your Allah talk. Now that you know who has your balls, will you do the needful?'

You are too numb to answer immediately. Jumbo's eyes are starting to go wet. You get a hold on yourself. You sense the anger rising in your blood.

'Major, you know what, you've done what you had to do. Now I have to play my part out,' you say.

'*Touché*,' says Major Rodriguez. 'An asshole with a philosophy.'

'Major, if your generals want me so badly why don't you come and get me?' you say. Rodriguez goes silent for a while. You know the idea appeals to him. Perhaps he gets a green from Colonel Ray Chowdhary who would, undoubtedly, be listening in. A motherfuckers' final round.

'Where are you?' asks Major Rodriguez.

'Now, Major, I might be an asshole but I'm not foolish,' you say.

'MM, you bastard, we have this signal traced right to your ass. You can't fart without the 15th Corps waking up,' he says.

'It's about time they did,' you say. You want to make sure Rodriguez comes after you. 'And now you listen, you goddamn toy soldier. You're still a cadet, aren't you? Cadet Rodriguez. You Goan piece of shit. Or should I say Portuguese? You think nobody knows who got Shomali. What was she? Your aunt. All I know is she was the best lay in the whole wide world.'

You hang up after that. You switch off your instrument. When the time comes you'll switch it back on, but today there's a lot to be done. This wasn't the way you had ever imagined you would use Shomali's name. But it was important that Rodriguez come after you. You can't split all the

333

acts of your life into probability equations. Some things you do because it's in your nature. And before you crossed the border you had a score to settle with Rodriguez.

You regret that Jumbo's IEDs were on a forty-eight-hour fuse. You now wish you could advance them by a day. You spread your bed-sheet on the floor. The two of you have never prayed together but there's always a first time. You face Mecca and word the Hadith.

You hit the road in the Gypsy with Jumbo driving and in army fatigues. Though you too have the option of a uniform you decide to forgo it for the time being. The Gypsy will give you swift access through checkpoints and your cover story of being a *Times of India* journalist will provide passage to unit commanding officers in their camps.

In the back you have your cargo, equipment, arms and other paraphernalia. The Hindu *kafirs* have obviously struck gold in their ploy of using a thief to catch another thief. You are sure both Major Rodriguez and Major Kohli will now be utilised by Military Intelligence and RAW to get at you. Or a spy, rather. You are not quite sure where to slot yourself. And now, of course, anger is fogging your brain.

Your first task is to do a recce in Drass. Look for tell-tale signs of the Indian timing for the Tiger Hill assault. The route as well. There are three possible routes to the top from the Indian side. After the fall of Tololing to the Indians all three sides are completely blind to your spotters. The Indians could spring a surprise or two, and it is your job not to let it be a surprise for your side.

It's a two-hour run from Kargil to the Drass Brigade HQ. On the way you see two Bofors guns being towed towards Drass. Ominous signs. You pass an artillery convoy. More importantly, two multi-barrel rocket-launching trucks. The Indians are gearing up their direct-fire artillery.

At Drass you see other signs. Bunkers being beefed up and two 15th Corps top brass staff vehicles parked at the local school. Of course, you know through your network that the commanding officer of the Drass brigade HQ, Brigadier Aul, isn't really in charge of the Tiger Hill operation. The operational brigade is the 17th of 26th Division with Brigadier Tejvir Singh as the officer in command. The HQ of the 17th is in the school that you saw the cars parked at.

You then proceed to the 2nd Rajputana Rifles camp. You have to return part of the way you came for that. The 2nd Raj Rif was the spearhead Indian unit in its successful assault on Tololing Ridge on 12 June. The unit had taken sixteen hits in all, eight of them officers, on that single night. But it had performed its task. Now the men lay in stupor at the spur of the ridge they had fought on, mourning their losses and awaiting further orders.

You are escorted to the commanding officer, Colonel Vinod Tewari. The colonel is courteous and accepts your media credentials at face value. He warms to you and orders breakfast. You are there ostensibly to do a Tololing reconstruction. Also, a piece on what moves men in battle. The colonel warms to your second stated objective.

'I have come to believe', Colonel Tewari begins, 'that nobody can fight a war without having a belief in God.' The colonel has arranged chairs for you in the open and you have a panoramic view of the Tololing Ridge.

You scribble furiously. The colonel goes on to enumerate instances in the Tololing battle that support his war theorem. You nod vigorously.

'An officer from our unit was three feet away from one of the militants. He was totally exposed. The AK-47 of the militant jammed. They had a hand-to-hand combat and the militant died. You see that rock there. My battle HQ was there. I sat there for ten hours on the night of the 10th. No shell landed within fifty yards of where I was. That night I got a message on the wireless and went to confirm the message to my radio tent. A shell landed bang in the middle of my battle HQ at that moment. Four of my men died. What would you call that. Luck? No, sir. It's not luck. It's the invisible hand of God. It was an aerial burst. My men turned into lumps of meat.'

You take fifteen more minutes of Colonel Tewari's battle-logue. What you have come for would take possibly a minute but you have to till the ground first, to sow bonhomie and trust.

'It must have been quite an experience, Colonel,' you say as awe-struck as possible.

'It was, son,' he says.

'I have some friends at 18 Grenadiers. I hear they are taking Tiger Hill tonight,' you mention casually.

'Yes,' he says. 'I just wished Thakur the best of luck. He's the commanding officer. We were together at IMA.'

'It's going to be a steep climb,' you say. 'It's 16,000 feet, isn't it? Won't they need oxygen?'

'No, not really. The high-altitude instructors are going to be laying the ropes,' says Colonel Tewari.

You have got more than you expected. That the dolly was on for tonight you already knew. More importantly, what the colonel has indirectly revealed to you because of his mention of the instructors from HAWS is that the Indians will be taking the steep side, the back of the Tiger route, the near-vertical east face which is hardly protected at all.

You take your leave of the colonel after presenting him with a collection of airline liquor miniatures and a carton of Rothmans. He's overwhelmed.

'Leave me your number in Delhi so I can look you up when I am next there. When will this appear?' asks Colonel Tewari.

'Shortly,' you say. You leave the colonel your number, for whatever it's worth. You have one last request.

'I have a friend in 7 Sikh. Could you patch me to him on your secure lines?' you ask.

'Sure as hell,' says Colonel Tewari. He picks up the phone on his table and asks Drass exchange to put him through to Major Raunaq Singh. He hands over the handset to you.

Jumbo gets the colonel out of hearing range. 'Would you like to check out some other brands, Colonel? There's Dunhill in there and some packs of Marlboro,' says Jumbo. He hauls out a bag from the back.

There's a background hum in the headpiece and then noise of artillery. Major Raunaq is obviously in the thick of things. 'Colonel Tewari?' he asks twice.

'Hello, Major,' you say. 'MM here.' There's silence at the other end. 'I have some news for you, Major.'

'I am listening, MM,' says Major Raunaq.

Obviously, the major is a bit stunned at your access to the secure line. You come straight to the point. 'I heard you are having big fun at Tiger. Some of your friends want to join you. Would you like to play host to Rodriguez and Kohli?'

'Does a man want a million bucks?' replies Major Raunaq Singh.

You are driving down to the Drass helipad. You have to go through two checkpoints at Drass HQ but with 15th Corps markings on your Gypsy you have no problems. Cramped in the back of your Gypsy, you have already managed to don the uniform of a major. There's been a sudden switch in your plans. When you dialled out to your network through your Iridium the call instead got transferred to Major Rodriguez. You could hear the whine of helicopter rotors as the major came on line.

'MM, you piece of shit, one hour and we have your Mossie ass,' says Major Rodriguez.

This had been an unexpected hindrance. The Indians have obviously worked Motorola fast. You now have no way of telling Skardu when they'll attack Tiger Hill or how.

This is when you think of taking the battle to Rodriguez very early in the game. Right when his chopper lands at Drass. The surprise element is too great an advantage to be ignored. You can then hijack the chopper to cross the LoC or fly to somewhere near Tiger Hill. The risk is obvious. Without your having informed Skardu of your plans your troops will have no way of knowing you were in the chopper. You'll have to brave missile fire from your side. That is a risk you will have to take. You thus abandon your earlier plan of a trek to Tiger Hill – the way, incidentally, Major Raunaq is expecting you. You will now provide a surprise to 7 Sikh.

The Drass helipad was a dangerous zone itself till Tololing was taken by the Indians. The choppers had then given up landing at Drass because of the shelling and fear of shoulder-fired Stingers from Tololing top. Nothing can put a crimp in a pilot's mental make-up swifter than news that he could be chased around by infrared missiles.

You notice a detachment the size of a company at the helipad. You recognise troops from 5 Kumaon whom you know are in the region. You also spot Colonel Sangma, the 5 Kumaon commanding officer, in the ATC hut. Major Rodriguez has obviously organised his dogs of war to come after you. His last ace in the hole to earn some brownie points for himself and 5 Kumaon from the army top brass. Earn some clemency where none should exist.

This introduces a snarl into your strategy. Though you are in uniform there exists the possibility the troops might recognise you if you step out of the Gypsy before the chopper arrives. After it does, there would be the dust swirl and other distractions to capitalise on. You put on your dark glasses for added camouflage. Jumbo parks the Gypsy out of line of direct sight of the troops, behind the ATC hut.

You hear the sound of the rotor blades after five minutes of waiting. You have already screwed silencers on to your weapons. As the MI-17 hovers above the runway you enter the aviation hut and take out the two radar controllers and Colonel Sangma. You don't bother to fall to the temptation of introducing yourself to Sangma, rekindling his memories. There is no time now for a cat-and-mouse game. You go for the brains. You don't even have time to watch the blood oozing from their foreheads as they slump on their chairs, and Sangma falls to the ground.

With Rodriguez, of course, it is going to be different.

Jumbo, meanwhile, is already walking to the chopper before the dust has settled. He walks unencumbered by the kit bag, which you carry slung on your shoulder twenty paces behind. You can see Major Rodriguez unstrapping his seat belt. There's Major Kohli as well, the way you have anticipated. They are making it a party. The doors are opening but Jumbo is through before they realise what is happening.

They recognise Jumbo too late. Rodriguez and Kohli are in the backseat, Kohli nearest to the door. Jumbo has already opened a gash on Kohli's right eyebrow with the back of the Glock. You too greet Major Rodriguez with a swing of your Glock. It takes out four of his front teeth.

'Hello, Major,' you say. Then you swing around and take an MP5 out from your bag. You squeeze your trigger on the 5 Kumaon welcome committee advancing towards the chopper, as yet unsure about what really is happening. Now they know.

You get a dozen of them in the first volley. The others scatter for cover. Jumbo's made quick work of the co-pilot and throws his body on to the tarmac. At ten thousand feet there is only so much freight that a chopper can take into the air.

Within two minutes you are flying again. Jumbo sits in front setting the course for the pilot while you glare at Rodriguez and Kohli at the back.

'Welcome, Major,' you say. Rodriguez's mouth is bleeding and he's pale but he still manages to give you a toothless smile.

'Ha, MM,' says Major Rodriguez. He spits out a tooth. It falls on his lap.

'A bit of a turnaround, eh, Rodriguez?' you say. You're keeping a close eye on Kohli. He's juke-box solid, though now he can hardly see through his right eye, swollen and bloody as it is.

You put the barrel of your Glock on Rodriguez's temple. The way you are you wouldn't mind firing. But that would be too smooth an end for a bastard like Rodriguez. You plan to turn him and Kohli over in one piece to the 7 Sikh. Let things take their natural course.

Rodriguez's composure is slowly returning to normal. There is one thing you can't call Rodriguez and that is a sham.

'How long have you been in this game, MM?' he asks.

'Long enough,' you say. 'How are my parents?'

'The last I know the MI was having another go at them,' says Major Rodriguez.

You grimace. Jumbo looks back with concern.

'Sorry, MM,' says Major Rodriguez. 'I know how you feel but that's the way it has to be. It was RAW's idea, anyway. Some Colonel Ray Chowdhary who's in charge. He just missed getting on to this chopper. They just got me in the game when they had cracked the whole thing.'

'Thanks,' you say.

Rodriguez's gums are starting to bleed. 'Where are you planning to fly us, MM?' he asks.

Jumbo is moving the chopper around on the Indian side, deciding the best way to go behind Tiger Hill without getting picked up by air defence units. Jumbo's done some fixed-wing flying and he can read the gauges. He flashes five fingers thrice. You guess fifteen minutes of fuel is more than enough to get you where you wanted.

'Major Raunaq wants to hold a welcome party for you,' you say.

Major Rodriguez pales. So does Kohli.

'You got your money, MM. And now you have a chopper. Why don't you just fly to Mossie country while your luck is holding? Seeing you can't fly yourself we will give you a lift. We will try our luck coming back. Dodge the missiles,' suggests Major Rodriguez.

'It will suit me better if you try your luck with the 7 Sikh. Try dodging Major Raunaq and his men,' you say.

'If we live to do it,' says Major Rodriguez. He grins and points his hand westwards.

Jumbo and the pilot are already panicking.

'Incoming,' says Jumbo and then you realise what's happening. A ground-to-air has locked on.

The pilot's discharging flares left and right and he goes in a steep dive, now skimming the valley floor. You are flying two yards above boulders in the valley behind peak 4875.

It's a near miss. You hear the explosion of the missile as it zeroes on one of the flares. Next time none of you may be that lucky.

The event has engrossed you and diverted your attention enough for Major Kohli to think he can take advantage. He spins on you, his torso picking up momentum. His right hand has grabbed your Glock and he's fisted you in the plexus with his left. You butt Kohli with your head but then as the helicopter banks sharply to the left you get flushed out from your seat as you haven't got your safety belt strapped on. You have lost your balance and are now half kneeling on the floor. You haven't lost your grip on the Glock though Kohli's twisting your wrist.

Jumbo meanwhile has taken a kick on the head from Major Rodriguez. The major has unbuckled his harness and has launched himself on Jumbo, going over your head. You feel the pilot pull up on the throttle. He's hovering now, preparing to land. You feel your grip on the Glock beginning to loosen and nearing the point where if in the next couple of seconds you do nothing to retrieve the balance your way you will surely end up as bug kill on the mat. You squeeze the trigger of your gun. The trajectory is lethal for everybody on board but apart from the fact that Kohli's grip on your wrist allows few other angles, you have also taken into account the facts that you are probably just a yard or two above ground level, hovering, and with little gas on board to go up in flames on impact.

You see the pilot's head slump on his chest. You hear something snap above your head where Jumbo is dealing with Rodriguez, or the other way around. And then as the chopper veers to the ground without control you hear the blades hit the rocks and you can feel the flying machine going head over heels and then as it tumbles your head hits the seat frame in front of you and you lose consciousness.

When you come back to your senses you are lying amidst twisted metal. There is smoke and the faint odour of petrol in the air. There are splinters of glass embedded in your face and hands. You don't yet know whether all your bones are in place. There is a gash on your left forearm and blood is dripping from your nose. Major Kohli is slumped over you. You don't know whether he's alive. You are surprised you are. What you see of Jumbo is making you nauseous. A broken piece of rotor blade is sticking out of his chest. His neck is at an unnatural angle and even though blood is clouding your vision you see in him no signs of life.

Of course, what matters most in the way you find yourself is that Major Rodriguez is not where you saw him last. You are finding it difficult to turn your head but by slanting it a few degrees you have him in your vision. You can see him outside. He's looking at you and smiling. Even though it's a toothless smile. He's rummaging through your kit bag or what's left of it. You surmise that the crash flung him outside. Your feet are suddenly cold. Water's making its way into the helicopter. It's crashed into a small rivulet. You look around for your Glock in desperation.

'Looking for this?' asks Major Rodriguez from the outside.

He's palming your piece. Obviously you have been unconscious for long and have slid into the category of the fucked. He's aiming at you now. The sonofabitch even squeezes the trigger. The bullet hits the twisted and charred cockpit controls which have buckled and are now hardly a foot from your face. It ricochets off behind you.

Unexpectedly, you don't flinch. For two reasons. You are suddenly weary and don't care to live any longer. Jumbo's death is getting at your yin and yang. Two, you don't think Rodriguez would relish writing your final chapter so early in the game. He is too much of a cat-and-mouse man to let go this opportunity.

You somehow manage to extricate yourself from under Major Kohli. Kohli copped it from the back. A strip of metal, part of what component you don't know, entered his heart from between his ribs. His jacket is all soaked with blood and you see the expression on his face for the first time. Not horrific or pained but puzzled. You glance at his wristwatch. Your own is broken. But Kohli's Timex ticks amidst all the death and mayhem. The time tells you that it could be an hour since you came down. You are surprised some troops haven't made it to the crash site yet. You figure distances take a long time in terrain such as this. The Indians would be eager to know the fate of their helicopter and the officers in it. Your own side would be determined to know it first themselves. Information such as this could be spun for huge propaganda depending on which side of the LoC the machine had gone down. The Indians will be aching for a CNN trip to the site if indeed the wreckage was on their side of the border.

But first there is the looming problem of Major Rodriguez. He is lining you up in his sights once again.

'MM, your time has come. Say your prayers,' he says.

'Hey, Rodriguez, what about your money, you don't want your cut any more?' you ask. 'Your money goes with me.' You have meanwhile twisted and contracted the various muscles of your limbs to check for injuries. You are badly bruised but your bones seem to be holding. On what remains of the cockpit floor, in areas that are still dry, you see the flares that you had been carrying in your kit bag. You sense an opportunity. They were special non-cartridge flares, having little brass toggles at the end of strings to set them off. The charge propels the flare six kilometres into the sky before setting it off. It then comes down tied to a mini-parachute even as thick orange smoke emits from the canister, leaving a colourful trail in the day.

'You know what, MM? Why are we two the only guys coming out of this crash alive?' asks Major Rodriguez. The major is in a philosophical mood.

Your back is towards Rodriguez. You are now shielding the flare with your forearm and the tattered remains of the sleeve of your uniform. Though you would like nothing better than to deliver Rodriguez to the 7 Sikh you also realise that in the flare you have one slim chance to avoid such a dreary end yourself.

You pull the toggles as you turn and the flare fires from between your ribs and elbow. You feel the shearing heat, the incandescent burst of red, and as you charge the major and butt his pelvis with your head you can see the flare has embedded itself in his chest and his clothes are on fire. Shortly, you feel your own scalp burning. And soon the smell of burning flesh from Rodriguez's chest.

You have taken the major down with you in a roll and though he has yelped in agony he soon locks himself in a silent death struggle with you. You have taken two rolls in the stream locked chest to chest with Major Rodriguez. The flare has burnt you as well and Rodriguez jabs you ferociously in the ribs and face and flings you loose.

Somewhere in the tussle the Glock has slipped from his palm and while he looks for it desperately he's also lying chest down in the stream to douse the fire engulfing his chest. Then there's the smoke from the flare. Billowing incessantly it takes Rodriguez in and out of your rather groggy vision. But now you have a two-foot-long jagged piece of metal straddling your arms and through the smoke, the hiss of steam and the loathing that you have borne for Rodriguez for many years, you swing it in an arc and bring it down in lethal fashion over his chest. You think you have gone through his heart for a spray of blood hits you. Your palms, too, are cut from where you held the metal.

And even as you lie panting from your exertions and watch life ebb from Rodriguez in shudders and from the blood oozing from his mouth, what stays embedded in your memory is your brief glimpse of the fearless gaze in his eyes even as they glazed.

Though you are glad that Rodriguez is no more you feel you have lost a kindred spirit. In another time and age and if the shadow of Shomali hadn't been there you could have been brothers.

You are fading out yourself now. The crash and the fight are getting to your head. And as you slip into that zone where you don't know whether you are conscious or asleep you can hear the boom of artillery echo through the hills. What you can also hear, magnified, by the hills around you, are the war cries *Jo bolo so nihal, sat sri akal.*

You pass out with the selfish knowledge that with the 7 Sikh going into battle at Tiger Hill there will be no spare troops in the vicinity to come hunting for you. Of course, you also know that your Mossie brothers will be out looking for you and you hope they find you before all is lost as the battle waged through the night.

When you come to your senses, you are surrounded by soldiers. You recognise the uniform of the Special Services Group (SSG), the élite forces of the Pakistani army. Dawn is breaking too and the guns are still booming. You sense from the sombre mood that things haven't gone well for your people. It's a while before they notice your coming to consciousness. You feel in one piece and strong, except for the burn on your chest and some cuts on your forearms and palm. While they have kept you on IV for what must be close to forty-eight hours, you get up in the bunker that you are in. You can hear a machine gun rattling from an adjacent area. You can hear shells flying across and exploding near by. Near, very near.

'Sir, how are you?' asks a voice. You can see he's the medic.

You ask questions and learn about the shit you were in. Of course, it was nothing new except you are now with a different cast of characters. You learn that a platoon strength of the SSG had been flown in on two choppers on the west approach of Tiger Hill. Eighteen men had been dropped off to locate and extricate you. Each of them had been shown photographs of you and when they clambered to inspect the ruins of the downed Indian MI-17, which Jumbo had managed to crash about three kilometres from Tiger Hill, they found you instead, tattered, bruised, burnt and unconscious.

This was some time in the night. They lost three men, two of them officers, in sniper fire from the 7 Sikh, who were packing the western approach to Tiger Hill, in just getting you to a fortified bunker two thousand yards from where hell was breaking loose in the night.

You learn, as you knew from two days back, that the Indians had launched an assault up the north-eastern face of Tiger Hill, a sheer vertical face of rock and the least protected side.

What you knew then is not intelligence now. Your army has already suffered from the lack of reliable data. Here you might have been to blame. Even in dying, Major Rodriguez ensured his victory, albeit indirectly. Tiger Hill has been captured by the Indians. A speedy thrust up the vertical face coupled with diversionary attacks on the western flank of the hill, which drew the bulk of your troops away from where the action was. The 7 Sikh apparently shouted their war cries on megaphones to convey the presence of large numbers. A very kindergarten-level deception. But very effective.

Followed, of course, by suicidal tendencies where they started radioing for artillery on positions close to them with the logic that more of ours would be killed than their own. Having successfully dislodged the Northern Light Infantry from the peak they are now engaged in mopping-up operations.

A window of a few hours remains, however, to launch a counter-attack before the Indians consolidate the area with reinforcements to seal their victory over an army dedicated to Jihad.

The SSG who had been tasked to get you out A.S.A.P. have, in light of the humiliating scenario, been retasked to lead the counter-attack. You know it's a matter of great shame for an army to be dislodged from an entrenched position, specially one so prestigious and which gives a commanding view of Drass.

The SSG have already committed half a dozen men to lead you away to Skardu by foot. The rest prepare for battle.

But in a way you have known what you were going to do before the plans for your flight were disclosed to you. You have had this premonition from the moment you hit the hills. You have known you won't get off them in one piece.

As the soft light of the dawn turns harsh, you take over the reins of the SSG. With their officers dead it is easy. In fact, and you are faintly surprised by this, the top brass of the Pakistani army actively want you to do so. Obviously, ground realities have been conveyed to them and in you perhaps they see some hope of redeeming lost honour.

They even patch you in to army chief General Pervez Musharraf. The general attempts to pump you up.

'I have wanted to talk to you for a long time, MM. I have read your file. You are a legend. What would we have done without you? The honour of Pakistan and its army rests in your hands. The international situation doesn't allow us to commit any more troops to Kargil. The Americans are push-ing us to de-escalate. If we can regain Tiger Hill we will fight on, but if we lose the Americans are going to push us to withdraw. You have trained with the officers of the SSG, and with you guiding them I am sure we have a chance,' he says.

You are amused. Now that the shit is about to hit the ceil-ing the general is reluctant to commit élite forces to the field. Musharraf, you surmise, doesn't know you from shit. He doesn't know, for instance, that you are worth more to Pakistan alive than dead. That if you lived Pakistan would live and fight another day and possibly win. Of course, you won't be on the field any more. You are too burnt for that. But even that, why not? There is plastic surgery. You don't, however, enlighten the general on these thoughts of yours.

'General, I shall do my best,' you say. 'Inshallah we shall drive them out.'

It's not that you haven't pondered upon what you have decided to do. You aren't about to attempt to do anything that you haven't been trained for in some measure or other. But in this thing, as in any situation of life, it's your state of mind on which things pivot.

And yours has, perhaps, undergone a paradigm shift. The Americans will call the same thing blowing a fuse. But the

349

shift that has happened is basically a little technical in nature. From being somebody who played the probability game you are now embarking on something in which you are reducing probability to a sucker's pastime. And you aren't a sucker.

It's actually simple to explain, but the fact of the matter is that it can only be understood by the few of us who belong to this trade in the world. The best of us don't ply our trade for ideology or pay or women or whatever else. That could be a reason for joining. You do it for the rush that comes from a job well done.

It's this philosophy that has permeated the various strands of your life.

Of course, there comes a point, as it had come with you, when you even tire of the rush. That's when the intelligent among us walk out, for the danger after this point is that you don't care any more whether you score a ten or not. That too is a kind of rush – not caring. Actually, this explanation might be a trifle unfulfilling. You could even be aching for one big rush, the mother of all rapids. A rush like this comes just once in your life and it can only come when you don't care for the consequences.

Which is where you are placed, exactly. How you build up to that point is a matter of individual make-up and circumstance. In the case of yours truly you are perhaps so meshed up with guys like Rodriguez and Kohli that maybe you are missing the bastards for the fun they gave you. Now, rather than suffer withdrawal symptoms, you just want to have one final roller-coaster ride that ends up with the trolley car running out of rails. Besides, no umbilical cords remain for you. You know your adoptive parents will soon be history.

You are with strangers now but it's an outfit that belongs to Islam. There are twenty-seven of you and all of you take turns in batches to offer final prayers to Allah the Almighty. You have taken off your Indian army uniform and have slipped into a dead soldier's one. Some of your men are apprehensive that it would bring bad luck but you can't be bothered with such banalities. The job at hand requires you to function at optimum efficiency and you want all the totems of military motivation to come to your aid. You are now Kamal Sher of Delta Company of the 12 Northern Light Infantry (NLI). The name is threaded on your khaki shirt. You have the stripes of a captain and you are leading men of the SSG into battle.

At noon you have gathered your men around you. You acquaint them with what awaits them. You brief them about the enemy. They are from the 7 Sikh, you tell them. What you omit to tell them is that in late April you polished off three of the 7 Sikh in your solo run away from Rodriguez's pack. That was your atonement for the incident where you went on patrol with Rodriguez and watched him slaughter five Mossies who had just crossed a stream. Your solo had left Rodriguez bewildered. He then didn't know the blood that flowed in your veins. That was your first taste of Sikh blood.

But you tell your men about the historic battle of Saragarhi in the nineteenth century, where twenty-two Sikhs fought till the last man and the last bullet against a superior force of Afghan tribesmen.

'You are going to face the same here. They are a brave people. But we are braver,' you tell them. Though if someone asks for an explanation from you as to how a corrupt army unit can offer war that is so gallant you would have no reasons to give. Except pride in their unit and race.

Somewhere behind the rocks in front was also Major Raunaq Singh. It will be a charming, lead-filled encounter, you muse.

You then go into your battle cry of *Allah o akbar* and it resonates around the hills and the valley. The Sikhs go silent. Some last rites remain. You proceed into the bunker where you gained consciousness in the morning. As you go inside

351

you see written in chalk across the entrance the number the NLI had given to this place of refuge from Indian shelling: Bunker 13. You smile at the coincidence. You remember the same number from the place where Major Kohli initiated you into bunker politics.

In privacy you tear your chemical kit from your underwear. You take your last infusion of heroin. With heroin you have passed the stage where the chemical affects the clarity of your mind. This was to blunt the pain that you knew would come your way as you launched into battle with the Sikhs. You are about to lead twenty-six men to their deaths. And the chances of success for your band depends on how long you are able to stay alive.